David and Troy Stansel-Garner, and Trent Garner.
Great guys. Great friends.

Acknowledgments

As *Fortress Republic* heads into editing, *Sword of Sedition* is not long out and *Daughter of the Dragon* is new on the shelves. So I've had the chance to gauge reaction from many readers, and from everything I've heard, the response is overwhelmingly positive. Not only did the readership roll with the sweeping changes we've started to implement (breaking up The Republic and marching onto the stage more of the large Great Houses), they embraced them. A benefit of writing inside a universe at war. Change is to be expected. Which makes my job even better, as I am able to enjoy a fresh challenge with every novel.

And not just for myself. At some point along the journey in each and every book, dozens of people lend a thought, a whisper, a hand or two. Only some of which I'll be able to thank here:

Jordan and Dawne Weisman, Mort Weisman, Maya Smith, Mike Mulvihill, Kevin Goddard, Kelly Bonilla, and everyone at WizKids who continues to work very hard on this universe. And especially Sharon Turner-Mulvihill, who I owe big time for her patience and often great efforts on my behalf.

The staff at Roc books, which now includes Elizabeth Scheier. Jen and Laura Anne, you will be missed, but I have been left in good hands.

The usual suspects who often walk through my office, my

MechWarrior: Dark Age

FORTRESS REPUBLIC

A BATTLETECH® NOVEL

Loren L. Coleman

A ROC BOOK

ROC
Published by New American Library, a division of
Penguin Group (USA) Inc., 375 Hudson Street,
New York, New York 10014, USA
Penguin Group (Canada), 90 Eglinton Avenue East, Suite 700, Toronto,
Ontario M4P 2Y3, Canada (a division of Pearson Penguin Canada Inc.)
Penguin Books Ltd., 80 Strand, London WC2R 0RL, England
Penguin Ireland, 25 St. Stephen's Green, Dublin 2,
Ireland (a division of Penguin Books Ltd.)
Penguin Group (Australia), 250 Camberwell Road, Camberwell, Victoria 3124,
Australia (a division of Pearson Australia Group Pty. Ltd.)
Penguin Books India Pvt. Ltd., 11 Community Centre, Panchsheel Park,
New Delhi - 110 017, India
Penguin Group (NZ), cnr Airborne and Rosedale Roads, Albany,
Auckland 1310, New Zealand (a division of Pearson New Zealand Ltd.)
Penguin Books (South Africa) (Pty.) Ltd., 24 Sturdee Avenue,
Rosebank, Johannesburg 2196, South Africa

Penguin Books Ltd, Registered Offices:
80 Strand, London WC2R 0RL, England

First published by Roc, an imprint of New American Library,
a division of Penguin Putnam Inc.

First Printing, October 2005
10 9 8 7 6 5 4 3 2 1

Copyright © 2005 WizKids, Inc. All rights reserved

 REGISTERED TRADEMARK—MARCA REGISTRADA

Printed in the United States of America

Without limiting the rights under copyright reserved above, no part of this publication may be reproduced, stored in or introduced into a retrieval system, or transmitted, in any form, or by any means (electronic, mechanical, photocopying, recording, or otherwise), without the prior written permission of both the copyright owner and the above publisher of this book.

PUBLISHER'S NOTE
This is a work of fiction. Names, characters, places, and incidents either are the products of the author's imagination or are used fictitiously, and any resemblance to actual persons, living or dead, business establishments, events, or locales is entirely coincidental.
   The publisher does not have any control over and does not assume any responsibility for author or third-party Web sites or their content.

If you purchased this book without a cover you should be aware that this book is stolen property. It was reported as "unsold and destroyed" to the publisher and neither the author nor the publisher has received any payment for this "stripped book."

The scanning, uploading and distribution of this book via the Internet or via any other means without the permission of the publisher is illegal and punishable by law. Please purchase only authorized electronic editions, and do not participate in or encourage electronic piracy of copyrighted materials. Your support of the author's rights is appreciated.

FORTRESS REPUBLIC

Dividing his attention between the water-softened world he saw throuh his ferroglass shield and the iconic layout on his heads-up display, Erik throttled forward into a hard run to lead the Condors forward after the retreating vehicles. Both Demons and the Shandra had fallen back down the slope onto a secodary line held by a fifty-five ton *Griffin* and two captured Haseks. Like the others, all three combat vehicles had been painted with tan and green colors being used by these supposed "Capellan irregulars." Skirmish troops thrown at Tikonov in advance of any main thrust. Poorly trained and mostly disposable freedom fighters.

"But they don't fight like it." he whispered, careful of his voice-activated mic.

In fact, reports of House Liao's wellorganised probing assault were what first tempted Erik away from Terra and what might very well be the high-level political event of the decade. Leaders from every Great House and most of the smaller realms, all converging on the capital of The Republic? At a time when the Senate was disgraced and disbanded, and starting what amounted it a civil war? Seven months ago, Erik, would have been hard pressed to imagine turning his back on such an opportunity.

Seven months ago, however, he had not yet learned to look at the larger picture.

Seven months ago, his uncle Lord Governor Aaron Sandoval, had not nearly gotten him killed.

A lot had happened since then. Erik had developed the first of his own intelligence assets. He'd made contact with one of The Republic's largest subversive organizations. These were both secrets he now kept from his uncle.

And both were reporting to him the same thing. House Lia's puch forward at Tikonov was larger, and better organized than The Republic credited. Which meant Tikonov—and the Sandoval hold over the Swordsworn faction—was in danger.

So Erik had come back. And without his uncle. The better to make his own mark now, while so many eyes were watching.

home, and my life. Allen and Amy Mattila. Randall and Tara Bills, with Bryn and Ryana and now Kenyan Aleksandr. Phil DeLuca, Kelle Vozka, Erik, and Alex and Logan. David and Troy and Trent who are now that much closer that I can come visit my "fourth cat."

Of course: Mike Stackpole, Herb Beas, Chris Hartford, Chris Trossen, and our cartographer Oystein Tvedten. Team BattleTech members Pete Smith, Chas Borner, Warner Doles. The new generation: Kevin Killiany, Ilsa Bick, Phaedra Weldon, Louisa Swann, Steve Mohan, Dayle Dermatis, Dan Duvall and others who are joining the ranks through BattleCorps.com; welcome to the neighborhood.

Always the deepest of appreciation for my wife, Heather Joy, without whose support none of this would be possible. My children, Talon, Conner, and Alexia, who are still growing up far too fast (my wife is starting to look up at our first). And yeah, the cats. Chaos, Rumor and Ranger. Our local "nobles." And Loki, our neurotic border collie, doing a study in three parts on how to herd cats; how he suffers for his art.

THE REPUBLIC TERRITORIES

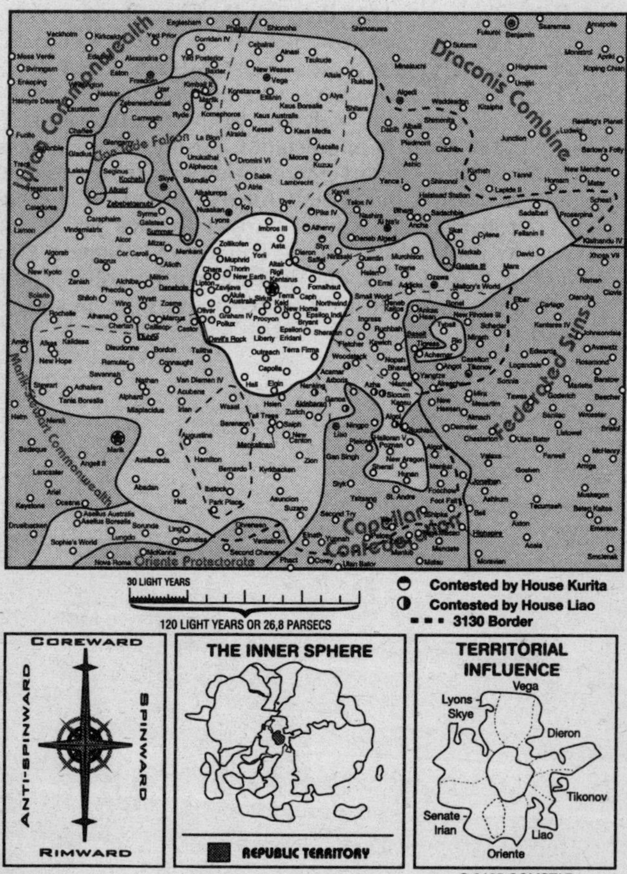

- ◐ Contested by House Kurita
- ◑ Contested by House Liao
- ▪ ▪ ▪ 3130 Border

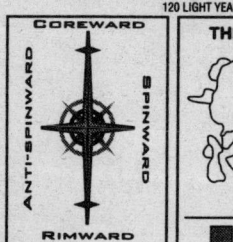

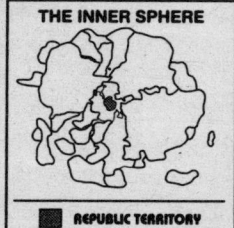

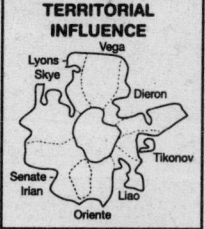

© 3135 COMSTAR
CARTOGRAPHIC CORPS

BUILT ON QUICKSAND

These are the times that try men's souls.
—Thomas Paine, "The American Crisis,"
    19 December 1776

There are always trying times that must be faced, and conquered. How we rise to meet such challenges, that is the true test of our strength of character, of will. As chaos rails against the fortress of the mind.
—(Acting Prince) Caleb Hasek Sandoval Davion, "A
    Public Address," Terra, 2 June 3135

1

With few loyalist holdouts left, it seems certain that life on Terra can be expected to turn once more towards calmer waters. In fact, can a reconciliation with the rogue Senators really be that far off? Now that the insanity has nearly run its course?

—Excerpt from the *Terran Times* editorial page,
8 June 3135

Siberia, Terra
Republic of the Sphere
9 June 3135

"Incoming!"

The warning crackled in Julian Davion's ears amid a wash of static. And already too late.

Missiles flashed across the low, barren ridge in overlapping waves. Fell over his position in a smothering blanket. Bright blossoms of fire gouged into the Siberian tundra's permafrost, threw smoking earth and blackened gravel against the lower legs of Julian's eighty-five ton *Templar*.

One flight of warheads and then a second slammed against his BattleMech's right side. They blasted away armor and shoved Julian hard to the left. Straps on his safety harness dug in at his shoulders, his waist. The quick-release buckle was a hard knot pressed into his gut.

The prince's champion of the Federated Suns wrestled

against his control sticks, working hard to keep his *Templar* on its feet and moving, shuffling forward, fighting its way up the slope. His muscles ached with fatigue and more than a few bruises. The cramped cockpit stank of old sweat, the ozone flavor of warm electronics, and a recent application of conditioner that some over-eager technician had used on the supple neoleather wrapping his command chair. The conditioner's acrid stench burned Julian's sinuses, scratched at the back of his throat. He desperately needed a swallow of water.

A final flight of missiles hammered into the *Templar's* right shoulder. Two warheads slammed into the side of its head, just back of the cockpit's ferroglass shield. A deep, metallic gonging rang in Julian's ears.

The 'Mech wrenched to one side as if shoved, but never faltered a step.

"Still here," Julian managed between dry coughs.

Already toggled to the First Davion Guards' common channel, he relied on the voice-activated mic built into his neurohelmet for hands-free comms.

"Still good."

His warriors were on edge as it was. They didn't need to worry overmuch about their commander just now. Especially after Prince Harrison's recent accident.

Julian could do with fewer reminders of his uncle's condition as well, and living in the moment was his first, best defense. Always checking his heads-up display for an update on the approaching battlefield. Keeping an eye on his OmniMech's waste heat buildup, the wireframe schematic that darkened as he lost his armor, his speed, and his supporting forces.

A pair of Kinnol battle tanks struggled alongside Julian's position, one of them responsible for the earlier warning. Seized in last week's battle near Chateau-Thierry, both had been striped blue, white and red across one fender to match the *Templar's* parade colors. They'd also weathered the storm of warheads, though one of the vehicles chuffed great gouts of sooty, black smoke through a gaping rent in its side. Still it pushed forward.

Behind the Kinnols, spread in a loose skirmish line, followed a double-squad of armored infantry. Heavy-footed Hauberk on the left. Standard Infiltrators on the right.

In their slow-moving wedge formation, Julian led his Guards up and over the ridge.

Down into battle.

The Western Siberian Lowlands near Salekhard were Terra's latest (and near last) battlefield. Senate loyalists pressing to the end their ill-fated resistance against The Republic of the Sphere. Already driven from their stronghold near Sverdlovsk by a joint operation between Julian's First Davion Guards and a large Republic force, this particular group had broken the cordon and fought their way along the eastern side of Russia's snow-capped Urals. Pursued by Paladins Avellar and Mandella, nearly escaping several times, only to be trapped here. A barren, desolate basin cut by icy rivers and thin woodlands. Few places left to run. No place left to hide.

"Bugs caught on the walk," Sergeant Montgomery had said.

The veteran non-com wasn't far off. Wide arctic plains and sinks of frozen marshland stretched near as far as the eye could see save for the Urals rising in the west. A few exposed ridges like the one Julian had slipped behind, but not many. Below, spread out over several kilometers, a dozen BattleMechs stormed those desolate flats. Three stories tall and clad in composite armor, many of them walked and ran in the close approximation of giant knights. Others stalked about the battlefield on reverse-canted "bird legs." Sleek and deadly. At a glance it was difficult to tell ally from enemy as the machines challenged each other with fists full of lightning and lances of jewel-tone lasers. Avatars of war, let loose into the world of men.

And they weren't alone. Between these battling titans, companies of armored vehicles reeled back and forth like metal-shod herds caught between mighty predators, mixing and clashing and then breaking apart again as they sought flight in a new direction. Overhead a few remaining aerospace fighters stooped out of a pale blue sky to scream over the battlefield, laying down long strafing runs that burst through enemy lines and carved up the frozen ground.

Missiles rose and fell, rose and fell. Their gray contrails streaked the sky. False thunder rolled across the open plains as warheads and autocannon argued with each other. Angry, hellish streams of particle cannon energies scourged the war machines of one side, then the other. Lasers bit back and forth.

Into this Julian Davion led the Guards' second thrust of the day.

A *Catapult* held the lower slope, flanked by two JES crawlers. Between them, capable of throwing out an umbrella of over two hundred warheads, they could pound an area flat with deadly saturation. Launching waves of indirect fire over the ridge had softened their blow, but Julian knew better than to let them have a second bite.

"Suns, concentrate fire on my target," Julian ordered as the *Catapult* hammered at him with its twenty-millimeter autocannon. He drew his crosshairs over the closest JES missile carrier. Waited for the targeting reticle to burn the deep, solid gold of a hard lock. Quickly toggled for his all-hands circuit.

"Swords—"

"Hammers!" *she* interrupted.

"Dammit, Calamity! Wheel in and hook them. Now, now, *now*!"

On that last "now" his crosshairs gave him good tone, and Julian eased into his triggers even as a wailing alarm warned him of missile lock. Of *multiple* missile locks. But he edged out the Senate loyalists by a good second or two, which so often made all the difference in combat.

His particle projector cannons, one mounted in each arm, spat out twisting streams of hellish energies. They twisted and snaked their way across the frozen ground as if with a life of their own and cored in through one side of the missile carrier, blasting away armor in shards and molten spatters.

The Kinnols added one more PPC each, and threw a flight of long-range missiles into the air. The sleek warheads drew a tight line on the wounded carrier. While one of the battle tanks missed wide with both PPC and warheads, the second made up for it by following in Julian's initial strike. Its PPC sliced through one tracked belt, crippling the JES crawler, stranding it in place.

As if that would matter, as the Kinnol's missile flight hammered in through the gaping wound Julian had already carved. Filling the crew compartment with a raging storm of fire and shrapnel, it killed the crew instantly and cracked one of the crawler's ammunition bins.

Several tons of warheads detonated in sympathetic explosions, ripping away one whole side of the vehicle, tossing it into the air as if it were a child's toy. Trailing a gout of fire and belching oily, black smoke.

The crawler—once a solid piece of machinery, now a mangled, fiery ruin—landed a good twenty meters away with a pancaking belly flop.

Then the second carrier and the *Catapult* disappeared behind clouds of exhaust smoke, and all Julian could do was tense and ready himself to ride out the terrible pounding he was about to take.

Better than one hundred warheads slammed in around him, blossoming in fireballs across his shoulders and chest, digging through the armor on his arms, his legs. Tearing up the ground as smoke and blackened earth geysered into the air.

Two missiles hammered into the side of the *Templar's* head, shaking Julian against his restraints as if he were a rag doll being whipped around at the end of short rope.

Another flight cracked a flaw through his centerline armor, and the physical shielding that protected his 'Mech's fusion engine. Coupled with the power draw spiked by his PPCs, the reactor's surging waste heat bled upward through the cockpit's diamond-plate decking.

Julian gasped, his breath pulled from him to be replaced by hot coals burning in his lungs. Fought his control sticks even as he felt the eighty-five ton machine overbalancing to the left. Ducked back the other direction, as the bulky neurohelmet he wore translated brain signals from his own equilibrium into the regenerative feedback loop being fed down into the massive gyroscopic stabilizers screaming in the *Templar's* gut.

No joy.

The slope, the heavy damage, the ringing in his ears from the pummeling he'd taken—Julian abandoned his fight against gravity and surrendered his *Templar* into a controlled fall. It slammed hard against the frozen ground, digging its left shoulder through the permafrost. Bounced Julian twice more against his harness as darkness pushed in at the edges of his vision.

"Jules!" Callandre Kell again. This time with far less polish. "*Verdammt*! Guard-one is down."

"Pushing forward *now*," a second voice promised, static bursting around every word. Faint. Another woman. "Rendezvous in two minutes."

Too soon! Julian shook his head, fighting off the numbing blackness that threatened to roll over him. Something about the timing of their assault . . . tried to remember . . .

It was a blur, but he knew there was a problem if Lady Zou pushed forward too far, too fast.

"Still . . . here."

His mouth was pasty-dry and tasted of blood at the back of his throat. His tongue throbbed where he'd bitten it. Every joint and muscle ached. He levered the *Templar's* arms beneath him, careful as both limbs ended in weapon barrels, not hands, fighting his way back to his feet. Getting into a four-point crouch.

The *Catapult* continued to hammer at him with its autocannon, the stream of slugs pounding around his shoulders with deep, ringing peals.

"Still alive," he told his warriors. If barely. "Keep to the plan."

Then the next salvo of missiles fell over him, and the world disappeared in a halo of fire and smoke and smoldering rubble.

But Julian was in a more stable position to ride out the missile barrage this time: 'Mech crouched down on one knee, both arms pinned against the ground. The *Catapult's* missiles hammered in hard and heavy, bursting across his back and down his left side. The JES crawler, already taking savage counterfire from the Kinnol MBTs as well as the Hauberk's LRM packs, had less luck, rushing its followup salvo and spreading more damage over the tortured landscape than actually fell on Julian's position.

Hanging forward in his harness, swallowing against the taste of fresh blood, Julian did not fight the tremors but instead rode through them. He checked his heads-up display and saw Callandre Kell racing back towards him at the head of a scattered column of armor, leading the charge in her SM1 Destroyer. Two of Julian's MechWarriors, both in *Centurions*, had been left behind, but not by far. With a lance of heavier armor, they fought a rearguard action against the advancing loyalists.

Worse news on his HUD was the cluster of golden, glowing icons moving forward out of the west, at the far reach of his sensors and on the other side of the enemy line. His tactical computer tagged the lead machine as a fifty-five ton *Griffin*, which belonged to the Republic Knight, Lady Ariana Zou. Zou's push over the Urals from Vorkuta had started this latest running battle, heading off the retreating loyalists while Julian threw his Guards up the Ob' from Berëzovo to form an anvil against her hammer.

It had worked, trapping the loyalist force between them.

Except Lady Zou's rush to defend the Davion champion threatened to wrench the trap back open or, worse, deliver herself into the teeth of the enemy. Her push speared into the loyalist gut, throwing the enemy line into disarray. But a full lance of enemy 'Mechs and a good number of armored vehicles now curled back in her direction. They would isolate and cut her command to pieces.

And The Republic and Federated Suns both had lost too many good men and women of late.

"Don't think about it," Julian whispered. Careful of his voice-activated mic. "Not now."

Action was the best therapy. He pressed forward with both arms and levered his *Templar* back to its feet while blossoms of fire still walked across its back and shoulders. Leaving the remaining JES carrier to his Kinnol tanks and his advancing infantry squads, he throttled into a forward walk and pulled his crosshairs over the *Catapult's* boxy outline.

Not waiting for a hard lock, trusting his own instincts as well as the advanced targeting computer to make any fine-tuned adjustments, he snap-fired one of his PPCs. The lance of particle energies drilled in over the *Catapult's* right side, slashing armor from ferro-titanium bones.

Pushing his heat curve, he toggled and triggered his second PPC right after, this time cutting heavily across the other BattleMech's left leg.

Four . . . three . . . two . . .

Julian shoved his throttle forward, timing the next wave of missiles nearly to the second. Pushing his *Templar* up to its maximum speed of sixty-five kilometers per hour just as the crawler spread out a third, wide spread of LRMs, he ran out from beneath the umbrella and slashed two more particle cannon streams across the *Catapult's* profile.

"We have their attention." Callandre again, reading her own HUD as more loyalists turned from the advance of Lady Zou to drive forward to the aid of their missile-carriers.

Thinking to push through and seize Salekhard? Run hard and hope to lose themselves in the thick woodlands below Gory Putorana?

They would never make it.

Julian's cockpit was a sauna. Sweat poured off his arms and legs. Burned his lips with a salty taste. His damaged shielding and overuse of the *Templar's* particle cannon had driven his heat up to dangerous levels. Every step came with greater difficulty as heat-addled control circuitry slowed the 'Mech. Still he slapped at the shutdown override, wrenched his crosshairs over and again slashed out with both of his primary weapons.

One cut hard across the *Catapult's* chest. The other sliced clean through one of its arms, cutting free one of its LRM launchers, which crashed to the permafrost in a ruined, smoking heap.

Then Callandre's Destroyer skated up fast on its cushion of air, autocannon blazing as the hundred-twenty millimeter gun finished the work Julian had started on the *Catapult's* leg, cutting through a titanium femur.

The *Catapult* toppled over, crashing hard against its remaining arm and burying that limb beneath the full weight of its body. It was not going to get up again.

The loyalist 'MechWarrior quickly cut his active targeting system, surrendering before any follow-up salvoes took out his fusion reactor or came slashing through his cockpit's ferroglass shield.

And, left alone on this stretch of the open tundra, the remaining JES carrier did the same before all weapons turned on it next.

A pair of Infiltrator troopers jumped up onto the vehicle's top and wrenched open a hatch, ordering the tank crew out onto the cold flats.

In a high-speed turn, Callandre Kell spun her SM1 end

for end and used the powerful drive fans to brake her headlong flight from the far side of the battlefield. Like most vehicles in Julian's command, Callandre's Destroyer was painted with a desert-tan camouflage. Until recently, the Guards had been secreted away in the American southwest, training alongside Republic units. The first step in a budding alliance between House Davion's Federated Suns and Exarch Levin's Republic of the Sphere. Called up the week before to help defend Paris against a major Senate offensive, there had been no time to worry over such details as proper camouflage.

No time for most. Julian did notice Callandre had again found some spray paint. Never content with painting out the sunburst-and-sword crest of House Davion, on the side of her Destroyer she'd also filled in a large red triangle. Then, in black, she'd covered it with a "V" shaped hound's head with red slits for eyes.

Not a Davion insignia. Nor the crest of the Lyran Commonwealth, either.

Kell Hounds. One of the Inner Sphere's elite mercenary units.

As easily as one should expect from an heir to the Kell name—as well as being a former drill commander of the Nagelring's elite parade grounds cavalry team—Callandre slipped her assault-designed hovercraft into perfect formation at the side of Julian's *Templar,* just as he stepped back down to a casual walk.

"You're hot," she said. Her voice had the high-gain strength of their private channel.

"Yeah." His voice was a dusty croak. "I do look pretty good."

Though he could imagine how his assault 'Mech showed on her thermal scans. Blazing white, very likely.

"Catch your breath. I've got your back." She actually sounded concerned for him. How touching.

In answer, Julian turned towards the advancing line of loyalist forces. He throttled back into a slow run, then pushed for his best speed. "No rest for the wicked," he said.

Though he did not specify which of them he meant. He didn't need to. Seven years since they'd schooled together or seven days, Callandre could still read him.

Of course he'd meant her.

She powered past him in a race for the loyalist line. "You'll pay for that."

Probably. But still, "Rein it in, Callandre." She was getting too far up front.

Julian checked to see that the Kinnol battle tanks had come up off his left side. Now he counted another trio of armored vehicles trailing back on his right. "Dawkins." Julian's command was filtered by the communications system and automatically selected for the right channel, putting him in touch with his personal intelligence aide and the mobile HQ that crawled across the permafrost farther afield. "Is our artillery in place?"

"Affirmative, Sire." Leftenant Todd Dawkins rarely let something so minor as a raging firefight discourage him from formality. To him, Julian was Lord Markeson and cousin of the first prince as much as he was the honorary commander of the First Davion Guards. "Awaiting your command."

They'd have to wait a moment longer with Lady Zou forcing her way through the loyalist cadre. Julian put them on standby.

Ahead, his *Centurions* stiffened up their resistance against the loyalists as the rest of the First Davion Guards raced forward to regroup. A second SM1 Destroyer powered in from the side to flank Callandre. Then a third. This last one had a large white star on the back. Major Dwight Hastings of the First Guards. Julian's man.

But far from blocking her off, they joined in a wedge formation with Callandre at the head.

"Callandre. Hastings. Rein in!"

But he knew better, even as he wasted time on the order. She'd slipped her leash. Again. Dammit. And Hastings had taken as much of Callandre's showboating as any good line officer could without also catching the bug.

The trio of Destroyers powered right past the *Centurions* at flank speed, barreling into the enemy line.

Julian swallowed dryly, anticipating a quick and vicious slaughter. He did not give Callandre enough credit to know her business, or the Senate MechWarriors for possessing enough survival instinct to know when to get out of the way. Three Destroyers, each with a twelve-centimeter bore autocannon that could cut the legs out from under an assault 'Mech in one pass, were not to be taken lightly. With the heaviest unit fielded by the loyalists currently a beat-up *Legionnaire*, most of the enemy quickly scattered away from the Destroyers, not wanting to be first.

Most. Not all.

A thirty-ton *Spider* was slow lighting off its jump jets. It delayed long enough to slash a scarlet laser across the front of Callandre's Destroyer and never mind how quickly it raced forward. Armor composite splashed over the ground, burning quickly down to smoking cinders.

Not enough to stop her, though. At point-blank, Callandre ripped a long, deadly burst dead center into the *Spider*. One of the other SM1s stitched its own autocannon fire into the *Spider's* side, while Hastings (Julian thought) also managed a centerline punch.

The *Spider's* armor wasn't about to stop one Destroyer from gutting its torso. Two was overkill. Golden fire shot through the gaping wounds as the fusion reactor burst free, gobbling up any material it could find as fuel. For an instant the *Spider* glowed bright and dangerous, just as Callandre's Destroyer shot between its legs and the others raced by on either side. Then it flew apart in an explosion that rocked the entire battlefield and nearly caught the suicidal SM1 in the expanding fireball.

Callandre's Destroyer trailed smoke and a few bright flames as it raced on. But it was still in one piece. And it had made rendezvous with Lady Zou's advancing thrust.

In fact, with resistance scattered away from that part of the battlefield, Zou's Republic warriors had an easy push through the center, leaving the wounded mob of loyalists scattered in their wake.

"Calamity Kell strikes again," someone said.

Julian smiled, but only because he knew Callandre would be grinding her teeth inside her Destroyer, hearing her old nickname thrown at her yet again.

"If you are done grandstanding," he said, and toggled back over to an all-hands circuit. "Leftenant Dawkins. Retard distance negative two hundred meters. Shift two points off the centerline of NavSat coordinates two nine zero point one five and point five. Drop the hammer!"

Ariana Zou and Callandre Kell led forward a strong column of 'Mechs and armor, approaching Julian's position as the order was relayed. The first artillery shells fell to either side of them and smashed into the regrouping loyalists. One heavy payload landed between the feet of a limping *Mad Cat III*, throwing it back and down, minus a leg. Other shells worried some scattered infantry, and overturned a Demon fast-attack vehicle.

Julian read the battlefield with a practice eye. Saw where the loyalists maintained their best order. "Shift all assets to the eastern zone. Saturate for thirty seconds. Now!"

A moment later, that part of the tundra erupted in a wall of fire and smoke and the detritus of broken machines. It forced the remaining loyalists right where they did not want to go. On a reckless charge into the teeth of a combined Republic-Federated Suns force.

"Remind me never to get on your bad side," Lady Zou said. She stomped her *Griffin* up next to Julian's *Templar*, helping set their line against the coming charge. "I would hate to see what you do to people you do not like."

There were a few laughs of black humor, but not from Julian. Or Callandre either, he noted. Both of them knew that Lady Zou hit close to the truth. Julian did not care for the loyalists, true, but neither did he hate them. Opposed their politics, yes. Would meet them on the battlefield and strip away their ability to make war, certainly. But as champion of the Federated Suns, he was merely exercising the will of his prince and ruler, Harrison Davion.

His prince's order had been to assist The Republic.

Perhaps the last order Harrison Davion would ever give.

"Let's finish this," Julian said. Unable to keep the demons at bay now that they were loose once more in his mind, his tone was short and clipped.

He breathed easier with his *Templar's* heat levels having fallen away, but there was still a tightness in his chest that had nothing to do with the battle. He pulled his crosshairs over the stumbling *Legionnaire*. A ruined 'Mech leading forward warriors without the sense to realize when they were beaten.

It was his job to explain it in a way they would understand.

"On my mark, silence artillery and all units advance. We

hold the line unless and until the loyalists break. Then it's hunting by pairs. All units respond."

He waited as Callandre and even Lady Zou had checked in with affirmative votes. Hastings and Dawkins and Montgomery. All lance leaders. All support auxiliaries.

"Now!" he ordered, and throttled his *Templar* into an easy walk.

The first salvo of concentrated fire knocked the *Legionnaire* back and put it down hard. Not to rise again. Their second shattered a Behemoth II assault tank, stripping it down to a ruined pile of scrap.

Return fire was light and sporadic.

A moment later, with two more tanks destroyed and a *Pack Hunter* torn down to spare parts, it was not even that. A very few units fled on wild escape paths across the tundra. Most dropped their active targeting systems and powered down in surrender.

"Not a bad day's work, Jules." Callandre cranked her steering vane over and spun her Destroyer through a couple of victory circles. "What do we do now?" she asked.

But with the demands of battle fading, and the questions rising once more, Julian Davion sagged back in his cockpit seat. Reaching forward, he toggled off the comms board, not yet ready to answer. What *should* they do now?

That was the question. Wasn't it?

2

That's the trouble! No one believed he could *do it, not that he* would. *Some great political grandstanding. Slap the nobles around a bit, and why not? But to enforce it by the military, and with no court to redress the conflict?*
What is Jonah Levin really *about?*
—Filmmaker Wendell Stone, on Lawrence King's *Speaking Out*, Towne, 12 May 3135

Genève, Terra
Republic of the Sphere
13 June 3135

Exarch Jonah Levin once considered the Chamber of Paladins his final refuge.

Some of that was simple architecture. To his mind, the Chamber possessed a mixture of senatorial grandeur and Arthurian legend. Thick doors of silver ashwood letting onto a tall, domed room. Brightly illuminated. A wide, ferroglass skylight that opened up a large portion of the wall as well. All surrounded by white stone and blue-gray marble, much of it carved in ornate decoration and often inlaid with delicate gold and silver filigree. Stepping across the threshold, guarded from the Hall of Government's Rotunda by nothing more than velvet ropes, he'd traded the minute cares and worries of the day for loftier goals, walking softly on runners of plush, crimson carpet as he made his way to his place.

As a knight of the Sphere he'd spent many years in the gallery. Large enough to seat several hundred knights, the assembled champions of every Republic world, the gallery seating circled the outside wall on a set of shallow risers.

Elevated to paladin, Jonah had then taken his place at one of the seventeen private stations arranged on the main floor. Here the paladins met, and reported, and worked together (mostly) to support the ideals and tenets as laid down by Devlin Stone, grand architect of The Republic.

Twenty-five years of service. Half his life.

And all of that had changed when his peers elected him to The Republic's highest post in December.

As the second of Stone's successors, and the man presiding over The Republic's darkest hours, he'd known little peace and even less rest since ascending to Exarch. One crisis after another. Until he dreaded setting foot in the Chamber, to hear what his paladins had to report, or suggest. The room would never again be the sanctuary it once was.

It was hardly recognizable now. It still looked the same, but the inviolate calm had been stripped away by an invasion of aides and clerical staff and harried knights who served the working paladins. The place was now more of a war room—a crisis center—than any refuge of thought and careful debate. Sullied. Poisoned, even.

"Not that we were given much choice," he said. Then he sipped from the nutrient drink his chief of staff had thrust on him, and made a face. The frothy, green beverage tasted like grass. As always.

"Exarch?"

Paladin David McKinnon waited at Jonah's side, looking up from the noteputer he'd loaded with reports of the latest fighting and clean-up efforts all across Terra. Oldest and now "Paladin Exemplar" with the recent passing of Victor Davion, at one hundred four years of age Sire McKinnon had the vitality and strength of most men fifty years his junior. Snow white hair and a weathered face, perhaps, but a strong bearing and still a dangerous, catlike grace when he moved.

"Apologies, David. Fatalistic thinking has no place here."

The venerable warrior shrugged. "Things change," McKinnon said.

But not always for the better.

"You were saying?" Jonah cradled the steel mug in one hand, brushed flat the front of his suit. "Another month?"

McKinnon hesitated. Then, "Less, I'd think. With the First Davion Guards on hand, we've moved harder and faster against the loyalist holdouts than I'd originally estimated. If you would care for a formal report?"

The paladin gestured to the exarch's dock. A raised dais at the focus of room, surrounded in a half-circle by the paladins' stations. Jonah's formal "chair" for presiding over the chamber.

Jonah shook his head. "I step up there and the doors close. Every paladin evicts his staff. We lose hours of productivity." He felt the muscles tighten and pull at the back of his neck. "We've been running behind since December. Let's try to catch up."

McKinnon glanced between his noteputer and his exarch. Then he gestured towards the station on the far end of the wide arc where Gareth Sinclair, one of the younger paladins, worked diligently over a holographic keyboard. Knight Lady Zou stood by to assist him.

"I believe Gareth has most of the data plugged into a world map."

The way McKinnon said it, he might as well have called Sinclair "the boy." Though in an avuncular kind of way. Gareth had certainly proven his chops in the recent fighting, after all. It was a vote of confidence that McKinnon deferred to the younger man, and solidarity among the paladins was a desperately needed commodity these days.

Also, Jonah needed more time in the company of Ariana Zou.

He nodded, and the two men stepped over to Sinclair's workstation. Jonah also caught Paladin Heather GioAvanti passing by. With a gesture he pulled her into the small gathering. Of all his paladins, he trusted these three the most. And while it dug at him to make such distinctions these days, it was a point that the paladins had not proven immune to the politics of destruction currently being played out across The Republic.

Ariana Zou stiffened to formal attention as Jonah

stepped up behind Gareth Sinclair. Her dark, almond-shaped eyes held tiny flecks of gold in them. She glanced sharply at the Gallery, and the door, no doubt expecting to be dismissed.

But Jonah ignored her for the moment. He watched as Sinclair continued to work, fully absorbed in his assignment and all but oblivious to the exarch's presence. The younger man had only recently ascended to the small circle of paladins, but already the stress told on him. Heavy shoulders. Weary eyes. Sinclair would come out the far side of these hectic months a great deal stronger, or utterly ruined.

"Where are we, Gareth?"

"Sir," Gareth said. But it took the young paladin a moment more to put the finishing touches on his project. He hit the command key and stepped back as the holographic projectors built into his workstation erased the keyboard and instead projected a fully formed globe of Terra into the air above the lectern-style desk.

The world rotated at an accelerated pace, turning fully around its axis every twenty seconds. A great golden star centered over Geneva, capital of Terra and the seat of power for the entire Republic. Several political districts around the world flashed with cautionary amber. One in danger-warning red.

"These are all that are left," Gareth promised. "Loyalist remnants scattered across Europe and Asia. A few holdouts in the Australian outback. The Americas are clear except for the area around Sao Paulo." He nodded at the one red-flashing district, nestled along the eastern coast of South America. "It's a stronghold similar to the one we broke in Germany."

"And a high cost we paid for it," Heather GioAvanti reminded them. "Sire Jorgensson was only our most high-profile casualty."

"Where did this start?" Jonah asked of no one in particular. "When did it spiral so completely out of our control that it came to this?"

Not that he expected a response. He'd spent months working on answers to those questions, and was no farther along than the day he'd taken office.

On the face of it, of course, all of The Republic's woes might easily be blamed on the still-unresolved crash of

ComStar's HPG network; a blackout on nearly all interstellar communications throughout the entire Inner Sphere. With hardly one station in ten still working—still attempting to keep the infrastructure of star-spanning nations functional—on that larger stage The Republic was one realm among several facing the same problems.

At a closer look, however, The Republic was actually an amalgam of the many different realms. Having been carved from the center of the Inner Sphere only seventy years before, following the great Jihad, the identity of its peoples was still wrapped up in those surrounding nations and cultures. House Davion's Federated Suns had given up dozens of worlds to the forming Republic. Same for the Draconis Combine, the Lyran Alliance, and the shattered Free Worlds League. House Liao's Capellan Confederation had fought long and hard to resist the annexation of their territory.

So what followed the Blackout might have been predicted. Perhaps. Centralized government quickly breaking down. Powerful men and women taking more authority upon themselves at a local level. The fracture lines deepened, widened, forming divisive gulfs, until all the old hatreds and suspicions flared up in armed conflict and political revolution on many worlds.

House Liao had been first to come back for their former territory. But not the last. There were also the Steiners to worry about. And Clan Jade Falcon, which seized on the opportunity to carve a small island of power within The Republic's outer prefectures, and now House Kurita's recent encroachment.

The rise of powerful warlords within, set upon by larger realms without, The Republic of the Sphere had reeled from one crisis to another in the last several years.

So, no, Jonah did not expect an answer. But that wasn't going to stop his paladins from rising to his challenge.

Paladin Sinclair ran fingers back through his dark, unruly hair. His nervous green eyes danced around, always searching the room now that he had surfaced from his work.

"If you are truly asking, Exarch, I believe it still comes back to the Senate. Mallowes. Derius. Riktofven. They undermined our strength when we needed it most."

"A simple plan," McKinnon agreed. "As the best ones always are. Buy deep into the next generation of officers. Leverage them into situations where they can shine, and draw attention, and suddenly you have access to the knighthood." He nodded easily to Sinclair, though his eyes were hard and unyielding. Gareth had been just such an experiment, though one that had backfired. "Raise one or two as paladins, you can influence policy. Maybe even handicap the election of an exarch."

What had Heather GioAvanti called it on the day of Jonah's election? A conspiracy to control thought?

Which was exactly what the Senate nearly accomplished. And might have, if Paladin Exemplar Davion had not tumbled to their machinations. The cabal silenced Victor before he brought his evidence to light, but an investigation into the paladin's death uncovered enough of the plot to force a confrontation between the Senate and the Executive branch.

The Senators—nobles all—were heirs to long family histories and traditions of wielding power. They resisted Jonah's efforts to bring them to heel, to the point of directly confronting him with a political censure.

"You did not have a choice," Heather GioAvanti said.

Her voice was strong and certain. The quintessential paladin, Jonah could not remember the last time she evidenced even the slightest measure of doubt in her duties.

"The Senate overplayed their hand. And if you had backed off, Exarch, they would have castrated the Executive branch and seized complete power."

"So instead," Jonah said, "I do the same to them. I disband the Senate on the eve of the greatest political summit of our generation. And in return their rebellion, however brief, has hijacked a great deal of our agenda."

Such an opportune moment it had been. Victor Davion (Victor *Steiner-Davion*) had lived a life of legend within the Inner Sphere. Related by blood to two of the Great Houses and having ruled both the Federated Suns and Lyran Commonwealth, there were few leaders who had not fought with him or against him (or both) at some point during the last century. Jonah had capitalized on this by organizing a state funeral to which nearly every Inner

Sphere realm and Clan had responded. A chance for real dialogue, to reaffirm old alliances and set out bold, new agendas in this uncertain time.

And it had been working! That was the galling part. Slow but certain, several larger realms had relaxed their guard and put forward tentative feelers that might have led to a restoration of peace and cooperative effort.

Then, Prince Harrison Davion had fallen from the chateau balcony at Thonon-les-Bains.

On the very eve of victory over the Senate loyalists, in fact. By all reports a stupid, tragic accident. Sitting or leaning back against the low stone balustrade, waiting for Julian Davion to report back. Had he seen the lights of Julian's car on the road? Leaned back a little too far, impaired by the glass of bourbon he'd enjoyed earlier?

Failed to grab the railing as he overbalanced?

Three seconds. At best, according to the initial report Jonah had read and reread. That was what Harrison had been given, to realize what had happened. Cracking his head hard against the edge of a stone balcony on the second floor. Pinwheeling through the remaining drop. Slamming hard into the ground.

The prince's own guard handled the investigation, aided by the best forensic team Jonah had to offer. But all the king's horses and all the king's men . . . No matter the exact circumstance, Harrison Davion remained in a coma in Genève's Sisters of Mercy Hospital. Hanging on, but weakening every day.

And any alliance that may have come from their talks and pledges of assistance hung in the balance.

Jonah took another sip from his nutrition drink. Grimaced. Grass again. He set the steel mug on the edge of Sinclair's workstation, stared at the turning globe.

"So what's left?" he asked. "We can root out the remaining loyalists, but Senators Monroe and Derius—among others—made it off world and are likely to continue their resistance. The Capellan Confederation has eased back their aggressive stance, but I expect that to last only so long as Daoshen Liao remains a willing guest. And in their place, House Kurita pushes hard through Prefecture II."

Heather GioAvanti tugged straight the hem of her dress jacket. "Coordinator Vincent Kurita plans to leave Terra within the week," she said. "He reminds us there is little he can do while isolated here."

"Convenient." McKinnon's leathery face wrinkled into a deep frown. "He relies on his absence from the Combine as proof against his participation in the attacks. Now he leverages that same argument to safeguard his own return." The paladin's hand knotted into strong fists. "I don't believe him."

"What would you have me do, David?" Jonah's hands were tied. And everyone—most everyone—standing nearby recognized that. "Hold the Coordinator of the Draconis Combine hostage against the cessation of all hostilities? And Chancellor Liao as well? Do we violate our pledges of safe conduct and grab up every ruler? We might be able to do that, yes. And then were would we be?"

"The Great Houses would all turn on us then," Heather said.

Sinclair's green eyes shifted from exarch to paladin to paladin. "I'm not sure we'd even get so far. Communication intercepts and readiness postures of the honor guards for several visiting rulers indicate that many of them have anticipated such extremes. Daoshen Liao has already removed himself from the Capellan Cultural Center here in Genève, isolating himself with his DropShip. Khan Becker of the Dominion as well. And BattleMech patrols around the natural preserve above Ishinomaki Port have doubled." He kept his voice very soft, and even. "Worse than holding such leaders hostage would be killing one in an armed attempt to take them."

Which was why Jonah had never seriously considered it. And despite McKinnon's usual hard-line stand that victory at any cost was acceptable in the preservation of The Republic, even the venerable warrior nodded to the truth of the matter.

But, "What do you think, Lady Zou?" Jonah asked.

As tactical surprises went, Jonah achieved complete victory. Ariana Zou had maintained a stiff and formal bearing, ready at the slightest nod to stand dismissed. Only her intense gaze, following the conversation, betrayed her complete devotion to every spoken word, every facial expression.

Jonah had noted her hard glare at the mention of Senator Monroe. And the very slight shift in her stance as she witnessed the small group so easily discussing (and dismissing) even the possibility of taking an Inner Sphere leader hostage. She had strong opinions. One way or another. But would she voice them?

For an instant, it seemed she wouldn't. She clasped her hands behind her back and stared straight ahead. But what Jonah initially took as reticence was really a measure of time in which she ordered her thoughts.

"I think, Exarch Levin, you should put your own realm in order before meddling in the affairs of others."

Her voice was soft yet strong. A woman who knew the worth of her own counsel, regardless of whether it would be weighed and fairly considered.

"The Republic is too fragile, at the moment, to withstand further aggressive policies."

A moment of silence followed Zou's calm argument. McKinnon was first to respond. "Glass houses and throwing stones, eh?" He tasted the words, and obviously found them not to his liking. "You do not think passive policies will only encourage our enemies to begin lobbing bricks of their own?"

"Why should they? When the Senate nobles are more than willing to do the heavy lifting for them?"

McKinnon folded arms across his chest. "Abandoning an aggressive foreign policy in favor of domestic policing is risky. If the nobles resist our efforts for too long, we will look weak."

Now that McKinnon had drawn Zou out, Jonah slipped back into the discussion. "If the nobles resist us long," he said, "we *are* weak." He reached for his mug again, if only to have something to do with his hands. The steel sides were cold and sweating. "We need to build on our recent victories. And quickly."

Zou nodded. "With respect, Exarch. Regarding victories or alliances. Quickly built means quickly abandoned. You want a strong house, you begin with a strong foundation on good ground. A fortress built on quicksand is no bargain at all."

That Zou had so closely mirrored his own thinking was enough to startle Jonah. And her choice of words was eerily on target. A stronghold was exactly what The Republic needed. And exactly what Jonah had set in motion last month, secretly laying the groundwork for one of many failsafe plans prepared against such a day as this.

As indicators went, Zou's stated opinions were all strong votes in her favor.

Still, he was not quite ready to commit. There was one question more he must have answered.

"Let me ask you, then, why you risked your life and your own warriors so easily on the Siberian plains." He'd reviewed the battlerom footage and read reports from everyone involved in the operation near Salekhard. He had his own thoughts about what had happened. But he needed it direct from Ariana Zou. "You broke from the battle plan when Julian Davion fell. In what seemed to be a sharp, emotional reaction. It happened to work. But you would not call that hasty? A 'quick' victory?"

"I would," she admitted. "We were fortunate."

"*Very* fortunate," Heather GioAvanti said. If it were possible to scold Zou and reward her for *chutzpah* all at the same time, Heather accomplished it with her tone.

"Or," Sinclair offered, "one might say 'instinctive.' A leap to sudden knowledge based on experience and conditioned skills."

Jonah sipped his nutrient drink, and barely tasted its green flavor with the thrill of the hunt on him. "So which was it, Lady Zou? Luck? Or skill?" Every word fell heavy from his lips. Most everyone knew how much was riding on her answer.

If *she* knew, she hid it well behind a mask of serene contemplation. The exarch and three of his most trusted paladins were giving Ariana a full-court press. Guiding her in the direction they wanted. Prodding and poking at her. Gauging her response. Certainly, she earned high marks for her composure.

"I'll take both in my corner any time I can, Exarch. And be glad for them." She drew herself back to formal attention. "But that isn't exactly the question you've been wanting to ask me. Is it, sir?"

If she hadn't fallen back on cadet-level formality, Jonah would have ended their conversation quickly. But he had to appreciate her ability to cut through to the chase, *and* maintain a proper level of respect. So be it, then. Bluntly.

"Why did you risk Republic lives for Julian Davion?"

"Because he deserved from me *exactly* what he stood ready to pay, especially in a fight not necessarily his own." Fire flashed behind her eyes. "Such men are rare, Exarch. And at that moment I believed his value to you, and to The Republic, at a much higher worth than me and mine."

"You would not rethink your strategy and actions now with time to look back on them?"

"No, sir." She did not hesitate. Not for a single heartbeat.

Jonah looked to McKinnon first. Saw the man's grudging nod. Heather GioAvanti and Gareth Sinclair were more circumspect. Each tipped their chin down only slightly, satisfied, though it was his vote, and his alone, that counted in the end.

And Jonah liked what he saw.

"Admirable," he said. "Heroic, even if touched with a bit of conceit."

"I did not mean to—"

He interrupted her with a raised hand. "These are also traits I've found in the best of my knights . . . and paladins. Meraj Jorgensson had both in abundance. You just might do as his replacement." He nodded to McKinnon. "Have her tested," he ordered. And saw Ariana reeling behind an expression of wide-eyed incredulity.

"I believe you may be right about Julian Davion," he said. "But it is just as hard on The Republic to lose a *paladin*. Remember, in the coming months, that I cannot afford to discard any of you so casually."

Then he turned and left Ariana in the care of the others, struck dumb and likely half-blind as well. As he had been when the offer of a paladinship first rolled over him. She wouldn't regain her equilibrium for days, he knew. Not with the battery of tests and the strains to which she'd be subjected in short order. The mounting mental and physical exhaustion. The psychological strain running her ragged, until she failed or came through the far side baptized by fire.

Cleansed.

Ready, he hoped, as there would be little time to recover. Ariana had the right of it. The sands *were* shifting beneath The Republic's feet. Jonah Levin felt them moving every day. Felt them now, in fact, as he stepped across the threshold that divided the Chamber of Paladins from The Republic's Hall of Government. His unsteady footing, threatened by a gathering storm.

If The Republic were to survive, it needed allies. And anchors.

Like Julian Davion.

And Ariana Zou.

3

Still no word on how the tragic accident that has befallen Prince Harrison Davion will affect The Republic's relations with the Federated Suns. Sources close to Julian Davion, Lord Markeson, remain hopeful of a continued and strengthened relationship.
—Thoman Clarke's *Inside Politics*, Genève, Terra, aired 10 June 3135

Thonon-les-Bains, Terra
Republic of the Sphere
14 June 3135

Caleb Hasek Sandoval Davion paced the chateau's third-floor balcony at Thonon-les-Bains, drink in hand, staying well away from the stone rail yet unable to take his eyes from it. By now he knew every chip, every last moss-filled crack. And as the sun fell towards the snow-capped crowns of distant mountains, and twilight's coming gloom gathered in the doorways and tall shadows behind the estate's many trees, he wondered again how his father could have done something like this to him.

"All of it so magnificently unfair," he complained. "So . . . treacherous!"

The sour taste burning at the back of his throat had not lessened in the last two weeks, no matter how he tried to soothe it. The smoky flavor of his whiskey masked it with every swallow, but too quickly the warm glow faded and left him shivering despite the beautiful, cloudless day.

He paused mid-stride. Stared down into the wide highball. Swirling the amber liquid, he watched the ice dance through a small whirlpool. The oval cubes tapped musically against the heavy glass, then settled again.

"Treacherous," he whispered. And couldn't help his glance towards the nearby door that let into his private suite.

The stain had faded, finally. The dark wash of bourbon he'd smashed against the wall, splashing fine Syrtis liquor over the flagstone patio and the leading edge of plush, gray carpet. He remembered his anger, and shifted uncomfortably from one foot to the other.

It didn't help when Mason Lambert stepped from the room and stood right where the spilled alcohol had pooled. Best friend or not. A piece of gravel caught in the sole of Mason's boot crunched against the gray flagstone. Gravel. That's all it was.

Though it sounded like glass. A shard missed by one of Levin's expert forensic teams. Pieces they had collected with due solemnity, as if weighed down by the tragedy that had occurred here. A sorrowful event.

Treacherous.

"It may seem so," Amanda Hasek said. She moved to his side from one of the umbrella-shaded seats where she'd waited out his silence. Duchess of New Syrtis and Caleb's aunt, she was part of the Federated Suns' contingent to visit for the funeral of Victor Davion. "But truly, Caleb, these things happen without nefarious design. No malicious intent."

Which hadn't stopped her from doubling her personal guard. As if she suspected foul play. Though with tragedy striking so close to home, who could blame her? Amanda Hasek ruled over the Capellan March, fully one-fourth of the Federated Suns, and after Harrison Davion was likely the most powerful among all the Suns' nobility. Only Corwin and Victoria Sandoval came close.

And Caleb! Heir to the throne, and now the acting First Prince. *De facto* if not *de jure.*

"It was so hard to believe," Caleb said. "All happened so fast."

"I know. I know." His aunt raised a hand to smooth back her coal-dark hair. As a nod to her years, she had finally allowed a touch of gray to creep in at her temples. But no more than that. "Harrison was always so healthy. So alive! Hard to imagine him any other way." She patted his arm. "I know."

But she didn't! No one did. Though Amanda stayed at the Thonon-les-Bains chateau as part of the prince's retinue. Had been here *that* night, asleep, when Caleb also paced his balcony. Waiting for his cousin to arrive from Genève, that great and honorable champion, the hero of the hour.

A traitor to his blood.

And as difficult as the late hour had been on Caleb, they were the last moments in which he had felt in any way normal. Before then, at least the household had existed in an uneasy peace. Amanda Hasek quietly at odds with her brother-in-law's choice of consort, distracting herself by working hard to marry off Sandra Fenlon and Julian when anyone (other than the duchess) could see the two of them were merely humoring her. When Harrison was not entertaining Sterling McKenna, he kept himself busy with matters of state. Julian as well, with the prince's champion of late taking on more duties than usual.

And despite his personal gaffe, the near-disastrous relationship he had unknowingly started with Danai Liao-Centrella, Caleb had been given his freedom to roam and explore and indulge himself. As an heir to the throne *should* be allowed.

And after . . . After . . . The instant paranoia and worry that Harrison had fallen victim to a Republic plot. Or one of the Raven Alliance! Amanda quickly expelled Sterling from the chateau, not taking any chances with Harrison's "poor judgment." Sandra Fenlon was moved to Genève, if only to get her out from underfoot. And Julian—he was kept under close watch by Caleb's own honor guard officers. Waiting to see what the "champion" might do. Might try.

Might *accuse*.

The sour taste burned at the back of his throat like a rising gorge. His skin tensed and tingled. A few places on his arms and the back of his neck pricked as if stuck by the tip of a blade. Caleb shivered, swirled his drink, then tipped it up and belted back a healthy slug of the warming amber.

He resumed his slow walk along the stone balustrade. Always at greater length than an arm's reach from the railing. Not wanting to look over the edge. Never again wanting to see that three-story plunge his father had taken.

The wild fear in Harrison Davion's bright blue eyes.

The short yell, cut off as the large man cracked his head against a second balcony far below.

The heavy crash of the prince's body hitting the slope, and rolling down through the brush to fold around one of the large pine trees that isolated the château.

"I think I should be alone for awhile," Caleb said. He tried to put the authority of the Prince behind it. Nearly got it right. It only sounded a touch empty. Hollow.

"Of course," Amanda said. And gave him another pat on the arm. As if he were still fifteen, and spending the summer on New Syrtis. Not a man twenty years beyond those visits.

Not a prince.

He waited as Amanda collected her personal bodyguard from the far side of the open-air patio and led the way back inside. She hardly gave Mason a look, obviously trusting her nephew's judgment in friends more than his own father ever had. The security guard was not so easygoing. He did raise a hand near his breast lapel, as if ready to reach inside his suit jacket for a weapon. But Mason made not one movement as the duchess passed by, quiet and respectful as always.

"Has to be difficult for her," Mason said once the duchess had passed inside, out of earshot. "Losing her sister, and her prince as well."

Caleb resumed his slow pacing. "I'm her prince now."

Prince of the Federated Suns. Leader of House Davion. He had waited his entire life for this. Had never known a moment's doubt of it, actually. Not one day of his thirty-five years. With ties to the three strongest noble lines within the Federated Suns—the Haseks of the Capellan March and the Sandovals of Robinson and the Draconis March—

he had always seen himself as a unifying figure. A living truce among the powerful nobility and the ruling line on New Avalon.

He'd never had reason to doubt. Until recently.

"What do I do about him?" he asked. He reached the end of the patio, near a corner where two of the stone walls met. Stayed away from both. Turned and started back the other direction. "What do I do about Julian?"

Halfway back he stopped. But not to wait out Mason's answer. Caleb spied a small tag of bright yellow crime scene tape stuck to the balustrade cap, caught in the slight evening breeze and fluttering up from the outside edge.

He shuffled half a step closer, craning his neck. The breeze kicked the tape up again. Yellow, with a piece of red lettering. And taped to the rail just at the point where his father had gone over. Where he had—

Fallen!

"You do what you have to," Mason said. "Just like that night, you did what had to be done."

Caleb remembered his friend saying just that to him. Stepping up at his side and laying a friendly hand on his shoulder. Comforting him on the loss of his father, who had thrown Caleb over for a cousin! A *distant* cousin who had taken advantage of the prince's generosity and sponsorship to eat away at the love Harrison Davion had once known for Caleb.

The finest schools and training hadn't been enough for Julian. Nor being named the youngest prince's champion in the Suns' long history.

No. Julian had wanted it all. Had stolen it all.

Caleb edged up towards the rail. Held the heavy, chilled highball in his one hand. Reached out carefully with the other towards the fluttering tag of tape. Yellow. Bright yellow. A warning. But it wasn't red lettering, he saw now. It was blood. A smear of blood on the end of the tape. His father's blood, of course. Right where Prince Harrison had gone over the rail.

Right after he had told Caleb the chilling, damning news.

Julian will be my heir.

His hand trembled as he leaned out towards the balustrade's stone cap. The sour taste flooded through his mouth, turning bitter, like spoiled adrenaline. Caleb remembered how his father had simply blurted out the truth as if it was the most obvious thing in the world.

Never mind the years Caleb had spent touring the realm, cast out among every backwater world, getting to know the nobles.

Never mind how hard he had worked to get his officer's commission.

Never mind that Caleb was his *son!*

We'll help you understand. We will. And then he had tried to pull Caleb to him. Reaching out. Grabbing hold. Just as Caleb reached out for a handful of the prince's silk shirt, driving forward . . . shoving . . .

"No!"

Dashing his drink to one side, leaping forward, Caleb snatched at the fluttering yellow tape. Tore it from the stone railing even as he overbalanced himself and collapsed. Folding over the balustrade, his hips pressed painfully into the stone as he leaned far out over the drop-off to stare at the ground swaying sickeningly far, far below. A shadow fell down and away from him. A large shadow, quickly swallowed up by the night. One short yell, and the sound of the prince's head smashed against the second railing below, and then silence.

Silence. And the headlamp from Julian's car sweeping up the chateau's long drive.

And Caleb standing there, watching his father's body roll down the slope, to lose itself among the brush and trees.

The scent of spilled whiskey was strong. The ground swayed back and forth, back and forth, as Caleb slowly caught hold of his bearings and hauled himself back from the overhang. Back from the same long, deadly fall his father had taken that night after dashing all of Caleb's dreams and desires as if they were a mere favor to be dispensed to another as easily as Harrison might grant land or title to some upstart warrior.

Back from the truth of what had happened.

That Harrison and Julian had conspired together to rob Caleb of what was rightfully his. His birthright. His people's need for a strong ruler to unite the realm and lead it into a glorious future.

Stumbling back from the rail, Caleb sat down hard on the flagstone patio. Silence descended. The world swayed once more, then settled firmly back into place. Leaving Caleb on the cold, wet patio, sitting in a spill of fresh whiskey, and clutching at . . .

Nothing.

No yellow tape. He had grabbed it. He was sure. He had snatched it from the rail and dragged it back with him. If he had lost it, dropped it down among the tall gasses and brush, he would have to send someone to find it.

"Mason . . . ?"

But Mason had disappeared as well.

A good friend, not wanting to see Caleb caught in a moment of weakness. Yes, that was what had happened. Mason would retrieve the yellow tape, and dispose of it. And Caleb could move on from what had occurred.

When he did what had to be done.

4

Shinonoi, Biham, Ancha . . . Three more worlds fallen to the Dragon! As the march of House Kurita pushes deeper into Prefecture II, and Paladin Marik returns under orders to Terra yet again, we are left to ask: Where is our Exarch?! Where is our rescue?
— Assistant Governor Kalvin Montgomery, Al Na'ir, 7 June 3135

Genève, Terra
Republic of the Sphere
18 June 3135

Julian walked slowly along the dove-gray corridor at Sisters of Mercy, Sandra Fenlon's long, slender hand clasped tightly in his own. Two knight-errants of The Republic, stationed at the security post that let onto this private floor, pulled the doors closed behind them. Their cold, impersonal stares followed after, raising a prickling feeling at the back of Julian's neck.

Sandra shivered. Whispered, "I always feel guilty when they look at me that way."

He nodded. Squeezed her hand. "Human nature," he said.

Most people tended to feel uncomfortable under the direct gaze of authority figures such as police, politicians, or military officers. Among the things Julian had learned in the course of his early officer training was recognizing this effect, and understanding how to use it. It had also helped him banish such reactionary impulses of his own. As an officer and especially as prince's champion, being stared at—studied and weighed—was the norm. *Came with the name*, as his father would have said.

So why, then, did it bother him now?

Partly it was the hospital, he decided. Partly. The astringent scents in the air. The heavy silence, broken as the sharp step of his leather dress boots against the terrazzo floor echoed down the length of the empty hall. Julian half-expected a nurse to leap out of a doorway with padded mufflers and a stern warning, that the prince required peace and quiet and a tranquil environment for his recovery.

And for the first time that day, he smiled. Thin, tense, but a smile nonetheless. Anyone who could say such a thing truly did not know Harrison Davion.

He squeezed Sandra's hand again.

Third door down on the right. One of the executive care rooms. Julian kept his gaze locked on the door handle as they approached, and startled when the door suddenly swung inward as if expecting them. Then Amanda Hasek stepped into the corridor, stopped. As surprised to see Julian and Sandra as they had been.

Sandra hesitated for a heartbeat, then dropped Julian's hand to quickly step forward and embrace the duchess. Though Sandra had come into her full majority the year before she was, legally, still a ward of Amanda Hasek. And would be until married off. Matchmaking Sandra with Julian was the duchess's chief endeavor. Usually. Today, though, there was no hint of a prideful gleam or any need to push Sandra back on Julian's arm as quickly as possible. Amanda accepted the offered comfort. She looked as if she needed it, with her face more drawn and pale than usual, her upswept hair in slight disarray, reddened eyes from crying.

Amanda broke away, hands on Sandra's shoulders as she held the younger woman at arm's length. With motherly care she reached up to smooth the side of Sandra's long, ash-blonde hair, worn in a straight fall down to curvaceous hips. She tucked a few strands back behind Sandra's ear, giving her ward a touch of girlish charm. Then she divided her gaze between Sandra and Julian, forcing a smile at seeing them together.

"He looks better today," Amanda said. Julian heard the lie in her voice. "A spot of color in his cheeks. Hands are warmer."

If so, it would be the first positive sign in two weeks, among Julian's six visits. Every time he looked for improvement in the prince's condition. Some sign that the prince would struggle out of his coma. And when he couldn't come himself, he read a daily report prepared by the hospital staff. So far, nothing.

"He'll be happy to see you, Julian."

Nodding, he leaned forward to embrace the duchess. No matter that six months before Prince Davion had considered this woman—his sister by marriage—a potential threat to the stability of the Federated Suns. Now, in such a tragedy, kinship mattered more. And for the first time he could recall, she felt fragile in his arms.

Julian stepped back, smoothed down his pale red uniform dress shirt. "I don't come by often enough."

"Nonsense." She tapped him hard on the chest, briefly showing a measure of her old strength. "You have military operations to see to, just as Caleb must handle the political fallout of such a disaster. If you shirked your duties for one minute, Harrison would have your hide later."

Perhaps he would at that. Harrison Davion might be beloved by his people—"old bluff and gruff," the gentle giant who'd inspired the latest fashion travesty he had (willfully) engendered—but those closest to the prince knew he had a ferrosteel spine and a warm temper. And zero patience when it involved matters of duty.

"He's a strong man." Julian embraced the duchess again in comfort. "He'll pull through."

"Yes. Well. I'm back to the château." Amanda stiffened her spine. A cagey look flared behind her eyes. "Trillian Steiner will pay a call today. I'd like to be there to sit in on any discussion." She shrugged. Politics as usual. "She might even offer true condolences."

More than a little catty. And not without cause, Julian

knew. For two states which had once worked together hand-in-glove, formal relations between Houses Davion and Steiner were currently cool. At best.

"Would you like me there?" Julian asked.

Amanda glanced at him sharply. "Caleb has it." But she softened again at once. "You've been busy enough, dear boy. Don't borrow extra troubles."

Julian hesitated, then nodded. He could not say why, exactly, but he felt that Harrison would have wanted him there. Perhaps it was a holdover of the prince going out of his way to involve Julian in so many political meetings those last months before the terrible accident. Perhaps it was . . . something else. That sensation of shifting sands beneath his feet. The uncertain political landscape.

Regardless, he would not press the issue. Not here, especially. The door loomed very large in Julian's peripheral vision. "Then I'll be staying in the city this night. Tell Caleb I look forward to seeing him tomorrow."

"Tomorrow?"

"Ariana Zou has completed her formal testing. She ascends to her paladinship. I know Caleb received an invitation."

Amanda frowned. "And you have already accepted yours?"

"For Sandra and myself. Yes." Ariana was a comrade-in-arms. They had fought together on the Siberian tundra. Soldiers beneath them both had died together. Of course he'd be there to see her promoted. As would many of the visiting dignitaries, he imagined.

It had never occurred to him that Caleb might deign to refuse.

"I will tell Caleb," Amanda said. Stiff and formal.

Julian and Sandra exchanged goodbyes with Duchess Hasek, then watched her down the corridor. Sandra stepped in close to Julian, keeping up pretenses. Amanda glanced back once from the security station, and she did seem pleased to see them together.

Once she was past the heavy doors and behind the watchful guard of the two Republic knights, Julian turned Sandra through the nearby door before he lost his nerve.

Another guard stood watch inside the room, as he'd expected, this one wearing a similar uniform to Julian's. Dark green stirrup trousers and dress boots. A pale green shirt instead of red—the difference between infantry and MechWarrior. He had lieutenant's bars and wore a shoulder patch for the Davion Heavy Guards. Part of the same combat command in which Julian served as a regimental officer for the First Guards. He didn't recognize the soldier right away, but knew him to be part of the prince's security detail, which was one of the combat command's many responsibilities.

For a hospital care room, this one was lavishly appointed. Gray and blue marble tile covered the floor, dotted with chocolate-brown throw rugs of synthetic, non-allergenic fibers. Faux-wood paneling decorated the walls in what appeared to be golden oak, coated with transparent aluminum-oxide to keep a sterile atmosphere. A holographic fireplace crackled softly against one wall, and large windows across the room let in plenty of natural light.

Only the scent remained the same. Antiseptic. Scrubbed. It reminded Julian a bit of the recycled air in a DropShip, though without the underlying smells of machinery and men working.

But the anticipation, that was there. A nervous tension. Julian felt it from Sandra, as well as from the soldier on guard.

"Oh, Julian."

Sandra sagged against him, her light perfume warm and flowery and seeming much stronger than it should in the room's antiseptic atmosphere. Her arms encircled his waist, and she lay her head against his shoulder as she looked at the large man resting in the double-wide hospital bed, draped with strong-bleached sheets and a warming, red-gold duvet. Julian walked them closer to the bedside, ignoring the I.V. standing its own silent sentinel and the bedside monitors that constantly checked pulse, breathing, and brain activity. Trying to look past the breathing tube stuck up into the patient's nose and the electrodes taped to his temple and the shaved patches on his skull. Wanting to see a positive change—anything!—in the pale, wax-like skin.

Harrison Davion. Prince of the Federated Suns.

A large and active man in life, there was no mistaking the weight Prince Harrison had dropped in the last two weeks. The skin on his face was too loose. Arms too thin, and dark circles under sunken eyes. His hair had yet to grow back on the right side of his head where the doctors had shaved it away as they worked to repair the fractured skull. Nurses had also shaved away the thick, dark beard Harrison had worn most of his life, and the stubble was coming back with more gray than Julian would have thought. He had never considered Harrison vain enough to trouble with dying his beard, though why that should surprise him—or bother him—he did not know. It was like discovering your father had kept a secret from you. And while most fathers did, when one of them tripped into the light there was always that moment of disillusionment.

"Dammit," Julian whispered. It was a shock, each and every time, to see his prince in such a condition. As if someone had taken a sledgehammer to the foundation for Julian's world, smashing it anew.

What he had told Amanda Hasek had skirted the actual truth of the matter. He did visit as often as he could, though it wasn't often given his workload coordinating military actions between the on-planet Guards and Exarch Levin's regular line forces and leading forays such as the one that had run the Sverdlovsk loyalists to ground. But what truly bothered Julian were the shadows of doubt and helplessness parading through his mind on every visit. As if he should have been there, *done* something—anything!—to prevent this.

But there was no turning back the clock. Now, it felt as if he were drowning in military routine, tiredly treading water and trying to keep his head from going under for the last time. Living in the moment to prevent thinking about how they could have come to this, or where the future—any future without Prince Harrison—might lead.

This was one moment he could not escape, however. The nightmare from which he could not awake.

His duty.

Sandra stepped forward, moving up to the bedside to take one of the prince's hands. She held it between both of her own. "We are here, my prince. Julian and I." She seemed at a loss for what to say next. "We arrived together."

Julian had moved to the foot of the bed, standing stiffly as if ready to deliver a formal report. There was that prickling sensation again, crawling with a clammy touch along the back of his neck, over his scalp. A bitter taste dried out his mouth, and he swallowed roughly past the knot in his throat.

"That's right," he finally said as Sandra nodded encouragement. "We're still faking it."

"Julian!" Her whisper was full of embarrassment.

"He knew, Sandra. Knows!" Cursed his awkward tongue. "That we play it up for the duchess. Called me on it over a month ago." Right about the time they were making planetfall over Terra, if he recalled correctly.

"Did he?"

It had been their private little drama, letting Amanda Hasek play at matching them together to prevent more disastrous pairings the duchess might have made. Amanda saw what she wanted to see. Harrison was not so easily fooled.

"And I suppose he approves of Callandre Kell?"

That nearly made Julian laugh. Nearly. "Faith defend! He does not." He glanced down, thinking to find Harrison ready to leap up for a new lecture. Nothing. Not so much as an abnormal blip on the nearby monitor. But at last Julian had found his distraction. "No one can fault Callandre's skills as a warrior, but given our . . . awkward history together—"

"You were *expelled* from the Lyran Commonwealth, you mean."

"It's enough of a black mark against me that Calamity and I are still friends," Julian said as if she'd never interrupted. He saw Sandra's appraising gaze. "Friends, Sandra. Nothing more."

"I believe the charges against you at the Nagelring's honor board called you co-conspirators."

Callandre had been telling tales again. Julian winced. "Water over the dam," he said. And smashing down among the rocks.

Sandra shrugged. Leaned down at the prince's bedside and kissed him lightly on the brow. Then whispered something in his ear that Julian could not hear. Her gray-blue eyes never left Julian.

Having smashed through the awkward moment, Julian relaxed. Slightly. He leaned forward, resting his hands on the bed's footboard. Felt the warmth of hidden electronics beneath the thin veneer.

"I keep wondering." He spoke directly to the man who had become his patron as well as his prince. "What you would tell me to do. Which direction we should lean . . . whose play we will back. Everything stands at the cusp now. The exarch's move against his rogue senators. The tentative alliance you put into place with T. Even our own . . . troubles back home."

Meaning the powerful March Lords. Duke Corwin Sandoval, who ruled the Combine border fist-in-glove with Victoria, the Duchess Woodbine. And Amanda Hasek, who managed the same task on the Capellan border, but alone. Amanda would shake off her own grief soon enough. And the throne had been weakened *before* Harrison's tragedy.

"How do we do this without you?" he asked.

It was a question very similar to one he'd asked before, wanting to know the mind of his prince. Wanting to learn so badly the lessons being pushed at him. *How do you do this,* he'd asked.

He recalled the answer as fresh as if Harrison spoke the words now.

"You make it happen, Julian. You do it because there is no one else."

Julian had braced up to attention. "I understand." Turned to leave.

But Harrison had held fast to his arm. "Not yet, son. But you will. Get used to it. *You* need to learn how to make it happen. As . . . a leader."

Harrison's final words. They rang inside Julian's mind like a tolling bell, echoing far, far back into the shadows of his thoughts. Stirring up dark whispers even as he worked hard to fulfill that last promise. But there was no road map and no clear direction. He ended up feeling his way through with Exarch Levin, with Amanda Hasek, with Caleb.

And he couldn't help feeling that something important had eluded his grasp.

"How do we do this?" he asked again.

But Harrison Davion lay still, and silent.

5

Senator Lina Derius has called for all military and civilian assets uncomfortable with the recent direction of leadership from Terra to rally to a new alliance of Senators. "The nobles are not a simple cog to be yanked out of the great machine of government and cast aside by some fumble-handed mechanic. We are the very spark that turns the motor! Without us, The Republic will stall. The Republic must fail."
—Covering the public motion to censure Exarch Jonah Levin, Action Newz, Liberty, 3 June 3135

Genève, Terra
Republic of the Sphere
19 June 3135

Julian's questions did not give way with the short night's sleep, though he managed to shove them into the back of his mind on the drive from Hotel Duquesne to Magnum Park.

He and Sandra Fenlon rode in the back of a chauffeured limousine sent to pick them up. Holding hands as they rested back against dark gray leather, staring out their own windows at Genève. Except for a few pre-dawn commuters, the city still slept beneath a black, storm-heavy sky.

"She's been out all night?" Sandra asked. She sipped at

a strawberry-flavored breakfast drink, having chosen to sleep in rather than awake for a 4:00 a.m. breakfast.

Julian nodded. He had also foregone an early meal, settling for a glass of juice and the promise of a large brunch with Sandra and Lars Magnusson and Callandre Kell. He watched as morning dew evaporated off the limousine's warming windows. Checked the sky again as if he might divine the storm's intentions. Not the most auspicious signs for the ascension of a new paladin.

"Her choice," he said, speaking to Sandra's question as well as his unvoiced thoughts.

Past the abandoned Senate and they were into Genève's "political district." A telling sign, that Julian counted two BattleMechs on guard near the gates to the Hall of Government—a *Black Hawk* and a *Centurion*—as well as a full armor column idling at the ready on one side street. And that was what he spotted without much of a search.

Magnum Park stretched out next to the Hall of Government. A huge spread of cultivated grounds, it included some of the nation's most respected monuments as well as the display of Trees from Every World. Julian recognized a Caselton red cedar, and the nearly extinct flowering acacia of Outreach. The limo slowed to a crawl as it entered the line of cars pulling up to a small roundabout, which turned beneath the spreading branches of three different varieties of thick-boled oak.

No gala event, this morning. The press had been kept away, Julian knew, save for two veteran journalists who would be allowed to quietly observe the event to later write about it for posterity's sake. The arrival of so many dignitaries was kept sedate as each car pulled forward to be screened by security and then allowed into the roundabout to drop off passengers.

The limousine swerved around a large, half-shell motorcycle that someone had jacked up onto its stand within the roundabout. A single guard was posted next to it, waving vehicles past.

Julian noticed the hound's head crest on the cowling as he stepped from the limo. Shook his head.

A short walk, then, along a cobblestone path that meandered into a grove of silver aspen. The sky had lightened to a bruised purple. Thunderclouds massed heavily, though not one drop of rain had yet fallen. More than one anxious face turned to stare up into the storm-swollen sky. Julian recognized Nikol Marik, arriving on the arm of her mother, the Lady Jessica Marik and one of the so-called Captains-General of the shattered Free Worlds League. Also Jasek Kelswa-Steiner, who prowled the gathering crowd like a stalking cat in search of prey. Looking for Tara Campbell, no doubt.

And there was Callandre Kell. Waiting for his arrival and having already collected Lars Magnusson as well as Yori Kurita.

Callandre had dressed down for the occasion, separating herself from the nobility by keeping to her riding leathers. Matte-black pants and jacket, with a red "V" plunging deep from shoulders to navel. A red scarf knotted about her neck and cherry-red highlights dyed in her hazelnut hair. She held her riding helmet by the chin strap, swinging it back and forth, back and forth.

Just like her, Julian decided, to throw at least a small wrench into the arrival proceedings by riding up on her own.

"Couldn't leave the helmet with the bike?" he asked, he and Sandra joining the small group. He eyed the swinging cap with distrust and ran fingers back through his reddish-gold hair. "Not going to start trouble today?"

"You never know, Jules." Her smile was bright and cheerful, her doe-brown eyes far too innocent to be believed. "Personally, I'm just waiting for the next time Erik Sandoval mouths off." She swung the helmet a bit higher. Lars laughed.

"You would not," Yori said.

Some distant relation to the Draconis Combine's ruling house—second? third cousin?—Yori Kurita wore a heavy red kimono with a golden obi overcoat wrapped about her. Julian was surprised, actually, to see her separated from the Kurita contingent. But then, she had already admitted among her peers that her name was not highly favored at court.

In fact, the other Combine samurai barely tolerated her.

"Don't encourage her," Julian said as Callandre smiled. There wasn't much beyond the Nagelring's "darling rogue," he knew. And once upon a time, he'd risked everything his prince had invested in him just to try to match her. "And you," he eyed Callandre, "not today. Not this morning."

She huffed an exaggerated sigh. "I have the helmet with me because I forgot to lock it to the bike and don't want to go back now. Okay? That, and I wanted to have something handy for when you start making my life miserable again. I don't have a roll of kroner coin today."

Making *her* life miserable? If that wasn't the *Atlas* calling the *Awesome* large . . . And he still had not forgotten the welcoming smack she'd given him with the rolled kroner balled up in her hand.

"What have I done—recently!—to make your life miserable?"

Her smile blossomed full and bright. "You got up this morning, didn't you?"

"Nice." Walked into that one.

With a laughing Sandra in tow, Julian turned them all towards the lower path, leading the others through the aspen grove and into a wide, grassy clearing that had been trimmed close in anticipation of today's event.

The crowd gathered in three deliberate rings as directed by officers of ceremony. The first, spread around the entire clearing at the edge of the treeline, was comprised of visiting nobles and the many off-world rulers visiting Terra. A second group, closer in, was mainly officers and the knights currently on-planet. Then, finally, the paladins themselves. There were six of them in attendance today, circling a low, wooden dais at the cardinal points, Exarch Levin at their head.

On the dais, Ariana Zou knelt in quiet meditation. After choosing the site of her ascension, she had spent the entire night here in contemplation of her life and military career, and her future responsibilities as a Paladin of the Sphere. She had knotted her raven-black hair into a bun at the base of her neck, but several strands had escaped and were matted to her skin by the morning dew.

She did not appear to notice.

Julian's small group were among the last to arrive, which was fine as his place was reserved near the back of the third tier regardless, at the center of those off-world dignitaries who had been invited and chosen to attend. Julian noted two of the three Captains-General, jockeying for position within the swelling crowd. Trillian Steiner holding court with Aaron Sandoval and some minor nobility from both sides of that border. And Caleb and Amanda Hasek.

Alaric Wolf, holding himself apart from the rest, snarling when approached too closely by other Clan warriors, including those from his own Clan Wolf. A savage animal ready to break his restraints at any time.

Coordinator Vincent Kurita with his New Samarkand warlord.

And Sterling McKenna of the Raven Alliance, who appeared isolated and alone. She had spent a great deal of time in the company of Prince Harrison this last year, traveling with him as friend and consort after four years of the prince mourning for his wife, Isabella Hasek.

No sign of Daoshen Liao. Or any of the Capellan nobility. With a year of open war flaring between the Confederation and The Republic, if the Capellans were even onplanet Julian had to guess they had not been invited. Just as well. Caleb did not need Danai Liao-Centrella distracting him further. Such a near-disaster *that* had been.

"He is not even here, quineg?" Lars Magnusson asked. Whispering as a quiet settled over the assembled witnesses. Things were about to start.

Callandre looked over. "Who?"

"Erik Sandoval. I recall him from the grand ball. And he was there when Julian and Yori annihilated each other in the simulated War of '39. But not at the funeral. Nothing since, in fact."

Julian had taken his mark, shown to him by a young lieutenant in The Republic's Triarii Protectors. He glanced over, but kept watch on the upper paths as well, waiting for the cue to his small part in today's ceremony. "No. Erik left Terra nearly three weeks ago. Before the big showdown."

But that was Lars Magnusson, as Julian had come to know him. A Ghost Bear warrior, he certainly looked the part. Well-muscled. Platinum-blond hair worn parted down the middle and long to his shoulders. Pale skin and heavy nordic features and thick, white eyebrows. He had a tattoo of his Clan crest centered on his right temple, with two of the six "arms" reaching across part of his face.

But to concentrate on the physical and forget about his

mind was a mistake. No missed detail escaped the younger man for long. His mind was always at work, looking at problems and even simple conversations from every angle.

"Still getting daily intel feeds from Riccard Streng?" Callandre asked.

Julia shook his head. "No." Those had stopped right after Prince Harrison's accident. Julian assumed Caleb was being quickly brought up to speed, though he had not seen Streng, the Federated Suns' spymaster, in several weeks. "No, I spoke to Aaron Sandoval, briefly, last week. Erik left quietly for Tikonov, to stiffen resistance against the Liao offensive."

Quietly, and secretly. Which had the lord governor of Tikonov concerned but not so much that he rushed right after his nephew to hold his own fort.

"Julian?" Sandra prompted. Thunder rolled overhead as the storm finally spoke.

"I thought that brushfire had burned down into a lull," Callandre said.

Fourteen months of hard fighting and a dozen worlds retaken by the Confederation. Julian wasn't so certain it could be called anything but a major offensive. "If there was any lull, someone apparently forgot to notify the Liao agents on Tikonov."

"Julian." Sandra's whisper was quieter, yet more severe. She nudged his elbow and nodded up the path where Paladin Heather GioAvanti had stepped out from beneath the low aspen branches, bearing a sword.

It was starting.

"Yeah, Jules. Pay attention."

Heather GioAvanti wore the gray uniform and full scarlet cape of rank allowed her position. She wore her frosted hair down, swinging straight over her ears. Her blue eyes fixed on the sword she carried balanced across both palms, as if she had the path memorized. Likely, she did.

With slow, stately grace, the paladin approached. By the time she had fully emerged from beneath the aspen, not a single whisper could be heard. Only a distant grumble of thunder. All eyes were riveted on her as if scope-locked on a target, including Julian's.

He waited, counting her measured paces as a way to still the dark whispers stirring at the back of his mind in this moment of silence. Forty-three from the edge of the grove to his position right at the back of the third circle. And Heather GioAvanti stared up at him.

Julian looked down at the sword. Nothing too special about it, except that it had been well cared for. No jeweled hilt. No engraved blade. A good field saber, which Devlin Stone was said to have commandeered on his flight from the Word of Blake reeducation camp during the Jihad. The man who had eventually led the Inner Sphere to victory, and later fought to form The Republic of the Sphere. A modern-day King Arthur, forging his Camelot by sheer will and determination.

Now this blade was all that was left of such a powerful and charismatic man. A symbol of what he had accomplished. A reminder of the responsibilities to every caretaker who followed.

Julian bowed forward from the hips, more in the manner of the Japanese courtesies followed in the Combine than a courtier's bow from the Davion court. Then he turned and raised his hands to the crowd, which parted to allow the sword to pass through. That was Julian's sole duty in the ceremony. Simple enough, though sweat beaded at the nape of his neck as the weight of the moment rolled over him like Juggernaut's carriage.

He paced forward ahead of Heather GioAvanti, traversing the dozen paces that made up the entire thickness of the outer circle. Then, as he'd been instructed, he stepped aside to allow the sword to pass.

Heather continued, approaching the second tier of witnesses. The captains and majors and generals of The Republic's line regiments. The knights and knights-errant of at least half a hundred worlds.

This time, it was the youngest of the assembled knights who stepped forward. A tow-headed youth, he barely looked old enough to shave. If the boy was twenty-one yet, Julian would have been surprised. Though his own cynicism surprised him more. As if the extra six years he carried conferred the wisdom of the ages! Prince's champion or no, at times he had to remind himself that he, too, wasn't much more than a young heir to ancient traditions, and it was that heritage which spoke with power, not necessarily him.

The young knight-errant passed the blade through, letting Heather approach the exarch and the rest of the assembled paladins. Jonah Levin stepped up to silently accept the christening blade from her hands, and then passed himself through the third and final tier to set foot on the dais with Ariana Zou.

For all the attention Ariana paid, Exarch Levin might as well have been passing by on a stroll through Magnum Park. Even from his new position at the leading edge of the third tier, Julian saw how her eyes were unfocused, her face without animation. It was as if she had truly cast off her past, and was waiting to be reborn.

In a way he envied her that, remembering how Prince Harrison had finally bestowed on him the title of Prince's Champion. Harrison had not stood on ceremony with family. He'd called Julian into his private quarters one day, and handed him the title without fanfare.

"You're it," he'd said. "Until you die or I find someone more deserving. Don't let me down, Julian."

Again. That had been the unspoken caveat. Of course it had. The sorrowful tone. The recriminations in Harrison's eyes, as if he knew what he did was more politically motivated than necessarily the best choice. Julian had repledged himself then and there to always stand worthy of such trust, and responsibility.

And, he believed, he always had.

But here, this day, the ceremony carried the weight of nearly six decades of tradition. And three years of desperation as The Republic fought to hold onto its strength. Raising a new paladin was no light matter. These were some of the most powerful men and women within the Sphere. The military and political elite. Each one was looked upon as a new, potential savior against the dark times rearing.

Timing was measured down to the last second, for the precise moment when dawn's light would have broken the eastern horizon and warmed the top spires of the Hall of Government. And though stormclouds shrouded Genève, Jonah Levin raised the sword at what should have been that moment, and laid the tip lightly on Ariana's shoulder.

She slumped as if he'd laid the full weight of his person against her. In a way, perhaps he had.

"Ad securitas," he whispered, and shifted the blade to Ariana's other shoulder. She began to weep. *"Per unitas."*

It carried over the entire clearing. *Through unity, freedom.* The Republic motto.

Or, looked at another way, *through security, unity.* A warning? Or a threat?

Exarch Levin brought the blade up to a simple salute. "Ascend," he commanded, "and attend your duties. Lady Paladin Ariana Zou."

6

The flow of information from Lord Faust's oversight government is thready at best, but we have been able to confirm that among the black-painted raiders are a few machines and 'Mechs bearing the dao-sword crest of the Confederation.

House Liao, it seems, has returned to New Hessen.
—Maya Smith, Political Correspondent for WXTV,
New Hessen, 8 June 3135

Tikonov
Republic of the Sphere
23 June 3135

A silver-gray drizzle swept across Tikonov's latest battlefield. The Jurai Foothills. Territory Erik Sandoval-Groell knew well, having led several training exercises into the region on more than one occasion. Lightly wooded slopes favored wide infantry dispersal. Hovercraft were at a severe disadvantage, with little room to open throttle and run, confined to streambeds and gravel roads. Dry washes. Choke-point ravines. Many, many shallow valleys running alongside easy slopes. And a few high-ground vantage points from which a BattleMech might control half a klick in any given direction.

As good a place as any to die.

Tracers converged on Erik's position—streams of violent

fireflies that flared briefly in the light rain, swarmed, and died. Hunching forward, Erik ducked his new *Enforcer III* beneath the hailstorm of autocannon rounds. The white-hot sparks chewed through the air over his BattleMech's right shoulder. A few stray slugs *pinged* off his arm and chest.

He dry-swallowed past the knot in his throat, knowing how close the Capellan irregulars had come.

Alarms rang out for his attention. Threat indicators. Missile warning locks. An ammunition cautionary. Of them all, this last one worried him most. His fifty-ton BattleMech had already taken severe damage down its right side, with the armor composite protecting his flank little more than a memory. It left the ammunition bin for his Mydron Exel autocannon vulnerable. One or two more solid hits and the bin would rupture, and by the time the explosion finished ripping through his BattleMech's chest there wouldn't be much left of it.

Or him, likely.

"Alphas, guard my back." Erik already had his communications system toggled for an all-hands command frequency. He called up the pair of Condor hover tanks that were left to his personal fast-strike lance. "Bravo and Charlie, swing inside. Now, now, now!"

The Condors raced up from behind, skating alongside and through a wide, shallow stream. Their lift fans cast up a wash of dirt and small pebbles and water. Their push threatened the Capellans' forward line, driving back a pair of light Demons and a Shandra scout vehicle. Everything but the Defiance Industries Schmitt. Like a shark scenting blood, the wheeled tank powered forward, crushing several small pines beneath its carriage and digging deep furrows in the soft, black soil.

Erik sidestepped to his right, clearing a path for his Condors and presenting his left side to the Schmitt. And just in time. Long tongues of fire licked out of the tank's rotary autocannon, spitting terrible streams of fifty millimeter slugs. These hammered at the *Enforcer's* left leg and arm, with a few rounds chewing in against the left chest as well.

Then the Schmitt's turret disappeared inside a cloud of sooty, gray exhaust as it spat out a flight of fifteen long-range missiles. With barely enough distance for the warheads to arm themselves, they speared out on a flat, shallow path. Chewing into the ground around Erik's feet, blossoms of orange fire threw scorched earth and gravel into the air.

Half a dozen warheads shattered armor from his legs, his lower torso. Shards and splinters rained down over the ground, littering the Jurai Hills with more detritus.

Erik rode out the worst of it, shaken against the straps of his restraint harness. He pulled his crosshairs across the Schmitt's blocky nose and settled them right over the triangular crest of House Liao. The reticle flashed from red to the deep golden hue of a hard targeting lock.

"My turn."

His *Enforcer III* was a good, well-vetted design with seven decades of combat deployment recommending it. Its right arm ended in a large-bore Mydron Excel ultra-class autocannon. The left arm opened into the barrel of a Blaze-Fire extended-range laser. Erik toggled for both of his main weapons, speared his arms forward, and eased into his triggers with a veteran's calm.

A ruby lance of energy slashed across the Schmitt's nose, slagging through armor composite, dripping fiery globules down to the ground that quickly crisped over with coal-black husks. Then his autocannon dug in right behind, hammering hard with an extra-long burst of fire. Chewed through scarred and pitted plating. Pounded hot metal deep into the tank.

Spiking through the main crew compartment.

No glorious explosion. No tall column of oily smoke. The Schmitt's turret simply sagged downward, pointing at the ground.

"Hit them!" Erik commanded. "Hit them hard."

Dividing his attention between the water-softened world he saw through his ferroglass shield and the iconic layout on his heads-up display, Erik throttled forward into a hard run to lead the Condors forward after the retreating vehicles. Both Demons and the Shandra had fallen back down the slope onto a secondary line held by a fifty-five ton *Griffin* and two captured Haseks. Like the others, all three combat vehicles had been painted with tan and green colors being used by these supposed "Capellan irregulars." Skirmish troops thrown at Tikonov in advance of any main thrust. Poorly trained and mostly disposable freedom fighters.

"But they don't fight like it," he whispered, careful of his voice-activated mic.

In fact, reports of House Liao's well-organized probing assault were what first tempted Erik away from Terra and what might very well be the high-level political event of the decade. Leaders from every Great House and most of the smaller realms, all converging on the capital of The Republic? At a time when the Senate was disgraced and disbanded, and starting what amounted to a civil war? Seven months ago, Erik would have been hard pressed to imagine turning his back on such an opportunity.

Seven months ago, however, he had not yet learned to look at the larger picture.

Seven months ago, his uncle, Lord Governor Aaron Sandoval, had not nearly gotten him killed.

A lot had happened since then. Erik had developed the first of his own intelligence assets. He'd made contact with one of The Republic's largest subversive organizations. These were both secrets he now kept from his uncle.

And both were reporting to him the same thing. House Liao's push forward at Tikonov was larger, and better organized, than The Republic credited. Which meant Tikonov—and the Sandoval hold over the Swordsworn faction—was in danger.

So Erik had come back. And without his uncle. The better to make his own mark now, while so many eyes were watching.

Whatever the case, the Capellan MechWarrior—a true irregular or not—led the defense. Holding back his defensive fire until Erik ran into range. The *Griffin* lanced out a scarlet beam, slashing wide of Erik's path, but the Haseks more than made up for it as a pair of particle cannons slashed out with manmade lightning, blasting and melting armor all up and down the *Enforcer's* front.

"Pop and fire!" Erik called out, tightening down on his own trigger.

His laser's ruby spear dug into the *Griffin's* centerline, carving away valuable protection. On his thermal scanners, the heat bloom at the core of the machine jumped several levels, from a warm yellow to hot orange.

He followed up with more hammering slugs from his autocannon, walking their destructive power from waist to shoulder on the fifty-five ton 'Mech.

The Condors cut loose with their own autocannon as well. And on Erik's command a dozen battlesuit infantry broke cover from the wooded slopes on either side of the Capellan station. Hauberk infantry shouldered their own long-range missiles, and let fly with a number of warheads. Infiltrator designs worked their way in closer, using their arm-mounted lasers to splash away more armor composite.

It had the desired effect, painting multiple threats across the enemy HUDs. The Demons raced out to challenge Erik's infantry. The battlesuit troopers quickly faded back into the woods to shift and then pop and fire again. The Swordsworn Condors used their clustering munitions to sand down the armor on the *Griffin*. Erik turned his own weapons against one of the Haseks, stranding it in place when his fifty-mill autocannon cut through one of its treads.

Like wolves on a wounded bear, Erik's battle armor shifted their fire against the Hasek.

It bought them time.

Just long enough for Bravo and Charlie lances to break over the hills to the east and west, charging in at the Capellan flank in a classic pincer. A *Packhunter* led Erik's eastern force, bringing in a Fulcrum heavy hover tank and two tracked Jousts. The western charge had less mobility but more raw firepower. Two JES strategic missile carriers and a Behemoth II assault tank closed the trap, parking themselves on a low ridgeline.

The Behemoth by itself could match both Haseks for particle cannons. The Jessies spread out an umbrella of eight score warheads, raining down a barrage of fire and destruction few combat vehicles could withstand.

One Demon overturned as half a hundred warheads pummeled its right side, blowing two wheels off their axles and caving in the crew compartment. Even more warheads fell over the crippled Hasek. Blossoms of fire ripped open the armor from front to rear, scraping away every last ounce of protection.

Erik divided his own fire, slashing another ruby blade across the *Griffin's* chest and digging at the wounded Hasek with his autocannon.

The Hasek hadn't enough life left to give. Erik's autocannon slugs found the vehicle's ammunition magazine. A side panel blew outward on a gout of fire and debris, rocking the tank up onto its side and then over in a slow, fiery death roll. The Capellans had just lost one of their hardest-hitting weapons. And if there had been armored infantry inside the carrier, they were dead now as well.

Poorly disciplined troops would never have stood up under such an assault. Erik would expect true irregulars—thrown into an impossible situation and faced with crippling losses—to break in a rout.

But not these. The *Griffin* staggered back under the blistering assault, but did not fall. The Hasek threw itself into reverse, crawling away slowly, slowly, but always keeping its best armor forward until it gained the cover of tall woods. The other vehicles—and now some infantry breaking cover as well—retreated in good order.

They fell back on the *Griffin's* position. Rallying. Making it clear that any attempt to rush forward would be met with a strong defense.

Certainly they convinced Erik, who honored the retreat. He'd been able to pull his other two lances in, leveraging maximum force. But there were other Capellan troops out there in the Jurai Hills. It wouldn't do to charge forward now and risk the day's victory. One mechanized combat vehicle destroyed. The Schmitt and possibly a Demon medium tank salvageable. He'd take the trade against two crippled Scimitars, which were his worst losses for the day. Definitely a net positive result.

But he still knew less about the invading forces than he'd like. All he'd managed today was to find another question. Which meant operating in the dark, or going deeper into debt with his newfound sources for information.

Had there ever been a choice?

7

Al Na'ir has fallen! Al Na'ir has fallen! And the Combine sweeps forward! How does The Republic justify such large resources spent over the last year to defend against House Liao, while House Kurita marches on against a threadbare defense?
—Commentator Jackie Jones, News Bulletin, Saffel,
26 June 3135

Lausanne, Terra
Republic of the Sphere
27 June 3135

The gravel path turned up and around a tight corner, leading Yori Kurita and Kisho out of the secluded shade garden, back into Lausanne's bright morning sunlight.

A hidden gem, this garden; one among many on their walk so far. She nearly stopped, thinking to enjoy the secluded glade—this one moment—without the crunch of gravel underfoot. Tall, fragrant foxglove bloomed in a wide array of velvet colors over red, white, and blue columbine. Stargazer lilies and ballerina roses nestled among shoots of fern and bushy, pale hostas.

A western garden. Grown in a chaos of fragrant perfumes and a riot of color. So unlike the much simpler, more orderly zen gardens she had enjoyed on the preserve above Ishinomaki Port. The gardens there had spoken of home, of the Draconis Combine, and lent themselves so easily to quiet contemplation. Here, the lush growth inspired one towards passion. And indulgence.

Glancing back, however, she saw how the path had turned down from an earlier view alongside Ouchy's marina. Twisted in along the shallow hillside, it deliberately took advantage of the low light. It reminded her of the twists and turns within her own life, and how even a moment's indulgence often had far-reaching effects.

A luxury she could hardly afford, as a samurai.

As Warlord Toranaga was often glad to remind her.

"It is allowed, you know."

Kisho did not turn to look at her. Did not directly intrude upon her *wa*. The Nova Cat mystic might have been talking aloud to himself, for that matter. Yes, it would be easy enough to let it go at that, without any loss of face.

"What is allowed?" Yori asked, bending to the barest forms of courtesy. She plucked at the wide sleeve of her silk kimono, brushed flat where serpentine dragons coiled around her right arm. Showing disinterest. Allowing Kisho to continue the conversation, or decline. Again, without shame for either of them.

He looked over, his gray eyes the color of storm clouds. "To stop and smell the flowers along the path." His mouth showed the ghost of a smile at one upturned corner. The closest thing she had seen to a smile.

Trapped. "This is what passes for mysticism in Clan Nova Cat these days? Proverbs old enough to have traveled from Terra itself?" She brushed her thick fall of dark hair back over her shoulders, enjoying the cool morning air against her throat. "You may be in need of more training, Kisho-san."

He shrugged. Nodded. "Which is what Oathmaster Kanaye said when he sent me along as part of the Coordinator's retinue. I am to be a student of the world on this journey. And you, Kurita Yori-san, are one of my many teachers."

Glancing over sharply, she searched for sarcasm amid his dry wit. Kisho certainly was not what she had expected in a mystic. A man who did not truly believe in his own supposed gift. Who doubted more than she did, in fact. Still, there was a vulnerability just beneath the surface. The kind that only appeared between friends—or at least between two people on the path towards becoming friends.

Yori settled her gaze on the path ahead. "I am no teacher," she said.

"We are all teachers." His whisper was too soft. Not necessarily meant for her.

She let it go.

Following the gravel path up and around, they broke from the tree-shaded walk out into an open park of grassy lawn and low-lying shrubs that sloped right down to the water's edge of Lake Geneva. Now Yori Kurita did stop. The scene was breathtaking. The warm sun soaked through her kimono's thin silk. A quaint marina peeked around a spit of tree-shaded land on their left—all they could see of Lausanne's Ouchy resort. Deep blue waters of the lake lay sun-dappled and still. And mountains. High, snow-capped peaks that framed the lake on all sides.

Her samurai heritage nearly demanded that she create a haiku.

But the moment was stolen from her as Kisho nodded to one side. "He is there."

She followed his gaze back away from the lake and the postcard-perfect view. An area of lawn closed in roses and a decorative marble wall. Circular, like an arena. Inside, a man in close-fitting exercise clothing spun and whirled and struck out at the air with fists and feet in a shadow-sparring workout. A long one, given the way his brown outfit was soaked dark with sweat and his long, golden hair lay matted against the back of his neck. But little exhaustion showed yet as he spun and threw himself into a new series of violent strikes and kicks, bounding forward like a savage animal fighting for his life.

There was little grace in the flow of one move into the next—none of the "art" Yori knew from her own extensive training. More of an explosion of martial prowess. And it suited him.

Star Captain Alaric Wolf.

He saw them approach in the next moment, and stopped. Cold. Like a thrown switch, he simply turned it off in the same way Yori might choose to stop walking. But to go from such a high-energy state to placid calm—she admired the level of control that required.

"*Konnichi-wa*, Alaric-san." Yori paused near the edge of the grassy arena. Bowed politely. "We did not mean to interrupt your exercise."

The Clan Wolf warrior watched them carefully, always studying. His blue eyes never blinked enough, to the point your own eyes started to water in sympathy. Young—no more than twenty-two or twenty-three by the reports Yori had been allowed to read—he carried himself as a man more advanced in his years. Heavy scar tissue marred his knuckles, and twisted in a braided rope along his right forearm. A deep, crescent-shaped scar puckered the corner of his left eye as well. The result of a hard life growing up in a Clan sibko, Yori guessed.

Alaric nodded curtly, not quite a bow, but did not otherwise complain of the interruption. "Comrades in arms can always make time for each other," he finally said.

She felt a small measure of relief at hearing it, too. A strong part of Yori Kurita had argued against coming to Lausanne, to say her farewells to this man. Aloof to the point of being cold, Alaric was not easy to understand. There were no strong ties between them. No history. Only a training battle fought for honor, in which Yori had faced off against Julian Davion. Kisho and Alaric had fought by her side. And even if it was a simulation only, honor demanded she extend the courtesy to her temporary ally.

"I saw your name on the report for those leaving Terra this week." Yori nodded to Kisho. "We thought to say good-bye. And to thank you for your assistance in the reenactment of the War of 3039. You handled yourself with great skill and bearing."

The Star captain smiled, baring his teeth. "Someone needed to show that Lyran how to fight."

Meaning Jasek Kelswa-Steiner. As Yori and Kisho charged the Davion line, Alaric had sidelined himself with the commander of the Stormhammers, chewing up Jasek's small command with savage ferocity.

Kisho tugged at his dark uniform jacket. He had not dressed well for the day's weather, and it had to be warm. "I hear Jasek is actually a very good MechWarrior," he said. "Fought the Jade Falcons on Skye."

"And lost," Alaric reminded him. "Skye is in the talons of the Falcons now."

Yori nodded. "You are well-informed." Especially for a man who only recently tested out as a warrior.

"I am a Star captain of Clan Wolf." He turned away. "It is not hard to learn what I wish to know."

Perhaps. But there was more that Alaric was not saying. Of that, Yori felt certain.

She and Kisho followed Alaric into his arena, towards the small pack he had thrown at the base of a rose bush full of blood red blooms. He dug inside and came out with a folded terrycloth towel. Rubbed himself down. The scent of his sweat competed briefly with the nearby roses, but lost as a light breeze strolled through the park and stirred the fragrant blooms.

"You chose a picturesque dojo," she said. Reaching for a compliment. "The distraction must be good for your *wa*. Your inner harmony."

Alaric glanced around, as if noticing the lake and the mountains for the first time. He stared back at her quizzically. "I have not thought much about them. I chose this area to work on ignoring such distractions."

An awkward moment enfolded the trio. "Your form?" Kisho then asked. "I did not recognize it at once. Kenpo?"

"Dragon style." Alaric looked sidelong at Yori. "No offense."

But said in such a manner as to imply insult to the name of Kurita, House of the Dragon. Or skirt it, at any measure. Yori hesitated, unsure of whether or not to take personal insult, and decided that she had no right. As Warlord Toranaga was always quick to point out, her personal honor would always be suspect. And to put it before diplomacy here, with the two of them representing different Inner Sphere powers as well as themselves, would not be prudent.

"None taken," she said. Teeth clenched.

Alaric hesitated, then admitted, "I also glanced at the reports coming out of Genève. Coordinator Vincent Kurita left Terra over a week ago. Why are you still here?"

Careful. "Not all from the Coordinator's retinue followed him back to the Combine. A small group stayed behind, to continue working with the exarch and his aides. To seek a diplomatic solution to the violence in Prefecture II."

"Understandably," Kisho said, "having Warlord Sakamoto striking deep into The Republic does not bode well for future relations." He stared into the nearby rose bush, eyes losing focus.

Slicking his long, sweat-damp hair straight back, Alaric wrapped the towel behind his neck. "And The Republic has been painting Katana Tormark and her Dragon's Fury faction with Kurita colors as well." He understood the problem well enough. "They believe she is a cat's paw, meant to incite the recent violence."

"The Coordinator would never sanction such a strategy," Yori said, defending Vincent Kurita by reflex.

Alaric showed his teeth in another predator's smile. "I would have."

"One cannot paint a Republic faction and forces from within the Draconis Combine with the same colors."

"Though if it is to be done," Kisho said, not addressing anyone in particular, "it may well be Yori's hand on the brush."

It wasn't the first time a strange comment by Kisho had brought conversation to an awkward halt. Alaric glanced sharply between Kisho and Yori, while she waited to see what the Nova Cat mystic might make of his own strange words.

As usual, not a great deal.

"*Sumimassen*, Kurita Yori-san. I did not mean to be so forward as to imply you would ever work against the Coordinator's wishes. Merely that . . . Soon you will be the only ranking samurai left in The Republic. If something is to happen, anything, it will be, of course, by your design."

Yori wasn't so certain. Warlord Toranaga had left her behind for a reason. Isolating her from her nation, her peers. Kisho and Alaric and Callandre Kell were no substitute for the company of like-minded samurai. Even if they were like-minded only in their distrust of Yori's blood lineage.

"Kisho leaves as well," Yori explained to Alaric. "End of the week. Regardless of the progress of any talks, he returns to the Combine."

"And you? What happens to you?" Alaric asked.

She did not know. But her entire life she had lived with such uncertainty. What was an extra week, or a month, spent alone? If nothing else, she gained time to learn more of the Combine's potential allies, and enemies. Like Alaric Wolf. Like Julian Davion.

"It shall be as fate, or the Coordinator, wills," she finally said.

Or, Warlord Toranaga.

= 8 =

It has been weeks since the last heavy push, with violence flaring only in isolated battles on New Aragon, Hunan, and Pleione. There is little doubt that Liao is mustering its strength, but to where and for what purpose? When the Capellan Confederation decides to lash out again, what worlds will feel the bite of its bright blade?
—Jackie Blitzer, Freelance Journalist, an editorial replayed on Genoa's "O'Hennesy Factor," originally posted at blitzer//battlecorps.org//on 22 June 3135

Genève, Terra
Republic of the Sphere
4 July 3135

High up in Genève's Hall of Government Julian Davion waited in the company of Héloïse Montgolfier, Exarch Levin's chief of staff and all-around *majordomo*. The two of them stood quietly off to one side in a large executive office, the room warmed by pale yellow wallpaper and tight-knit carpeting of burnt gold and staffed with half a dozen executive secretaries, all of them busy confirming schedules or maintaining records or researching questions brought to them by the exarch himself. A beehive of constructive activity.

Julian approved.

There was little in the way of casual conversations, he noticed. Little of the usual office environment chitchat. When necessary, questions flew back and forth with sniper-shot accuracy, most of them directed at one silver-haired woman who looked to be in her late nineties; old enough, apparently, to have read—and remembered!—most every detail about The Republic from its formation to modern hairstyles and music.

"Ms. Lane, the gift received by the exarch at last week's meeting with the ambassador from Tall Trees?" This from an older man with a wireless headset tucked into his ear, his hand curled around the microphone tab to prevent being overheard.

Ms. Lane barely slowed her rapid-fire input into the desk's built-in keyboard. "Silver statuette of the plains lion, currently on the endangered species list for Tall Trees." Now she did stop and look up. "Do you need the inscription, Michael?" She sounded like a mother offering her child a cookie.

Michael shook his head without looking back, already returned to his own conversation.

"With her around," Julian asked, "why do you need a research staff?"

"Ms. Lane *is* impressive," Héloïse agreed, sitting back casually against the edge of an empty desk. Perfectly at home.

To Julian, from the half dozen or so times he'd met with her, Héloïse Montgolfier appeared most relaxed when surrounded by purposeful activity. Empty rooms and quiet moments—these were the things that worried her. Somewhat strange, but likely a useful trait in a woman who worked in such close proximity to the exarch. With her around, nothing seemed left to chance.

She even dressed politically; in a subtle, charcoal gray dress suit and sensible shoes. The only splash of color came from the golden scarf she wore knotted about her neck. Gold with red sunbursts, he'd noticed. Very similar to the House Davion crest. To make him feel more at ease, no doubt. She wore her red hair bobbed conservatively at her ears, and simple, tasteful, golden studs for earrings. No other jewelry except for an engagement ring.

The way she constantly toyed with the ring, as if checking

to make sure it was still there, Julian guessed the engagement was recent.

He spotted the signal only because he'd been watching for it, and guessed that it would come from Ms. Lane. The elderly woman looked up from her holographic display, where words danced along the page as fast she typed them, and gave Héloïse a smile and a nod. The chief of staff did not hesitate, but moved right for the nearby door, which Julian knew from past experience opened onto the exarch's public office. He followed.

Unofficially, the exarch's office was known as the Bullet. As soon as Julian had heard it, he'd understood why. The long, rectangular room was capped on one end by a semicircular glassed alcove that looked down over Magnum Park. Bullet-shaped. But there any military allusions ended. Levin's office was richly appointed with red cherry wainscoting and walls of deep, dark gold. Wood polish and leather flavored the room. Two cases of leather-bound law books and the exarch's baroque desk of mahogany and bronze ran about as far as one could get from the utilitarian designs favored by the military.

Exarch Levin did not wait behind his desk, but instead met Julian in the comfortable sitting area arranged beneath a wide skylight. Out of respect, Julian walked around the carpet inlay, which displayed the Great Seal of The Republic—an outline of Terra, surrounded by ten golden stars and run through the middle by a knotwork banner. And around the outside, its Latin motto. *Ad Securitas Per Unitas.*

He certainly hoped so. As he continued to sink in the quagmire of politics, a little security would seem a welcome gift about now.

Julian shook Levin's hand. "That must bring you some small measure of relief," he said, nodding back towards the seal. When last he'd been here, the stars had burned red, not gold, and the banner had been replaced by a sword. A traditional change to always remind the exarch that fighting had come to Terra.

"Some very small measure," Levin admitted. He smoothed the front of his suit and gestured them into seats, taking one of the two oversized armchairs while Julian accepted the other and Héloïse perched on the edge of a leather divan. "But Tara Campbell mopped up the last resistance around Sao Paulo, which officially puts Terra back at peace."

"I read about it." He smiled, though not with much humor. "How can one not? The news media loves her. Several outlets are calling her final salvo the 'shot heard 'round the Sphere,' as if she ended all The Republic's troubles right there."

"I believe that may be wishful thinking. A few pro-Republic agencies trying to influence—or intimidate—the debates on Liberty and Markab."

"Senators Derius and Monroe." He nodded. Two Senators who'd led the recent call to arms against Exarch Levin. Conner Rhys-Monroe was also an ex-knight, and had taken to the field himself in the final assault.

"I'm not sure we can call an ongoing conspiracy to unseat the exarch a 'debate,'" Héloïse said. "But it's worth noting that similar fires are burning on Park Place and Augustine and Kervil as well. The Senators are organizing as best they can. For once, the Blackout is working in our favor."

"A thin silver lining if ever there was one." Levin nodded towards an antique Chippendale that crouched between the glass-fronted bookcases, sending his chief of staff to play bartender.

"Kervil?" Julian asked. Something about the name of the world sparked a memory.

Levin pursed his lips, as if he'd bitten into something sour. "Senator Melanie Vladistock. Someone I thought I knew. She was part of the original cabal, loosely associated with Mallowes and Derius. A minor player, much like Gerald Monroe."

Of course. Kervil was Jonah Levin's homeworld. And while it was safe for the moment from the encroachment of House Kurita, among his many worries Levin must be wondering when the other shoe would drop as the Dragon continued to press forward through Prefecture II.

"I'm not certain how to say this, Exarch."

"Straight out tends to work well with me, Julian. Prince Harrison . . . he thought well of your gift for brutal honesty."

"Yes, sir. Well, then, I'd suggest you stop thinking of

Kervil as home and Senator Vladistock as an old friend. There are no minor players on this stage. Not anymore. Not since the Senators pushed an army out of Germany with every intention of staging a military coup. If there was a final line to cross, that was it. Anyone who stands with the cabal is now your sworn enemy."

Levin accepted a clear glass from his chief of staff and took a small sip. "I guess I asked for that," he said. "But it is not so easy, to tell our real enemies from our possible allies. By your litmus test, I should have arrested Lord Governor Sandoval unless he turned all Swordsworn resources over to The Republic. Instead, we sent him home to Tikonov. Because without him, the world *will* fall to Liao, I've little doubt. Or will be held by Erik Sandoval-Groell, in whose love of The Republic I have less confidence."

A fair analysis. Erik held his citizenship from the Federated Suns, and was certainly an agent for Corwin or Victoria Sandoval. How far he'd follow his uncle was always hard to gauge.

Of course, Duke Aaron Sandoval was no guarantee either. The lord governor was still young and ambitious as well, and in the end would swing with prevailing winds, Julian had little doubt. Looking out for what was best for Aaron Sandoval.

Accepting a glass from Héloïse, he said as much to the exarch, who nodded and managed a short-lived laugh.

"Yes, I think you have that pegged fairly well. Which is precisely the reason I asked you to join us today. To discuss the Sandovals, the situation developing on Tikonov, and the unstable border The Republic now shares with *your* Federated Suns."

Julian's drink smelled lightly of citrus. No alcohol, for which he was grateful. He took a sip of the flavored water, letting a fresh, orange taste wash away the bitterness. The glass had a thick, heavy base. The kind that felt just right in his hand. A pleasant distraction, though Jonah Levin's emphasis could not be overlooked. Not for long.

"It is not my Federated Suns, Exarch. I am prince's champion, but without a prince to champion. A murky situation, with Caleb as acting First Prince and Harrison still hanging on in a coma."

Levin was quiet for a long moment. Chewing over Julian's words and considering his approach. Julian saw the exarch begin to speak more than once, then resist.

Héloïse Montgolfier toyed with her engagement ring. Brushed back long bangs from her pale green eyes. Glanced several times towards the door as if wanting to return to the bustle and activity of the outer office. Or perhaps she wanted to go ask Ms. Lane for any precedents on the division of power within House Davion. If an easy answer existed to be found, no doubt it would be part of the older woman's encyclopedic knowledge.

Then, "Certainly you have *some* influence with your cousin."

Which was not what the exarch had considered in his long silence, Julian felt certain.

How much to admit? That was the question. How far should Julian go in following the last wishes of Harrison Davion? The prince had admitted to putting a tentative alliance on the table with Exarch Levin, which was how Julian and his Davion Guards came to be fighting alongside Republic troops in the recent troubles. But there were no formal declarations. Nothing recorded at all, of which Julian was aware.

"Truthfully, Exarch, I have not had much access to Caleb in the last few weeks. He grieves, of course. And he has been sequestered away on many days with his intelligence aides, coming up to speed as quickly as he might. I know you and he have spoken on more than one occasion as well."

"Ceremonial demands," Levin said. "Expressing my personal condolences, and offering the resources of The Republic to do all that can be done for your prince."

"Then I should not step too far outside of political channels." He balanced the glass at the edge of his lips and took a long, satisfying pull from the sweetened water. Then he set the glass on the low table dividing the armchairs from the leather divan and made a decision. "I *can* discuss military coordination and some other matters, however, which do fall within the scope of my position. Prince Harrison made it clear to me that we were to work together, and Caleb has not countered that position as yet."

On shaky ground, perhaps. But Julian could almost feel Harrison Davion prodding him from the hospital bed.

"Tikonov is critical to our border defense," Héloïse said, taking up the discussion for the exarch. Eager, in fact, now that the awkward moment had passed. "Our latest reports indicate that what we first considered probing assaults may be a much stronger—more heavily supported—push than estimated."

Levin set his glass down as well. "The Capellans are sitting in strong positions on Algot, Menkar and Foochow." He counted those worlds out on one hand, raising three fingers. "They've pushed as far as Buchlau and Halloran V. Even made a stab at Kansu." Three fingers on the other hand. "But that's as far as they seem to be reaching along that front. They've put most of their effort into reinforcing the world of Liao, and isolating our stronghold on New Aragon."

"So what you are missing," Julian said, taking up the narrative, "is any direct line from, say, Algot, through to Tikonov. Which would support your earlier reports that the forces there are irregulars sent to cause trouble."

"Except . . ." Héloïse began.

"Except," Julian agreed. "You are thinking of Demeter and New Hessen."

Worlds of the Federated Suns, where some of the recent fighting had spilled out of The Republic. En route to Terra, in fact, Julian had dropped on New Hessen with some of his Guards and routed (with the help of a Republic knight) a well-organized band of Capellan irregulars. New Hessen would be a perfect jump-through system to reach Tikonov.

The exarch nodded. "We are thinking exactly that," he said. "Though knowing the history between Houses Davion and Liao, I feel fairly comfortable in assuming that no one is actively working within the Federated Suns to support Capellan aggression."

Even better, Julian knew. Before Victor's death and this trip of necessity to Terra, Harrison had been working to fortify the Capellan March. Not just in anticipation of Daoshen Liao turning an eye on Davion worlds, but in preparation for a flanking attack into *Confederation* space. A perfect, political necessity to drain resources from the

Draconis March, and to occupy Amanda Hasek with visions of conquest. Distracting one. Undercutting the other. And keeping either powerful March Lord from turning their own eye and ambition towards the Davion throne on New Avalon.

But one did not discuss "family" matters in front of strangers. "I would consider that a reasonable assumption," was all Julian said.

Héloïse toasted him with her own glass of sweetened water. "Then I see no reason why we cannot work together on this."

Julian had no choice but to correct her. "I will take it to Caleb," he said. And they all knew it was no adamant pledge. "I will argue strongly in favor of the proposition. In fact, if he can be reassigned, I recommend putting Sir Raul Ortega after this. He has been our 'guest' on New Hessen once before, and has at least the beginning of a working relationship with the local garrison commander and planetary lord."

"A good suggestion, Julian." The exarch nodded his confirmation to Héloïse. "It will be done. At once."

And with that, Héloïse stood. "Thank you, Exarch. And our appreciation, Lord Davion, for your assistance."

Julian stood with her. And then Exarch Levin. They exchanged handshakes, Levin lingering over the clasp for an extra heartbeat. "I truly am sorry, Julian. And I hope the best for you and yours."

"Prince Harrison is a strong man." Julian's stock answer these days. Though he did not miss the loaded glance Levin traded with his chief of staff. Clearly, he'd been speaking of more than Harrison's condition.

As . . . a leader.

Harrison's voice again, whispering from the dark shadows within Julian's mind.

"Thank you, Exarch Levin."

Julian again walked around the great seal, being escorted out by Héloïse Montgoflier. He made it to the main door, had his hand on the bright brass handle, before the exarch spoke up.

"Julian."

He looked back, pausing with the door barely cracked open. "Yes, sir?"

Jonah Levin stood just the other side of the seal, the toes of his patent leather shoes scuffing the Latin motto. The one-time paladin and current exarch matched gazes with Julian, held him. "What will Caleb do?" he asked. Held up a hand before Julian could respond with any pat answer. "Tell me what you think."

It was the kind of order Harrison might have given. Not caring for the political niceties. Or any bruised egos, including his own.

"Exarch Levin, I truly wish I could tell you. I do. But right now . . ." He shook his head. "There is just not any knowing Caleb's mind."

Not at all.

Thonon-les-Bains, Terra

"What do you think she wants?"

Caleb Hasek Sandoval Davion paced in front of the chalet's massive, darkened fireplace, back and forth across a thick floor rug of tightly coiled braids. Hardly a need to watch where he was walking. He'd already kicked back the low table with its delicate, carved legs. And when his dress uniform boots fell sharply against the brick-tone ceramic tiles, it was time to turn sharply on his heel and pad softly back to the far side of the large, lodge-style room.

A fire burned on the flagstone hearth behind a wire mesh screen. Not yet built up for the cool evenings that came to Thonon-les-Bains even in summer, the fire looked small and inconsequential within the cavernous opening. Not that Caleb trusted it. At every pop, every hissing crackle, he veered aside, the legs on his green dress trousers warm—too warm—with the spreading heat and tiny sparks of hot fury stabbing into the sides of his legs. First the left leg. Then the right. He never saw a spark jump out through the wire mesh, but they were there.

And he still did not trust it.

"Amanda told her—warned her—to stay away."

He stepped onto the tiled floor, paused in front of a wall-mounted mirror. Shifting from one foot to the other, he checked his uniform one more time. He hadn't bothered with the parade-dress since leaving Firgrove, after his brief remarks made in front of a local military academy. It had mattered less to him these last several months to be seen as an officer in the New Syrtis Fusiliers than it had to appear as Harrison Davion's son. Heir to the throne of the Federated Commonwealth.

"But Sterling." He tugged his jacket straight. "She looks at things differently. Right?"

Mason Lambert waited on one end of the long sofa, perched on the arm, not *quite* sitting in the presence of his new prince. But their long-time friendship allowed for a few concessions, so Caleb let it slide.

"That's what I think," Mason said. There was the sound of a heavy engine outside on the circular drive, then silence. He glanced meaningfully at the door and nodded. "And one would hardly call her subtle."

Mason had never voiced much of an opinion about Sterling McKenna before, one way or the other. He rarely acknowledged the Raven Alliance khan at all, though she had become a favorite subject of many public and pundit debates after taking up with the widowed prince. So Caleb had known a moment's surprise when Mason stepped forward earlier to recommend he take the meeting despite Amanda's standing objections to the woman.

"The duchess is an astute leader," he'd said. Treading cautiously. "With her in charge of the Draconis March, likely the Federated Suns would still hold the Draconis Reach worlds."

Including Harrow's Sun, on which the Lamberts had been part of the local nobility. It wasn't often that Mason played *that* trump card, reminding his friend about the losses he—like Caleb—had endured in life.

"But when it came to her brother-in-law, your father, she was understandably biased. Let Sterling McKenna have her say. Then you can act on it or dismiss her counsel as you decide. It costs you nothing."

And Caleb trusted Mason's counsel above all. A friend in the long, dark years of his Periphery tour, his *exile*, Mason had been there after Julian pulled away and Caleb's father had apparently all but forgotten him.

Footsteps on the far side of the double-wide entrance. A rapid tattoo knocked on the far side, and a security agent from the Davion Guards opened the door to lean inside. One of Caleb's long-standing guards. One of his faithful.

"Khan McKenna?" the agent said.

A sharp glance to Mason, who stared back with encouragement. Caleb nodded.

Letting the heavy door swing fully open, the guard stepped aside to admit Khan Sterling McKenna. A tall woman, several centimeters over Caleb's medium height, she carried herself with poise and a kind of stealthy grace. As if barely restrained strength lurked beneath her calm. Luxurious, blue-black hair hung in a thick, straight sheet down the back of her neck to her waist. Stormy, gray eyes, like those of a hunting falcon. And young. Too young, many had said, shocked to see her accompany a man twice her age. She had learned to eschew Clan leathers in the company of Harrison Davion, though had never mastered (or never bothered to care about) the idea of political dress. Instead of a conservative business suit, McKenna wore a tailored design cut along Capellan fashion and in the striking, bold colors of blood red and dark blue, a broach fashioned after the Alliance crest, and dangling earrings that dropped down into razor-sharp talons.

No subtlety. None at all.

Caleb found that refreshing.

He also expected an awkward moment—the silence that usually descended the first time someone came to grips with addressing him in his father's stead. The quiet comparison, and the just-barely-perceptible shrug of acceptance in the end. He'd learned to hate that moment, but hide his displeasure.

So he was surprised the second time this day—and pleasantly so—when Sterling McKenna did not hesitate, but crossed the room with long, determined strides. Her hands warmly grasped his shoulders, her gray eyes soft and sympathetic, but never showing one ounce of pity. Or regret.

"Prince Caleb. I am so sorry for your loss. Highness."

She held his gaze, smiled when he put hands on her waist just in a need to do *something*. To return her heartfelt embrace. Standing so close, he smelled the lavender soap on her skin, or maybe it was her hair. He allowed her that moment of intimacy, stared over her shoulder as Mason stood up and quietly left the room to let the two leaders talk. From the bottom of the stairs, Mason nodded again, once.

He would wait near the top of the staircase, Caleb knew. Listening in. Ready to offer his advice the moment Sterling left.

"Thank you," he finally said, separating the two of them with a short step backward.

He gestured to the wide sofa covered in brocaded fabric and easily large enough the two could sit comfortably, and intimately, but still maintain a distance of respect. They sat, turned towards each other with just the right amount of mutual attention. His aunt would be proud of him for his complete mastery of the situation.

His father . . . as proud as a man might be, when he had already decided his son was unworthy. Caleb frowned. Shook his head to clear such a thought.

"Formally," Sterling said, "the Raven Alliance extends its condolences and pledges its support in this difficult time. Prince Harrison was a fine leader."

She was the first person, after Mason of course, to refer to his father in the past tense. In *his* presence, anyway. "He's not dead yet," he reminded her.

Sterling's upper lip curled ever so slightly, and Caleb knew at once what he had done. Contractions were frowned upon among Clan trueborn as the sign of a weak and lazy mind. And he was neither! Resolving to do better, he repeated, "He *is* not dead yet."

Crossing one arm across her middle, she propped her right elbow up and tapped her fist against the point of her chin. A strong pose. Sterling McKenna nodded. "You will forgive me if I speak frankly, Prince Caleb. *Quiaff?*" She obviously did not care if he took exception or not. "The Clans do not hesitate to accept and move on. We are a warrior-based society, bred for war, and with us it is the prerogative and the duty of the younger generation to step up to supplant the elder. Which is why Julian Davion still has a great deal of support within the alliance. True, Harrison may recover. But you know as well as I that he will never be as fit to lead. To command. The Federated Suns demands a strong leader."

"I hadn't—had not!—considered looking so far ahead."

Though hadn't Mason warned him of this after the two of them had reviewed Harrison's full preparations in the Capellan March? This need for an appearance of strength. Of continuity on the throne? "Of course I expect my father, should he recover, to continue to rely on my steady hand. Your counsel, and your support, is appreciated." And it was. It was. But . . .

A warning flare went off in his head. Like a strobe flash, temporarily blinding him to all else. His vision swam with a overcast haze, as if all color had drained away to leave a world of blacks and whites and many, many shades of gray. Sterling glowed a soft, subtle shade of dove gray.

"Julian?" he asked. "You mentioned Julian just now, as having support within the Alliance."

She nodded. "He was prince's champion. Paraded as an example of youth and excellence. Harrison showed him great favor, and it is difficult for a certain amount of power—of authority—not to rub off onto him because of that. Quiaff?"

Was prince's champion. He did not miss that emphasis. If one looked upon the situation as Caleb ascending—even temporarily—to the full throne, what was Julian's official position?

"Aff," Caleb said. Frowning. "Aff." That was the proper response to a Clan rhetorical, wasn't it? "I suppose it must."

"Which is why he continues to take meetings with Exarch Levin in your stead. Is that not so? One today, in fact?"

He had not known about *that*. Though certainly he hadn't forbidden Julian from taking meetings—Caleb assumed with regard to the local deployment of the Davion Guards—shouldn't he have been kept apprised of such talks?

"I should've been," he said softly. "I should've."

A lot of things should've been brought to him, in fact, but hadn't. Only an off-chance remark by his aunt had brought the Capellan March preparations to his attention. And he had demanded an immediate report. It had taken time, as Riccard Streng was still nowhere to be found. *Dr. Strange*, his father's master of spies, had slipped away without word or warning. Where was the Suns' chief intelligence officer? Why wasn't Julian here to tell him of this meeting with the exarch instead of Sterling?

Why did it seem as if there was an effort going on to keep him isolated *from his own legacy*?

". . . things that need to be done," Sterling said.

Caleb blinked long and slow. When he opened his eyes, color had returned to the world. Sharp and vibrant and even painful. Dark, bottomless blues and sharp reds in Sterling McKenna's outfit. The burning, buzzing oranges and yellows of the fire—a snap of golden sparks and a whispering hiss as pitch boiled out of a split seam in one log.

The sofa's golden brocade, writhing like serpents over the fabric, slithering over his hands. Biting at his wrists. His legs.

Caleb stood, brushing off his trousers with sharp, violent swipes. Stopped. Fixed his green uniform jacket with a careful shrug and tugging down the hem. "You said?"

"That there are things that need to be done." Sterling stood. "I have taken up quite enough of your time, and have done what I came here to do."

She stepped in towards him, raised a hand and laid it against his chest. "Thank you for taking my audience." She began to move away.

Caleb caught her hand, clinging to it with both of his own. "No. That is . . . Neg—is that how you say it?" Her hand warmed between both of his. "I appreciate your candor and . . . I apologize for the way you have been treated of late. This cannot be an easy time for you, either."

Though it was becoming harder and harder to imagine his father with Sterling McKenna. Woman and warrior. Khan of the Raven Alliance. Now, one of his peers.

And her smile, when it came, was slow and full. Showing white, white teeth. "Prince Caleb. You do your realm credit." Her smile faltered slightly. Her eyes darted away. "If only."

And with that she withdrew. Slipping her hand free of his, though the warmth of her touch lingered. And her scent. Nothing so flowery as perfume, but the honesty of soap and just a touch of wintergreen. A breath mint? A cleanser? Caleb wanted to know.

Now was not the time, however. Now he let her retreat, following her with hungry eyes as she glided across the room and let herself out the château's wide entryway doors. He stood there, transfixed, considering, as Mason slipped back down the staircase and leaned over the lower rail to watch him. Waiting for his friend—his prince—to speak.

Sterling had been more right that she likely knew, Caleb decided.

"There are things to be done."

9

"I did not ask for this position, nor would I have sought it. I would have given my life in service to The Republic, and counted myself fortunate to be allowed to serve. But when the tyranny of small men usurps the Faith-decreed right of Republic citizens to be represented by those they have chosen to speak for them, this . . . this is what brings us here to the brink where we must and will accept the necessity of a hard course of action!"
—Senator Conner Rhys-Monroe, Viscount Markab,
Inaugural Remarks, 4 July 3135

Tikonov
Republic of the Sphere
7 July 3135

"You've done well, Erik."

Studying, manipulating data on the blue, holographic screen shimmering in the air above the glasstop desk in his *supposedly* private office, Erik Sandoval-Groell startled at the strong voice with its familiar edge but not-so-familiar note of praise. He caught himself between stabbing for the power switch and slamming a fist into the intercom panel glowing to one side, and instead settled his hands flat against the cold, smooth glass, swallowing back the bitter taste of adrenaline.

A light push, and he half swung his chair around to face his uncle.

Duke Aaron Sandoval leaned through the door, one hand to either side of the frame. Lord governor of Prefecture IV and leader of the Davion-inspired Swordsworn militia, he had blond hair shaved into the traditional topknot favored most within the widespread Sandoval dynasty and had grown a light, well-trimmed beard since their visit to Terra. Intense blue eyes. A paramilitary uniform complete with a noble's cape. He looked young and strong and every centimeter the leader people touted him to be.

Erik didn't exactly hate him for that. But they were hardly endearing traits in the man he was beginning to look upon as his competition as well as his mentor.

"Was that a compliment?" Erik held his uncle's gaze for a steady moment, fighting the guilty flush that burned its way from the back of his neck, spreading over his scalp. He caught the edge of Aaron's smothered glower.

"Could not have been," he said. He turned back to the holographic screen.

He felt Aaron move into the lavishly appointed room, but did not hurry as he ran two fingers in a swiping motion over one of the larger blocks of suspended text. A white haze swirled around the blue-glowing words—an excerpt from Gavin's latest report—and he tucked it away into a sidebar folder with a casual press, drag, and double-tap.

"Would you like a lollipop, Erik?" Aaron Sandoval's voice had a harder edge to it now. Dark. Cold. "Or would you prefer to be treated like an equal? A partner?"

Erik tapped his chin, as if considering, then raised a finger for patience. Swiped over a small, electronic post-note, tucked that into a secondary open window, and then double-tapped it closed as well. Hiding it among a series of tabs at the bottom of his screen, this one labeled as nothing more sinister than "Weather."

His own private code. Reports from LI ANN, the Capellan agent he had subverted and was now running as his own asset behind Confederation lines, came in under the less-than-impressive codename South Wind.

Which left one confidential report open and vulnerable, peeking out from behind a partially collapsed window. His uncle would find it.

"You've never treated me as an equal partner, *cousin*. Shensi made that much clear to me."

Erik stood, swinging away from his chair and sitting back against the edge of the desk in time to catch Aaron's flash of surprise. Since Erik's arrival, his exile from the Federated Suns' Draconis March, he had referred to Aaron as his uncle, though only six years separated them and their family tie was actually distant cousins, four generations back. But "uncle" was a more respectful title, they'd thought. *Aaron* had thought. Erik never realized how subservient that simple decision had made him. Until recently.

Aaron veered away just short of the desk, stepping up to one of Erik's several bookcases. He browsed the leather-bound histories, with a finger trailing along the edge of the shelf. "You are still angry about that?" He glanced over. Shook his head. "You prevailed, Erik. You proved your ability and your worth." He pulled one tome from the shelves and thumbed through it. "At that point you made yourself my partner. And if you doubt me, ask yourself why I stayed on Terra for so many weeks *after* I learned you had returned to Tikonov."

"You nearly got me killed."

"And you neatly subverted two of my most loyal intelligence officers. If I wanted you dead, Erik, I'd shoot you now with the hold-out needler I've holstered at the small of my back."

The casual threat of death instantly convinced Erik of his "uncle's" seriousness. He steeled himself against any rash movement. Swallowed dryly against the knot scratching at the back of his raw throat.

Too late to reach for the intercom panel, to call for help or at least berate the guards at the door to his personal apartment for admitting *anyone* without announcement or warning. He made a mental note to have the men assigned to front-line infantry duty at once.

"You'll leave them where they are," Aaron said, as if reading his mind.

"Why would I do that?"

"Because you know one or both of them belong to me. And the Davion you know . . ."

"Beats the Davion you don't," Erik finished. True, by

keeping them around, he had a pipeline back to his uncle's side of the Swordsworn camp. That might come in handy.

Aaron snapped the historical volume closed, replaced it on the shelf. The dry, musty scent of aging paper and warm leather breezed past Erik. "Never, never assume I have nothing left to teach you, *cousin*. It's a dangerous assumption to make."

Point. But hardly game. "All right, then. Why *did* you stay on Terra? You saw the reports. Tikonov is being pressed harder than the exarch knows. It's like an infestation. I stamp out one threat, one *nest*, and another pops up elsewhere. Fast."

But Aaron ignored him, stepping close to the desk, bending at the waist to lean in towards Erik's floating screen of text and numbers. Force estimates and recent partisan activity reports from all across Tikonov. Cost estimates of the fighting for the next six months. The next twelve. Force depletion and economic impact reports should the Swordsworn involve itself in the escalating feud between the exarch and the disaffected Senate.

And the private correspondence Erik had left intentionally for Aaron to find. Brisham Vicore, Count Caselton and Republic Senator. Aaron saw the iconic crest of Caselton and thumbed the panel to the front of the holographic screen without so much as an apologetic glance to be reading through Erik's files.

"Is this confirmed?" Aaron asked. "Erik? Count Vicore has pledged his resources to the Swordsworn?"

"And the quiet support of two other worlds," Erik said. "If we agree to stand for them against any military option Exarch Levin may choose to use against them. Vicore would prefer *not* to stand noble's court."

"Faith defend, who would? You've done well, brokering this arrangement. I had hoped to meet again with Harrison Davion. I did spend more time with Julian."

Erik could not shift gears so quickly, and took an extra moment to separate out the two conversations. "Thank you," he said, accepting the praise. And, the prince's champion? Not Caleb?"

Aaron shifted some of the open panels around on Erik's screen, never coming close to the dangerous files hidden right in front of him. He rubbed one hand along his fringe of golden-blond beard. Tapped the side of his nose in thought.

"No. Well, once. Just long enough to pass along condolences on Harrison's accident."

He stopped, as if tripping over an idea, then shook his head.

"Caleb has been reclusive. Not exactly approachable. And not someone I'm sure we can easily deal with."

"He's family," Erik reminded his uncle. "If not with him . . ." It was as far as he was willing to push. Not yet wanting to admit that he had made overtures to Caleb Hasek *Sandoval* Davion at Victor's viewing.

"I'm telling you, Erik, there is—was—something more going on in that family. Prince Harrison pushed me off towards Julian more than once. And you recall the simulated honor battle between Julian and Yori Kurita."

"Caleb was absent," Erik said, remembering. "You remarked on it then, too. But what does it *mean*?"

Then Aaron said something that had to be hard for him to admit. "I don't know."

Neither did Erik. Yet. But he had resources now that Duke Aaron Sandoval could not tap.

And if knowledge was power, then secrets were the currency of position.

10

And why shouldn't the Senators stand forth against Exarch Levin's excesses? His haphazard leadership? Prefecture V is afforded a better defense against House Liao, which has fallen quiet, than Prefecture II against House Kurita. Denebola is slowly turning into an armed camp... with no aggressors in sight, mind you... while Irian is stripped of its garrison. We must demand answers! We must demand a change!
  —Senator Michael Riktofven, Augustine, an address, 4 July 3135

Annemasse, Terra
Republic of the Sphere
9 July 3165

A bright, summer sun blazed directly overhead, assaulting Annemasse's Interplanetary DropPort with relentless determination. Baking the landing field until temperatures pushed upwards of forty points Celsius and the air shimmered with sixty percent humidity.

Julian Davion paced the black, sweltering tarmac outside

of the gold-and-black painted security post, grinding his mounting frustration beneath the heels of his dress boots. His sweat-damp uniform stuck to his skin. Circling Sandra Fenlon, who waited with hands clasped in front of her in a greater display of outward calm, he divided his attention between the armed soldiers nearby—the ones with the Roman profile crest of the Principes Guards stitched to their shoulders and safeties on their laser rifles thumbed *off*—and the nearest skyscraper-sized vessel nested within a shallow, ferrocrete bunker.

When he moved too near the security gate, or any of the armed soldiers, the Guards stiffened to greater attention and shifted their grips on the rifle stocks.

"Perhaps you should practice a bit of that diplomacy Prince Harrison often remarked on," Sandra whispered as he stomped by her again.

Perhaps he should. The guards grew more agitated with each passing moment. But despite any implied threat the DropShip still pulled at him most. An *Overlord* some forty stories high, it towered above the "city block" of smaller *Union*- and *Seeker*-class vessels to either side. Light gray trimmed heavily in dark green (nearly black) around the upthrust bow, there could be no doubt about the *First Sun's* nationality. Slashed across the upper hull, in a corona of reds and golds, was the sword-and-starburst crest of House Davion.

And swirling about the base, seeping up out of the shallow blast-trenches, was steam used to warm thrust nozzles and expandable joints in preparation for the fusion-hot thrust.

In preparation for take-off.

"This is ridiculous." He stopped near the post officer, a smooth-faced lieutenant with a boy's shy smile but cold, killer's eyes. The ID patch sewn onto his right breast read: Stansel. "Have the tower patch you into the *First Sun's* communications. Caleb Davion *will* pass me through."

"I apologize for the delay, Lord Davion. But when the tower has cleared you, they will call us."

"Do I need to get my wireless from the car?" In moments he could have Exarch Levin (or at least Héloïse Montgolfier) on the line. He resisted the temptation to use his position for what seemed so trivial a matter, but the

First Sun looked ready to blast away from Terra at any moment.

"I will have to ask you to remain away from your personal vehicle," the lieutenant said. He slipped a finger into the trigger guard.

Even Sandra noticed that, and stepped forward to place a cautionary hand on Julian's arm. Still, Lieutenant Stansel did nod at a nearby corporal, who unclipped a radio from his belt and stepped to one side for the illusion of privacy.

Julian understood the need for security, at times *and within reason*. And if this had been his only delay he certainly wouldn't be feeling the pressure of seconds ticking away. But Switzerland's Annemasse DropPort had been put under heightened protocols, apparently at the direct request of Caleb Davion, holding Julian up at three different checkpoints as his bonafides were checked again, and again, supposedly in conjunction with Caleb's security detail already aboard the blast-prepped *Overlord*.

"He's cleared," the corporal said, lowering his radio.

The lieutenant nodded Julian towards his car. "With our apologies, Lord Davion."

With his release, and no more security between him and the DropShip, Julian could afford to be more forgiving. "Doing your duty," he said, feeling slightly guilty he had given the officer trouble for following orders.

He slipped into the driver's seat of his Eridani Slipstream, a hovercraft coupe provided to him for the duration of his stay and from which Riccard Streng's people had removed or neutralized all active and passive listening devices (a *pro forma* necessity, on both sides). He waited for Sandra to buckle in, then toggled the roll-back doors closed and engaged the lifters. The coupe lifted easily, floating on a cushion of air.

A foot pedal redirected thrust out of rear ports, pushing the vehicle forward hard enough to press Julian and Sandra back into their seats for a short, high-speed race across the black tarmac, and finally into the DropShip's wide shadow. For a moment he thought he saw a laser battery emplacement tracking them from the upper decks, but decided it had been a trick of the sun and shadow.

Still, rather than coast down to a manageable speed for braking with the forward thrusters, he waited until the last moment and bootlegged the hovercraft into an end-for-end swap and used the larger, rear thrusters to dump speed quickly. He'd seen Callandre pull this maneuver often enough. His wasn't quite so smooth, but it worked, braking them to a stop at the foot of the single, lowered ramp connecting the landing pad's reinforced ferrocrete with an open bay door.

Julian goosed the throttle, spun the coupe around, and pushed it up the shallow slope into the gloomy cave of a portside cargo hold.

Where Caleb waited with a full security squad of seven uniformed, well-armed members of the Davion Guards. And Khan Sterling McKenna.

Where was Duchess Amanda Hasek?

Cut power doors rolled back. Julian grabbed a handhold built into the roof and levered himself up and out of the low-profile hovercraft. He listened to the fans spinning down, and the engine pinged as it cooled. The cargo bay smelled of grease and plastic cargo containers and dust accumulated from a hundred different worlds. Cooler than outside, by a degree or two. Enough to make Julian glad to be out of the direct sun.

He nodded to his cousin. Glanced among the faces of the honor guard. "Paranoid much?" he asked. Dialing for humor.

Failing completely, from the glower that settled over Caleb's face. "What do you want, Julian?"

To be back outside on the baking tarmac, with a 'Mech company backing him, for all the warmth in Caleb's voice. He swallowed the knot in his throat. "Sandra came for me at the hospital," he said, feeling his "fiancée" move up on his right. He shrugged. "I was not told you were leaving today."

"I do not report my schedule to *you*. When I want you to know something, you will be informed."

"For security's concern, Caleb—"

"*Prince* Caleb!"

Julian took an actual step backward at his cousin's outburst, at the vehemence and indignation lurking behind it. As if Julian had offered serious insult. He glanced sidelong at Sandra, saw the same confusion and a touch of concern mirrored on her face as well. "Pardon?"

"Prince Caleb. It is a form of address you need to reacquaint yourself with, apparently."

"No. It is not. Prince Caleb." He pulled himself up to strict attention, divorcing himself from the blood ties as well as sixteen years of shared family. "I was not expecting a formal report, but the courtesy of knowing the plans of the acting Prince of the Federated Suns whose position it is my pleasure to serve."

"To serve?" Caleb asked. He glanced back, seemingly looking past Khan Sterling, into the darker shadows of the massive cargo bay. Nodded. "We're not so certain anymore. I know we do not like finding out third-hand about meetings one of our commanders has taken with the Exarch of The Republic. Chasing his own agenda."

Julian felt the blood drain from his face, and a cold tingle at the ends of his fingers. A shiver raced up his spine, slamming into the base of his skull like a hammer blow. In his six years two months and . . . eighteen days! . . . as a fully commissioned officer in the Armed Forces of the Federated Suns, no one had *ever* come so close to calling him disloyal. And Julian could hardly believe it was Caleb doing it now. The man who had been one of Julian's idols after his coming to the Davion palace.

Almost a brother.

Certainly a friend.

"I chased after nothing." He spat out the last word as if it had turned rancid in his mouth. "I followed the agenda laid out for me by your father."

"Tying the millstone of The Republic around our neck." Caleb shook his head. "This may not necessarily be in the greater interests of the Federated Suns just now. You did not consider that we might not agree?"

"Honestly. Prince Caleb. I did not." A dry, bitter taste coated the inside of his mouth. Adrenaline. A fear-anger response to Caleb's threatening posture. The guards. McKenna. The blind reversal of Prince Harrison's agenda.

"And you feel you should not?"

"Your father is still alive," Julian said. A thrill of anger softly warmed his voice. "Until his death, isn't it your mandate to support all policies as begun?"

"You think to tell us our job, cousin?"

"If need be. *Cousin*." Several of Caleb's guards took a

step forward, through none of them moved past their liege lord. And there was still a large divide separating Julian and Caleb. A no-man's-land into which neither of them appeared ready to venture. Five meters of nonskid surface, glistening with a deceptively oily look.

It might as well have been five kilometers.

"Even if not," Julian continued, taking a small step forward, "it is *my* job. And I filed my reports through our MilNet secure data system. You would have had instant access to these here on the *First Sun*, or at Thonon-les-Bains using your father's passcodes."

A pregnant silence. Then, "I do not have my father's passcodes."

He did not? "Then Riccard Streng could have passed them along to you," he said, naming the intelligence chief, Prince Harrison's spymaster and personal advisor.

"*Dr. Strange* has dropped out of sight." Caleb dropped yet another bombshell. "We've had no official contact for weeks. Though he was still tapped into our secure data system, and accessing all MilNet information until we revoked his clearance two days ago. Are you working for Streng?"

"No!" Julian shook his head as Sandra snuck her hand into his, gave him a squeeze of assurance. He wanted to step forward, cross to his cousin, but he felt as if his feet were mired in quicksand. "Faith defend, Caleb, why would you think me a threat?"

"As if you did not already know!"

Caleb's dark brown eyes were bright and alive with rage now. He stalked forward, crossing the gulf that had stretched out between the two men. Sandra pulled Julian to her side, and he felt her tremble as Caleb stalked within reach. Behind him, several guards brought their laser rifles to the ready and Sterling McKenna glanced between Caleb and the security escort as if suddenly uncertain of what might happen. Worried, as was Julian, that things had somehow escalated too far.

"By the Unfinished Book, Caleb, I have no idea what you are talking about. Go read the reports! Everything I've pursued in the past month and a half has been in accordance with your father's wishes, to promote a military alliance between our nation and The Republic. It's my job."

"Was."

The word slipped out with the whisper of a sniper shot, striking Julian in the center of his chest. A cold ache gripped him, as if tight steelbands had suddenly wrapped around his body. Squeezing. Slipping further into the sinking sands.

"Sorry?" he asked. Wanting to believe he'd heard incorrectly.

"Was your job. Commander. We relieve you of your duties as prince's champion and ask you to resign the post. Immediately! If the need arises for a new champion, we will appoint one as necessary. In the meantime, you are to retain local control of the First Davion Guards on Terra until and unless we see evidence of any lack of ability to command." Caleb smiled without humor. "It is not 'our' nation, Julian. It is *my* nation. You may reflect on that while continuing to watch out for my father."

Julian felt as if he'd been struck by a bolt of lighting hurled down from the sky. A PPC blast, at the least. Rooted to his spot and sinking quickly in the quagmire, he struggled to free himself, his thoughts, from the situation's unyielding grip.

Failed.

As the acting Prince, *could* Caleb actually remove him as champion? Certainly he had the force of arms behind him here, and some political weight as well with Khan McKenna looking on, but the legal niceties might be harder to control. If Julian were to contest his forced resignation, on the grounds that Caleb had no authority . . .

He'd be undermining his cousin, and the throne of the Federated Suns! Not a path he'd willingly walk, no matter how dark the outlook.

But he could still hope for calmer heads to prevail. Couldn't he? Someone to intervene and mediate this sudden, hostile conflict between Julian and Caleb. Someone to whom Caleb would listen.

"Duchess Hasek?" he asked. "Caleb . . . Prince Caleb . . . where is Amanda?"

But his cousin was not in any mood to reconcile or even press their debate. Caleb stared coldly at Julian, his eyes dark and hooded. His face was pinched in a mask of contempt.

"We sent our aunt ahead to prepare a proper reception on New Avalon and to bear our personal report to the High Council. And she would not plead your case even were she here, Julian. She would agree that our need for a strong transition is paramount to all other concerns. And this decision was reached in consultation with my own security personnel, with Mason and even with one of our allies." He nodded back over his shoulder in the general direction of Sterling McKenna. "It was not made lightly."

"Mason?" Something niggled at the back of Julian's mind. A mention of that name from before . . . "Who is—"

"Who we choose to consult is our business. I suggest, cousin, that for as long as you remain an officer of the Federated Suns, you begin to warm to this fact." Caleb stepped forward, shortening the distance between them. Sandra Fenlon gripped Julian's hand and arm tight, tight. "I am prince. Me! Don't you ever question that again."

Then Caleb slowly and deliberately turned his back on Julian. An obvious gesture of dismissal. A message that Julian was now behind him. Far, far behind him.

"Now," Caleb said. "Get off my ship."

And the sands closed in around Julian's head.

GOOD FENCES

Wars cannot be avoided, and can only be deferred to the advantage of others.
—Niccolo Machiavelli, "The Prince," 1513

One can afford the luxury of patience only when commanding an unassailable position. At such a point, the best offense is a strong defense. But the trouble with living behind fortress walls is that at times you begin to wonder if you are holding the enemy out, or if they have now caged you within.
—Erik Sandoval-Groell, "Quoted in the Kai Lampur Daily Sentinel," Tikonov, 23 June 3135

11

We saw Ohrensen fall. We saw New Canton sit by, appeasing House Liao with worlds to be used as staging grounds for attacks into Prefecture V. We watched as such moderate and fair-minded leaders as Lina Derius and Geoffrey Mallowes were branded as traitors and even subject to arrest without recourse! You tell me. How long do we wait? How much more rope do we offer Exarch Levin, before he has finally tied a hangman's noose large enough to fit The Republic entire?
—Senator Therese Ptolomeny, Park Place, 4 July 3135

Undisclosed Location, Markab
Republic of the Sphere
14 July 3135

"Really, Conner. Blacked-out windows and circling VTOLs? Why not blindfolds while you were at it?"

Senator (and now Viscount Markab) Conner Rhys-Monroe leaned back against the tram's cold, ferroglass window, ignoring the bumps and rattles and a sudden stomach-dropping sensation as the vehicle lurched down the ramp into an underground garage. Arms folded across his chest, a tight smile glued to his face, he stared hard at Melanie Valdistok as if appraising her idea.

"If I'd felt it necessary, I would have," he said, taking Melanie's sarcasm at face value. He glanced between her and Usuha. "It is not too late."

Subhar Usuha shook his head. "I would rather forgo that experience."

Usuha had yet to evidence any sense of humor; or much, in fact, except the dispassionate, business-like manner that had gotten the man elected as Ozawa's senator after the Spirit Cats' Kev Rosse was finally voted out of office. Usuha had a cold, if distinctive, style. A Nehru jacket only a few shades darker than his coffee-brown skin, cut for his linebacker shoulders. White, white teeth, which showed when he talked but never in a smile. Braided black hair, corn-rowed back and left to drop down in a professional length of only three inches, weighted at the end of each thin braid by an ebony bead. The style kept his hair out of his eyes and when he shook his head the beads clacked together softly.

In contrast, Melanie Vladistock could not have been more his opposite. The senator from Kervil, a world in Prefecture II, was tall and lanky and moved like a classically trained dancer. Which she had been, at one point in her life. All poise and grace, and soft, appealing edges surrounding a core of solid titanium. She did not bend. At best, she allowed others a comfortable grip.

Just now she toyed with her hair, twisting a long reddish-brown curl around her finger. Such a schoolgirl habit made her appear younger than her thirty-eight years. Much younger. A private image Conner found immensely appealing. Most days.

Days when he could push the events on Terra far back in his mind.

Days when his father's memory did not plague him. Gerald Monroe's voice echoing in his mind like

(*a gunshot*)

distant shouts.

The ramp leading into the underground bunker was shallow and just long enough to drop them into a garage full of GI trucks, half a dozen tracked tanks, three SM1 Destroyers, and a pair of JES II strategic missile carriers. Two laser turret emplacements guarded the entrance.

"No BattleMech company?"

"South-side bunker," Conner said, deadpan. Melanie glanced sharply at him, but he left her wondering if he had told her the truth or not.

The tram followed its preprogrammed path, making a switch from one overhead rail system to another with a scrape of sparks. Coiling around to the backside of the garage, past three darkened alcoves, it finally pulled up in front of a dimly lit station where a single armed guard waited with his hand on his holstered pistol and a communications wire stuck into his ear. Raising his hand, he clenched it next to his mouth and spoke briefly through the hidden mic.

Conner nodded the others ahead of him. "If I'm first out the door, the guard will assume I am under duress and shoot anyone behind me."

Even Subhar Usuha blanched a bit at the idea of being shot so cavalierly. He stepped up to the door as it slid back on hidden hinges, and was first onto the platform.

The garage wasn't much more than one would expect of an underground facility. Lots of gray concrete and a few metal pipes and conduits for wire runs pulled across the ceiling. A high ceiling, to fit the tall profile that came with most turreted tanks. And it smelled of more than exhaust fumes and spilled gasoline and concrete dust. An acrid tinge flavored the air. The taste sat on the back of Conner's tongue like rotten eggs. It had drifted through his father's office in the Senate, that touch of sulfur. From gunpowder.

He swallowed. "I apologize for the stringent security."

"You don't really mean that," Melanie said.

"No."

In fact, he'd learned from his time as a knight of The Republic to never, *never* modify security protocols for the convenience of guests. Or himself. And in dealing with the different "flavors" of senators involved in this stand against the exarch's abuse of power, he'd found it convenient to remind them from time to time that he had been a military man before his father's suicide landed on his shoulders the full weight of his family's titles. Viscount Markab and a distant heir to the Dukedom of Mallory's World, yes. But also *Sir* Conner. The wild knight.

He had reveled in his reputation, in fact, with his mohawk and non-conservative dress. Until the political pressure leveraged against Senator Gerald Monroe pushed the man over the edge and Conner had left military service for the political arena.

Except, if that were true, how had it ended up with him leading a desperate, violent charge out of Germany to take Paris? His attempt to capture political leaders as bargaining chips?

How many more good men and women had died since Conner's agreement to serve out the remainder of his father's term?

Shaking the questions from his head, Conner led the other two senators into the nearby alcove and down a short hallway lined with closed, steel doors. The ceiling was low here. Barely high enough for a good-sized man to stand upright with the pipes and electrical runs suspended overhead. Near the wall, a steady trickle of water drip-drip-dripped into a small puddle spread over the floor. He'd have to get that seen to.

"This was the Monroes' fall-back position during the Jihad," he said. Sixty years before. When the Inner Sphere had burned under Word of Blake's scorched-earth campaign. "Complete with defensive systems and storage, and apartments for several hundred families. A base of operations from which we expected to fight an ongoing resistance. We've kept it a closely guarded secret."

"So you have your own private bunker." Usuha shrugged. "In itself, not so noteworthy."

The corridor ended at a double-wide steel door, reflecting back stretched images of Conner and the other two senators. If Melanie or Subhar noticed the murder holes to either side, out of which sentries could thrust muzzles of assault rifles at any moment, they did not say anything. So neither did he.

Instead, he placed his palm on the inset piece of dark, charcoal-tinted glass next to the security door. A light flashed behind the glass, outlining his palm. Then the door slid back into the wall with a hiss of driving pneumatics.

"Perhaps not. But I do get a sense of security while here," he admitted, leading the two inside.

Then he smiled as the room's "presence" washed over his two comrades. It stopped them cold, leaving them both momentarily speechless.

The room was a command center, full of communications boards and tactical plotters and satellite imaging stations. A large holographic projection table rested on a raised dais at the center of the room, its glasstop screen glowing softly amber in the dim light. Fully operational, the center would have been the envy of any planetary defense force and likely competed with anything less than the exarch's own situation room on Terra.

In enough space for fifty or more staffing officers and technical crew, just now a skeleton team of three junior officers and one staff sergeant worked the various boards, panels and computer interface screens. Most of the equipment sat dark and lonely, often covered by a plastic shroud. The entire room had a fresh-from-the-factory smell. Plastics and cold steel, mainly. The scents had yet to be overpowered by the ozone taste of warm electronics, the human touches of old coffee and nervous sweat.

"Well?" Conner asked, breaking the silence.

Subhar Usuha nodded. "I take it back."

Melanie was also impressed, walking out among the aisles between dark screens and chairs still wrapped in thin membranes of shipping plastic. "This must have . . . How could you . . . Years. Decades. Conner, this cost a fortune!"

And was never to be used except in the most dire emergency. Had his father ever considered that the actions he had taken, along with the rest of the Senate cabal, would initiate just such a crisis as this? Their "victimless plan" to influence the military, and the government, at the highest levels. And Conner's strong defense against the exarch's high-pressure tactics.

"Sergeant," he said. "Throw The Republic onto the main table please."

He walked over to the large holographic array, stepping up on the dais and waiting to be joined by Melanie and Subhar. She was slow in coming, stopping to pull up the corners on a few plastic shrouds. Checking . . .

"Matsushita. Kamaharra. These were manufactured in the Draconis Combine."

And imported illegally. She left off that part of her accusation.

"Mother was much more the careful one," Conner admitted. He stared down into the table as the amber glow parted into a soft, blue background and tiny suns winked into existence. "Over the last twenty years, I believe we've upgraded or replaced every piece of equipment in this room."

It helped that his mother was also a Combine citizen, and the head of a very large merchant family, influential on both sides of the border.

As Melanie joined the two men, Conner adjusted some holographic controls projected into the air above the table's edge, and a fully detailed starmap of The Republic of the Sphere slowly coalesced into being. Not fully three-dimensional, as the emitters were good for only eighteen inches above the table's wide, glossy surface. But good enough to give some depth perception to the starfield. Nearly three hundred burning suns in hues of yellow and red and a few bright white or hard blue. Terra pulsed at the very center like a miniature strobe. Then the prefecture borders sketched in with thick, golden lines, fencing Prefecture X within a circular wall, stretching spider-like arms out to divide each Republic district into its own place. Border worlds from neighboring realms peeked out like eyes watching from the edge of the dark.

"Sergeant." He did not look back, but studied the starmap with intense concentration. "Add the latest strategic overlays."

Several dark cancers ate into the bright field. Stars dimmed in Prefectures V and VI as House Liao pushed out from their Capellan Confederation. The Oriente Protectorate swallowed two worlds as well. In Prefectures VIII and IX, the Jade Falcons carved out their own territory. And the Draconis Combine border shifted as well with their most recent military drives chewing deep through Prefecture II.

Melanie shivered. Gripped her arms in a solitary hug. "Watching that happen is enough to give one chills. How many worlds has The Republic lost to outside aggression?"

"Twenty . . . ?" Subhar looked to be counting. "Thirty . . . ?"

"Now," Conner said, as he performed his own input over the projected control surface. "Let's see where *we* stand."

A silver halo glowed to life around half a dozen worlds spread across a large part of The Republic.

"Markab," Conner said, "and Ozawa." He nodded at the two worlds marked out of Prefecture III. "Kervil." Melanie's homeworld in II. "Liberty and Augustine and Park Place." Senators Lina Derius, Michael Riktofven. Therese Ptolomeny.

Their new Alliance of Senators.

"Far flung and unable to support each other," Subhar said. "The Blackout notwithstanding. You are isolated and ineffective." He spread his hands as if to encompass all of the displayed Republic. "When we gather together in the Senate, we speak with a voice Exarch Levin is forced to heed. There, we have a solidarity of purpose and will."

Very careful uses of "you" and "we," Conner noted. Subhar was not yet on board. But he would be. He had no choice.

Fortunately, Melanie had recovered well enough to answer the Ozawa senator. "What else would you have us do? Let Jonah Levin run roughshod over our rights and responsibilities? He *disbanded* the Senate, Subhar. He took away the voice of the people. Can we really trust that he will simply give it back?"

That rattled the man's composure. He laid a hand to the side of his face, slowly rubbed it along his jaw. Thinking. "I am not saying I agree with his methods. But I see no call to join you in what I perceive as a mutual suicide pact. I do not fear Noble's Court or a military investigation. And I am responsible to the people of Ozawa as well as to the benefit of all worlds in Prefecture III. This . . ." he waved his other hand at the disparate worlds with their solitary halos, "is not convincing."

"All right." Conner stepped up his program to Stage Two. Gestured at the starfield where the silver halos suddenly expanded into a web of thin strands, tying other worlds together.

Markab grabbed Mallory's World, Cylene and Ronel. Ozawa tied in Towne and Addicks. On the other side of

The Republic, Liberty pulled in Outreach and Hall. Augustine tied itself to Irian and Hamilton.

"See it yet?" he asked.

Subhar looked the map over. Shook his head. "Senator Derius has no impact on Hall. You've no influence on Ronel either. If I'm not mistaken, Ronel was recently fought over in a three-way struggle between Katana Tormark's Dragon's Fury, the Swordsworn and the Steel Wolves. Tormark holds it for now."

"For now," Conner agreed. "Then how about this?"

He advanced the network to the next stage. Filling in a few more worlds between Augustine and Liberty. Scooping up a wide swath of systems at the inside border of Prefectures III and IV. And a few along the border of II and III as well.

"This assumes, of course, that we can successfully shift Senator Vladistock from Kervil to Markab, where she can continue to influence worlds such as Ancha and Sadachbia."

Suddenly, two distinct shapes took form within The Republic's chaos of stars. A triangular wedge, anchored between Irian and Park Place and crowned by Liberty. And a sweeping field from Markab down through Ingress and Sheraton. Drawing final lines through Epsilon Eridani and Capolla formed a network of worlds that sliced away fully one-fourth of the existing Republic.

Watching it happen, Conner felt a stir in the dark recesses of his mind. A black argument, worried that taking such a step would be the beginning of the end for The Republic of the Sphere. But watching it die a slow death, devolving into a military police state where the ages-old system for giving voice and protection to the people was traded for a false sense of security held even less appeal.

The lesser of two evils. That was always the argument.

"Do you believe the exarch could possibly ignore this?" Melanie asked, her voice dark and honeyed. Her eyes were aglow with the possibilities laid out in Conner's bold plan.

Subhar appeared suitably impressed. "You can support such a network?"

"There are weak areas," Conner admitted. "We skirt close to Swordsworn-held worlds and, of course, the advancing Liao menace. Coordination is the key, and lack of

HPG communications hurts us almost as badly as it does The Republic entire. *Almost.* These borders were chosen with great care to take advantage of the few ComStar stations still in working condition. And with two JumpShip bridges here, and here," he pointed out two open stretches of space, which included the territory surrounding Liberty, "we can maintain a solid arterial stretching from Markab to Irian."

Melanie nodded. "Of course, Ozawa is of great importance, Subhar." She leaned over, almost against his side. "Your leadership would figure heavily in any plans."

And Conner thought they had him. Caught up in the scope of such a resistance to the exarch's totalitarian grip. Able to leverage their political muscle as well as any military strength necessary, the former having been what was lacking when they fought for their cause on Terra. Not this time. Now, with a few months of preparation, Exarch Levin and his paladins would be forced to meet them on equal footing!

But, "No. You don't have it yet." Subhar shook his head. The beads weighting the ends of his thin braids clacked together, rattling a soft dissent. He folded his arms across his chest. "Too many holes in your current infrastructure. Too many chances we'd have to take, warning the exarch of our plans."

Our plans. Conner caught Melanie's raised eyebrow and nodded. Perhaps Subhar Usuha was not fully committed, but he straddled the fence and leaned far to their side. Ready for the last push.

"Do you have any suggestions?" he asked. Sometimes, a man merely needed to tug against the leash. A little slack could go a long way.

His father had taught him that.

"Move carefully. Move quietly. Don't reach too fast for the brass ring." Subhar stepped away from the table and turned to face them both. "Show me you can accomplish even part of what you've laid out here. And I will deliver Ozawa."

"Ozawa?" Melanie asked, letting a touch of regret tell in her voice. Of disappointment. In the great Subhar Usuha.

Conner nearly laughed when the large man recoiled as if slapped. "And Towne. Addicks. Small World. Give me a foundation to build upon, and I will raise a magnificent fortress."

"I knew you were the right man for the job," Melanie said. She placed a hand on each of his wide shoulders, looked up solemnly and gave him one regal nod. A vote of confidence.

And when she looked away, she slipped Conner a pregnant wink. One he returned.

Let Subhar remain distant. Let him play lord of the manor, if it catered to his ego as well as his sense of caution. In the end, hard-line practicality would force him into this new alliance as one of its strongest members. Conner had no doubt. But let him believe it was his own choice, and that he competed with Lina Derius to be the one to sit highest atop the dais. Conner did not mind. Because he and Melanie knew the truth of the matter.

When Exarch Levin finally came to realize what had happened, and approached the new alliance, Levin would not worry about who sat isolated within the fortress.

He would deal with those guarding the gates.

12

Sources will not say where Countess Tara Campbell has been sent. Only that she continues to "champion The Republic's interests." Speculation, of course, knows no bounds. Liberty, Markab, Tikonov, and Skye are high on the whispered list. Skye may be most likely, as it is known Countess Campbell was seen with Jasek Kelswa-Steiner during his recent visit to Terra. A relationship that may have begun much earlier . . .
— The Terran Tattler, 12 July 3135

Genève, Terra
Republic of the Sphere
16 July 3135

Julian Davion enjoyed the feel of a good gym.

Not the solemn, antiseptic rooms of an elite center, with social class requirements, private rooms and a personal trainer standing by. Another supposed perquisite of the nobility, where the latest in soft and silent machines provided a manufacturer's promised "strength training resistance."

Give him time-tested counterweight machines—and free weights!—any day.

Silva's Gym was exactly what he had been looking for. And it had the added bonus of being only half a dozen blocks from the Sisters of Mercy. Mirrored walls made the room feel about ten times bigger than it really was, which was large enough to start. Coming in right behind the early morning crowd, there were enough people working out to give the place a well-used feel but not so many he had to wait long for any machine or free weight station. The open room smelled of honest sweat and the not-so-honest body sprays some men and women used when they approached the gym as a pick-up point, rather than to lose themselves in an hour of exertion.

Julian was here for the burn.

Coming off of squats, thighs throbbing with a deep, dull ache, he straddled a plastic-covered bench for his second set of presses. Pooled his terrycloth towel onto the floor by his feet. Dropped his Vita-Sports bottle into the soft nest. Laying back flat, muscle shirt bunched at the small of his back, he braced his arms beneath a rough-textured bar loaded with ninety kilos of old-fashioned steel disks.

With a soft grunt and a shove he popped the bar loose and balanced it over his chest. Eased it down. Pressed it back up again. Down. Then up. Sliding into a rhythm of piston strokes, giving it an easy set of ten repetitions. The weights rattled together at the top and bottom of each press, joined the metallic scrapes of other weights being loaded onto a nearby leg press, the sharp *chinks* of dumbbells touching at the top of a press, and an occasional *slam* as someone let their counterweights fall back too hard on one of the many machines.

Thirteen . . . fourteen . . . fifteen!

Holding the bar at full arm's length, he rocked it back to slip easily into its cradle. He sat up, careful not to knock his head (again) against the bar. Grabbing his towel and his plastic bottle of Vita-Orange from the floor, he dabbed his face with the sweat-damp terrycloth and sipped. Staring straight ahead into the mirrored wall, he met his own gaze.

His reddish-blond hair was mussed to one side, and he didn't care. His muscle shirt stuck to his body, soaked through, and his skin held a healthy, ruddy glow that came with a good workout. He recognized the strong chin and hazel eyes he had inherited from his father. And although Christoffer Davion had died when Julian was thirteen, sometimes he still heard his father counseling him.

Sometimes, his father spoke with Harrison's voice.

A good prince serves the people well, uses the person badly.

Had his father actually said that? It sounded like Christoffer, who had much preferred his elected post as World Chairman of Argyle as opposed to any hereditary title his name had brought him. Still, he had given his warmest blessing when Harrison showed an interest in Julian's upbringing. And Julian liked to think his father would have been proud to see him graduate, to become the youngest Prince's Champion ever. He would have liked that.

This last week? Not so much.

Julian took another hard swallow of the sports drink, grimaced at the too-orange taste and checked the label out of habit. The ingredients list promised real oranges, but even the feel of the beverage—oily slick as it washed over his tongue and slid down his throat—was artificial. Had to be all the rest of the junk they packed in. The sodium and glucose. The electrolytes.

A decent sweetener was too much to ask?

He snapped the top down, buried the bottle within his towel and dropped them back to the floor. Lay back again. Flexed his hands and took a good grip on the bar. Ninety kilos. Plus another five in bar weight. Another set, easy.

Uses the person badly.

He glared at the bar, popped it up and levered it directly above his chest. Lowered it and then *shoved,* rattling the weight disks. Lowered. Shoved again. He powered through four quick reps. Five. Six.

At that place in the count, Callandre Kell suddenly appeared. Red leather pants, glossy jacket zipped all the way up to the base of her throat, black gloves. Riding gear. Her tangle of hazelnut hair streaked and tipped in wild, bright red highlights today. A storm clouded her face, turning her doe-brown eyes hard and dark.

She threw one leg across the bench, and him. Straddling

his stomach, she leaned down, grabbed hold of the bar and forced it right down against his chest before he could think to react, adding a good measure of her own weight.

"You self-centered sorry-for-yourself petulant child!"

Julian huffed a quick breath, barely able to keep the bar from crushing his chest as he strained against her. "Good to see you too," he said in a rush. On a short, sharp exhale.

So close, her breath felt warm against his cheek. Smelling of . . . licorice? She glared. "What are you doing, Jules?"

"Currently? Being assaulted. Before your arrival?" The bar slipped back a few centimeters. Pressed against his chest. He chuffed and shoved back. "Trying to work out."

She eased back only slightly, but kept her hands wrapped around the bar on the outside of his. Fully in control.

"You don't return my calls. You don't bother to tell me that mutt of a princeling *fired* you. I have to hear it from Sandra?"

"Sandra called you?"

"No I caught her on a talk-show exposé." She shoved down on the bar, bouncing it against his chest. "Yes, she called me. She's worried. Ducking calls from Exarch Levin? Avoiding your staff officers for the Guards? She thinks you're feeling undermined by Caleb's action and are making bad decisions. I assured her that it's not likely a recent thing. You've always been pretty dumb."

"Thanks."

"Don't mention it."

"Everything all right here?" a new voice asked. Above Julian's head.

He craned his neck back far enough to see one of the gym's managers in baggy shorts, a lifting belt and a ripped muscle shirt with the Silva's logo scrawled across the front. Arms too thick to comfortably fold across his chest, the manager hooked his thumbs into the leather belt. Two other men waited not far behind him—customers whose workouts Callandre had interrupted.

"Fine," Callandre said. "Just fine. I'm his spotter. See?" She pulled up on the bar, helping Julian lift the weight back to near-full extension. Then she settled her own weight on it again, levering it down until it sat atop Julian's chest. "How many is that?" she asked with false sweetness.

"Seven," he grunted.

The manager wasn't buying. "Look, ma'am. I'm going to have to ask you to leave."

Callandre looked down into Julian's face. "Ma'am?" she said.

Now *there* was a way to get on Callandre's bad side in a hurry. Julian craned his neck again. "It's all right," he said quickly. "Just a little motivational help. Really. Leave us."

The guy didn't leave. But he didn't push, either. Maybe he had heard Callandre's earlier mention of the exarch. She had not exactly been subtle. Julian shoved hard against the bar, and Callandre. "C'mon," he said. "Eight?"

She helped him lift the bar and spotted him back down. Again. Then again.

"Ten," Julian counted. Then gasped as she pressed down hard again. "That's ten, Calamity!"

"You've never done sets of ten since I've known you," she said. "Jules." She forced him through another slow and painful five reps, grinning down at him. Her leather jacket creaked as she twisted with his piston-like presses.

"Fifteen!"

Julian grunted with relief as she helped him lever the bar back into its cradle. She swung off from above him and let him sit up, then grabbed a seat at the foot of the bench and sat with her right side to him. She smiled hard at the gym manager, who shrugged and left them to their games. The other customers had already returned to their own workouts, the sounds of dropping weights rising again, though more than once Julian caught an interested glance in their direction.

His chest ached and his shoulders felt as if they might fall off at any second. Bending to one side, he scooped up his towel and his Vita-Sports drink. She took the bottle from him and popped open the cap, took a long swig.

"Have a drink," he said. His voice warmed with a touch of anger now that he was out from beneath the weights. "Were you trying to kill me there?"

"Put you out of your misery," she said, and handed him back his bottle with barely a swallow left in it. She stood and stepped away from the bench press station, moving closer to the mirrored wall where she had thrown her helmet. Then she did something very female and played with her wildly tangled hair.

Julian stood and followed. He dropped the bottle in a nearby receptacle and laid the towel across his shoulders.

"Not that it is any of your business, Callandre, but my continuing role here on Terra has been pretty narrowly defined by my prince. I'm a soldier. I follow orders."

"You're sulking, Jules. And I have to say it was far sexier back at the Nagelring when we were waiting for the honor board to convene. Now . . . This reminds me of how you looked after. Those few days when you thought your entire career was crashing down around your ears. What am I going to have to do this time to shake you out of it?"

"We are *not* going on a three-day drunk."

"Like I would even suggest that." Her reflection in the mirror smiled hard at him. Callandre turned to face him. "This time," she amended.

He relaxed. Tension bled out of his shoulders, leaving only the raw, pounding ache from straining against the weights and against his friend. He *had* been thinking of their wild year at the Nagelring, actually. How good it had felt to cut loose, even if for those few, ruined months, with the darling rogue of the Class of 3129 . . . and 3130 (thanks to their suspension).

He leaned up against the cold, mirrored wall. Swallowed dryly.

"I'm not here looking for a date or for a wild party, Jules. I'm looking for the Prince's Champion. How you've been acting lately, from what I've heard . . . this isn't you. Prince Harrison expects better."

It was a sharp jab to the stomach. Hollowing him out. Steel bands tightened around Julian's chest, making it harder to breathe. "You don't know anything about Harrison Davion. How could you possibly know what he'd expect?"

"I know more about him than you'd think. The best measure of a ruler is the people he keeps around him, isn't it?"

"I'd accept that as a maxim," he said, cautious.

"Well, then. From everything I've heard and seen, Harrison kept no one closer to him than you. Not even his own blood. So put that in your Gauss rifle and launch it."

Not even his own blood. Callandre's words.

As . . . a leader, Harrison's voice whispered from the back of his mind.

Julian swallowed. Hard. "I'd have to say, you're likely a bit prejudiced towards my case. Honor among thieves, so to speak."

She smiled. "Harrison didn't care for me, did he?"

"Not even a little bit," was his quick response.

"And I'm okay with that as well. If I were Prince of the Federated Suns, given our reputation together, yours and mine, I'd not like me much."

"Yeah, well, I've never really liked you, either."

"Right. You wanted me so bad, it must have made your teeth hurt." She bent down to scoop up her helmet by the chin strap and swung it lightly against her leg. Possibly—possibly!—daring Julian to deny it.

Calamity Kell could do a lot of damage hanging onto the helmet by the strap. He'd seen it before.

"So," she said. "Even if you are a second-rate 'Mech pilot and a dog at heart, you still mean quite a bit to the man lying in a hospital not a two-minute drive from here. And I have to say, Jules, letting Harrison's agenda stagnate is poor service from the Prince's Champion. Especially when there's not much else you can do for him just now."

The only jab sharper than her calling Julian a second-rate MechWarrior was her pointing out how he had failed his prince. Because Callandre Kell was absolutely right. Not that Julian would give her the satisfaction of admitting it. Never that! But it pained down deep, at the core of his being, making the aches of his workout and even the hurt of Caleb's accusations pale by comparison.

"I suppose you have some grand scheme all planned out?" he asked. "Your bike waiting at the curb, probably in a no parking area? Ready to drag me off?"

Callandre stepped in close. She smelled of leather and . . . yes . . . licorice. "Sandra said you cabbed it over, so I thought I'd drive you to the hospital. Long as I'm in the area, that is. And just *maybe* there's a dinner this evening. A bunch of us getting together. Lars and Yori. Sandra. The few of us that are left on Terra, skulking around Genève."

Skulking was certainly a word that oft applied to Callandre. "Fine," he said. A visit to Harrison's room had been last on his list for the day. But not anymore. "Then you can drop me at the Hall of Government. There are some things I need to do." Things he had put off for too long. "And if I can catch up to you for dinner, I will. Otherwise, make my excuses for me."

"Like I'm not used to that."

Julian decided to let her have the last word. It was the least he could do. He'd visit Harrison. Then Exarch Levin if possible; Paladin Ariana Zou or Heather GioAvanti if Levin was busy. Because there *were* important events still afoot. And "watching out" for Harrison, Caleb's orders, could be liberally construed. No matter what else Julian might be, he had an obligation. To his prince.

And . . . as a leader.

13

Will I answer the charges Lina Derius and others have levied against me? As they have preferred not *to subject themselves to a proper investigation and the nobles' so-called* honor *court, I can only say that they will have my answer in due time.*

—Exarch Jonah Levin, Q&A press conference,
19 July 3135

Genève, Terra
Republic of the Sphere
2 August 3135

"You must be kidding me. Him? The Ghost Paladin?"

Jonah Levin watched his chief of staff stagger back from the holographic table, her pale green eyes fixed wide and staring on the man who had just palmed open one of the most secure locks in all of The Republic. The base of a deep leather chair struck Héloïse Montgolfier in the backs of her calves. She collapsed back into the seat with a soft fall and a groan of protesting leather.

The man Jonah (and so many others) had for years

known simply as "Emil" let the door close behind him. Stood there in a dapper, dark suit with feet together and hands clasped in front of him. The picture of self-effacing. He gave her a slow smile and a single nod.

"It does lend itself to a certain amount of incredulity," the ghost paladin agreed.

"Yes."

It was apparently the only thing Héloïse could think to say. She looked to her exarch, and Jonah shrugged.

He'd been leaning over a glass-topped desk, a modern sculpture of metal and glass which, with a few codes tapped in, converted to a fully functional holographic display capable of accepting battle-rom footage, hyper-detailed maps from the World Cartography Office, or feeds from any military satellite in orbit over Terra. Just now the scaled miniature of a large battle stood in frozen display. Half a dozen 'Mechs, including a scarred *Hatchetman*, and two dozen or so armored vehicles. Infantry at this scale were little more than ants, scurrying around the feet of metal-shod titans. Jonah and Héloïse had been in the middle of a strategic review, but she didn't seem to be in a . . . receptive mood . . . at the moment. So he shoved himself away from the desk and crossed in three long strides to the door, to shake Emil's hand in a quick, two-hand clasp. Welcoming him to the meeting.

Although officially known as the exarch's private study, the windowless room was Jonah Levin's inner sanctum among the many public and private offices dedicated to his position within the Hall of Government. Appointed in the same cherrywood paneling as the Bullet, the same bronze accents and leather furniture, it *felt* like an extension of his main office and yet at the same time was so much more.

Armored and shielded against anything short of a direct nuclear blast, it was Jonah's first-line bunker where he could retreat with relative safety in the event of any surprise attack against Genève.

Other times it served as a meeting chamber. Or a strategic and tactical planning center where the exarch could run simulations on, say, an invasion of the Federated Suns—without any possibility of the idea being leaked.

It was the room Jonah retreated into to watch worlds

fall, and to plan where and how to send men to their deaths in battle.

A room filled with secrets.

And several of them were on display this late, late evening. A bank of plasma screens covered one entire wall in lieu of windows. Four of the nine monitors displayed a composite map of The Republic, the borders shifting slowly in a kind of time-lapse motion that swelled Prefecture X by as many as a dozen systems. Two more scrolled through bios of various command-level officers, flashing pages out of their personnel files for exactly six seconds, then moving on to the next.

Another screen did the same with political figures. Lord-Governor Aaron Sandoval held the place of honor at that particular moment, but was quickly replaced by Senator Lina Derius. Then a sketchy page on Caleb Hasek Sandoval Davion. Jonah saw his ghost paladin frown at the sparse information.

The final two screens compiled several lists. Of military forces and their current strength. Stockpiled resources. Monetary worth of The Republic's largest defense contractors, and a rating of their overall value in terms of military readiness.

Say what one wanted about Héloïse Montgolfier. Nothing kept her down long. She shifted her weight in the leather chair, sitting forward now as she studied the man who strolled casually around the room. She brushed a few strands of red hair back from her face, tucked the short bob behind her left ear.

"For how long?" she asked now, glancing between the two men.

Jonah was not surprised when Emil said simply, "Long enough." Uncomfortable giving too much away at once, his master of spies and champion of the ghost knight organization. The secret, eighteenth member of the paladin corps.

And *concierge* at the Duquesne, Genève's most prestigous hotel. A place uniquely suited for the ghost paladin to monitor so many visiting dignitaries, as well as so many knights and even the other paladins who came and went beneath Emil's watchful gaze. *That* was what had floored Héloïse so easily. The ghost paladin being such a nondescript man—a minor-level functionary—whom she must have talked with and dismissed hundreds of times.

In other words: perfect.

Emil paused at the desktop projection. Studied it with quiet intensity. Looked up at Jonah.

"Liberty?" he asked.

Not in any doubt as to the world. Asking after Jonah's intent on sharing the information with his chief of staff. Who, until today, had not been privy to all his secrets.

"If we are going to bring others inside, we can't hold back on such details."

Jonah crossed to a sideboard table where he had left some tea to cool. He found his white china cup and cradled it in both hands, then blew across the still-steaming beverage. "Tara Campbell must and will figure into any plans we have for The Republic's future."

Héloïse thrust herself out of the chair. She stood motionless a moment, as if unsure how to act in the presence of the ghost paladin. Then she paced a tight square around the room. "Except that according to what you just told me," she finally said, "The Republic has no future." She spoke to Jonah, but rested her pale green eyes, sharp with accusation, on Emil. She seemed to blame the ghost paladin, though Jonah assumed the man was merely a convenient target.

A decision Emil made very easy. "It does not," he promised. "Unless we find a way to make one for it."

"We *could* try to save what we already have." But her voice was small.

"A feat of which, I promise you, no one in this room is capable."

Jonah stepped between the two. He recognized what his ghost paladin was doing, drawing Héloïse out. Exposing any prejudices and testing for weaknesses that might poison her against the exarch, and their plans. But that wasn't what he needed here and now. He needed a friend. Someone he trusted. Someone he *knew*. Héloïse Montgolfier did not belong to the entrenched Republic bureaucracy.

She belonged to him.

"The time for that debate has passed, Héloïse. The Republic is dying. Andrew Redburn held it together for what short time he could, and I'd hoped to cut out the sickness before it spread too far. Like the cancer it is. But we all came to the party too late. The Senate cabal was too firmly entrenched. The factional politics too rampant. And the Blackout . . ."

She nodded. Stopped pacing and hugged herself. "The Blackout lit the fuse. And we can't stamp it out. *This* part of the conversation you've shared with me before. When things stop working—the basic things we all take for granted—people get nervous. They get *defensive*. And far too many of them still have weapons." She sighed and reached up to tap a finger against her brow. "I know that. Intellectually."

Then she lowered her hand to her heart. Made a fist. "But it's still hard to accept."

He gestured her back to the chair she'd found earlier against the wall. Sank into the one next to it, letting the warm leather mold against his body in a comfortable grip. Emil remained standing. Taking a sip of his tea, he let himself enjoy the taste for a moment. Just that. The golden aroma and the spiced blend that would soon be a treasure lost to him as the plans for Fortress Republic moved forward.

"It gets easier," he finally said. "I fought it for half a year. I'm sorry, you don't get that kind of time."

"Yes, sir." But she still wasn't accepting. Not yet.

"You know. For all his great efforts, all his political insight, Devlin Stone worried that The Republic could not stand." He saw her eyes widen at his mention of the great hero of the Jihad. The Republic's founder. "It's true. In his private notes, he called it the 'momentum of ignorance and fear. *Plaga factiosus*. The plague of factionalism.'"

"If it worried him so much, why did he abandon us?"

"He does not say. Though I believe it was the only way to finally test his creation. His social reengineering. And he left behind several contingency plans to deal with possible failures along the way. But the Blackout, that he did not predict. So we are thrust into his greatest nightmare with very little to help guide the way. Only a last-effort fallback position."

She nodded at the screens, and the information they held. "Fortress Republic."

It was all there. The troops they had available. The resources, both public and secret, that could be leveraged to complete the plan. Pull up the drawbridge! Fire the nearby woods!

"Now I need your help," Jonah said. He gestured with his tea cup at Emil, who had moved to a computer interface to adjust the program that shifted the borders on The Republic map. "*We* need your help. And that of some paladins. A few knights. As many political leaders as we can trust."

Héloïse shook her head. "There won't be many of them. Especially as you begin redrawing the borders of Prefecture X. Our political fences built good neighbors, all right. Not counting the extra boost in impetus you will hand to our exiled Senators, you'll meet resistance across the board." Standing, she crossed to the wall of plasma screens. Stared at the shifting border. "Dieron being the most obvious problem."

It was a treat, watching the mind of his chief of staff at work. Héloïse had a gift for politics the same way paladins Heather GioAvanti or David McKinnon had such a natural feel for the battlefield.

He stood and followed her over to the screens. They were joined by Emil, who continued to study, crosscheck, and make subtle adjustments to the computer models. And pretended badly that he was not listening.

"Why Dieron?" Jonah asked. He had his own idea of where the trouble spots were going to flare. Dieron did not rate. It was already within the fence of Prefecture X's border.

"Because Lord Governor Copland and Prefect Nakano won't want to give it up, and we are going to lose it."

"Are we?" Jonah asked his ghost paladin.

"Yes." A simple declaration.

Héloïse rubbed her hands together, warming to the analysis. "The Draconis Combine, on the Coordinator's order or not, has retaken eight . . . ten worlds surrendered to The Republic during our formation. We may yet win a peace with them, but it is naïve to assume that any brokered deal would not include Dieron and possibly Altair as well. They want back their fortress world. Their lost military district."

That bumped Dieron towards the top of the list, then.

"So any strategy has to take increased Combine aggression into account. All right."

She studied the map. Saw where the border stretched, bent, consumed. "Now Imbros III *might* be possible. Okay . . . Okay . . . Zollikofen, sure. That's Paolo Yngvesson. You can buy him or bully him. But Denebola, that's your biggest key."

"Why is that?" Emil asked, caught up in the analysis despite his earlier misgivings at involving Héloïse. Involving anyone, Jonah knew, until it was too late.

"Because Lord Governor Roxanne Waters believes the sun rose and set on Devlin Stone. Stone rescued her father out of the Zaniah reeducation camp, and he helped champion *any* reform no matter how unpopular. Show her an excerpt from Stone's private journals, and she'll make water flow uphill for you. And Prefect Buralli is a cousin. Between them they'll carry Lipton, Chara, Oliver . . . maybe Zavijava, but politics on that world are Byzantine on a good day. They can even put pressure on Pollux in Prefecture VII. Devil's Rock, though, will be a problem."

"Devil's Rock is non-negotiable," the ghost paladin said. He offered no explanation. Jonah already knew, and Héloïse simply accepted the demand at face value.

"Well, don't expect much political coverage on that. Hall and Elgin . . . okay. Nanking? With the local BattleMech factory, you'll need Prefect Sebhat in your pocket, in the early stages at least. Politics will take a back seat."

"Emil?" Jonah asked.

The ghost paladin clasped hands in front of him. His dark eyes rarely blinked as they studied the map, and the force-strength tables on one of the other screens. "We've already begun concentrating troops on our 'staging worlds.' Hsien. Connaught. Milton. These are the prefectures where our line regiments have been least affected by the growing conflicts. And Northwind, of course."

"Of course."

"Northwind?" Héloïse asked.

He hesitated. "Originally we looked at Small World or Errai. But Northwind is heavily pro-Republic and has another good recommendation." He pointed at the screens, drew an imaginary line from Liberty to Markab, passing right through the Northwind system.

Emil turned towards her, distracting her, for which Jonah was grateful. "The alliance of exiled Senators is picking up strength, especially in Prefectures III and VII. Their most vulnerable point is the fragile link tying Liberty to Markab."

"Senator Derius to Conner Monroe, the new Viscount Markab." Héloïse nodded back towards the holographic projector. "Which is why Tara Campbell will follow up our reconnaissance-in-force. To take down Derius. That will go a long way to settling any final unrest in Prefecture X. But . . . what about Monroe?"

A touchy subject with Jonah and Héloïse knew it. He heard the hesitation in her voice. Monroe had been a knight—popular and successful, a rising icon in his own right—before pressure brought to bear against his father forced Gerald Monroe to suicide. As if Jonah would not already carry that black stain to his grave, he had to live with the fact that it had ruined another good man as well.

And because of it, Conner Rhys-Monroe might be one of the most dangerous men alive in The Republic.

"We know *Sir* Conner has been working closely with Senator Vladistock, and approached half a dozen others including Ozawa's Senator Usuha."

"The paladins are dealing with him?"

"Lady Ariana Zou is on it." He took a long sip from his tea. It had settled into the perfect temperature. On the lower edge of hot. Ripe and golden. "She was sent to Northwind as well."

"A bit junior for such an assignment?"

"She's a paladin," was all Emil said. He turned back to the screens.

"She is," Jonah admitted, despite Emil's subtle glance. "But she'll have help. Julian Davion came to me, and volunteered his Davion Guards to pursue an alliance between The Republic and the Federated Suns. I sent him to Northwind as well. Callandre Kell is with him. And I received immediate requests from *both* Magnusson of the Dominion *and* Yori Kurita to have their BattleMechs released for travel with the Guards. Julian has been making friends, it would seem. His ability to draw together such a varied pool of talent, and from what we saw last month, we couldn't have a stronger piece set on the board in our favor."

"His orders are to engage the Senator?"

"My *request* was that he work with Paladin Zou or on his own authority to maintain the peace and stabilize the area." Levin tapped a heavy knuckle against the nearby screen. "He'll draw out Conner Monroe. Of that, I have little doubt. A vital role . . . and unfortunate."

"Sir?" Héloïse and Emil asked at the same time, with slightly different inflections. Hers an actual question. His, a caution.

One he heeded. Partly. "Julian has been a friend of The Republic. He represented Prince Harrison's efforts faithfully and well. But this time, he's acting without a strong mandate. How that will affect his ability, we have no way to tell. We've sent along what help we can, including our strongest endorsement. But the rest is in the hands of fate."

"Can't that be said of all our endeavors?" she asked.

"True enough. A moment of regret that has passed." Jonah drank down the last of his tea, which was quickly turning bitter as it cooled, and grimaced. "It is simply a fact of our position, that we must abandon so many good men and women. What Julian might have been—should have been—no longer matters. What matters now is what is. And we'll have no room for regrets.

"Soon Julian Davion will be among the many . . . on the outside, looking in."

14

> *News of troop movements within Prefectures VII and VIII continue to come in. Garrison forces pulled back, concentrated on only a few, select worlds. And the office of the exarch still refuses to comment.*
> —Kasey Black, The Military Morning, KMLT, Terra, 4 August 3135

Northwind Academy, Northwind
Republic of the Sphere
7 August 3135

The red desert protocol stretched barren plains of hard-packed, cracked earth and upthrust ledges of red, crumbling rock between the Senate loyalists and Julian Davion's overmatched motley force. No large hills. No dangerous ravines. An occasional, shallow arroyo that might fill with raging waters during a desert storm but were, at the moment, dry as Julian's parched, scratchy throat.

Vegetation was sparse. Barrel-shaped cacti painted in their own camouflage of sage and ochre-brown. Tinder-dry brush that burst out of shadowed crevices to bake under an angry sun and break free. A stiff wind pushed these skeletal tumbleweeds across the desert, jumping them off ledges and occasionally swirling them up into the air on a short-lived dustdevil. Driving them under the feet of marching BattleMechs, or into the fans of armored hovercraft where the high-speed lifters slashed them apart like grass under a mower's blade.

Laser fire cut across this no-man's-land, sparking rainbow flashes in the wavering, heat-baked air. Missiles arced up on gray contrails, bleeding their exhaust across a hazed, pixelated sky. Particle projector cannon hurled Zeus' own lightning back and forth.

"A terrifying beauty," Julian whispered. He licked sweat from his upper lip and blinked away the burn stinging at the outside corners of his eyes. "Faith defend, why are we so attracted to the terrible light of war?"

"*Wakarimassen?*" Yori Kurita asked. And, "What was that, Jules?" at the same time.

Not quite so soft as he'd thought. The voice-activated mic built into his bulky neurohelmet had picked up at least part of his muttering.

For better or worse, he was saved from an answer as warning alarms wailed for his attention. Filling the cramped space of his cockpit with shrill, biting tones to give him a casual second to react before a seventy-five ton *Tundra Wolf* lumbered far enough forward of the loyalist line to slash a scarlet blade across the front of his *Templar*. The blow shoved him backward as the laser boiled away armor composite. Molten droplets splashed against his upper legs, cooling quickly to a dull silver wax, and raining down to the ground where they would (normally) smolder and crisp into cinder-coated slag.

Throttling into a backward walk, Julian pulled back to escape the *Wolf*'s follow-up barrage of long-range missiles, the warheads falling short to erupt across the desert's rocky floor in a violent line of fire, smoke, and flying gravel. He was less successful against the enemy's advanced tactical missiles, which drilled in on low, flat arcs to hammer him across the shoulders and slammed two warheads into the side of the *Templar*'s head. His cockpit bucked hard to one side, the straps of his restraint harness digging in at shoulders and hips, pressing the quick release buckle into his abdomen like a hard fist.

"Pressing hard from the southwest," Julian broadcasted across the Guards' common frequency being shared with Yori Kurita and Lars Magnusson. "Swinging wide. Hold the line!"

Planting one of the 'Mech's shovel-bladed feet hard behind him, he slammed his throttle forward and quick-shifted from a backward walk to a forward run. Wrenched against his control stick, dragging his crosshairs against the left-hand side of his viewscreen, he caught the advancing *Tundra Wolf* in the middle of a turn, holding relatively motionless.

The targeting reticle burned the long, lingering gold of a hard lock as his targeting computer adjusted for the slight oblique. The *Templar's* arms shifted by a fraction of a degree.

Just enough.

Easing into his triggers, the barrels ending each of the *Templar's* arms glowed with a cerulean nimbus. Julian's communications system crackled with distortion as twin arcs of manmade lightning burst from the particle cannons, streaming downfield over tailings of a collapsed ledge and a large patch of burning tinder-brush to slash along the *Tundra Wolf's* right side. Burning deep into the leg, the arm. Ripping blackened wounds into pristine armor.

Hardly enough to drop the Clan-designed machine, it at least made the other MechWarrior think twice about a weakly supported advance. The Demon and a pair of VV1 Rangers trailing along in the *Tundra Wolf's* wake were not so impressive as Callandre slid her SM1 Tank Destroyer into the *Templar's* shadow.

"Got your back," she said. On his heads-up display, Julian saw a few other Guard units swing away from center, following Callandre's lead.

Failing to notice what that did to Yori Kurita's side of their abbreviated line.

The *Wolf* hesitated, right on the edge of effective range. Julian hot-cycled his PPCs to lash out again. Then again. Drilling megajoules of destructive, blazing-white energies into the machine's centerline, then slashing low across both legs.

That decided his opponent, who back-throttled for the safety of his own line while Julian and Callandre Kell continued a flanking swing out to the south and west of Julian's entrenched force. A classic stand-off, with the Guards (and friends) holding to a strong central position, ready to choke the loyalists should they try to swarm forward and swallow them whole.

Also known as the "chicken bone" defensive strategy.

A strategy that fell apart not ten seconds later, as Julian got caught out of position with his fusion reactor spiking high into the amber band. The *Templar* moved sluggishly, its myomer musculature and joint actuators addled by the high-heat conditions. Sensors crackled with a light frost of static. Waste heat dumped into his cockpit, blasting at the back of his neck, his arms, and flash-drying his sweat into a white scale.

Julian swallowed, dry and painful, and traded another long-range salvo with the cautious *Tundra Wolf*. His particle energy streams were joined by a *Centurion's* hammering autocannon and the blood-red laser from an advancing Joust.

At that point he first took real notice of the swinging line. The Davion Guards had shifted away from center, following his leading probe and stringing themselves into a long, westward-leaning crescent. Thinning their ranks to the south and east . . .

. . . where the *Rifleman* on the far side of the loyalist line led a sudden, devastating charge, backed by a pair of *Enforcers* and half a dozen medium weight, fast-strike tanks.

"Beware!" Yori shouted over the channel, followed by a string of Japanese curses.

Julian had no idea what Yori Kurita said, but guessed it was neither complimentary nor hopeful. He read the same looming disaster on his HUD that she saw forming in front of her *Grand Dragon*. The enemy commander had played it well. The *Tundra Wolf's* hide-and-seek game with Julian had pulled him farther and farther out of position, while the loyalists waited to see if the Guards held or—as they had done—shifted their track to pull way from the supernumerary forces added to their roster. Leaving Yori Kurita and Lars Magnusson with no eastern flankers, and now without much backup as the loyalists collapsed against the eastern end of Julian's line.

Jumping his throttle forward, he shifted his march to suddenly slash back across the front of his own troops. But sluggish. Slow. "Lars! Push wide now, now, now. Draw them after you. Yori, with him. Turn the loyalists. Guards, at them!"

He snapped off the commands as fast as he could, sensing more than seeing the only possible escape from the mistake his allied force had made. If his plan could be wrenched into place in time. If Lars and Yori trusted him as a commander. If his own warriors could be expected to react as strongly for a temporary ally as for one of their own.

Too many ifs.

Lars did break hard to the east, his sixty-five ton *Arcas* shuffle-stomping through a rill of red rock and gravel. His lasers fired as he sniped at the *Rifleman,* cutting a shallow wound over the other 'Mech's chest and then the right leg.

But that was as far as his plan held. Yori hesitated, drawn between her own desire to charge forward against her enemy and Julian's order to divide their forces in front of a numerically superior opponent. She shuffled a few steps east. Paused. Traded her PPC and long-range missiles against the *Rifleman's* rotary autocannon, and came out the worse for it as the hammering slugs ripped terrible wounds up both sides of her *Dragon*. She staggered back, cut east, and then held again as Lars moved farther and farther away. The Ghost Bear was completely unsupported.

And Julian's warriors did move, but not as he'd hoped. They slid further west still, in a comfortable hook to come up on his side, forming a new line *behind* him rather than pincing across the middle.

Which forced Julian to take a steeper angle into the midst of the nearest loyalist forces. Still attempting to salvage a standoff, risking a minor defeat against a spectacular rout. Losing his wager.

The *Tundra Wolf* powered right for him, lasers biting out with a savage, scarlet edge and missiles slamming down all around Julian's position. They were joined by a *Pack*

Hunter as well as a pair of *Hatchetmen* (of course the loyalists had been given *Hatchetmen*!) and supported by a sudden swing of JES strategic and tactical missile carriers. Julian stepped straight into a firestorm.

A wreath of fire and black, sooty smoke obscured his forward screen, and gravel pattered against his armor as hard as any autocannon slugs.

A deep, burning wound across his centerline carved deep into his engine shielding, and temperatures jumped again as more heat dumped across his neck and shoulder. The *Templar* stumbled.

His PPCs slashed out hard, one of them drawing a terrible scar from the *Tundra Wolf's* left shoulder up and across its face. But too late. It was his last act of defiance, as two JES strategic carriers overwhelmed him with overlapping missile barrages, more than two hundred warheads slamming into the rocky terrain, walking blossoms of fire and shrapnel up his legs and chest, pounding with violent hammers across his shoulders and head and forcing him first to his knees, then flat out in a long, metal-grinding skid with his *Templar's* chest to the desert floor and a fury of enemy firepower drawing down a violent curtain.

One final glance at his tactical display showed Callandre following into the furious assault, right behind him.

Which was the point at which the simulator's programs simply gave up on him. Unable to match the kind of beating he would take as the *Templar* ground to a halt beneath such a furious assault, his screens simply blanked out as the computers turned their resources to those warriors still active on the allied side of the battle.

Cursing, Julian slapped at the toggles on his communications board. Cut it from IN-SIM mode to COMMAND-STRAT.

"Give me a live feed!" he ordered the technicians overseeing the training session.

Slowly, his HUD warmed back to life, then the large monitor screens that had simulated a BattleMech cockpit's ferroglass shields. But instead of looking face-down into fire-blasted earth and cratered ledges, he had a "God's Eye" view. As if the *Templar's* head had been torn away from its body and set as a stable platform eight meters over the desert's battle-scarred floor and the smoking ruin of his *Templar* (and Callandre's overturned Destroyer). A true ghost in the machine. He could spin about effortlessly, zoom in on any part of the battle, and request wireframe schematics on any of the combatants. He just could not interact with his people.

So he sat there, and watched them get torn apart. Hands clenched into fists with fingernails cutting small crescent-shaped bruises into his palms.

The *Tundra Wolf* was not faring well, staggering forward against heavy fire, but having taken down the larger *Templar* its purpose was certainly fulfilled. Still, there was no denying the *Wolf's* strength as it laid into one of the Davion Guards' *Centurions* and, with the aid of those same missile carriers, laid it out for scrap as well.

"Damn," Julian whispered. "What a waste."

On the far side of the field, where the charge had begun, there wasn't anything left to cheer about either. Lars had managed to pull the *Rifleman* after him, finally, but his *Arcas* wasn't much more than a walking skeleton of its former strength. And what few Guard units had rallied to their allies' side were blasted apart and burning, raising dark pillars of oily smoke into that hazed, pixelated sky.

Only Yori Kurita remained as any threat, laying about her with her PPC and a trio of medium lasers—two firing against any vehicle eager enough to slip into her rear quarter. A VV1 Ranger and a Fox armored car had already discovered the folly of that. Both lay overturned and out of the battle.

But now the loyalist *Enforcers* came at her head-on, with two Condor multi-purpose tanks as well as a Hasek MCV spilling out a squad of heavy, Hauberk infantry.

"Mine!"

Yori throttled forward, no longer caught between conflicting orders, or trying to uphold a battle plan gone to the devil. Her *Dragon* spat out a gout of fire and smoke as missiles launched from the forward-thrust profile. The right-arm PPC chased after them, laying open the skirt on one of the Condor hovercraft, spilling the air cushion in a violent exhale and sending the craft tumbling end over end until it blossomed into an orange and yellow fireball.

The *Enforcers* got some of their own back as they caught Yori in a tight crossfire. Their autocannons hammered out with thunderous applause to strike sparks and shards of armor composite from the chest and shoulder and arms of her *Dragon*.

The barrage staggered her charge. Slowed it. But could not stop her now that she had sixty tons of determined machine aimed right for them.

Five hundred meters . . . Four hundred . . . Three . . .

Like metal filings drawn to a magnet, both *Enforcers* collapsed against the *Grand Dragon*. Bending the loyalist line. Opening up a new break through which the Guards might have rallied and—if nothing else—turned a coordinated enemy offensive into a free-for-all slugging match.

"After her," Julian urged his unit. "Follow, follow, follow."

But he saw the moment come, and go.

Two hundred meters. An upthrust ledge of red stone sloped away from the desert floor, rising away from the *Dragon* and towards the *Enforcers* where it finally gave way to a seven-meter drop. The two loyalist 'Mechs slipped in tight towards the side of the ledge, possibly thinking to hunker down and wait for the *Dragon* to deliver itself at point-blank range where their greater maneuverability and close-in weapons would give them a definite edge. Letting their Hauberk infantry and remaining Condor challenge the Dragon's approach. Turning to cover either direction, ready, no matter which way she came around.

But Yori Kurita stormed right up the slope and over the far side. Julian held his breath.

"BANZAI!"

A seven-meter sheer drop. Surrendering sixty tons of machine to gravity was not going to end well for Yori. But rather than worry for it, the Combine samurai embraced it. Full-throttle and not one ounce of hesitation this time.

A throaty yell.

An extra-long stride that pushed the *Dragon* well over the crumbling edge.

Out just far enough to stomp a thick, wide foot right into the face of the nearest *Enforcer*. Delivering a kick that crushed through armor composite and ferroglass and the titanium framework beneath. Caving in the cockpit, and continuing on through one side to tear away half of the *Enforcer's* head.

The *Enforcer* toppled over backward, falling as fast and as hard as the simulated gravity could pull it down.

Yori's *Grand Dragon* listed in mid-air, came down on its left side right on top of her victim.

The MechWarrior in the remaining *Enforcer*, stunned, took two extra heartbeats before he moved in against the downed machine, weapons blasting and ripping down through shattered armor and cutting free a severely twisted leg.

Julian saw that not one of his Davion Guards had moved a meter in Yori's direction during the entire charge.

Not one.

"Call it," he ordered. And shook his head out of frustration as the screens blanked once again, technicians shutting down the simulation.

He sat there a moment in the near-dark, an outline of the cockpit's escape handle backlit by a small blue LED, and worried once again how he could ever—ever!—integrate Yori and Lars into the battle order of his First Davion Guards. Whatever possessed them, either one, to volunteer to accompany him to Northwind, it no longer mattered.

Everyone had their reasons. His in keeping with Harrison's final wishes. The Guards in following him, possibly to Caleb's displeasure. Callandre Kell in taking her temporary leave from the Kell Hounds.

"All that is left," he decided, reaching for the handle, "is making it work."

15

As the news of Harrison's tragic state reaches further into the Federated Suns, you can expect more outbursts like the one that happened today in Jarman City. Anger and frustration, and the overriding question of why Prince Harrison left New Avalon in the first place during such troubled times.
—The Daily Planet Editorials, New Hessen, 6 August 3135

DropShip First Sun
Zenith Station, New Hessen
Federated Suns
9 August 3135

It was one of Caleb Davion's smaller fantasies. Just on the edge of propriety. Not necessarily difficult to arrange, but—for whatever reason—one he had never indulged in by chance, nor had he gone to any lengths as yet to plan ahead.

And it might have continued in that manner, had she not come to his private cabin aboard the *First Sun* so late.

Brought along a nippled bottle of Pajarito Smooth Agave (with the pickled cutworm floating inside) and two bulbous glasses with zero-G seals. Been so close to a KF drive jump.

At the time the first cautionaries rang out over the ship's PA system—three long, baleful tones meant to alert, not alarm—Caleb was splitting the worm with a great deal of appreciation and rising interest. Sorry to see it slip into her glass on one of the final pours, he'd watched her hold it up to the light in his spacious berthing compartment, staring through the golden, glowing amber swirl. In microgravity, the Smooth washed around the inside of the glass with a captivating oscillation.

Then Sterling had swirled it down into the bottom with a practiced motion, and sucked it all quickly through the wide drinking straw. Swallowing the Smooth but catching the worm between her teeth, looking the question at him.

By the time of the second, near-jump alarms, his skin burned as raw and as deep as his throat where her hands touched, explored. She tasted of Smooth. When he buried his face into her luxurious, blue-black hair, he smelled the lavender of her shampoo as well as the light tang of sweat damp behind her ears. Her breath came in short, sharp rushes in his ear. Long, silver-painted nails clutched like talons into his shoulders.

He chewed on her hair and swam in her clean, honest fragrance, warm and drunk and powerful.

And they'd *jumped*.

Caught between heartbeats, between breaths, Caleb sank into his partner as they were both suspended in that one interminable blink between stars. As the JumpShip *Avalon-One* powered up its KF drive and tore a rent through space and possibly through time as well. Twenty-eight light years, from Tigress to New Hessen, the *Invader*-class star traveler carrying the *First Sun* and the *Blood Raptor* as well as a *Leopard CV* escort. Twenty-eight light years *ad coitus*, with the stars swimming around inside Caleb's head like some great galactic waltz.

Or, possibly, it was just the Smooth.

It wasn't as he'd ever thought it would be, this fantasy. Like the golden shock aftertaste of the best Pajarito Agave, reality slammed back in at the base of Caleb's skull. A swell of weight and warmth that shook through his body and out his arms and legs to the very tips of his fingers and toes, and then collapsing back into one final spike of excitement that hollowed him out. Left him barren and dry, floating above the world in a tangle of (sweat-slick) skin and damp sheets as his blood pulsed loud and strident in his ears. A steady ringing of (sirens) and the distant shout of voices—

—yelling in his ear, "Battle stations!"

Hands clutched at him, wrestling him around in the sudden zero-G environment as vertigo washed him up against the cold, metal bulkhead and Caleb tried to form words around a thick, numb tongue.

"What?"

"Battle stations!" Sterling McKenna *shoved* herself away, clawed past the safety net that surrounded Caleb's shipboard bunk space and drifted free into the room. "We are under attack!"

The *First Sun* shuddered in a series of light tremors, then bucked once in the telltale hitch that even Caleb knew was a DropShip detaching from a JumpShip docking collar. He clutched at the safety netting, pulling it aside and himself halfway out of his rack before Sterling twisted in the air to see him.

"Wait!" she called. Too late.

When the DropShip's fusion drive lit off, gravity returned in a rush that made the earlier vertigo seem a blessing. Because suddenly "down" was a concept at the whim of the main drive and maneuvering thrusters. And it caught Caleb half in and half out of his bed, legs tangled in the zero-G netting as his body was wrenched down suddenly and firmly. His head bounced hard against the deck. He could have sworn he heard it shatter like a glass ball.

Sterling landed cat-graceful on her hands and the balls of her feet.

She scrambled to one side and grabbed up the one-piece body suit she'd worn beneath her uniform. Hitched her long, well-toned legs through, and quickly peeled the rest of the suit up her hard body and slipped arms through the tank-style straps. She pulled her long hair out, and had it tied in a loose knot before Caleb had recovered so much as a sock.

"Who . . . who would attack me? Here in the Federated Suns?"

"They are attacking the vessel," Sterling said. Shoved a jacket and pants in his direction. Pulled her own boots on over bare feet. "Soon as we jumped in-system. Had the Zenith Station under patrol. But they made a mistake, filthy *surats*. *Aff*, they made a grave, grave mistake."

Caleb smelled golden Agave. Buttoning his shirt, he glanced around. Saw his glass bulb (or Sterling's, it could have been) rolling on the floor back and forth near the bulkhead. Nearby, a spreading puddle leaked around broken glass and a lacerated, sopping, red label.

The Pajarito Smooth. It had floated away from the table, and smashed itself against the deck when gravity returned. That's what he had heard earlier. Not his head breaking.

Though he still wasn't certain that hadn't happened as well. He pressed the heel of one hand against his temple. "Ahh. Someone silence those infernal bells!"

"When they stop ringing, the ship will be locked down." Sterling leaped for the berthing door. Punched the faceplate of a small lockpad. "You may want to be on the bridge when that happens," she said as the door whisked open under pneumatic pressure.

The ship lurched sideways again, swinging around onto a new course. Caleb grabbed for a stanchion. Sterling rolled with it, literally, tumbling through the door and slinging herself by the frame into the corridor.

"Wait! Where will *you* be?" he called after her. But no answer came back.

He grabbed for his boots. Cursing the Raven Khan and the fates and the broken bottle of Smooth, the heady scent of which burned his sinuses with liquid fire. It was another thirty seconds before he stumbled out the door and into the corridor, yelling for Mason. Carrying his boots and jacket and trying to tuck his shirttail in one-handed.

As fantasies went, this one would certainly need revisiting!

Though by the time they made it to the bridge, Caleb liked to think he had reassembled himself after their disconcerting arrival in the New Hessen system. Dark hair smoothed back. Boots yanked on and trouser legs tucked inside. Only one button on his jacket not properly fastened, and that because he'd popped it off while wrestling with it during another awkward ship's turn.

Mason Lambert did not look much better. Red-eyed from interrupted sleep. A faint shadow of beard darkening his chin. His friend rubbed gingerly at the knot swelling beneath his left eyebrow, spreading into a dark bruise along part of his forehead (that same ship's turn).

Stumbling through the open door, Mason caught himself on a stanchion just back of the captain's chair. Caleb pulled the bridge door closed behind them. An armed marine slapped at the quick-release buckle holding him into an acceleration chair and leaped forward to help Caleb secure the manual dogs before Mason could turn to help.

"Prince Caleb!"

Captain Shaun Marti twisted around to stare back over his left shoulder. Instead of the usual spacer's pallor, he had tanned arms and a freckled face, acquired under the suns of a hundred different worlds. Dark eyes. A broad, generous mouth good for smiling, for frowning, and for pulling into a thin line of displeasure at seeing the prince on *his* bridge.

"Sire, I recommend you return to your stateroom at once."

"Not bloody likely," Mason muttered. Still holding onto the stanchion, eyes closed.

Caleb left his friend to his recovery. "What is happening, *Captain*? Who dares to attack us?" He spoke slowly and clearly, preferring not to slur his words. The taste of the Pajarito Smooth sat on the back of his tongue like acid now.

The *First Sun's* captain obviously knew better than to waste time arguing with his lord and master. Having voiced his objection, he waved Caleb into the empty chair next to him. Likely reserved for the executive officer during non-combat exercises, it was safer than fighting the shifting gravity of a vessel under combat maneuvers.

"Liao," Captain Marti said once Caleb was securely buckled down. The four-point harness bit in at his shoulders and all but cut off the circulation to his legs. "An *Okinawa*-class DropShip and two *Lung Wangs*. A dozen aerospace fighters." One of the ship's officers crowed and the sound raised a small cheer on the bridge from those around him. The captain smiled, thin and serious. Nodded. "Make that eleven."

"Liao? In the New Hessen system?" he asked.

Shaun Marti nodded. "Again."

Again? Then Caleb remembered some of the talks at Thonon-les-Bains. The conversations he'd overheard while resting up from some late night party or other. "That's right. Julian came through here on the way to Terra. And there were Republic troops as well. I thought they threw some irregulars back into the Confederation."

"Apparently it didn't take," Mason said. "Another job left half-done. What do we have in the air?" he asked Marti.

But the ship's captain was busy taking a report from his communications officer. "Tell them to launch the ready fighters whether she clears that bay or not!" he ordered.

"Captain?" Caleb prodded. "Our forces?"

"Half a dozen *Corsair* heavy fighters, already deployed, and two ready-flight *Daggers* I'm trying to shove out the airlock aboard *First Sun*. Our *Leopard CV* is dogging one of their *Lung Wangs*. Khan McKenna's *Bloody Raptor* has engaged the second."

He gestured onto the bridge's wall monitor, currently split between a live camera looking out onto the vacuum of space and a tactical display showing four large icons playing chase on the other side of the local Recharge Station as well as two wasp-shaped bodies being protected by their respective guardians. *Avalon-One* by *First Sun*, and a *Merchant*-class vessel by the *Okinawa*.

Between the two JumpShips, a host of small, dart-like craft danced and circled in a silent ballet.

"Give me the odds," Caleb said. Aerospace was not his specialty. Like any good warrior, give him real earth under his feet any day. Here, he was better working in the abstract.

The captain shrugged. "Five to seven," he said. "Against."

"Swinging about," the navigator said, calling out the move without so much as a by-your-leave. "Aft thrusters dark. Fore-port jets on burst."

"Does that mean another—"

FORTRESS REPUBLIC 137

It did. Vertigo swam over Caleb as zero-G returned. Or, worse, not *quite* zero-G. There was a shifting center of gravity stapled somewhere to the ceiling just now, as the DropShip flipped end for end and centrifugal force roiled Caleb's stomach. Bile rose in the back of his throat, and the Pajarito Smooth pounded in his temples.

Then the screen caught Caleb's attention, and he forgot all about the disorientation of a three-dimensional battlefield. On the live-camera side of the monitor, a blue-and-silver painted *Corsair* fled from a pair of angry *DFC-O Defiance* fighters painted green with white trim. The camera operator worked to keep the fast-moving, jinking craft in focus.

Caleb divided his attention between this and the tactical screen, which showed the *Corsair* trying to make the safety of the *First Sun's* weaponry. He then felt a slight sideways jolt as the *Overlord* shuddered, and two new icons leaped onto the tactical display. The ready-craft had finally launched. They sped out on an intercept course with the *Corsair* and the paired *Defiance* fighters.

•They weren't going to make it. The *Corsair* was in trouble now, as the Liao fighters' pulse lasers chewed on its tail. It was too far away.

This Caleb understood.

"Can we drive forward to provide covering fire?" Caleb asked. Thinking like an armor commander. Move your artillery base up. Give your crews an umbrella to escape under.

"And leave the JumpShip vulnerable to capture?" Marti asked. "Not even by direct order, Highness."

"We can swing back after."

The captain stared at him, dumbstruck for all of two heartbeats. "An *Overlord* does not change vectors as easily as you throttle a tank into reverse, Prince Caleb. I have six overlapping spheres of containment to coordinate. Sire, please, let me fight my battle!"

Caleb's ears burned with the rebuke. As courteous as it could be under the circumstances, and as necessary as it might have been, a darkness stirred within him to hear a man so subordinate to his position talk to him so. Who did Shaun Marti think he was? *His* battle? The Federated Suns was Caleb's, and his alone!

"What do you mean she threw him out of the cockpit!?" Marti railed at his comms officer with a string of inventive curses Caleb had never heard out of a line officer. Very little of it complimentary. Caleb was not certain what had set the stoic man off, in fact, until he ended his rant with, "Faith-cursed Raven bitch!"

Sterling!

"She's in one of the *Daggers*," Mason said, coming to the same conclusion as Caleb at roughly the same time. Leaned forward for Caleb's ear, though he still clung to the stanchion for stability. "She's going to get herself killed. Natural selection in action."

The ready fighters. *That* was where she'd run off to, then. Unable to sit back with an aerospace battle in hand, separated from her own DropShip, which was almost certainly going to claim a *Lung Wang* "kill" without her (never, never bet against a Raven Alliance pilot!), she had commandeered one of the *First Sun's* ready-launch escorts.

"Which one?" Caleb asked, leaning forward to stare bullets at the monitor. "Which, which, whichwhichwhichwhich . . . ?"

On screen, the *Corsair* had finally given up on escape and had cut his own thrusters, flipping end-for-end to trade blistering salvoes with the two pursuing *Defiance*. The end came quickly then, with the green blades of the Liao pulse lasers slicing into the nose, and through the cockpit's ferroglass canopy.

Oxygen burst into space, freezing instantly into a shower of small crystals. The pilot might still have his flight suit, Caleb knew, but that also became a moot point a moment later when one *Defiance* showered the cockpit with blistering energy, gutting the interior and leaving the fighter a dead hulk flashing silently through black vacuum.

Now the *Defiance* craft and the *Daggers* were head to head and closing extremely fast. Almost at once, lasers lit up the vacuum between the two flights, green pulses flashing from the Liao fighters in towards the Davion craft, which answered back with furious, white-hot tracers spit from their rotary autocannon. One *Dagger* churned through his ammunition quickly, almost recklessly. The other concentrated on short, controlled bursts while at range.

"That's her," Caleb said, spearing one hand forward to

point at the controlled gunnery. "That kind of fire discipline has to be Sterling McKenna."

But the concentrated firepower of both *Defiance* fighters proved too much for the second *Dagger*. Or he had jammed his RAC with the long bursts. Squaring a turn against his own flight path, he powered away at a ninety-degree angle, taking himself quickly out of range from the Liao fighters.

The second *Dagger* stuck. Used vector thrust to wobble against her own flight path, avoiding most of the emerald laser fire as she held her own fire to those same short bursts.

Luring them in!

Surging in at point-blank range, Sterling finally opened up with full weapons. The bright, ruby daggers of her medium lasers flashed forward to carve deep into the nose of one *Defiance*. She followed up with a long, steady burst from her rotary AC, which hammered its way along the starboard wing, walking large, gaping rents into the armor as it clawed over the fuselage and finally tore apart the cockpit in savage retribution for the *Corsair's* earlier death.

Caleb nearly cheered her victory, but sat rooted in sudden fear as he saw Sterling's *Dagger* suddenly roll over on one wing and quickly veer into a collision course with the second *Defiance*.

Her lasers chewed away at the nose and port wing as the two fighters skimmed in *very* close to one another. For a moment, it seemed as if there could be no other outcome but a fiery collision and fast death for both pilots. But the *Defiance* pilot flinched away at the last second, thrusting beneath Sterling's flight path . . .

And right into Captain Marti's own "sphere of containment." The veteran spacer leaned forward, hand gripping the air in front of him. "Take it!" he ordered. And the *First Sun* rained out with its heavy weaponry, filling the dark vacuum around the *Defiance* with violent energies and hard-hitting autocannon. It gave Caleb a fair impression of the captain's earlier jibe about momentum and space combat tactics, because now the *Defiance* was trapped by its own maneuvering. Caught inside the *Overlord's* reach, it could not maneuver away fast enough, but had to try to tough it out as it flashed close by. Too close.

A pair of particle cannon streams reached out to swat it

hard, finally carving through one wing and completely killing one thruster. Throwing it into a death spiral. The DropShip's next salvo blistered the fighter across its port and aft, caught the fusion engine.

Caleb watched as it came apart at the seams, erupting into a silent fireball of brilliant, blinding, silver-white.

Now there were cheers. Several shouts on the bridge and some heavy glad-handing. Captain Marti was already ordering the *First Sun,* "End around and after that *Dagger.* Get ready to catch the next one she throws our way!"

Caleb settled back, suddenly a great deal more calm. He glanced behind him to Mason, just the one time. Whether his friend saw the conviction written on his face, or simply sensed what Caleb meant to do, Mason nodded. Once.

Caleb faced forward again, saw Shaun Marti staring at him quizzically. Gave the ship's captain his best cold smile. "So. How would you rate our odds now?"

Nodding, Marti merely said, "Better than even."

Still selling the Raven Khan short. But victory went a long way towards silencing naysayers, and proving a warrior's—or a *prince's*—worth. Sterling would certainly disabuse him of that before they left New Hessen.

And so, next, would Caleb.

16

News of a large buildup of military forces within the Federated Suns has been grossly exaggerated. Count Brisham Vicore has personally verified and attests to the situation. Count Vicore has worked very closely with local government administrators in recent months, putting to rest any rumors that he had considered fleeing into Davion space to escape the exarch's wrath.
—What You Don't Know, Station Break XLTV, Caselton, 3 August 3135

Tikonov
Republic of the Sphere
12 August 3135

Standing atop the western tower of the Dao Xi office complex in Kai Lampur, Erik studied the overcast skies in every direction. Hard and gray, nearly black, as if steel wool had been used to scour the skies clean of all color. The edge of a major storm front was sweeping in from the northern ocean. There were reports of funnel clouds as far south as Jiaten, but nothing local. Here the clouds held still, and despite the cover the day was hot and muggy and tasted of sweat in the way only a summer storm could.

Nothing moved in the skies. Not a speck on the horizon. Not a flash of red running lights out of the east where twilight gathered early this day. Erik checked his watch again, shrugged. Gavin was not often late, but it happened. Occasionally.

He moved to the steel rail that fenced in the rooftop landing pad. Leaving the large, white "X" behind him, he gripped the cool pipe railing and leaned out over the twelve-story fall. Halfway down was the sky bridge, a glass-encased walkway connecting the two towers. People moved within the enclosure, oblivious to his presence high above. Going about their lives—their work, or thoughts possibly turning towards home and dinner with the evening drawing nearer. Wondering whether or not to bet the spread against Hektor in this week's grudge match on Solaris VII—being billed as the summer's number one blockbuster. Thinking about the terrible weather and how it would affect weekend plans.

Did any of them worry about the military operations taking place on their very own world? A few, certainly. Those with friends or family in the military, or living in a district under assault.

How many worried about the Swordsworn? The direction it took as government from Terra grew more and more distant?

Fewer.

And the war being waged in Prefecture V? The Capellan front stalled out as it backbuilt energy in the same way the overhead storm waited and gathered more strength before unleashing hell on this quiet city?

No matter. Erik worried for them. Erik and Aaron. The men and women under their joint command. And Gavin, with his secretive, distant masters. They would do the worrying about such things, letting these citizens and residents of The Republic go about their lives. Walking to and from the different towers. Marching through the glass-covered sky bridge with the *thrump-thrummp-thrummmp* of so many feet against . . .

Not an echo of feet. Not only in his mind. Erik heard it

now, the VTOL. A dull, soft beat as rotors chopped up the air.

Still not a blur of motion on any horizon, and it sounded as if the VTOL was closer. Much closer than that. Erik looked straight overhead in time to see the Brightstar executive craft drop out of the cloud cover like a descending storm demon, calling out with its own whispered thunder, bullying the air.

Straight down at the western tower, and the white "X" glowing softly with inset lighting. The artificial winds stirred, then hammered at the rooftop pad. They whipped dust and grit into the air, stinging Erik's eyes. They tugged at his dark topknot, ruffling it with wild fingers, but he neither shielded his eyes nor brushed back his hair.

He held tight to the cool, steel pipe railing. Watched as Gavin soft-landed the sleek VTOL with a veteran's touch.

Only then did Erik move, ducking beneath the still-spinning blades to meet Gavin as the other man rolled back his door on the pilot's side of the cockpit and hit the tarmac with his usual confidence.

"Two days?" Erik asked as the two men walked towards the small dormer abutting the landing pad. "You drop out of contact for two days, and send me only a cursory note instructing me to change plans and meet you?"

The man Erik Sandoval-Groell had come to know only as Gavin stared right through him with flat, hazel eyes. He had slicked his chestnut hair back with some kind of cream today, holding it in place despite the air still being pushed around by the VTOL blades. He did not duck beneath the spinning rotors as Erik did. He did not seem to care one way or another about them now that he had abandoned his craft.

"Things change," he said. "You asked for concrete intelligence on the plans Liao has for Tikonov. That takes time."

"Three times we've come close to securing Tikonov again. Three times these 'Liao irregulars' have reinforced their position. Damn right I want to know the full extent of their involvement here. You are making me look foolish."

The small dormer was nothing more than a pair of swinging glass doors that let onto a small foyer with two chairs and a bench seat, and doors to an elevator. With the doors swung shut behind them, even the whisper of the slowing blades was lost, giving them a moment of quiet while waiting for the car.

"I warned you that Capellan involvement on this world was stronger than believed. If we had taken your uncle into our confidence, perhaps he'd have allocated greater resources to be put under your control."

Not likely. The lord governor had grown increasingly stingy with anything resembling shared power. Another reason Erik was disinclined to speak with his uncle about the inroads he had made with Gavin's organization of power brokers and information traders. That Aaron had even left Erik to mind Swordsworn business on Tikonov while he took his flying palace away again (to Northwind, this time, of all places!) had come as a surprise. But an opportunity he would put to the best use possible.

"My uncle and I will argue about what direction to take the Swordsworn later, Gavin. What I need now is a target. A victory. So tell me. How many worlds in Prefecture IV has the Capellan military dug its claws into?"

Gavin studied the digital readout, watching as the elevator climbed up floor by floor. Stopped to take on passengers, or possibly let some off. Climbed again. "How many?" he asked.

"Yes."

"In Prefecture IV?"

"Yes."

"Including Tikonov?"

"Yes," Erik said again. Letting a touch of anger show.

"One."

Erik felt the frown cover his face like a slow-moving avalanche. "One," he repeated. Wanting to take Gavin to task for the answer, but knowing the other man had never—not once—distorted information or failed to produce results. Information was neutral. It might have a price, depending on its difficulty to obtain, but it was never subject to debate once delivered. "They cannot operate so far in advance of their main lines without a staging world."

"Yes." Gavin nodded.

So it was a puzzle? Something Gavin's contacts had dug up that did not fit in the neat little box Erik had anticipated wrapping for his uncle. "Is The Republic selling us off to barter a peace with Daoshen?" If there was a crown jewel sparkling for the Chancellor's eye after the world of Liao itself, it had to be Tikonov. Could Levin buy peace by putting the Swordsworn up against the Capellans?

He might. But not according to Gavin. "I think I can safely say that the exarch has no interest, at this time, in Tikonov's troubles. Not for or against."

"That seems unlikely, with Senator Vicore joining his resources to ours. How can the exarch not see us as a potential ally or threat?"

"Answer that, and you will have solved Duke Aaron's greatest puzzle," Gavin promised. "But as to the Capellan threat, there is no great conspiracy within The Republic. And no advanced-staging world within Prefecture IV."

"Those DropShips do not appear out of blue sky. They are ferried in, dropped, and abandoned with regularity that worries my top officers. There needs be a staging world."

"And I'm suggesting it's time to stop looking under the stones in your own backyard to find it," Gavin said as the elevator car arrived. A soft chime sounded through the tiny lobby as the steel doors rolled back.

"Where else is there to look?" Erik asked, and caught Gavin's slow, secretive smile.

The information broker reached into a pocket and drew out a memory crystal. He passed it to Erik with an easy handshake.

"On another side of the fence."

17

LIAO RESURGES!
In a strong gesture, Capellan forces have struck out from the world of Liao in several directions against multiple worlds. The escalation of violence comes as little or no surprise, though the scope surely does . . .
—The Tikonov Times, Headlines, 18 August 3135

Northwind Academy, Northwind
Republic of the Sphere
18 August 3135

News swept the campus of Northwind Academy like a summer wildfire, burning low and fast through the dry fields as students carried rumors and the bits and pieces of fact they overheard from one small gathering to another. Jumping between treetops as faculty and staff clustered, broke apart, clustered again. Raging out of control with the story growing out of proportion, warped far beyond what simple facts supported.

Fortunately, as the flames licked up around Julian Davion and the others, its source was one of the primary embers. From a man who spent a great part of his life putting out fires. Near unimpeachable.

"How many worlds have they hit again?" Julian asked, speaking around a mouthful of pita sandwich. He shook his head, as if the news had not quite fit between his ears the first time.

Sir Marcus Crane, a local knight-errant called to service by Lady Ariana Zou, leaned down against the large metal table Julian *et al* had commandeered at the Northwind Academy's student union—part of an outdoor café. Marcus's curly blond hair glowed under the buttery yellow sun. A gusting breeze stirred a few longer curls, pulling strands across bright blue eyes.

"Ningpo, Azha, Arboris, Genoa, Nanking," Marcus said. "Five. And stepped-up operations against New Aragon and Hunan as well, if you want to count those."

An excited muttering buzzed through the small crowd of cadets quickly gathering around them in this public area. Lady Ariana Zou had half-risen from her chair at the news. The rest of the table sat thunderstruck, most of them staring over half-eaten sandwiches. Yori Kurita held her chopsticks paused in mid-dive at her rice bowl, hovering, like a stooping hawk suddenly uncertain which of the several thin slices of teriyaki chicken it had chosen for its prey. Callandre Kell was the only one finished, having wolfed down her food quickly to better concentrate on the chess match she'd taken up with Julian, against Sandra Fenlon's friendly advice.

"Five," Julian said. "All staged from the world of Liao?"

"As near as can be determined," Sir Marcus told them. He looked to Major Daniel Lewandowski, from the Academy Commandant's office, who had joined the small team for a morning intelligence briefing and for lunch. "The General had the same official news delivered to his office."

"I heard the list of targets included New Canton," one of the cadets volunteered from the innermost ring of audience.

"And that Oriente is working with them again. Like they did when they took Ohrensen." Another eager student.

Crane shook his head. "Unsubstantiated rumors. When the Capellans hit New Canton, believe me, we will hear about it in no uncertain terms."

When. Not *if.* Julian took note.

Lars Magnusson leaned back, arched in a hard stretch much like a large cat. Ignored the cadet input. "No one saw this coming?" he asked, in a tone that suggested he would have.

The idea of escaping simulator bays and closed-door briefing rooms for a casual meal and a moment to relax was fast becoming a hindrance. Leaving off the gusting wind that snatched at wrappers and had knocked over Calamity's styrofoam espresso cup more than once, the questions and the curious who stopped by to meet one of the young royals, or Lady Zou, what Julian wanted more than anything right now was a monitor screen and access to the academy's online resources.

He stood as Ariana sat back down. Swallowed hard, and washed down the oil-and-vinegar taste of his garden pita with a quick swallow of vanilla-flavored soda. The sandwich tailings went into a nearby trash receptacle, which swallowed more of the meal than Julian had. He kept the paper cup, holding it at his side as he paced a tight line next to the round table his friends and current allies occupied.

"Okay," he said. "Okay. Okay. That puts the Liao offensive within one jump . . . two? . . . of our own operations."

"Two jumps off from Northwind," a new cadet volunteered. "Liberty, too."

Who had mentioned Liberty? Was the grapevine solid enough to have winkled out news of Tara Campbell's mission? Probably.

"Should we have seen this?" he asked Lars. "Maybe. But everyone expected a huge push to come at New Aragon. To silence Prefect Tao once and for all. Now . . . Where is Ningpo? Would that backdoor New Aragon?"

He glanced around the table. Yori Kurita stared back impassively. Callandre gave him an exaggerated shrug that said she neither knew nor particularly cared at the moment. She was still entranced by Julian's sweeping attack across the chessboard, looking for a way out of the trap he'd laid for her.

Not happening.

Julian snapped fingers next to his ear and found his intelligence analyst for the Davion Guards in the final seat at the round metal table, trying to disappear between Lars Magnusson and Sandra Fenlon. Leftenant Todd Dawkins squirmed, his fingers twitching as if wanting to fasten onto something. A lifeline.

"Todd? Ningpo?"

"I could run grab a noteputer, Sire."

Of all the . . . Where was that kid? The one who'd known relative distances to Northwind and Liberty? Julian found him at the head of the crowd of students, which numbered close to thirty by now. Bright eyed and a confident smile. The kind of face that encouraged instructors to call on him, no doubt. Head of the class? Blowing the curve for others?

He remembered that smile from many years ago. He'd seen it more than once in a mirror.

"Ningpo?" he asked the cadet. The name tag pinned to the front of his service grays read MacDougal. Red hair and bright freckles on his cheeks. Good Highlander stock.

"Almost directly spinward of Liao," he said. "One jump coreward from New Aragon." A pause, then a hesitant, "Sir . . . Lord Davion . . . backdoor?"

So there were a few things left to teach him.

Julian stepped over to the table, where Ariana had been watching him put Callandre into a strategic headlock. He borrowed four white pawns and the bishop he'd already taken from her, plucking them off the side of the wooden board and arranging them on the table in a rough pattern.

"Liao," he said, tapping the bishop's head. Arranged the pawns in a broken line next to the bishop as the cadets crowded in around the table. "Arboris. Genoa. Ningpo? New Aragon."

He looked to the cadet, who managed to look apologetic as he leaned in and broke Julian's line a bit more by shifting Ningpo further out.

"All right. So The Republic has kept New Aragon well-supplied through Genoa and Ningpo would be my *guess*. Shortest distance between two points, and all that. They *could* shift from Genoa and run through Arboris, which is close by. But they still need Ningpo, unless they want to start bending further out towards the border. It can be done, but we're talking pressure. Constant pressure, leveraged against a world under siege. Any setback will be magnified out of proportion. Instead of attacking New Aragon, the Capellans are slamming the back door on them."

"Then Genoa and Arboris are feints," the cadet said.

150 Loren L. Coleman

That made Major Lewandowski and Ariana sit up straighter.

"Why do you say that?" the paladin asked.

The cadet looked about. It was as if a wide gulf had opened between him and the others, cadets who had pressed forward a moment ago putting half a step of distance in between themselves and the man under fire. He hedged, suddenly unsure.

"Lew?" Ariana asked.

Lewandowski leaned forward sharply. "Cadet Corporal MacDougal! Snap to and report!"

The boy recoiled as if slapped. All but jumping to attention. It was a reflexive reaction, sweeping back through the crowd. Authority had spoken. Any one of them could be next.

But MacDougal rebounded quickly. Stepping forward, he pointed to the two pieces Callandre had managed to take away from Julian. Both pawns. "May I?"

In response, Callandre upended the whole board and scattered the pieces into a loose pile. "Please," she said.

Julian frowned. Looked up into the sky. "I was eight . . . ten . . . twelve moves from checkmate."

"I guess we'll never know for certain."

Using the white pieces, MacDougal quickly built the lower half of Prefecture V—the worlds captured or contested by the Capellan Confederation. With the black, he stationed pieces for worlds of interest. These made up a large part of the upper half of the prefecture, and New Aragon, with placeholders for Northwind, Liberty, Tikonov and New Canton as well.

When finished, it resembled an awkward chessboard, with the black rook (New Aragon) surrounded by a field of white, about to be cut off completely, and the outlaying pieces threatened by a two-prong Liao attack.

"Go, Mac!" The cadet had at least one fan in the crowd.

"If you track everything by thirty light-year jumps," the cadet said, borrowing a french fry from Lars Magnusson. Not even thinking about it as he nibbled it down to the right length. Held it out to represent the span of distance that was roughly to scale with his map. "New Aragon is nearly cut off as it is. There are two worlds on the Capellan radar, then. Ningpo being first, closest to Liao. But Algol is a close second. With those, they no longer need Genoa or Arboris to close that door. So I'd say that those strikes are to pin troops in place and divert attention."

"But not Nanking?" Yori asked. She leaned across Lars, pointed out the threatened black knight. The cadet had given Nanking more importance than some other, likelier worlds.

Julian had the answer to that one, and beat the cadet to the punch. " 'Mech factories. Nanking has industrial facilities Daoshen Liao wants. He'll throw serious forces at that world. No mistake." He frowned at the table, the arrayed pieces, and then forced a smile for MacDougal and offered his hand. "Mac? Thank you for the help." He spent a sidelong glance on Major Lewandowski.

"Everyone back to your own meals and your own classes," the major said, putting an end to the large gathering. He chased off the junior students with a hard glare.

The senior cadets, MacDougal among them, dragged their feet just enough to see if they'd be asked to remain. When didn't a senior officer need support staff, after all?

Not this time. Julian waited until they had passed from earshot, drained the last sip from his vanilla soda, then whispered a short laugh down at the table. "Impressive. Reminds me of . . . someone."

"Yeah," Callandre said. She ran fingers through her hazelnut hair, the wild tangles highlighted with subtle, golden tips. "I was just thinking he needed serious help as well."

"Stay away from that boy, Calamity."

Ariana held up her hand for a moment of peace, then reached out to flick the crown of the black queen. "Liberty," she said, her thoughts mirroring Julian's.

"Or Tikonov," he said. "Given the Chancellor's preoccupation with old Capellan worlds, perhaps more likely."

Yori Kurita pushed her rice bowl aside, chopsticks laid across its rim. "What you are saying is that the Liao advance might interfere with your plans to disrupt the alliance of Senators, *hai*?"

Your plans. For all their training, for all that Yori and Lars volunteered to accompany the Guard on its mission for The Republic, Julian was no further along understanding why, or in making them a strong part of his team.

Sandra missed the underlying tension, but if nothing else

she did know Julian very well. She laughed, and all eyes focused on her for a moment. She blushed a light shade of pink.

"I'm sorry. Err . . . *sumimassen*?" Yori smiled and nodded, and Sandra settled back. "From a political standpoint, I'd say it could disrupt *or aid* any efforts against this alliance. But if I'm not mistaken, it's the not knowing that bothers Julian more than anything." She smiled, a touch sorrowful. "It's hard to plan for events of which you can never be certain."

Lars Magnusson sat forward. The winds tossed and toyed with his unruly, ash-white hair. "Always plan with certainty. A definite strategy placed against shifting conditions will always hold stronger over a shifting strategy lost among a hard-line situation."

Callandre snorted a laugh. "At the Nagelring, we referred to that as a 'duck your head and charge' strategy. I look forward to the Lars Magnusson-shaped hole you're going to leave in a wall somewhere."

The Ghost Bear warrior grinned, showing his teeth. "And *how many* extra years did *you* spend in academy?" he asked. Julian laughed. And Callandre, never one to hide from her own foibles, licked one finger and drew an invisible tally mark in the air.

Then made a gun with that hand, and shot Lars with it.

"Which gets us no further along where we need to be," Ariana said, wrestling the table back around to the point. "Liberty is in play, now. And we'll simply have to watch what transpires from the Capellan front. But where does that leave you, Julian?"

He shrugged. "Same place we've been for the last two weeks. Working to integrate our supernumerary forces—Yori and Lars, any of the returning Highlanders who can be spared—and waiting for the Senators' first move. We'll react to them."

"Going on the defensive." Lars all but spat out that last word as if it left a rancid taste in his mouth.

"A modified aggressive posture," Julian said.

"What does that mean?"

"It means we build up our strength and wait to select a target based on accurate and complete intelligence. And when we move, we do so with the express purpose of dealing the alliance a critical blow. This is one time when we do not need to win the war, Lars. Just a few of the opening battles."

"Rather win the war," Lars growled.

Ariana shook her head. "We might need to welcome these people back as allies one day. Some of them. Let's not burn bridges behind us."

Julian nodded. "Especially," he said, "when there are so many we're lighting on fire out in front of us."

18

Yeah, I hear we have Davion Guards standing in to help on Northwind. And I'm wondering why we need 'em at all? Don't we have other units pulling back to the world a'ready? Been on the news, ain't it? Don't need no FedSun fancy boy thinks hisself a dashing general parading across our worlds. We got paladins for that!
—Call-in listener, "Speak Your Mind," W7LA, Northwind, 17 August 3135

Northwind Academy, Northwind
Republic of the Sphere
20 August 3135

The secondary Strategy & Tactics Lab at Northwind Academy did not impress Julian Davion. Not with his time at New Avalon's premiere academy and the New Avalon Institute of Science, and his visiting year at the Nagelring. Without considering the equipment he'd had access to as prince's champion, the local facilities were . . . *lacking* would be a fair term.

Antiquated might be another.

Each cadet station was a mid-level computer disguised as a very poor facsimile of a 'Mech's tactical monitor. Several of the humming screens flickered with static or lost tracking from time to time as stressed electronics did their best to keep up with the heavy class use. The bitter taste of ozone, of slowly frying circuit boards, hung over the room. Not a way to inspire confidence in the equipment, or the instruction for that matter. The only extra step taken was the strip across the top of each screen, programmed to duplicate the readings found on a MechWarrior's HUD. A cluster of icons and information tags, dialed out of sensor guesswork and the occasional identification transponder. A large monitor took up a good portion of the front wall, where someone might dump large files full of auxiliary information into any of a dozen different "pages," throwing them up for study.

Cadets usually sat at their stations while an instructor used the front monitor and individual stations to feed strategic overviews or tactical situations from the master computer station at the center of the local network. In this case, however, with Julian commandeering the lab (and co-opting several students) for his personal operations center, he parceled out information on a need to know basis to see what some of Northwind's best and brightest might do with it. He let them feed final results back to him for review and discussion, and flagged the truly impressive results for later presentation to his motley command team.

James MacDougal set a high bar for others to follow, as Julian had suspected he might. The senior cadet had a head for strategy and tactics, a natural flair that could not be learned. He'd been born with it.

Which was why Julian kept the boy, dismissing all others, when his three o'clock appointment finally caught up with him at the lab.

"You never fail to impress," Aaron Sandoval said, waiting near the door as the last of the student-cadets filed out.

A few studied the lord governor of Prefecture IV with admiration. Even awe. But Julian saw more than one open glare of suspicion. The Swordsworn did not always receive good press here, on a world known for its devotion to Devlin Stone's Republic. The Highlanders had bled thick and heavy over the last few years especially, rising to its defense.

"Teaching?" Aaron asked. "Taking time away from your schedule to influence the next crop of Northwind alumni? Be careful. The exarch will disband your Davion Guards and exile you next."

A poor comparison to the actions of those highly placed nobles within The Republic Senate, and their cabal's plan to buy off prominent warriors in hopes of someday owning a paladin or three. "As an icebreaker," Julian said, "you might have done better."

"Poor taste. I agree." Aaron seemed genuinely apologetic. He tugged at the cuffs of his jacket. He wore a dark, double-breasted suit with a banded-collar shirt, his blond hair trimmed close and his beard tightened down to a thin mask. He spared a single glance towards MacDougal, then shrugged the lad's presence aside. "Too much time spent in the company of . . . well, cynicism does seem to run in the Sandoval bloodline, let's say."

"Many things run in the Sandoval bloodline." Julian's smile was not necessarily kind. "Loyalty and treachery. Bravery and cowardice." He forestalled any insulted outburst with a raised hand. "Like any," he said, "House Davion notwithstanding." *Let's play our game.*

Aaron conceded the point with a careful nod.

This was not Julian's first interview with Duke and Lord Governor Aaron Sandoval. Though one among a handful. And what had colored each meeting before was the cautious, well-hidden play of the duke—the tightrope he walked between ambition and outright treachery against The Republic. Not even Exarch Levin had been able to crack the man's shell, forcing him down on one side of the line or the other.

At that time, though, Levin had desperately needed the support of men such as Aaron Sandoval, courting him and the Swordsworn as well. There was little doubt that as Aaron leaned, so leaned most of Prefecture IV.

However, something had shifted in that relationship. The exarch seemed less and less concerned with the Swordsworn's internal politics, even as Aaron Sandoval courted Julian's favor (and through him, Prince Harrison's). He had little idea of any contact the lord governor might have made with Caleb Hasek *Sandoval* Davion, but assumed there were efforts along those lines as well.

Which was why Julian had seized the high ground right away, putting Aaron on his guard and letting him know up front that he would be as quick to lean against him as for him.

"I surrender the point," Aaron said. "The Sandoval dynasty has no claim to moral superiority." Though he said that softly, as if worried another family member might overhear. "Shall we say, then, that the Sandovals are instead in a position—as we have been for the better part of two centuries—to wield enormous influence? On either side of the border?"

Julian doubted he could have pulled such an admission, or the blunt appraisal, out of Corwin Sandoval. Or Victoria either. Duke and Duchess, the dynasty leaders who controlled the Federated Suns' Draconis March. It *was* a concession. Aaron admitting that he might—might!—require something from Julian.

"If you are asking me to believe that the Sandoval dynasty as a whole has interests within The Republic as well as the Federated Suns, I can safely say that I do. In fact, I'm fairly certain that is common knowledge within many political circles. Exarch Levin and I certainly discussed it."

"Then you can see how it behooves our mutual interest to keep Tikonov strong and secure."

Julian did not miss how the *you* could have meant Julian, Julian as representing Prince Harrison's interest, or as he might represent the exarch on Northwind and within Prefecture III. Classic fenceline politics. Give your neighbor a strong nod, but let him see you smile at the home on the other side of you and make him wonder what that meant.

"You are wondering about our response to the plans you forwarded." It was not a question. And it served the ball back into Aaron's court. *Our* might also refer to Prince Harrison, or Exarch Levin.

"Of course."

Julian nodded to young MacDougal, who had slaved his workstation to the master computer. On the forward monitor, a map of The Republic splashed itself over two-thirds of the screen space. Northwind glowed a bright, pulsating silver, along with Terra. Tikonov glowed golden and just as bright. Intentionally in competition with Terra's radiant light.

"You would like us to shift forces from Northwind, to Addicks and Mallory's World and a large force settled down on Yangtze specifically, in order to free up Swordsworn troops you can then concentrate on Tikonov." Force-maneuver arrows slid around on the map, striking like snakes among the mentioned worlds.

"Yes." Aaron made himself sound the very model of a reasonable man.

"No."

Julian did not care how he sounded.

The lord governor looked taken aback, as if a good friend had suddenly asked to borrow money. "I have to say. That is a very unreasonable position from which to begin negotiations."

He shrugged. "I am not negotiating. Mac, fill it in please." He waited as the lion's share of Prefecture IV colored over a dark, sublime gold. The shade spread out from Tikonov and Tigress and Tybalt, leaving only Achernar and Ronel untouched, and half a dozen worlds cut off by the line that stretched from Deneb Kaitos to Kawich.

Meanwhile, Liao green pushed up from Prefecture V, drawn to Yangtze like metal filings to a lodestone. And the border of Prefecture III lit up with red and silver sparks around Mallory's World, Ozawa, and Addicks.

"There is at least this one evaluation . . ." *at least* this one, hinting at more, "which considers the possibility of my Davion Guards and a few Republic troops drawing the full weight of House Liao's eventual push as well as clashing with Senate designs. Meanwhile, this leaves the Swordsworn free to consolidate their gains."

"That is a very pessimistic view," Aaron said. Though he seemed impressed with the analysis. More intrigued than insulted. "A fascinating piece of fiction. Though if the exarch is truly so paranoid after suffering under the depredations of House Kurita and the Liao, I suppose we must humor him."

"And that is *exactly* what I thought as well," Julian said, spooning some real *bonhomie* into his voice. Then darkened. "Until young MacDougal here discovered that you might have the extra resources yourself to safeguard those three worlds and free up regular Swordsworn forces."

"He found . . . I . . . The Swordsworn can . . . what?"

Aaron glanced between Julian, who dialed for a regretful expression, and the Northwind cadet, who had been schooled to show nothing but his usual grinning charm. Julian doubted it was much of a stretch for either of them.

"Mac," he prompted.

MacDougal nearly bounded out of his seat, ready for the call and with a real gung-ho attitude. "Aye," he said. His accent, nearly undetectable most of the time, took a slight Scottish tinge when excited.

"T'wasn't much, Lord Governor. I couldn't even be certain what it meant, when I dug up a report of Caselton's Legate Johnetta Popadic being dismissed from her post."

"Legate Popadic being an outspoken critic of Count Brisham Vicore and the Senate," Julian provided. Though he had little doubt from Aaron's cagey expression the lord governor knew exactly who Count Vicore was, and what the man meant to the Swordsworn.

"Do tell," Aaron said, recovered from his earlier aphasia.

The cadet had come to the front of the class, standing before the video map of The Republic to tap a finger against the screen's soft surface. A rainbow of color splashed out around Caselton, beneath MacDougal's finger, then Mirach and Schedar and even Sonnia on the Federated Suns' side of the border.

"Vicore has a wide range of influence in this corner of space," MacDougal said as if delivering a book report. Neutral. No agenda here.

Julian nodded. "And a long history of dealings with the Sandoval dynasty."

"Political cover," Aaron said, dismissing the close relationship between Brisham Vicore and the Sandovals. "The man does not want to stand noble's court should Exarch Levin prevail. Can you blame him?"

"He also has military forces under his control. Two companies. And, according to another report we dug out of the background noise, he recently hired two more companies of mercenaries off of Ruchbah." Ruchbah being the world in Prefecture IV with the strongest ties to the mercenary circuit.

Aaron's guarded look darkened. "I did not know this."

Julian paused. Then, "I believe you." He conceded that point, confident that he had taken control of their little game of *who knows what*. "But if I assume that Count Vicore *has* asked you for political cover. Or . . ." the insight came in a flash, "has been granted such assurances by Erik. Your nephew?"

"Cousin." Aaron's voice was flat and clipped.

"Then I assume these forces are also brought under your control. And if they are not being used to help secure Tikonov, Lord Governor, you see that I must wonder what they are being held in reserve to accomplish."

What indeed, if Duke Aaron was first learning about this from him. The man tapped the point of his chin with a thoughtful finger, studying the map for himself. His blue eyes were intense but gave nothing away other than his sudden interest. Certainly he was not about to let Julian move too far ahead in their contest.

"A masterful analysis, as always," Aaron finally said. Then smiled a politician's smile in MacDougal's direction. "And I see you have inherited Prince Harrison's penchant for surrounding yourself with bright and capable men. May I ask, is Caleb also privy to your counsel on this matter?"

"Not at this time. I believe Caleb is . . . No."

"Interesting." Somehow Julian felt that he'd surrendered a point, and had failed to even see it slip away. "Well, I would like a day to review this new data with my own counselors. If you would have any supporting data transferred to my staff?"

"At once," he promised.

"And can I assume from your candor as well as your demeanor, that a compromise may still be possible? If there is a way to support our efforts to secure Tikonov while not endangering the exarch's position . . ."

"*Quid pro quo*. It is the only offer you will see from me, Duke Sandoval."

The duke nodded. "And I would expect nothing less. Lord Davion."

Especially now.

"If you let my people know what you may need from us. And it is within our ability without compromising *our* position." He paused. Came to a decision. Nodded. "You'll have it."

"I'm sure the exarch appreciates your support in this matter," he said. "And so do I." Julian drew a definite line between Jonah Levin and himself this time, wanting Aaron to know that he accepted the man's pledge personally. It was the kind of politics Harrison had taught him best. Always, always collect the debts yourself!

Aaron Sandoval withdrew, pausing at the door for one brief look back. "You may do better than I thought," he said. Cryptic, but warm.

Julian let the other man slip away with having the last word. He turned to James MacDougal and gestured him back to his seat.

"Now," he said. "We just have to hold things together."

For a little while longer, at any rate.

Jarman City, New Hessen
Federated Suns

Nothing had yet gone right on New Hessen.

Caleb's DropShip had taken fire from a squadron of Republic aerospace fighters during atmospheric insertion, leading to a harrowing few moments as Captain Marti cut engines and dropped in a desperate freefall, then hit the crew and complement with three G's heavy burn to make up for it.

Sterling McKenna's covering flight ran The Republic pilots off, and a Major Thom Oakley did eventually transmit a "most sincere apology," but not before Caleb spent several excruciating moments plastered to his stateroom bunk: his heart laboring, every joint bruised from the stress, and wondering if he were about to die.

Major Oakely was on his list to find out how far a "most sincere apology" flew with the First Prince of the Federated Suns!

Then, to make matters worse, local control brought Caleb down in Weldon Port instead of Jarman City, necessitating a lift-off burn and a second landing (also without fanfare!). And another day lost.

Poor intelligence on the ground. No one certain of exactly what units from the Confederation *or* The Republic were at hand. A broken chain of command. The local lord sequestered at an undisclosed location. It took a summary order from his "lord, prince and master" to force the man back to his estates where he could receive Caleb properly.

Two cities burning thanks to collateral damage taking out a petroleum refinery in one case. A crashed *Claymore* in another.

And the local weeds had Caleb hacking hard enough to bruise his lungs.

"What do you call that . . . that filth!"

The door had hardly closed behind them: Caleb and Sterling McKenna, Brevet-Colonel Mark Hedges, Lord David Faust, all standing around the drawing room on Faust's Jarman City estate. Caleb wheezed deep as the filtered, air-conditioned room relieved him of the terrible cough and sinus squeeze that had pained him since leaving the *First Sun*. His breath came back slowly. His eyes still watered, though, as if not yet believing relief was at hand.

He caught Faust gesturing towards a seating area, where two suede couches faced each other over a low table. The steward of New Hessen was whipcord thin, with brown, almond-shaped eyes set in a round face. His black, oiled mustaches were weighted at each end by a tiny silver bead.

"Black creeper," the noble said easily. No doubt used to the question. "It is like Terran kudzu, pervasive. It constantly sloughs off its outer husk, like snakeskin, growing and spreading and rotting all at the same time. You are also here during its flowering season."

"You should slash-burn it out of existence," was Caleb's opinion.

"Oh, we've tried, Highness. Believe me, we've tried. Fortunately, it does not thrive away from New Hessen's white sun and greenhouse atmosphere. So as far as we know, it has not spread to other worlds."

If it could, Caleb had an answer for the military-industrial machine. Forget BattleMechs. Seed planets with black creeper, and the population would move out, clearing the way for an easy invasion.

Of course, that did not solve the problem of what to do once his forces seized control of the world. Ah well.

As it turned out, the suede sofas were extremely comfortable, padded with deep, overstuffed pillows. The low table between them would have been of a good height to rest his feet upon, if not for the chess set that stood ready right before him. Each side stylized after House Davion (black) and House Liao (white), with BattleMechs for rooks and pawns of saber-bearing infantry.

"Do you play as well?" Faust asked, nodding towards the board. Strangely phrased.

To which Caleb shrugged. "Who has time for games?" he asked. Lounged back, relaxed. Still catching his breath, he turned down the glass of plum wine offered by his host, but did not hesitate to ask for New Syrtis brandy, three fingers. His first sip cleared the rotten taste that lurked at the back of his throat. His second replaced the iron-wet stench with warm, smoky amber.

Then he allowed himself to enjoy it.

"You have a problem, Lord Faust."

The other three also sat, Faust and Hedges looking no more relaxed than Sterling, who sat next to Caleb on the edge of her seat as if she might spring to action at any time. Sterling had refused a drink of any kind, as had the local garrison commander. Faust enjoyed his dark, purple wine.

"I have many problems facing me and New Hessen, Prince Caleb. Which would you care to address first?"

The man's attitude might be slowly crawling up the list. But Caleb felt generous in letting it slide. Living on a weed-choked planet where a man couldn't draw a deep breath of pure air had to take a lot of the normal pleasantries out of life. He let the brandy warm his throat and gut. "Let's start with your inability to keep New Hessen free of invading militar*ies*, plural."

"Sire. It took your cousin the prince's champion, *and* a Republic knight, to kick the Liao irregulars off last time. Why it did not take, I can't say. I know the moment they left, we suffered considerable raiding by pirate forces bearing the insignia of a double-edged battleaxe. These raiders kept us off balance until the Confederation pushed forward once again, and then began to work *with* the Liao troops." He shrugged. "Then we lost Colonel Torris, and our small garrison could not summon the wherewithal to do much more than stumble about blindly."

"So you went looking to The Republic for help? Or did they come volunteering again, asking you to look the other way?" In either case, it was a grave assumption of risk to take such a step without consult.

"They did *not* ask, Prince Caleb." He took a sip of his sweet nectar. To Caleb, it smelled sickeningly cloying. "But yes, we did look the other way," he admitted. "And thankful to have them. Until the possible cure simply became a new disease."

"Where, exactly, do things stand now?" Sterling asked, a hungry look in her eye.

A good question. One Caleb would have gotten to. Still, absent Mason Lambert, who had chosen to remain at the spaceport to help organize the debarking elements of the Davion Heavy Guard and New Syrtis Fusiliers, it was good to have Sterling along.

Very good.

Brevet-Colonel Hedges rubbed his hands together, looking far too eager. Fresh-faced and clear-eyed, Caleb doubted he had seen much of the actual hard-line fighting being reported here.

"We've identified elements, some, of McCarron's Armored Cavalry, as well as a company, at least, of line troops. We think a battalion of irregulars, conscripted out of the cities and handed a rifle, basically. Nothing *too* much to worry about there."

Did the man have to qualify every statement?

"From The Republic, we're sixty percent certain there is no knight present to lead them. We believe they followed McCarron's out of Prefecture V, possibly from the fighting on Ningpo or Algol. Elements of the Fifth Hastati and Fourth Triarii Protectors."

"*If* their insignias can be believed," Caleb pointed out.

Hedges rocked back. "I hadn't thought of that."

No, of course not. Caleb traded a quick glance with Sterling, who nodded.

Whatever New Hessen had suffered in military leadership since the loss of Colonel Palos Torris, an able commander if Julian's reports were to be believed, it was about to change for the better again. He had come to a decision on *First Sun's* bridge during the aerospace battle—there could be no argument with victory.

Coming home to New Avalon as First Prince of the Federated Suns was not enough. Not with the dark cloud of his father's *accident* hanging over his ascension.

But coming home a hero as well . . . Proving himself on the battlefield . . . What more could a people ask for in a leader?

He sipped his brandy, letting the burning liquid coast past his tongue. Lost in his reverie so deeply, he missed Colonel Hedges's question.

"What was that?"

"I asked if you would like to see our latest battle-rom footage. It was captured from a Republic Joust. In it, you can clearly see elements of McCarron's Armored Cavalry, we are almost sure, and what we suppose are the Fifth Hastati Sentinels."

"*Aff*," Sterling said, though Caleb had less interest in it.

He could allow her these kinds of moments, however. A military leader of a martial people, of course she would take an opportunity to review battle footage. But as with the idea of staring at a chess board for hours on end, Caleb did not see the value in such time spent.

Not until Lord Faust used a remote to drop a hidden monitor down from the ceiling, and paged his way through several dozen files to find one dated the week before. He started it running, the scene jumping in through a snowstorm of static to track across a raging battlefield in slow pan.

The Joust's turret swung around, looking for a target.

Like any battlefield, this one was a study in chaos. Missile trails arced across a pale sky, the gray contrails spreading out into the building haze. Warheads dropped down across a riverbank and into the water, erupting in geysers of blackened earth and water and mud.

Streams of particle cannon energies skipped across a nearby lake, slashing deep scars into the side of a green-and-ochre painted *Centurion* wading ashore amid a flotilla of hovercraft: SM1 Destroyers, Regulators, and a lance of Pegasus scout vehicles.

Lasers slashed to and fro, jeweled hornets that flashed by so fast and cut so quick that a 'Mech or vehicle hardly knew it'd been stung until the molten armor began to cool against the ground.

The Joust's battle-camera washed out in a backflash of crimson laser fire, bled into grayscale for a few seconds, then colored in again as the (modified) *Centurion* limped off-camera stage right, favoring the left knee into which the Joust had cut deeply.

A *Spider* stepped in front of the Joust then, blocking the camera. The Joust rolled back twenty meters.

In time to catch the after-mod *Centurion* facing right at the camera. The square-faced *scutum* was emblazoned with the emblems of McCarron's Armored Cavalry and House Liao, as well as a swirled yin-yang symbol painted over its chest, quite obvious as the 'Mech swung its shield aside to fire a right-torso heavy laser. The deep, burnt-orange hue carved the front off a foolhardy Condor. LRMs erupted out of a chest-mounted launcher, spreading more smoke and shrapnel around the field. They drove the Spider back and sent the Joust fleeing backward as well, as the *Centurion's* battle-axe rose and fell, rose and fell, finishing the job against the Condor. Like a vengeful (Asian) god come to claim its . . .

A god!

"Back that up!" Caleb ordered, sitting forward suddenly as a bolt of lightning fired off in the back of his mind. He set his glass down hard on the center of Faust's chess set, slopping some of the smoke-filled brandy over the edge. Jabbed a finger at the screen. "That 'Mech. The *Centurion*. Bring it up again!"

It wouldn't be. It couldn't.

Faust worked the controls, slipping the video image back several frames to find the BattleMech in a full-on display. The yin-yang symbol, wreathed in an open hand. House Liao's triangular crest. The MAC's armored knight.

A mistake!

Brevet-Colonel Hedges cleared his throat. Smiled. "*That* is a 'Mech of McCarron's Armored Cavalry."

Oh, but it was also so much more. Caleb stared at the custom paint, the Asian logo that would have meant so much more on a world like Solaris VII where even the name of Cenotaph Stables was often enough to tip the bookmakers into laying off action.

"That," Caleb said, correcting the garrison commander, "is Yen-lo-wang."

She was here!

Danai Liao-Centrella.

19

With a great deal of pomp and ceremony, Senator and Viscount Conner Rhys-Monroe took leave of Markab in command of a healthy contingent of armed forces. The tearful farewell was the scene of several rousing speeches, and one violent demonstrator who threw a bottle of kerosene.
—Kent Clarke, Action News at Eleven, Markab, 6 August 3135

Ronel
Republic of the Sphere
26 August 3135

Wide, low-profile buildings stretched through the riverside industrial sector of Dargo City, making for a maze of wide, twisting streets and several alleys dead-ending into loading docks and utility service areas. They were blocked occasionally by a stalled tractor-trailer truck, or fallen roadway that had bridged one of the many dark-water sloughs and had never been meant to hold up under the weight of large

BattleMechs. Smoke piled into the sky from different areas: several gutted vehicles roiling with greasy flames; a stretch of green belt bordering the sector; a lumber warehouse, with enough treated wood set aflame to keep burning for days.

Here, a company of Dragon's Fury militia chose to make a stand rather than give up another of Ronel's larger cities.

Here, Conner Monroe intended to teach them their error in another lesson they could take to Katana Tormark and, if it became necessary, all the way back to House Kurita.

VTOLs buzzed down the low urban canyons, a pair of Cavalry attack helicopters skating by on either side of Conner's *Rifleman* as he pressed forward, leading a push for the local docks. Armored infantry scurried around his feet—Infiltrators mostly, leap-frogging forward to lay down suppressing laser fire against the enemy Hauberk—followed by their paired Hasek mechanized combat vehicles, which provided devastating fire support with their Johnston particle projector cannons. The vehicles ran their heat curves to dangerous levels, flashing arcs of manmade lightning again and again into the enemy line.

A single Defiance Industries Schmitt tank struggled at Conner's side, grinding forward on broken, left-side tracks while it added its two Mydron rotaries to the loyalists' firepower. Two JES II strategic missile carriers rolled up behind, flanked by Goblin APCs.

Despite such an impressive backing, Conner's forces should have been outmatched. Should have been. The Dragon's Fury *Vulture* and *Warhammer IIC* could easily have tipped the balance between the two sides. With six extended-range lasers between them, they dealt out serious hurt of their own, probing back with hot, crimson lances. Hauberk heavy infantry broke from a nearby parking lot into the shadow of some warehouses, joined by a squad of Elemental-style troopers. Two Shoden assault tanks and a large array of fast-attack vehicles. Demons. Shandra reconnaissance cars. VV1 Rangers. Half a dozen Pegasus hovercraft and a pack of hoverbikes.

"Pushovers!" Conner yelled, careless of the voice-activated mic built into his heavy neurohelmet. Letting his voice carry to each and every warrior under his command.

The unit's common frequency carried back a rousing cheer, broken only by a new crackle of static as the Haseks lit off another pair of hellish particle streams.

It quickly fell back to the curt, commonplace chatter of the battlefield. Still, he heard a surge of fresh confidence among the voices of his men and women. And that, he knew, was making all the difference.

The Dragon's Fury contingent was losing Dargo City because they *felt* defeated. Harried and harassed the entire day, as Conner fed mercenaries into the grinder as a way of flushing out enemy concentrations and absorbing the kind of losses a unit could rarely afford to take. Mercs, though, he could afford. What could not be repaired could be rented fresh from Ruchbah, or possibly Towne.

If men wanted to put a price on their lives, that was their business. *His* was taking Ronel as swiftly and solidly as possible.

Then let Subhar Usuha stand on the evidence and challenge him.

The local garrison held a choke point between two large facilities: a chemical plant and what looked like a fenced, secure warehousing district. The chemical plant was an exaggerated single story. Across the long, flat roof and a good half klick to the other side Conner saw his two mercenary *Pack Hunters* still chasing down the *Griffin* they'd cut from the Fury's line. Behind the enemy position, the terrain opened up to a long, paved riverbank. Docks. And water.

All of which disappeared in a sudden, billowing cloud of gray exhaust as the *Vulture* turned, hunkered down, and let fly with all four of its LRM launchers. Four-score warheads, rising on fiery trails, jumped up and over the no-man's-land to cascade down in a lethal rain of fire and smoke and scorched asphalt that flew through the air like shrapnel.

Conner welcomed the assault. Laughed at it. Throttled forward into its rough embrace, wrestling against his control sticks and working the steering pedals to sidestep and duck aside and charge on a sudden oblique. Then he turned and ran straight at them. His *Rifleman* responded to his easy touch with the fury of a machine with something to prove. Weathering the dozen missiles that actually slammed into it. Shrugging aside the loss of armor.

Spearing its arms straight forward, never giving up the offensive.

Two late warheads corkscrewed in on gray contrails, caught the side of the *Rifleman's* cockpit and erupted in two deafening explosions. They smashed Conner's ferroglass shield on the left-hand side, blowing razor-sharp shards through the cockpit. The impact shook him hard against his restraint harness.

He felt a sharp stinging in his arm, his shoulder. And a pinch, just below the lower edge of his neurohelmet.

No time to worry about it. With a half-twist against the force of the blow, Conner swung the BattleMech's upper torso around just enough to hold target lock as he ripped into the *Vulture* with both rotary autocannons in long, devastating blasts. Long tongues of flame licked out from the rapid-spinning barrels, spitting out overlapping cascades of fifty-millimeter slugs tipped in depleted uranium for real 'Mech-stopping power. One cannon walked a series of pits and deep gouges up the *Vulture's* left flank. The other crossed from shoulder to shoulder, tearing away armor, smashing it beneath the shower of hot metal and raining shards and splinters down into the street.

Several webbed cracks starred the *Vulture's* ferroglass shield, and Conner knew he'd given the other MechWarrior something to think about as well.

"Sierra-one! Sierra-one is crippled." Their worry overrode the background calls for med-pickups, for flanking support. "We're stuck!"

The Schmitt had not weathered the storm of warheads as well as the others, its left-side tracks finally blowing out completely. Now it was not much more than a stationary pill box, but one with quite a bit of firepower still at its disposal.

Conner traded a light pull from both RACs against the sudden charge of one Shoden. The tank took superficial wounds as ATMs hammered up the sides of both legs and carved away at the assault vehicle's armor. He retreated a single step, planting one leg firmly behind him, and did a quick check of his own wounds.

A large shard of ferroglass stuck into his left bicep, oozing blood but not too badly. Not yet. He brushed a careful hand across his shoulder and lower neck where the neurohelmet did not quite reach. Scraped away more splinters. His fingers came away smeared with blood, which he wiped across the front of his cooling vest.

Nothing he couldn't live with.

"Sierra-one, suppress those infantry positions near the warehouse. On my mark: Cavalry attack 'copters, clear, Jess-one and two give me full spreads on fast cycle and keep them coming. All other ground forces forward!"

Another hard shake as the *Warhammer IIC* moved forward to cover his comrade. The enemy 'Mech slashed down Conner's left side with all four lasers, putting two into his forward leg and carving out the upper leg actuator. Conner spent several hundred rounds in the *Warhammer's* direction, just to keep its attention. He toggled for one of his officers, cutting away from the busy chatter on the all-hands circuit.

"Lieutenant Minor? Minor? Blake!"

"Yezzir." A gunshot voice. Loud and violent. Blake Minor was senior mercenary officer between the two *Pack Hunters*. "Bit. Busy. Now."

"Break off, break off. Over the top and on my position. Go!"

A quick toggle, and he was back to the loyalists' common frequency. Waited. Waited. "Now! Now now NOW!"

The timing could not have come off better. Just as the *Vulture* threw up a new umbrella of eighty warheads, Conner shoved off his planted leg and into a run, pushing for the *Rifleman's* best speed of sixty-five kilometers per hour. Not quite reaching it as his left leg threatened to buckle with each hard plant. Mid-fifties was the best he could do. But it was enough.

With the Goblin APCs bursting forward, taking the point, and infantry scattering out of the way of the Hasek MCVs, most of his force pushed out from beneath the *Vulture's* chosen kill zone. Closing hard. Only the Schmitt and both JES carriers were left behind to weather the new storm. And they gave back twice as good as they got, throwing eight-score warheads back at the Dragon's Fury line.

Wave after wave of LRMs pasted the choke point between the two buildings. A few strayed, cratering large holes in the side of the warehouse, crumbling one wall of the chemical plant. Most fell in a wide line of death across the Dragon's Fury line. Blackened earth and fresh gravel geysered up on columns of fire and smoke, raining down over the battlefield. Dozens of warheads caved in one side of a Shoden, sent two of its large wheels tumbling off in different directions. Dozens more crashed down the *Vulture's* right side and knocked it backward to sprawl across the scarred roadway.

Four hundred meters. Three hundred.

A second barrage of warheads fell across the enemy line in a savage curtain, not quite as effective as the first as the Dragon's Fury spread out in a loose field. Some retreated back towards the docks. Others scrambled forward to avoid the rain of destruction.

A hoverbike swung out too far and powered right into a Hasek's PPC blast. It erupted in a ball of fire, tumbled end over end into a small cluster of Hauberk infantry.

Two Pegasus collided with each other and stalled out. One of Conner's Goblins shifted its track to slide up close. Drop-down ramps flew out, disgorging a squad of lightly armored combat engineers. They swarmed over the stalled craft, slapping shaped charges onto vulnerable points to disable the vehicles if they could not be captured.

"Warriors should realize when they've lost," Conner whispered. He kept the comment to himself as he stepped through a thick wreath of sooty, gray smoke and continued hammering away at the downed *Vulture*.

Two hundred meters!

The gunpowder stench of cordite and scorched earth was strong. It billowed in through the burst left-side shield in sooty clouds.

His rotary autocannon spinning out rounds, hundreds at a time, Conner drained his ammunition bins down towards empty as he pummeled the still-struggling *Vulture*. The bulk of the Dragon's Fury militia fell back, opening out towards the docks where the *Warhammer IIC* held a new defensive line.

Then Conner's two Cavalry attack helicopters swarmed in, autocannon blazing as they strafed the enemy units from behind. The 'copters overturned a VV1 Ranger, then chased down a Demon.

And with lightning in their grip came the two *Pack Hunters* as well. They'd left the slower *Griffin* behind, running up the far side of the chemical plant and then burning off jump jets to sail high overhead in a long, reaching arc.

Blake Minor's *Hunter* cleared the building, landing in a three-point crouch just off the plant's corner. His extended-range micro lasers worried an infantry emplacement, drove them back from even thinking about a mad, suicidal rush. His PPC slashed at the besieged *Warhammer*.

His merc companion did not fare as well, coming down too hard and not quite clear of the low-profile chemical plant. The second *Pack Hunter* crashed through the ceiling, trapping itself a little more than waist-high inside the building. It waded out slowly, kicking its way through several square meters of factory. Still, the particle cannon in its right torso lashed out in a coruscating whip, adding to the *Vulture's* misery even as the sixty-ton 'Mech finally climbed back to its feet.

Just in time for Conner to seal its fate.

Running up near point-blank range, he pulled into extra-long cycles on his two rotaries, spinning them to their maximum delivery. One of the autocannons froze up, pushed too hard too fast. But his second punched out with fire and hot metal, digging furious talons into the *Vulture's* right side.

The rounds clawed deep, deep through torn armor, into one of the ammunition bins that supplied the shoulder-mounted LRM launchers.

Any 'MechWarrior's nightmare. The fifty-mill slugs shredding the bin, cracking open fuel cells and slamming at the warhead tips. One spark struck against spilled propellant. A temperamental warhead. One explosion, to spark off a chain reaction of sympathetic detonations that cascaded through the ammunition bin like wildfire through dry grass.

A raging inferno of expanding fire that had nowhere to go. Bulging out one entire side of the stumbling BattleMech, until flames and thick smoke burst through seams, through rents, through rivet holes popped free by the pressure. The *Vulture's* cockpit canopy blew away on explosive charges, flipping forward end over end to clear the overhead. Its MechWarrior shot up into the air on his command seat's ejection rocket, pushing for as much sky as possible before his parafoil unfolded and gave him a chance to glide to safety.

Not a heartbeat too soon, as the explosion ate away the *Vulture* from the inside out, crashing through the internal shields protecting the fusion drive, tearing it apart like a child's toy. Orange, licking flames bled into the hard, golden light of a cascading fusion overload. The atomic fire burst free, gobbling up material for fuel. And the *Vulture* ceased to exist.

It erupted in one final, destructive blow that shook the ground and hurled flaming scraps for hundreds of meters in all directions.

So close, Conner felt the wash of intense heat slam through his shattered cockpit shield. He breathed deep and choked on the acrid stench of burning metal. A gritty cloud of hot ash and soot wreathed his 'Mech, pouring into his cockpit, jabbing needles into his eyes. As he powered forward, limped through the burning piles that had once been one of the most powerful war machines ever developed, he could only hold his breath and squint through tears of pain.

Walking out of the death grounds on the far side, expecting to see a ready line of Dragon's Fury warriors wanting vengeance for their lost avatar, Conner blinked his eyes clear in search of a target.

He had none. The *Warhammer IIC* had turned and raced for the water's edge. Stepping off the high bank to plunge down into the river's deep grasp, it waded out towards the main channel where it was soon lost beneath the gentle surface. Speeding across the water to either side, throwing off wide roostertails, were the Pegasii, the hoverbikes, making their getaway in the most direct route possible.

The light vehicles had less of a chance. The slow Shoden assault vehicle, no chance. It didn't even try, but instead powered down its targeting system in a sign of surrender. A ring of Infiltrators and both Hasek MCVs quickly surrounded it.

The other Dragon's Fury vehicles broke apart in a chaos of tangled paths, racing north and south along the water's edge in hopes of escaping the pursuing loyalists. Looking for one of the few bridges they might use to cross the wide river or, if nothing else, to lose themselves in the hills and forests far outside of Dargo City.

Several linked up with the *Griffin* on the northern run, forming an ad hoc lance that could give Minor's *Pack Hunters* some trouble. Conner called off Blake. Ordered him to monitor the enemy's progress, but if the *Griffin* kept to the river and exited the city, to let him go.

"That's good salvage we're letting walk away," the mercenary officer said.

Conner rested back in his command chair, breathing easier now that his life support system had cleared at least part of the acrid smoke from his cockpit. "Balance it against the damage your man did to the chem plant, which I'll cover, and we'll call it square."

An easy choice to make, given that all salvage was divided on a pro-rated basis for the entire field, and the loyalists' share would far outweigh anything the mercs might hope to claim.

"Besides," Conner said, softer but still strong. "We'll get another chance at it."

He'd call it a near-certainty, in fact. In battle after battle, the Dragon's Fury had proven a tenacious opponent. Never surrendering an easy victory. Always ready to push back should Conner or one of his senior officers take their eye from the goal for even a second. With no hope of relief or rescue—not with Katana Tormark busying herself with House Kurita—and certainly no hope of an overall victory, they fought for pride. They fought for *honor*. And glory. And just out of basic contrariness, he suspected.

And because they knew the stakes on Ronel. A world of secondary importance before the Blackout, it now possessed one of the most precious resources a widespread organization required.

A working HPG.

What the Senate Alliance needed. The reason Conner had come.

The prize, for which he was redrawing borders. As he had mistakenly tried to do on Terra, where the fences were planted deep. But outside of Prefecture X, especially, where the nobles had considerably more sway among the many worlds, he felt they reached for a much greater opportunity.

"We'll get another chance," he repeated.

They would!

20

> As remnants of the Highlanders continue to trickle in to Northwind, and in the continued absence of Countess Tara Campbell, Major Lewandowski from the Academy Commandant's office was quick to assure people today that the departure of Paladin Zou and the Davion Guards was not a significant loss to Northwind's defense.
>
> "With further elements of the local Hastati and Principes arriving within the week, Northwind will be well-garrisoned."
>
> —From the Office of the Commandant,
> for General Release, 23 August 3135

DropShip *Markeson Pride*
Zenith Station, Northwind
Republic of the Sphere
29 August 3135

A *Fortress*-class vessel, the *Markeson Pride* belonged to the First Davion Guards. And Julian.

Never as luxuriously appointed as Harrison Davion's *First Sun*, still there was a touch of extra effort to the gleam of brass fittings, the smooth operation of all doors, hatches, and machinery. Every stairwell, every maintenance ladder; when one stepped out onto a new deck there would always be a red sun painted on the nearby wall, reaching out with its flaming corona, with a simple numeral stenciled inside giving an exact position by deck and bulkhead number. Crew members hurried through the corridors with an extra bounce to their steps. Even the most junior astech pressed a military crease into his oil-stained coveralls.

Julian could hardly remember a time when it was any different.

So when Callandre asked, he actually had to think for a moment.

Paused at the hatch they had been about to drop through, he anchored himself to one of the convenient grips to keep from bouncing in the light gravity environment. He wore a dark green singlesuit with gold piping down the outside of his legs and arms, and a tight-fitting beret to keep his hair from becoming a hassle. He rubbed a hand against the side of his face, felt the light scratch of his midday shadow.

"In my first six months assigned to the First Guards," he finally said. "No one wanted a piece of me. I was Harrison's nephew, handed my commission and my command on a platinum serving plate. And the First Davion Guards were known mainly for the warriors who promoted up to the Davion Heavies, or the Assault Guards."

"The First was known for much more than that," Callandre said.

"Historically, yes. But they were virtually destroyed in the Steiner-Davion civil war. Then with the Jihad, and the later disarming, what was left of them, what got rebuilt, never regained that legendary status."

"So they had history, but lacked any current chops."

"Exactly." Julian nodded. "Morale wasn't bad. It was just . . . just. Down ladder!"

He shouted through the hatch, a spacer's courtesy, then stepped over the opening and dropped through.

Not that it took much to control his fall. At point-two gravities, a hand on the ladder's outside railing was enough. He bent his knees ever so slightly, and when his feet hit the lower diamond deck plating flexed deep to easily absorb the shock of landing. Grabbed hard onto a lower ladder rung to dampen the bounce-back. And stepped away in a half-walk, half-glide as Callandre followed right after him.

She actually fell head first, opening up into a brief, almost-comical swan dive. Then she shoved away from the ladder in a reverse tuck with her head swinging up and away. She landed in a stiff-legged bounce, reached out and accepted Julian's clasp, never doubting for a second that he would be there for her.

"Show off."

Unlike many "ground-pounders," Callandre had always loved space flight. Loved the travel between stars, and the privilege of setting foot on new worlds. It didn't hurt her that she had spent a few years in gymnastics training, or that she had voluntarily taken a course in zero-G combat.

"So?" she asked as Julian used the quick-release lever to access a nearby hatch door. A thick door, well fortified and insulated.

"Well, there were rumors following me out of academy—"

"I'll bet."

"—so it was apparently decided before my arrival to treat me with all due courtesy, but expect nothing much to change. Certainly no one was going out of their way to guard my back. I was a curiosity on a good day. In a combat environment, I was an unknown, and therefore a danger."

"And? How did you solve that?"

"With something my father taught me," he said, and cracked the hatch. He used leverage from a handhold to shove it open. He and Callandre slipped through and onto the observation deck that Lars Magnusson and Yori had already found.

Similar to Harrison's flag bridge on the *First Sun*, the observation deck wrapped around a good part of the outside hull and had a thick ferroglass wall for a direct view onto the hard vacuum outside. Cold, with shipboard heat radiating out through the glass, the room was kept warm enough only to prevent frosting on the inside surface. To keep a clear view.

Not that there was much to look at just now. With no atmosphere to soften their edges, here the stars were bright and violent and stared unblinking out of the black depths of space. And very, very alone. The ship had a slight roll to it, so eventually they would swing around to see the local recharge station with its solar-collecting panels and microwave dish for transferring energy to orbiting JumpShips. Like the *Northern Wind*, which would soon take them (and five other waiting or converging DropShips) on the first leg of their journey, a drop-off and layover at Addicks' nadir station.

Until then, they waited to dock. Patrolling the area at not much more than "station-keeping" thrust. Swimming in a low-gravity environment.

Like Julian and Callandre, Yori and Lars had also opted for single-piece jumpsuits—convenient when dealing with uncertain gravity conditions. Lars' was a solid, silvery-white, his name stenciled on the upper right breast and a Dominion crest patched onto each shoulder. His unruly hair waved in the low gravity, but apparently was not much of a distraction.

Yori, on the other hand, wore a hairnet to keep her dark fall of thick hair under control instead of slicking it back with holding gel as Callandre had done. Her jumpsuit was dark red, trimmed in black and with only the Kurita dragon on her breast. She bowed. Carefully.

"*Dozo gomenasai.* I thank you, Julian, for making the *Markeson Pride* available to us en route to zenith station. Do we know when the *Northern Wind* will be ready?"

"Six hours. Lady Zou shuttled over to shake things up." He saw Yori puzzling out the idiom. "She'll get them back on schedule," he promised.

"Ah. *So ka*? Then we shall enjoy your hospitality a little longer."

And then some. It would be a fast jump to Addicks, where two DropShips would be detached, strengthening the local Swordsworn garrison. Then a transfer to a new JumpShip, already charged and holding on station (supposedly) and a new jump just as fast as the *Markeson Pride* and escorts could detach from one docking collar and latch onto the second. But insertion on the other side was likely to take days—a week even—before making a new planetfall.

And then?

Who could say? The reports coming in were sketchy at

best. Even so, "The exarch, and I, continue to appreciate your assistance, Yori. And the forbearance of House Kurita to spare you. For however much longer that is possible?"

Wondering, waiting, but still without an answer as Yori shook her head. As she always did.

"It shall be for as long as it is. And no longer." She turned back to the window. Hooked her toes beneath a low railing which ran along the wall. Relaxed in a low-gravity posture.

Lars Magnusson studied her behind her back. He looked to Julian and shrugged. *He* was far more forthcoming as to his reasons for staying around so long. The Dominion was worried about the health and stability of The Republic. Lars hoped to learn differently, and take such knowledge home.

"Jules?" Callandre asked. Unlike the others, she rested in a comfortable stance away from any handgrip or toe rail. Quite comfortable at a fraction of her usual weight. "Your father?" she prompted.

He smiled. Nodded. Tore himself away from the puzzle that was Yori Kurita and returned to the simple enigma of Calamity Kell, whose primary guide in life seemed to be the mantra, *Do what you feel like doing.*

No. That was unfair to his friend. And for everything they had come through together, he knew better than that. Callandre had a deep sense of commitment, and the passion to make a difference, and damn the rules if necessary. Perhaps better would be, *Do what you feel needs doing.*

And don't forget to have a little fun along the way.

"My father," Julian said. He could hear *his* words in his head, as if they had been spoken yesterday. "The basis for *any* strong relationship is . . . ?"

"Respect," Lars said. Jumping in first, and with both feet. As if daring anyone to argue the point.

To which Callandre raised an eyebrow and asked, "But will you still *batchall* with me in the morning?" Lars' eyes grew wide, his own brows crawling for his hairline as he worked through the double-entendre.

She laughed. "I'd say it should be trust. Like knowing there must be a good reason a friend would go seven years without contact."

"Get over it," Julian groused.

"Mutual honor."

This from Yori Kurita, who stared through her pale reflection in the deep ferroglass and studied the harsh starlight outside. As usual, she held herself distant from the others, yet at the same time remained a part of them.

"Only when you are willing to put your personal honor in the hands of another can there be any level or trust *or* respect."

A sentiment not too far off from what Julian had been about to say. He nodded, considering. Then Callandre nudged him. Hard. "Unrequited commitment," he finally said, rubbing his shoulder where she had poked him. Shrugged. "At the core of any strong relationship is at least one moment of pure selflessness."

The others stared at him, curious. Julian found himself suddenly missing Sandra Fenlon, who had stayed behind on Northwind out of necessity. She had met Julian's father. Once. Would appreciate such a simple idea.

"I'm going to give you that," Callandre finally said. "But how did that help with the First Davion Guards? Or, at least, with the *Pride*?"

Now he laughed. Remembering. Feeling so foolish as he ignored the whispers and jokes behind his back. "I unpacked a set of dungarees. Working coveralls," he said for Yori's benefit. "Cleaned. Pressed. About as shipshape as you could want. And my first day I spent in the base 'Mech bay giving my own machine a thorough diagnostic and coolant flush."

A puzzled expression.

"The next day," he said, "I did the same for the scruffiest looking machine in the bay. And touched up its parade colors. I spent two days after that working in the motor pool, helping to rebuild an engine. Then basic maintenance on some infantry battlesuits."

"You are kidding me." Callandre shook her head. "Right?"

"It's not hard. If you're willing to take some direction from the techs."

"Lower caste labor?" Lars asked. The Dominion still strictly regulated a caste system between warriors and the military support branches. To him, it was an alien concept to worry about more than your own equipment.

"Every day. And every night I washed and pressed my coveralls, and shined my boots, for the next day. They would be stained, but never slovenly."

"And that did it?"

"Nope. A few warriors thanked me for cleaning up their machines. I think a tech or two had me on their 'favorite officer' list. But nothing I'd done was really . . . impressive enough to sway them. Finally, it did come back to the *Markeson Pride*. Sitting out on the landing pad and really not cared for too much, because the First Guards so rarely left Markeson. Fusion-scorched base. Faded battleship gray. Completely ignored."

The observation deck was dead silent. Julian held his audience in a firm grip now. Even Yori Kurita looked interested, turning away from the window to study Julian with dark, impassive eyes.

"*Iie*," she said. But it was half of a laugh. "You did not."

"I did. I got out a simple chipping gun and a compressor, a cherrypicker truck, and started the next day. It was a Saturday. Nice warm sun. A great day to begin prepping and painting a DropShip, I thought. I managed about one hundred square meters by the end of the day. About one fifty on Sunday, and that included church services, which I attended in full dress uniform with the insignia of the First Guards newly sewn to my jacket.

"On Monday, I had thirteen volunteers out there helping me. Everyone one of them in fully pressed dungarees. Not a shabby laborer in the lot."

Callandre shook her head. "*That's* where it started?"

"By week's end, the entire First Guards were out there. From the most senior MechWarrior to the most junior logistics clerk. We scraped and repainted the entire *Pride* by hand. No dock. No automated machinery. Lots of sweat equity."

"And when you were finished?" Callandre asked.

But Julian had a hunch that Yori Kurita knew the answer. He looked the question to her, and she smiled. Thinly. And gave him another bow. A deeper one, as she might have reserved for another samurai. She gestured around at the spotless room, the perfectly cleaned ferroglass wall.

"That," she said, "was when they started on the inside."

Lars and Callandre laughed, Lars so hard that he lost his grip on the toe rail and nearly fell over in his scramble not to fall off-balance in the low gravity. But Julian and Yori did not. He could not tell what Yori considered behind that mask she wore so often in public, but Julian felt a thrill of fresh expectation. Because she was exactly right. That was when they had moved to the inside and kept on working. As a team.

And *that*, he suddenly knew, was how he would need to work this motley array of forces into a coherent whole. Not as supernumeraries grafted onto his First Guards, but as full and equal members of a new ad hoc unit. He would dedicate himself to that cause. Never expecting anything.

Unrequited commitment. If anything, that was the key. But he had better turn it fast. There wasn't a whole lot of time left, and a great challenge rising ahead of them all.

On Ronel.

New Hessen
Federated Suns

"Back, back, back!" Mason Lambert yelled in Caleb's ear as the M1 Marksman trembled under hard-hitting autocannon fire. Desperate peals rang through the cramped interior, like a hundred ball peen hammers ringing against the upper turret assembly in a rapid tattoo.

"Po!" Mason said. Sitting in the tank's only passenger "jump seat", he had his helmet's facemask pressed hard into the padded finder on a telescoping viewer. "It's a Po. In our five."

"I saw it," Caleb yelled, his voice filling the Marksman without one trace of hysteria in it. You could not command in an armored corps and not learn to trust your machine. Its armor. Its ability to dig itself out of a scrape.

He swallowed dryly, using his control system to seize control from his main gunner of the right-side missile launchers. Ignoring a VV1 Ranger that jumped out of a nearby vale, sliding through the grassy field, he swiveled the weapons out from the turret on universal mounts to drop a flashing red crosshair against the broadside of a Po II heavy tank. The targeting reticle flashed amber and red, a partial lock. Best he was going to get on an override. He thumbed his secondary firing stud.

Overhead, the muted roar of warhead exhausts called out like a wounded beast. The Shigunga medium-range launcher screamed out ten fat-bodied warheads, the missiles slashing across his monitor in a blurred image of fire and soot.

They blossomed in bright flowers of destruction as they walked from fore to aft on the sixty-ton tank, cratering armor on the tread overhang.

"Got range and bearing," Caleb called.

In case his gunner hadn't noticed the override, and was deafened by the autocannon slugs pounding across the turret base, his voice-activated mic also kept him in constant contact with the driver and main gunner.

"Fergie. Chop back on the throttle and give us a right-hand turn. Maverick, bearing relative one, seven, two; range one hundred ten. Get there!"

Sergeant First Class Donald Ferguson rogered the order. "Let me get us around that burning Jessie . . . there!" Deep within the tank's guts a grinding sound tore through the machinery as he hauled the ninety-five ton vehicle into a tight turn.

Corporal Matt "Maverick" Rolph was already busy twisting the turret further around, bringing the Lord's Thunder Gauss rifle to bear against the Po. Each second counted off as the turret gearing *chocked* its way through the long turn.

The tank commander could do little else but wait.

Wait for the launcher to cycle a new set of warheads into their tubes, and then fire off a second flight to keep the Po busy. A second set of fiery blossoms.

Wait for reports to come in from his scouting flankers, who were circling around through the tall pines to find out how large a Capellan unit they had discovered within the Nashton Hills—a back door on Jarman City, according to the report Caleb had read from Brevet-Colonel Hedges.

Wait to see if the M1's legendary armor would fail now, of all times, filling the crew compartment full of hot shrapnel.

He didn't want to believe that. God would never be so cruel to a prince of the Federated Suns. The angels marched at Caleb's side!

And soon, he would notch another important victory on

his belt. His third in the last seven days, since taking command of New Hessen's armored corps. Since stepping *Brevet*-Colonel Hedges into a supporting role before the young officer (maybe, possibly, likely) ran this campaign into the dirt and buried it alive.

On his screen, a second set of targeting crosshairs edged into view, tracking quickly now as the main turret swung around to match the bearings on the left-side MRM ten-pack. He saw a three-tank set of Demons chase after one of the Capellan Shandras. A distant Regulator pounding Gauss slug after Gauss slug into one of his disabled Fulcrums, hammering it down into scrap.

Then the Po, with its low, classic profile. Box-shaped back end and the "trash-lid" turret centering its autocannon with a ten-centimeter bore directly at them. He was tempted right then to wrest full control away, take the killing shot himself. And might have, if Rolph hadn't been on the edge of his trigger.

The crosshairs did not quite match, but close enough, when the rail gun sliced out a large, ferrous slug at hypersonic speed. A silvery blur. The Po rocked laterally, jumped one side off the ground. Left a long, terrible gash in the rising deck on which the main turret sat.

Mason crowed and glad-handed Caleb on the back of the helmet, knocking the prince's head forward. The one man in all of the Inner Sphere who could have gotten away with such an act. He grinned with feral humor.

"Again," he yelled. Released control of the missile launcher. Allowed Rolph to add it back to the full spread. "Maverick. Hit it again!"

Rolph did, spreading two flights of medium-range warheads across the Po's side even as the other tank drove hard forward in a desperate bid to get out from under the Marksman's heavy weapons. The autocannon barrage trailed off, striking only an infrequent rhythm now.

The Gauss slug punched *through* the deck riser this time in a devastating riposte. The concussive force alone was enough to rattle skulls and certainly burst the eardrums of the crew inside. Then the shrapnel and shards ricocheting through the cabin . . .

The Po sat, silent. No targeting system tracking on the Marksman. No active emissions of any kind.

No more autocannon slugs hammering in at the—
WHUMMP!!

It seemed to Caleb as if God himself had reached down to pick up the Marksman, raised it above the battlefield several meters and then let it drop back down heavy on its left side. It rocked back over to slam down hard on both tracks. His head whiplashed, helmet smashing against the back of his padded seat hard enough to draw a gray veil over his vision for a moment. Then the hard bounce. His jaw came together hard, teeth clacking in a rifle shot loud enough to echo in his ears.

Mason hung halfway out of his chair. One strap on his safety harness had broken away from the left shoulder, and his faceplate had cracked against a nearby console. "That wasn't a Po," he offered, humor dry despite the blood flecks staining his lips.

"I know, I know," Caleb yelled back.

"Sire?"

Ferguson. From the driver's controls far forward in the tank's long body.

"I know it isn't a Po," he snapped.

"Yes, sir . . . Sire!" The sergeant sounded confused.

Rolph didn't. "Not a Po," he agreed, trumping the distant calls of alarm. Caleb's scouting forces. His few infantry skirmishers were trying to regroup at the rear of their column. " 'Mech! Breaking through the trees right on our six!"

Before he could say another word, or Caleb give the order, Ferguson cut the M1 hard left to spin fresh armor towards whatever Capellan machine had managed to get behind them.

"Got a . . . targeting info calls it . . . *Hatchet* . . . no . . . *Centurion* . . . what-the-hell?"

With Ferguson spinning the tank in a full turn and the turret already cranked over, the new machine slid under Caleb's sights quickly. A cold, hollow dread eating away at his guts turned to black ice as Rolph's hesitation and the targeting computer's confusion realized Caleb's fear.

Not God's hand. Not *the* God. Just *a* god.

An Asian deity. King of the nine hells, if he recalled correctly. Painted dark green and ocher, with a square-faced scutum and axe held in a high, overhead grip.

Yen-lo-wang.

"Danai."

Danai Liao-Centrella. Doing her Capellan best to kill him. Her missiles spread out a fresh volley, slinging the warheads in low and thick to slam in near the treads. Just short, in fact, into the same crater she had carved a moment earlier when the missile detonations had scooped up the ninety-five ton machine and dropped it several meters back.

The heavy laser riding over her right shoulder and side speared out in dark, deadly orange. Slashed across the M1's profile, slagging away armor with the faint shriek of tortured metal and boiling gasses. Alarms rang out, warning of an armor breach. One of the tank's sensors detected a drop in the cabin's positive atmospheric pressure.

Two toggles and Caleb could have taken control. Full weapons. The 'Mech right underneath the M1's primary reticle. Rolph had frozen, seeing the large machine bearing down on them. Caleb knew he had the time. Had the angle. Knew he could dish it right back at her.

Did she realize it was him? Even know he was on planet?

"Wouldn't matter if she did!" Mason yelled. "Caleb! Dammit."

"It might matter. It could!"

"Sire, is everything . . ."

Before Ferguson could question him, the shouting if nothing else had shocked Rolph back to action. Missiles spread out from the launchers, clipping Yen-lo-wang across the large shield, pushing past to slam a few warheads centerline. Smoke roiled out of the fissure. Too many craters in that armor to have been freshly paneled. And the 'Mech limped when nothing they had done had so much as touched a leg.

Caleb reached for the toggles. (To direct aim at the vulnerable points, or stop Rolph from heaping on more abuse?) Even he wasn't sure why, and even as he did so it was too late. A new slash of silver blurred on his screen.

The Gauss slug slammed into Danai's modified *Centurion*, at the junction where shoulder met main body. Too close to the cockpit. Too close to *her*.

His hand slashed across the communications panel without hesitation or thought, cutting over to a general frequency often used to negotiate terms of a cease-fire.

Surrenders. Challenges and taunts. He rode out a heavy pummeling as the *Centurion's* heavy laser carved more armor from the M1's profile. More warheads danced across their deck.

Caleb called out the only name on his mind. "Danai!"

Hobbling forward at a steady pace, Yen-lo-wang nearly upon them, arm up and axe held high, ready for a death-blow, something stilled the MechWarrior's hand. His voice? The familiar call of her own name?

A hesitation. Just enough for Rolph to cycle his weapons. Punching out with the M1's Gauss rifle. Shooting a silver mass into the upraised arm right at the elbow. Wrenching the entire arm back, too far, mangling the joint.

"Maverick, leave off! Leave off! Mason, go take the turret."

"Sire?"

Mason shook his head. "I'm with Rolph. Drop her, Caleb. Drop her *now*."

"No!"

He cut out Rolph's turret controls, taking remote control from his commander's chair. The corporal, shocked, beat on his now-useless equipment, screaming his prince's name again and again as the fifty-ton BattleMech loomed over them. The screen Caleb relied on for targeting dimmed as Yen-lo-wang's shadow fell over the outside camera eye.

Three stories tall. Broad-shouldered.

Wreathed from behind in a kind of holy fire . . .

Which blossomed full and angry as the *Centurion* stumbled forward. A few stray warheads slipped around from the far side, dropping down onto the Marksman's long deck, their explosions resounding through the cabin like the ringing of a giant gong.

"What the—incoming!" Rolph yelled.

Caleb saw it too. A dark haze against a bright blue sky. Missile contrails, feeding out from half a dozen or so warheads. Then another set. And another.

Cascading down. Crushing through the plate armor on Yen-lo-wang. Cratering deeper into the M1's ferro-fibrous composite. The tank shook with a fresh palsy. Rolph yelled, his voice rising high and shrill into a painful howl as the telltale *pinnggg-ping!* of shrapnel bounced around somewhere within the crew cabin.

And from behind Danai's *Centurion*, a new BattleMech lumbered up into view. Long-legged and gangly, with five lasers built into upswept shoulders and a blunt 'Mech-sized taser built into the right hand, the *Morrigan* knifed jeweled daggers into the back of Yen-lo-wang. A Republic machine. Bearing the crest of the Fifth Hastati Sentinels.

It was the choice of a moment for Caleb to twist his controls, slipping the turret to one side of the wounded *Centurion*. Centering golden crosshairs right into the *Morrigan's* chest and hauling back on the triggers to put one of his few remaining Gauss slugs on dead centerline.

Only now did the BattleMech seem to know he was there. It staggered back a pace, then put a firm leg behind it and pushed forward once more with weapons training down onto Caleb's M1. Lasers pulsed out with scarlet daggers as overhead a swarm of missiles dropped in overlapping waves.

Pounding and pummeling. With Thor's own hammer.

The missiles cracked the M1's deck, pouring fire and smoke and the scent of scorched earth into the cabin.

The impacts rocked the huge machine back and forth. Back and forth. Then it tipped high up onto one side as a full score of warheads blew off the left-side track. The tank hung there, suspended for one frantic heartbeat, as the last wave of missiles hit.

Then God's hand did reach down and scoop up the Marksman. Spun it around in a sickening turn, and dropped it again with a mighty fist beating down hard.

Shaken like a rag doll, neck lit up in terrible pain, Caleb flopped forward as his harness buckle snapped and he slid down onto the cabin's warped decking. He landed in a tangle of limbs and straps and (ironically) an evacuation pack. The gray curtain pulled across his vision once again. Growing darker. Leaving him with one last glimpse of the jump seat. Mason's seat. With four perfect straps still tightened down over an empty chair.

Leaving him alone.

Not even with the whispers of angels to comfort him.

21

Ningpo has fallen! Barely three weeks into the new campaign, the Capellan Confederation has seized another world. The decisive victory is credited to heavy civilian interference with local defenses. A few critics have also decried the light garrison force defending the world, claiming the exarch is not doing enough.
—General Release, //news//battlecorps.org//, 21 August 3135

Genève, Terra
Republic of the Sphere
31 August 3135

In his eight months as Exarch of the Sphere, Jonah Levin had seen his paladins disappointed, angry, elated and sorrowful.

He remembered them vengeful, as they had been after the betrayal of the Senate. Wroth, to lose one of their own. And then hopeful again with the birth of a new paladin in Ariana Zou.

He had known suspicions of them, even on the day of

his election as an unknown paladin left dark stains on the conclave. And days of reward when good men and women had stood up, despite any personal agendas, to trust his leadership and help him steer The Republic for what little remained in the way of safe waters.

But in his two hundred fifty plus days since taking office, Exarch Levin had never felt so close to losing the elite conclave, The Republic entire, to an outright mutiny.

The Chamber of Paladins was in full uproar, sure enough—with knights leaping to their feet in the Gallery, some arguing and shoving back their neighbors in brief and bitter feuds. A few dozen kept their heads, and some even kept their seats, though most still had action steeped in their blood and moved quickly to try to calm their brethren. Stepping in between the more aggressive gatherings, calling out for calm, for peace.

But not even the paladins were listening much to such a caution. Fifteen of the elite, nearly the full assembly, each manned his own station on the chamber's main floor, reacting as befit his or her own temperament.

Anders Kessel was expounding loudly, of course, and on the verge of insubordination as he cried out for "the loss of Stone's dream."

Gareth Sinclair, young and hot-blooded, jumped quickly (too quickly?) to Jonah's defense, eschewing the paladins' private messaging system to argue the merits in a boisterous rebuttal to Kessel's grandstanding. David McKinnon sided with Gareth, though more to oppose Kessel, Jonah guessed, than from any devoted consideration of the merits of the exarch's plan.

Heather GioAvanti stood in stunned silence, staring questions at the exarch before bending her attention to her private messaging board. Already rallying support among her peers in a quick show of leadership. But support for him, or against?

Thaddeus Marik knelt before his station in prayer. Tyrina Drummond and Janella Lakewood had moved to the Gallery gate, drafting half a dozen of the knights in attendance to hold the rest back from the floor. Keeping the disturbance contained if not calm.

And Maya Avellar wept openly, unashamed.

Having begun the chaos, Jonah waited out the worst of

it. From the exarch's dock, where he presided above and before every assembled man and woman, he had control of the entire room as needed. Locking it down. Summoning support. He considered using the built-in public address system to rise above the din, but adding to the escalating chaos and his followers' distress did not seem a well-reasoned course of action.

Meanwhile a hundred angry voices echoed back down from the chamber's gilded dome, adding to the cacophony, while on the other side of the giant ferrosteel wall Genève went about its business, unconcerned and unknowing. And so things might have continued.

But Jonah, having given them their head, now reined his people back in slowly but surely. With deliberate care, he reached down to tap one of the holographic buttons he had preprogrammed. A single light in the overhead dome faded to black.

He gave that a slow count of three. Then tapped the next.

Another light.

The next. And the next.

Slowly, overhead and around the room where glowing panels were spaced evenly against the walls, Jonah walked across his controls, blanking out the lights. A very few dimmed to a preset gloom that he had chosen specifically for its ambiance. Most, however, he let go completely.

Before he'd finished half of them, the furor had died down to those with (they felt) the strongest arguments. Two more, and even Anders Kessel had closed his mouth and turned to watch the exarch, who did not slow down or pause to acknowledge the sudden shift in noise level. With deliberate care he shut or dimmed every light in the room but one. The final one. The one backing his dock, leaving him a silhouetted outline to the paladins and knights assembled this day.

"That concludes our floor show," Jonah said. Not a bit humorous.

His calm sarcasm chastised the men and women charged with The Republic's defense more effectively than any tirade. Many of them hung their heads. Many knights.

The paladins all met his gaze. Every one. And Jonah returned a careful spotlight to every one of them, even to the absent stations where Ariana Zou and Kaffyd Op Owens were represented in spirit if not in the flesh. He let them stand forth once again from the knights who watched, who judged, and who would act based largely on their example.

"If you can say you did not see such drastic measures approaching, then you were willingly blinded by your own fantasy and not by this office. For weeks I have opened up files, sent you careful reports, and culled all the necessary facts out of the chaff of government to help prepare you. To let you see. I, and a small handful of advisors, have now taken this as far as we dare."

Anders Kessel leaned forward, hands gripping either side of his personal station. "Exarch. While I believe we would all agree that dark times are upon us, your proposal smacks of defeat. That we should give up."

"It is not my plan, but one of Devlin Stone's carefully prepared contingencies," Jonah reminded them. He swallowed hard, knowing his greatest opposition would come from Kessel. But in a way he welcomed it. Desperate measures should be challenged. Should be debated. "We are not giving up, Paladin Kessel. We are enacting a strategic retreat."

"But so many worlds?" Maya Avellar asked. Shook her head. "So many worlds . . ."

"With your forces spread out across several continents, and facing potential enemies that are, let me remind you, numerically superior, who among you would endeavor to hold an entire world? Or even more than a single base from which to concentrate, prepare, and then strike back at those who first prove themselves the greatest threat?"

He had several of them nodding along now. Having moved past their initial shock at his announcement, that The Republic had moved into its death throes and was in danger of failing altogether, some were once more beginning to think like military leaders. Like the great generals and far-sighted leaders each had proven themselves to be.

It was no mistake that The Republic's founder had established a governmental system based on martial prowess and a risk-versus-return mindset. Only in military operations could such a cold and clinical detachment eventually reign.

"This will not be an easy time. But it is a necessary evil

we have been faced with. The alternative being years of stagnation—at best!—followed by the long, painful slide backwards into the worst examples we could pull from history. The Succession Wars. The Pentagon Civil War. The Jihad."

A cold blue light had begun flashing in the bottom corner of the exarch's screen, hidden from view from those below. As he spoke, he tapped the icon, opened up an unsigned window and saw the brief message displayed for his eyes only.

WE ARE FIVE . . .

No doubt who had sent that. Jonah knew a brief ease as muscles in his back and shoulders unclenched. He had been hoping for such a message. A forward paladin who had not been so surprised, and who was willing to take those first drastic steps.

"Exarch." Tyrina Drummond. The large woman had always been one to sense the direction of events and position herself near the front. Half of leadership was knowing when to bend to popular will. Which ended up being part of her argument. "Exarch, how do you think the people will react? Such an iron-clad restriction on the borders? The political spin that will follow, casting us in a dark light indeed, Devlin Stone's blessing or not."

Jonah leaned forward. He used a slide-control to move the lighting back up by ten percent, restoring more of the chamber to something less than shadows and gloom.

"They will react poorly," he said, acknowledging the problem that was certain to come. "They will be frightened and ignorant of most of the facts. They will strike out blindly. For a time. But we must and will provide the leadership they have come to expect. We must be resolute and supportive. And when necessary, we will stand firm against any threat to our common goal: to keep The Republic's light burning for the future hope of all humankind."

SEVEN NOW. PERHAPS EIGHT.

A new message, scrolling into the same open window.

A consensus slowly built among his paladins. And, by extrapolation, his knights as well. It was a routine he expected to see repeated at many levels, on larger and larger scales the further they moved along. Shock. Resistance. Distress. Acceptance. And then . . .

"Can it be done?"

Leadership.

David McKinnon. Paladin exemplar, with the passing of Victor Davion. A man so many of them looked to for guidance. Pushing past the century mark was impressive enough, of course. But his greatest accomplishment was the spark of divine fire that still blazed in his eyes. That he still believed, after everything he had seen and experienced, including—as a veteran of the Jihad—some of humankind's darkest hours. That capability to keep seeking a better path for all. That gift drove people to support men like McKinnon.

"Can it be done?" Jonah asked.

"You hope to seal the borders. And security will be maintained with 'all necessary force' as you promise."

"Yes."

"Can that be done? Is it possible to create such a . . . star-spanning fortress?"

A practical question. Always a good sign. McKinnon might not be one of the seven or eight ready to follow him into the hardship ahead, but he was at least willing to consider the merits.

"It can," Jonah promised. "As much as I have given you, it is not everything. Not because I do not trust you." Though Jonah did not. Could not. Completely. "But there will be assignments, hard tasks, ahead for many of you. And some things that you could learn might hurt those missions. Could endanger us all, in fact." Playing on mission security was another tactic that could only work with seasoned veterans. The elite of the Sphere.

TEN.

"It remains to be seen if we can make it work, Paladin McKinnon. But I promise you, the resources *and* the technology exist to attempt it. If you are willing to pay the cost for ultimate victory."

Now *that* made an impression. The elder paladin recoiled as if struck, having his own Founder's Movement motto thrown back at him. Victory at any price. Nothing was worth more than the continuation of Devlin Stone's dream. The survival of The Republic.

CALL YOUR VOTE. NOW, JONAH!

"This can be done," he said. "It must be done. But, even

as exarch, I cannot do it alone. This august body; this circle of men and women, and the cadre of knights who support it, and still support The Republic, are the only ones who can make it happen. If I do not have your full support, if you no longer trust my leadership, then we are at a loss. What say you all?"

There could be no official vote. Not as such. There was not even a procedure to follow, except for the election of an exarch. But this was important. It was as close to a reaffirmation of the exarch's mandate as one could ever conceive. Jonah felt the incredible weight of his office, of the task left for him, settle down into his chest. For a moment, he found it hard to breathe as he waited for someone to make the first display of support. For, or against.

McKinnon surprised him. The venerable warrior was the first to nod his head in a bow of affirmation. Silent. Still.

Then Heather GioAvanti and Gareth Sinclair. Thaddeus Marik. Tyrina and Maya and Kelson Sorenson. Janella Lakewood. A cascade of support sweeping across the line of paladins as every one of them to the man bowed their heads and held the pose, hands clasped before them or spread out over their station panels.

Then, nearly as one, the knights rose from their seats in the Gallery. Standing in silent obedience to the will of the exarch and his paladins.

"Four weeks," he said. Mournful and yet not completely without hope. It *was* a death sentence, but as with any wake there remained a promise of the next life. "Four weeks until the completed shutdown. There is much to accomplish. Much to discuss. I am opening more files at every level, knight-errant to paladin. We need debate and challenges as to the specifics. And if any man or woman can find a better path, let him bring it forward. But no matter what, we shall endeavor to persevere. Many of you will have a special charge. They will not be easy. They will not always be clear. Trust in your fellow warriors. Trust in yourselves. The way shall always be open."

A flashing icon. A new one. Also unsigned. He thumbed it open as he finished his short speech. Read the entire text in a glance.

YOU HAVE MADE A GRAVE MISTAKE.

So not every paladin was with him. So be it. But as with

any challenge in his life, Jonah planned to meet this one with every weapon still at his disposal. And faith defend any man or woman who crossed him now.

"This is not the beginning of the end," Jonah promised, looking out over his paladins. Studying each one in turn. Fifteen pairs of eyes stared back in open support, or challenge. And either was fine with him.

"Merely the end of the beginning."

SOLITUDE

Never doubt that a small group of thoughtful, committed citizens can change the world. Indeed, it is the only thing that ever has.
—Margaret Mead, republished in "A Treatise On Leadership," New Avalon Press, 3066

Change so often comes by such difficult and painful means, that we take great pains to avoid it. We erect grand fortresses to safeguard our most cherished beliefs. But change will not be denied forever. Eventually, if they must, the heralds of progress take up arms to tear down the high walls of ignorance. Brick by painful brick.
—Julian Davion, Lord Markeson, "Theories on Political Upheavals by Military Means," published first on New Avalon, 12 February 3132

22

Civilian unrest on Hoan and Ankaa was quelled only when Swordsworn officers enforced the public's call for an airing of grievances against the local governments. Debate continues to rage over the likely need of a special election to recall the current world governors, both of whom are applying for assistance from Terra and Exarch Levin.
—ComStar INN, Ankaa affiliate, routed by JumpShip Silver Bell, 27 August 3135

Ronel
Republic of the Sphere
4 September 3135

Sho-sa Jirobi Katanga bought time for his warriors as he ordered the Dragon's Fury back another half kilometer. Throttling into a run, he raced his *Panther* across the Mitchell Dry Lake Basin at better than sixty kilometers per hour, swaying his head side to side in time with the BattleMech's swinging gait. Swallowing against the bitter, dry taste left behind from one adrenaline rush after another. Sweat-salt crusted at the corners of his eyes, dried to a flaking scale against the dark coffee skin of his forearms. Every muscle ached after ten hours in his command chair, overseeing this running battle, this rout. With no sign of relief on the horizon, not until every member of his unit was dead, destroyed, or captured, he accepted his karma.

Let it be him, then!

He moved laterally along the battlefront, pulling to his side a pair of Maxim heavy hover transports and his remaining SM1 Destroyer. A Shandra scout vehicle raced up from behind as well, arguing against his orders to fall back with a simple shout of "Banzai!"

Four armored vehicles and a lone BattleMech, holding their side of the basin. Challenging the mercenary Storm Chasers, the Senate loyalists.

Long-range missiles and light autocannon sniped at them, worrying away their armor a few kilos at a time. The enemy force hesitated, even outnumbering his force at better than two-to-one, and Jirobi smiled. If nothing else, the assault force Conner Monroe had brought to Ronel had learned to respect the Dragon's Fury. Knew better than to push forward blindly. Wait. Observe. Attack. These were the enemy's tactics now, which they'd followed dogmatically this day, pushing forward again, and again, and again.

A Condor's crew gave up on patience first, their vehicle sporting the blue and gray thundercloud colors of the Storm Chasers. They thought enough of themselves to probe too far forward, Arbalest launcher and Mydron Excel autocannon hammering away at Jirobi's ad hoc unit. He turned against them with righteous fury.

The *Panther's* Lord's Light PPC spoke for Jirobi's insult, slashing across the basin's dried, cracked mud to grind into the side of the Condor's primary drive fan. Sparks exploded and metal ran bright molten red to the ground where it smoked itself down to charred cinders.

The Maxim transports could do little from their range except add several handfuls of LRMs to the Condor's misery. The missiles cratered the hovercraft's deck, cracking its armored lift skirt. But an SM1 was never to be taken lightly. Skating forward on a cushion of air, its own drive fan reaching for a top-end speed of one hundred thirty kilometers per hour, the Destroyer broke from Jirobi's pack just far enough to grab range with its ultra-class one-twenty-mill autocannon.

A long tongue of flame ripped from the barrel.

A gray haze of hot metal and bright, white fire-flashes from tracer rounds.

With its furious razor-edged storm, the SM1 neatly sliced off one entire side of the Condor's skirting, spilling its cushion of air in a quick and violent dust devil. Digging the left-hand side of the speeding hovercraft into the lake's dry basin, sending it in a rollover tumble that spread scrap metal along several hundred meters of open, desolate ground.

Jirobi's communication system did not come with a voice-activated mic. He toggled for an all-hands circuit and left the channel open. "Back to the pack!" he ordered.

Turning his *Panther* to the southwest, he trailed after the much faster Maxim by an easy hundred meters and was quickly overtaken by the returned Destroyer as well. He left his throttle shoved up against the forward stop. Counted the distant silhouettes of two BattleMechs waiting at the head of a battered armored company.

All that was left of his garrison. His charge, given by Katana Tormark, that Ronel be held until further orders.

Now his failure and his shame.

"Jirobi-*san*! Our Shandra . . ."

By the Dragon's teeth! He'd not thought! Jirobi read his tactical screen with a trained eye, and pulled up a rear view just in time to catch the Shandra scout vehicle on a dead-center race back into the teeth of the advancing mercenaries. The death of their Condor had mobilized them, a few of their faster vehicles leading the charge forward to get something back for the dead crew, the destroyed machine. The Shandra, with its heavy minigun and two samurai-hopefuls armed with laser rifles, was no match for the Bandit hovercraft or even the Striker light tank that led the way.

Not that the two men had any thought of coming back from the battle.

Shedding armor composite and with smoke chuffing out from under the engine housing, the vehicle accelerated directly into the oncoming Striker, which was having trouble bringing its missile launchers down hard enough to anticipate the charging Shandra.

Two Streak-SRM warheads finally pounded into the Shandra's front armor, but too little, too late. The armored vehicle plowed into the front of the Striker at ninety-plus kph. It erupted into a soot-stained fireball that looked to Jirobi like a wilted apple blossom, overturning the Striker, leaving it tilted up on one side.

"A single measure of relief," Jirobi whispered. "One more day, and I shall compose haiku for their sacrifice."

"*Wakarimassen,* Jirobi-*san*?" Lieutenant Vallence in the SM1. Another samurai hopeful who had joined his honor with that of Katana Tormark.

He had left his communications open. "*Iie.* It was nothing." A warrior's final, desperate request.

Which the gods answered not a dozen heartbeats later as a fresh, strong voice crackled out over his antiquated comms system.

"Dragon's Fury. Dragon's Fury." A confident, female voice. Her *ki*, strong. "We have you holding the southwestern border of Mitchell Basin. If your honor permits, we stand ready to assist."

Was this . . . Jirobi knew the gods never looked kindly on distrust of their gifts. But this seemed too fortuitous. Assistance? By whom and from where? In every direction, nothing but sun-dried, weather-scoured plains that held water and life six months of the year, but now was a death land waiting to claim its next drink of blood.

He dialed over to a general channel, matching frequency with the original call. "*Hai!*" he said. "*Hai,* if this is real. I am Jirobi Katanga of the Dragon's Fury, and no one's honor is served in defeat to mercenary *ronin!*"

"Good enough," the new voice said. "I am Yori Sak . . . Yori *Kurita*! And I offer you a message from the First Davion Guards."

Jirobi throttled back as he raced up within the confines of his ragged company. Looked through his ferroglass shield at Lestrade's beaten *Griffin.* Olna Takari's limping *Spider.* The scarred and pitted armor on every vehicle left to their unit. Which was not many.

Kurita? The House of the Dragon! Here? And with Federated Suns troops? Well, why not. If the gods were to provide . . .

"What message?" he asked.

"To stand by and *hold*. Hold your line, Jirobi-*san*." And here Yori paused. Then, "We are about to . . . shake things up."

"Julian. Go."

Yori Kurita's assurance of a favorable beachhead was all he had been waiting for, though walking an eighty-five ton BattleMech out of an open DropShip hatch was by no means an easy step to take.

The *Markeson Pride* hovered nearly ten kilometers over Ronel's Mitchell Basin, camouflaged by the afternoon sun as it held station high above to preserve an element of surprise. Wanting to send a clear and challenging message to Senator Conner Rhys-Monroe, that the First Guards had arrived and their agenda was nothing less than taking Ronel back from him and his budding alliance, Julian and Yori had worked together to form a hammer-and-anvil strategy to do just that.

"But this hammer is about to take a nine-kilometer swan dive," he whispered, louder than he'd meant.

"You are complaining *again*?" Callandre asked. Fortunately his transmitter was dialed to a private frequency the two of them often shared. So only she had heard his last-moment misgivings. "Living in the Federated Suns made you soft?"

He'd show her soft! Stepping his *Templar* through a tight shuffling turn in place at the head of a short line, he faced his back to the open bay door and looked back across the nearly empty bay. No technicians. No support personnel of any kind after exposing the interior to such thin atmosphere. Just his waiting lance, a few battlesuited infantrymen, doing their best to wave vehicles into a double-column line, and on the far end of one line Callandre's Destroyer.

"You just wish you were along for the ride," he said. And levered himself back, taking the spill in a backwards fall.

Which was certainly true. Though his awkward departure rattled her for a moment.

"*Verflucht*! Jules, are you insane?!"

High praise from the Nagelring's darling rogue. The same woman who had once driven a Hunter light support tank out onto one of Tharkad's alpine lakes *and intentionally sunk it through the ice* to prove a bet on whether she would have enough time to power free of the freezing water before the engine drowned.

"No," he gasped. "Not insane." Just very, very stupid from time to time. Damn, but Calamity had a way of getting under his skin at just the wrong moment. Dropping through the thin atmosphere, Julian gritted his teeth as he went through the procedure for high-altitude insertion in a tumbled BattleMech.

Extending both the *Templar's* arms straight out to the side, increasing drag.

Pulsing his drop pack's burners for a few seconds at a time. Using them to cancel his 'Mech's end-over momentum.

Within thirty-five seconds he had easily brought the falling machine under control. Ten seconds to spare, in fact, before the full burn point. Which he hit, and let the drop pack's internal controls take over. All directional lifters fired, burning through their reaction mass at an incredible rate. They balanced him out by taking a feed off the *Templar's* internal gyroscope, which was in turn controlled by Julian's own sense of equilibrium as translated by the neurohelmet's sensors.

One of the lifters pulsed hard, steering him onto a level drop. It held him there for another handful of chest-bruising heartbeats. Then one final *hard* burn that pressed Julian into his command chair at four gravities, making it difficult to even breathe, much less raise a single hand towards his controls. The automatics would work, or they wouldn't. His ejection seat would fling him out of harm's way in the event of a catastrophic failure, or not.

His life was truly in the hands of technology and fate. Both of which had a tendency to fail, from time to time.

But not here. With a final roaring burn, the drop pack set Julian down in a hard but livable landing on the dry lake basin. His knees flexed deep as they absorbed what was left of his descent momentum.

Julian arched back quickly, forcing the 'Mech into a tall

stance, and slapped at a nearby control that sent a wireless signal to the drop pack (which could not be received unless and until all lifters had stopped firing). Explosive bolts fired, separating the drop pack from the *Templar*. And Julian took his first steps out onto a live battlefield.

He had already dropped his crosshairs over a gray-and-blue painted *Arbalest*, ripping his PPCs down either side of the twenty-five ton 'Mech, before he remembered to start breathing again.

"Guard-one, down and engaged!" he reported, gasping for breath, having toggled back over to an all-hands circuit. Though he swore he heard a distant *jerk* whispered through his neurohelmet's speakers.

Then, "Guard-two down. Engaging."

"Guard-three . . ."

"And four!"

A full lance of freshly armored 'Mechs. Hitting the field just as two companies of Storm Chasers and a few loyalist crews smashed into the ragged line set by *Sho-sa* Jirobi Katanga. Julian tried to imagine what it must have looked like to the mercenary commander, seeing four fresh machines crash down on long trails of desperate flame.

Especially when they began tearing apart his line.

The Guards' *Enforcer* quickly moved to aid a staggered *Griffin*, while their *Centurion* and a captured *Legionnaire* slashed into a mix-up of armored vehicles and scattered infantry that looked ready to bowl over what was left of the Dragon's Fury column.

Julian throttled his *Templar* forward into an easy walk, laying about on both sides with his particle cannons, his medium lasers. Tied his TharHes four-pack into his main triggers as he worried the *Arbalest* again, using his cannons and SRMs to give it a solid kick in the backside as it turned and fled north without waiting to see if any of the rest of the Storm Chasers would follow.

Julian let it go. He still had more than enough targets to worry him.

Like the engineer squad swarming up the side of Leftenant Sheila Hanson's *Enforcer*, using magnetic grapples as they clambered up towards the cockpit hatch. The young warrior tried to swat them away, but her 'Mech's arms could not reach far enough around on her flank.

"Hold still," Julian ordered. He climbed his crosshairs over her shoulder, settling them on the egress hatch. Waited until the first engineer slipped up to plant a shaped charge against the lock. And then triggered his single medium laser.

Light body shields or not, 'Mech weaponry was designed to burn through some of the best armor composites developed. The flash of ruby red cut the combat engineer in half, hurling his legs over the side of the *Enforcer's* shoulders. His head and arms and upper body fell away to the other side.

Only a light scorch mark nicked Hanson's 'Mech.

It might have changed the minds of the others, though that would never be proven as a squad of Raiden armored infantry leaped up into the side of the *Enforcer* and used their arm-mounted lasers to sweep away the rest of the engineers.

The Storm Chasers might have been caught completely unawares, but Julian had to hand them some credit. Except for the *Arbalest*, the unit held its ground well and shifted quickly to respond to the First Guards' sudden threat.

Which meant, of course, that they shifted quickly against Julian.

Lasers and missiles hammered in from all sides, in a last-ditch effort to take down the heaviest machine on the field and throw a measure of doubt into the new arrivals. It was a gamble, and one Julian might have made in their stead. But his *Templar* held up under the savage assault, rocked back by the physical force and the loss of several tons of armor, but never in danger of being dropped to the ground.

He could play that game as well. He dialed in his command circuit, overriding the combat chatter, and tied in a general-broadcast frequency as well. "The *Sun Cobra*," he said, choosing their first victim. Letting the Storm Chasers hear.

And from their various positions on the battlefield, all four Guard 'Mechs turned towards the fifty-five ton machine with its flanged head and the deadly bite from its paired PPCs. The *Centurion's* lasers sliced deep into its right side, while the *Legionnaire's* autocannon hammered the legs full of fresh, jagged-edged wounds. Hanson's *En-*

forcer used lasers and autocannon both to heap more misfortune on the *Sun Cobra*.

Julian took an extra second, weathering the storm of fire against his *Templar*, as he relied on his targeting computer to help lock in *precisely* on the right leg. The azure particle streams of both PPCs twisted together into a single, devastating whip, bursting through a weakened knee joint, blowing the leg in half without any seeming effort.

The fifty-five ton machine crashed over, not about to hold up under that kind of damage. It bounced twice against the dry lake basin, and was immediately swarmed by armored infantry.

To which Julian simply said, "Now. The Bandit."

A fifty-ton hovercraft capable of speeds in excess of one hundred fifty kph, the Bandit had been skating in closer and closer to use its lasers and short-range missile packs to devastating effect against isolated clumps of the Dragon's Fury infantry. Seeing the *Sun Cobra* dealt with so ruthlessly, and hearing its own name next on the hit list, it spun about in an end-for-end turn Julian had often seen Callandre pull in her Destroyer. But momentum was another factor. Before it could reverse on a one-eighty, it had to cancel its forward motion, and that took time.

Time enough for Julian's four 'Mechs, and a Dragon's Fury *Panther* to turn their weapons against the hovercraft. Ripping away the elevated turret. Carving off a steering vane and blasting terrible, gaping holes into the lift skirt.

The three PPCs between Julian's *Templar* and the *Panther* were enough to slag away nearly every ounce of armor protecting the Bandit's right deck. As streams of autocannon fire hammered in after, followed by knives of scarlet laser fire, the vehicle had no chance.

One scarlet lance cut deep into the lift vanes, and suddenly the basin to all sides of the craft was filled with high-speed metal as the spinning blades disintegrated into a blow-out of razor-edged shrapnel. The Bandit bottomed out hard, sliding to a rough stop but—fortunately for the crew—not rolling over. The mercenary crew managed to shut down their fusion power plant before anything worse happened.

Before any more of the mercenaries heard their name

called out next, they broke and ran. A few managed to hook up with a companion for safety in numbers as they beat a rapid retreat back to the north. But most cut loose from wherever they stood and ran far and fast in the opposite direction from the nearest enemy machine. Some went east and a few more, it seemed, westward. The bulk spread out in a wide fan heading north, towards the far side of Mitchell Basin.

"Do we pursue?" Sheila Hanson asked.

"No," he decided. "Let them run."

Any moment now the retreating forces would see the landing flare of the *Pride* as it closed the door on the north side of the basin. Yori Kurita and Lars Magnusson would lead out the Guards' armor contingent, spreading them into a wide net meant to trap every last loyalist and mercenary machine.

"They have nowhere to go."

23

New Hessen's name has come up yet again as a world also facing encroachment by House Liao. Or is that the truth?

"We cannot say for certain that Liao forces are not working hand-in-fist with the Davions," said Knight-Errant Bishop Reinhardt in a pubic statement released on Kansu. "New Hessen could well be a staging ground for strikes deeper into The Republic, with local garrisons simply looking the other way."

—Interstellar Associated Press, Algol, 17 August 3135

Kai Lampur, Tikonov
Republic of the Sphere
5 September 3135

The Dao Xi offices at Kai Lampur were in full operation, with data-runners carrying their noteputers from station to station and room to room, and swarming around any of half a dozen different individuals for final authorizations—none of them Erik Sandoval-Groell. Or his uncle.

Erik knew it had been set up this way on purpose, to prevent a breakdown in organization during those times he had to be absent. Gavin had explained it very carefully. Erik provided direction for his top advisors, was given twice-daily updates and sought for counsel only when an aide deemed it necessary for dire political ramifications. Usually, when the direction they leaned went against the grain of his uncle's plans. Then he weighed the risk versus return, made the call, and orders went out over his signature with an efficiency to rival any military-political organization Aaron had ever headed.

Which gave him time, now, supervising the work around him but not an integral cog in this growing machine, to take a moment for himself while the lord governor inspected reports flashing up on screen after screen on the computer stations they walked past. Erik's worry could only be measured in the damp sweat itching in his palms, the dry cotton taste sitting on the back of his tongue. His outward calm was perfectly in place, and he allowed himself just a moment to enjoy a quick flash of warm pride before returning to the present.

Returning to war.

Seize the high ground.

A military maxim at least as old as Sun-Tzu's *The Art of War*, he knew. When higher ground meant your archers could shoot farther—and kill at a greater distance—than your enemy's. When it added impetus to your charge, with soldiers and horse-drawn chariots charging *downhill* to meet the tiring warriors pushing *up* at your line.

Signing off on orders to move the Swordsworn's Schedar auxiliaries, splitting them between the systems of Ankaa and Hoan, he paused in the middle of his wide-looping scrawl, stylus scratching to a halt on the noteputer's glassy surface. Considering. Was there an older reference? Willing to bet that there was. Surely there would be appropriate Scripture in ancient biblical texts, thinly disguised in verse, or anecdote, which carried the same thought.

Or, perhaps not disguised. In the Old Testament days, hadn't violence often been preached hand in hand with tolerance and love? The gouging out of an eye for an eye. Stoning thy neighbor to death for such serious transgressions as planting the wrong crops. Somewhere, back in his youth studies, he was sure he had read that.

"Nothing has changed."

"Sir?"

A smart-dressed aide in a button-down Oxford and a blazing red power tie, the young man could have been equally at home running orders on the floor of Tikonov's common market stock exchange. It seemed to have been an easy lateral move to this political appointment, overseeing logistics or public relations or whatever new department the young aide had taken here as a home. Where had Gavin found such people so quickly? Two months almost to the day since Erik had authorized the man to build this secondary system, and it had the feel of a government long accustomed to power.

"Nothing," Erik said. "Nothing." He finished his signature with a quick flourish and nodded the aide on his way.

But . . . *Nothing has changed,* he admitted to himself again. Four thousand years of "progress" to come back full circle. So often still, might could make right, and tolerance and love only went so far before it was time to dust off the weapons of war.

"Everyone is still thy brother's keeper," Erik whispered. And laughed.

He watched as his uncle stopped the young man with the noteputer and checked the orders Erik had countersigned. Aaron's face clouded over with a dark pall, like a bruised sky promising a storm before the day was through.

Seize the high ground. And he had. Bringing his uncle into this nexus of Erik's own power base. Letting him see what his nephew—his cousin!—could do when well-funded and provided with the best intelligence (Aaron's) money could buy.

"You are thinning our border with the Federated Suns?" Aaron asked, his voice tightly controlled. Hardly a question, it demanded an answer in the same way a direct order would.

Erik nodded. "With Brisham Vicore in our camp, we have freed up resources best spent elsewhere."

"Best spent on Ronel, on Addicks." Aaron ticked off the locations of his "hot spot" priorities with the fingers of one hand. "Mallory's World. Kansu. Sheratan."

"Achernar," Erik argued. "Ankaa. On Sheratan we agree."

"Ankaa will not save us Ronel *or* Addicks."

Of course not. Ronel and Addicks were short-term objectives, and Erik was thinking far beyond his uncle's current reach. For once. "Ankaa will save us one of the most mineral-rich worlds in the region. It has no overwhelming exports, yet, but with key restructuring and one or two of those pre-fab factories developed by the Clans—which we will purchase from the Dominion—within the year it can begin producing war materials and operate as a base for logistics support."

"*Now* he looks ahead."

Aaron gestured to the organized chaos buzzing around them. "Read the reports, Erik. Realize. The Republic does not have a year left to it. This—*this*—is the moment for which we've been waiting. What I've been looking towards from the start, while you whined about our military setbacks and worried about a few minor pawns being lost on the board."

A few nearby men glanced over. Officers, wearing the modified Republic uniform common to most Swordsworn companies. Gray fatigues stripped of old unit loyalties, and green berets with a modified sword-and-sunburst crest patched to the side. The men's eyes widened with the insult aimed at Erik.

"Take care, Aaron." Erik's voice was only two notches above a growl.

"We must support Julian Davion on Ronel!"

Ah. Now that was what Erik had waited for his uncle to admit. Not the needs of the Swordsworn or even a particular world's worth (or lack thereof) in the greater picture. Aaron had cut a *deal*. Of course Erik knew it. He paid well to know such things now, and while his account might be accruing some heavy interest, it was all worth it.

"Why?" Erik asked. "Julian Davion has shown no sympathy towards our cause. Harrison Davion, when he held Julian's leash, hardly gave you the time for a meeting. Now Julian shills for Exarch Levin and The Republic and suddenly you are on board?"

"Julian Davion is his own man. He is a strong leader and has in him the seeds of greatness, I promise you. The time to make him our ally is now, while he struggles, not later, when he . . . when he gathers more power."

When he . . . what? What had Aaron been about to

say? Something his uncle knew about Julian—and Prince Harrison?—he had not confided in Erik.

"What of Prince Caleb?" Erik asked, attacking swiftly from the flanks. "He released Julian as prince's champion. Why wouldn't he see these 'seeds of greatness' in his own cousin?"

Aaron smiled slowly. Maddeningly smug. "Perhaps he did. And that is why Julian was released, and abandoned."

Something not quite right. A cog, half a turn out of position. Because Julian was young and strong and a fit leader, the Prince of the Federated Suns would *not* want him at his side? And Aaron would then risk Caleb's irritation by courting the young general who was so obviously out of favor?

"You are not making sense. If what you say is true, we should seek Caleb's support and leave Julian to wither. Why the sudden enthusiasm for this man?"

But Aaron closed up. A withdrawal Erik read by the way a blank mask settled over his uncle's face. "I've no need to explain myself to you."

Erik laughed. Not loudly, not enough to shame his uncle in front of the men and women surrounding them, but between the two of them, to share the joke. "What else have you been doing the last thirty minutes? If you do not need to explain yourself to me, then climb back aboard that flying palace of yours and pass along the orders to secure Ronel yourself."

But Aaron would not, because he could not. And that was what galled the lord governor and duke, Erik's superior in most every way, that he *had no choice* but to seek Erik's willing allegiance if he wanted things done his way and fast enough to make a difference. Erik had enough direct control over a percentage of Swordsworn resources now that Aaron had to take him seriously.

"You could not have picked a worse time to grow a backbone, Erik."

But Aaron sounded two parts impressed to his single part of annoyance. A master, finally forced to admit that his student had learned, and learned well enough to rise to the challenge of a game. He gestured to an abandoned computer station, one with a map of Prefecture IV projected a few centimeters into the air across the flat, glassy surface of a holographic display emitter. Using a light-tipped stylus, Aaron drew quick circles around five worlds. The five he had named before.

Those stars suddenly glowed brighter. Small information tags opened up in tiny windows next to each. Planetary names. Populations. Gross manufacturing capability. Strength of the local economy. Plucking an icon out of the window would bring a wealth of information to their fingertips.

Erik borrowed a stylus from a nearby station. With a glance, he sent the Swordsworn corporal manning that screen on a coffee break. With a quickly slashed "X" he closed the window over Kansu.

"Lose it," he said. "The Confederation has too many forces in play, spearing out from Liao, from Menkar and Algol. We cannot stand against the Capellans *and* The Republic."

Except that Aaron had put Kansu in play with his recent victories against the Confederation on Shensi, on St. Andres. Those victories had vaulted him onto a larger stage, and lulled Exarch Levin into giving him a large benefit of doubt. To go back on that stratagem now . . .

"Done," Aaron said in his characteristic decisiveness. Then visibly winced as Erik slashed away Addicks and circled Ankaa and Hoan in its place. "I may give you Ankaa," he said. "But Hoan?"

"Ankaa has the potential for massive industrial strength," Erik said. "Hoan, for its medicinal resources. These two worlds beg for strong military exploitation." Plus, for some reason, Clan Sea Fox traders were snooping around the world. And anything that attracted the attention of the Sea Foxes was worth securing for themselves. As a bargaining chip.

Not that Aaron needed to know the specifics.

Or care, likely. He simply said, "I made a tentative agreement to support the strengthening of a garrison on Addicks."

"Pull your Bright Guards Battalion off of Sheratan, then. I can cover their replacement."

He didn't say from where. And Aaron did not ask. "You can?" was all he wanted to know. It was a question that actually asked *why?*

Erik hesitated, then: "When The Republic makes a large push at us," not *if*, "Sheratan will be the first battlefield. I'd like to have the advantage of the high ground. Troops comfortable with the local territories. An on-site commander creating some kind of relationship with the local legate, the world governor."

His "uncle" nodded, blue eyes taking on a hard gleam. "And you will move quickly to secure Achernar because Raul Ortega and Anastasia Kerensky won the world away from you two years ago."

"*And* it has a working HPG," Erik reminded him, fuming. He used his stylus to draw a quick circle around that system, near the exact center of the prefecture.

"*Partially* working. According to the most recent reports."

"Which is better than anything we have on Tikonov, or Tigress. Yes?" To which Aaron could only shrug, then nod. "Achernar will be the key to securing the center of Prefecture IV. You knew this when you sent me to hold our claim there. And you shorted me the forces I needed to hold it. Because—!" he held up a hand, forestalling Aaron's explanation. "*Because* the Steel Wolves were too strong, and we could not afford a true struggle with them. So you planned to hand them Achernar, knowing that the Wolves would never be content to hold on to Prefecture IV. With a few victories to encourage them, they would turn their attention against stronger worlds. Toward Terra itself, eventually."

Aaron smiled. "Which they did, after losing Achernar to a Republic force. Either way, we fell off their radar as an opponent unworthy of their attention. Kerensky's disdain for you personally was our greatest asset, and her greatest mistake."

"Achernar is the key to the center of Prefecture IV."

"Yes."

"Then I will be the one to turn it."

Only a brief hesitation. Then: "Yes."

"As to the rest, we do not have the forces to divide our strength between Ronel and Mallory's World."

"What of the heavy forces released to you by Brisham Vicore on Caselton?" Aaron asked, spearing home with a sharp thrust.

Intelligence provided by Aaron's own spies? Or through

The Republic's interests in all of its wayward Senators? "What does not shift towards Achernar and Sheratan I will need to secure Tikonov once and for all."

This got Aaron's attention. "You have found the Capellan staging world?"

"I have a report from a Capellan double agent working for me—for us—off of Halloran V." Where she was at the moment, anyway. That would change soon enough that Aaron could not have time to get his hands on her.

Or so Erik thought.

"South Wind?" Aaron asked.

"How did—"

He stopped himself. Cursed his startled reaction. Aaron had used the code name Erik had shared with only one other person. Though it was far more likely his uncle had broken Erik's personal file security than that Gavin had let slip the secret, it was still a revealing fact.

"I've known of her for some time," Aaron admitted. He shrugged it aside. "So long as you keep your *head down* and she is not in position to betray us, your *affairs* are your affairs." Lending extra weight and an obvious double-entendre.

"She has provided critical information regarding Capellan interests. Enough for me to act."

Aaron shrugged. "That is your choice. However, I'll be taking two companies of troops with me back to Ronel. And shifting a third company over to Schedar."

A full battalion! That left Tikonov woefully unprotected, and cut drastically into any forces Erik might be able to send after the Capellan staging base. He'd have to give up Achernar, for now. Possibly roll back some of the strength marked for Ankaa as well.

"Two companies to Ronel?" he asked. Shook his head. "That is a mistake, Aaron. Ronel is a disaster looming on our border."

"It *also* has a working HPG. Which is a large part of your argument for going back after Achernar."

"And Dragon's Fury troops. And Senate loyalists. A Republic paladin and wayward Davion Guards. Who knows what other splinter factions? By your own report, Ronel is a military meat grinder that might rip apart a great deal of our strength. We won't be able to trust anyone! And we certainly can't take and hold the planet for ourselves."

"I trust Julian Davion."

There it was! Said flat out.

"I do not trust any man passed over by his own prince! Why do you?"

"You mean as much as I might trust a young officer set aside by his own family?" Aaron asked, clearly referring to Erik's status within The Republic, away from the main Sandoval dynasty.

Erik could not help his sidelong glances, to see if anyone else had overheard. "That was uncalled for. At least let me hold back the company being sent to Schedar."

"I do not like how open you've left our border with the Federated Suns."

"Only against the Draconis March. Viscount Elbar. Count Cartago. They are family. And if you can't trust family . . ." Erik smiled, and not with much humor.

Aaron nodded back, Erik having made the point for him.

"All right. Take a company off Ankaa, damn you." Erik raised a hand in surrender. Used the stylus gripped with white-knuckle strength in his other hand to sketch a line between Ankaa and Ronel. "I'll pass the orders today! And I'll hold back on Achernar until Ronel is secured or I find other forces. But you *will* leave me one of those companies."

"Or else?" Aaron asked, rightly reading the warning into Erik's tone.

He threw the light-tipped stylus onto the holographic table, the pen lost amid the light blue haze riding over emitter glass. Folded arms across his chest. "Or else you might find out what happens when you pull every last soldier loyal to you and you alone away from your own capital."

Right then Erik knew he'd gone too far, surrendering the high ground back to Aaron. Saw it in the way Aaron's eyes glinted cold and vicious with his sudden victory. The ghost of a smile turning up the left corner if his mouth. The sigh of contentment. The lord governor had marshaled his forces with better acumen, applied pressure in the right place, and—most important!—had outlasted Erik in a simple game of patience.

A strategy for victory that Aaron Sandoval had leveraged again, and again, and now again.

"Send your troops off Ankaa," Aaron said with an easy grace. He handed Erik his own stylus. "I'll *consider* what to leave behind. Given the troubles you've had with Capellan insurgents, a company would not be remiss."

He made it sound like a gift. And Erik, swallowing the hard knot lumped in his throat, nodded curt appreciation. "Thank you. Uncle."

Aaron's cold voice cut like a scalpel's edge. "You. Are. Quite. Welcome." Each word cut deep, deep. And Aaron certainly knew it. With a nod, he turned for the room's distant door. He paced off several long strides before stopping to look back.

"And Erik?"

"Yes?" A pause. "Yes, Lord Governor?"

"Would you ever be completely certain?" he asked. "That I had removed *all* the troops loyal to me. And me alone?"

Loud enough for several nearby officers to hear, Aaron left the entire room to think over that question. He turned smartly on his heel and left the room with a bold swagger and not another backward glance. Picked up his security contingent at the wide open doors, who clustered around Aaron as if preparing to run a gauntlet of enemy infantry.

Not a totally lost gesture, as a uniformed captain stepped up next to Erik the moment Aaron had cleared the room. "Do we take them at the elevator? Or the main door?" The two contingency plans Erik had put into place, should the meeting not go his way.

And it hadn't. No mistake. But enough had come down on his side of the line to still his hand. And his uncle had been right about that last—would Erik know for certain who was loyal to whom?

"Let him go," Erik said. "Our lord governor has tipped his hand, if nothing else. And if he believes that does not confer some advantage, he's going to be sorely surprised."

Because with all the back-and-forth, the shared data and the plans laid out from either side, Erik still had not given his uncle a look at *everything* he knew. Like Brisham Vicore's complete force strength.

Like the very close proximity of Caleb Hasek *Sandoval* Davion.

"New Hessen," Erik whispered. *That* was what South Wind had brought him. New Hessen and Caleb. Both within easy reach. And if Erik managed to secure one or the other—or both!—then he would certainly find a way to seize the high ground again.

He would!

24

With Liao forces scattered throughout the southern hills and valleys, Republic troops have established a firebase near Weldon Port, denying access by local garrison commanders, and aerospace forces belonging to the New Syrtis Fusiliers (and commanded by Khan Sterling McKenna) have made several threatening overflights in direct challenge to Brevet-Colonel Hedges' no-fly request. Whatever tentative peace once existed appears lost. Perhaps for good.
—New Hessen Explorer, Military Matters Page,
4 September 3135

New Hessen
Federated Suns
5 September 3135

Submerged, like a black coral reef under high tide, the ebb and flow of sleeping memories and the swirling eddies of pain-filled semi-consciousness washed over him in a blur of dark, timeless waters.

There was never a here or now. And no future. Only brief glimpses of *then*. The before-times. When his head had risen above the waters and a pale, distant sun had driven hot spikes through his eyes and into the fore of his brain. That's what he remembered first. New Hessen's pale, white sun.

And the stench. That too. A rotten, warm, ragweed smell, like

(*black creeper*)

composted dandelions. Choking him with the spoiled odor. Clawing at the back of his throat, with each coughing spasm lighting his body afire. A new bolt of pain that reminded him of a time when he'd been younger . . . thirteen? . . . fourteen? . . . and Mason had dared him to climb high into the top of an ironwood oak. Springtime on New Avalon, the tree's lush growth like a canopy overhead, but if he could just stretch a little further, reach for that next branch and hoist himself up, he could touch the sun and Mason would have to go away and be quiet be quiet (*be quiet!*) for the first time in years.

No more dares.

No long falls waiting for him, with branches scratching up the sides of his arms and legs, and that thick limb catching him right across the midsection, hanging him twenty feet over the ground (where his mother would find him half an hour later, shouting up at him to hang on, *just hang on*, and someone was coming to bring him down.)

Mason! Where the hell was Mason?

Another cough. Another lance of fire ripping through him as he lay over that thick branch . . . no, that stone railing of the château. At Thonon-les-Bains. Leaning far out over the darkness and the three-story drop as his father plunged with *his* arms flailing and a short, sharp cry interrupted as his head cracked hard into the stone balustrade of a second balcony deck rail. He leaned over the rail, hands tightened into the same claws he had used to seize handfuls of Harrison's silk shirt; dragging and twisting and shoving and *throwing* . . .

A yell of surprise. The sickening crunch of bone. The heavy fall and the long, tumbling slide down into the lower brush and trees.

Mason's hand on Caleb's shoulder. Comforting.

Bet you didn't see *that* coming! Stick that in your third eye!

"Caleb . . ."

No! His father's voice, calling to him from down inside the tangle of brush and trees. Still alive!

"Caleb . . ."

But not calling out to apologize to him. To take back his declaration that he would make Julian heir. Julian! And not him! Harrison called out not to him at all, but to Julian, whose headlamps illuminated the château's lower slopes as his car climbed up the long, twisting drive. Accusing his son. Letting Julian know who had done this. Always back to fault. Who to blame. Who had to be sent away, far away, so no one would be any wiser.

Mason!

"Caleb!"

High tide rolled back, and the waves of memories receded as he startled back to consciousness on her urgent whisper. He blinked, and the crust of sleep around his eyes scratched at the corners. A blurry image hovering over him. He blinked, and he saw her almond-shaped eyes staring out of an elfin face. Her mouth (that mouth! Tasting like grapes and raw spearmint) a tight, disapproving line.

Danai Liao-Centrella.

He lay on the filthy wooden floor of an old hunting shack, the one-room dwelling (if he could call it that) smelling of mouse turds and the rotting scent of black creeper. She knelt above him, still in MechWarrior togs and a heavy, tan windbreaker she had pulled from her own rescue kit. Still wore her cooling vest as well. For the ballistic cloth. The smooth, creamy skin of her bared legs showed several bloody scratches from fighting their way through the forest tangles.

"We have to move," she said. Poured some cold water onto her fingers from the canteen she carried, flicked it into his face. The droplets stung like the kiss of cold razorblades.

She poured out some more and patted his forehead, rubbed the crust out of his eyes. "Are you awake? Caleb. We can't stay here."

"Why not?"

His tongue felt thick and rough. But at least his mouth no longer tasted of blood, like it had after she'd slapped him back to a temporary consciousness inside the Marksman. She'd looked just as angry then. For her being there at all, as much as for his being a party to it.

"Patrols. In the woods. They found our tracks by the lower stream. Can you walk?" She paused, shook her head. "Check that. Can you *run*? Are you awake yet?"

He was. It rushed back fast. Spitting blood and chips ground off his teeth as Danai pulled him through the warped and ruined hatch on the Marksman. His left side on fire from broken ribs. At least two. Stumble-running across the pockmarked and fire-scorched ground, leaning heavily into Danai's arms as she helped him towards a distant stand of fire and pine.

He recalled stopping once when a large wall moved nearby, rising and then falling back with a ground-shaking *stomp*. Realizing it was a *foot*, not a wall, and the BattleMech it belonged to towered above them like a giant come to claim their bones to grind for bread. Then she'd dragged him on, while it was distracted by a retreating tank, away from what was left of the battlefield.

Seven days ago. Hiding out. Healing. Alone, the two of them, and hunted. Forced into a grave covenant of mutual assistance.

Though Caleb had done little so far by way of assisting.

"Yeah," he finally said. Awake. Though barely. Darkness surged up from the back of his mind and threatened to swallow him back down again. "Yes. I'm awake."

His voice was a weak croak, but stronger than it had been the day before, he thought. He'd managed to keep some food down in the last twenty-four hours. Something more than water and vitamin supplements from the survival pack she'd snagged from his tank. Freeze-dried apple. An ancient pack of peanut butter spread. And the gamey, wild taste of a rabbit she'd caught, skinned, and cooked on a small fire built just outside the ramshackle door.

"Come on, then." She grabbed the front of his uniform and hauled.

And he flopped back down hard, coughing, vertigo shooting off dark fireworks behind his eyes and his taped ribs jolting him with new waves of pain on every hitching gasp. Nausea clenched at his stomach. The sickness and dizziness were aftereffects of the concussion he'd taken when the M1 rattled through its death throes.

"Wang ba dan," she muttered beneath her breath. It did not sound complimentary. She hauled him up into a sitting position against the wall, and held him there until the worse of the dizziness had passed. Looked deep into his face.

"Not quite as polished as you were on the *Stargazer*."

The luxuriously appointed JumpShip on which they'd met. He remembered. That's where they had started their little game, two celebrities playing with their own temporary anonymity. Her, a champion gladiator from Solaris VII, the Game World. Him, the heir presumptive of the Federated Suns. A game of careful playacting that had come crashing down around both their heads at the Terran reception as each discovered the other to be a scion of a rival Great House.

He still couldn't say who the ultimate loser had been. Certainly no one had come out the winner, though.

"Look who's . . . talking," he finally said, panting. Their faces close . . . so close. Eyes staring. "When was the last time . . . shaved your legs?"

Leaving him against the wall, she quickly gathered together their combined survival kit. "Just now I'd settle for—" She stopped mid-sentence.

"Settle for wha—" Caleb started to ask, and was shocked when she leaped at him to clamp a hand roughly over his mouth.

Her eyes were rabbit-wide, searching each tiny window in the hut, he suddenly realized, for a face, an outline. Listening. Every sense on high alert.

Then he heard it. The sharp *cra-ack* of a breaking twig outside. The rustle of dry grasses as someone walked carefully—and at a distance—around the outside of the abandoned shack.

Mason?

Maybe it was. His friend had escaped the Marksman as well, hadn't he? Caleb thought he recalled an image of the jumpseat straps

(*fastened tight*)

hanging open, and empty.

He shook her hand away, and nearly blacked out again.

"Mebbe they won't come in . . ."

"They'll check," she whispered. "Not a lot of room to hide in here." She moved away from him on cautious hands and feet, distributing her weight evenly over the plank floor to prevent as much noise as possible. "Never should have stayed so long."

His fault! That's what she was saying. Because he was weak. Because he was *injured*. He struggled up the wall, getting his feet beneath him. He'd show her. They both would. Him. And Mason.

Where was Mason?

Caleb reached out as if expecting his friend's arm to lean against—Mason was *always* there when Caleb needed him—and stumbled forward from the wall only to crash down hard on his knees.

New jolts of pain ripped through his body. A loose plank jumped and rattled.

Two types of soldier. The cautious, and the commando. Tearing away the dark gauze wrapped around his brain, Caleb recalled that bit of wisdom from some long-ago instructor. Knew that a cautious soldier prowling outside would fall back and radio for assistance.

This guy was a commando. Running forward of a sudden, feet pounding against the ground. Maybe fumbling for his radio, maybe not. Caleb would have bet money (six to four and pick-'em) that the guy worked the action on a sidearm or his rifle instead, chambering a round as he stormed for the single door and Danai crabbed her way across the floor to crouch in the shadows just to the door's right-hand side.

The side *away* from the hinges, he noticed.

Smart girl.

Few MechWarriors carried a weapon in the cockpit, and Caleb did not make a habit of wearing a sidearm either. He supposed Ferguson or Rolph had been armed, and an M1 did have a small arms locker with two rifles and a collection of pistols in case of need, but Danai had not known or not thought to go searching for it.

Strange enough she had come to look for him at all. At least, strange at the time. Until she told him later about The Republic push that had broken through her lines and rolled over another local garrison patrol as well in a take-no-prisoners drive. The Republic owned Dargo now, and was making a push for Jarman City to seize control of the local government until "a stable defense of New Hessen could be implemented that would not look the other way while House Liao used the world as a means of staging flanking attacks against The Republic."

Caleb blinked away the vertigo, and the political rhetoric, as the door crashed inward and slammed back against wall, sagging desperately from one rusted hinge. Neither served them at the moment, in the situation they found themselves in now, which was absent any weapon other than the basic survival knife gripped in Danai's slender hands.

Against an Intek laser rifle held by the infantryman filling the doorway. Not a fair match at all. He wore a simple armored breastplate and a field helmet. Saw Caleb kneeling near the far wall. Levered his rifle down to cover him.

"Don't move!"

Never saw coming Danai's foot, as she exploded from the side wall with a full-force roundhouse kick. Swinging up and around. Snapping forward hard enough that her combat boot crunched the cartilage in his nose to paste and all but threw him back out of the shack.

The shock of the impact, the bodily force; the infantryman clenched down on his weapon and the Intek sparked a single ruby-edged dagger that burned through the air just to the left of Caleb's shoulder to char a round, smoking divot into the thin, plank wall.

The scent of scorched wood joined with the rotten dandelion smell of the local black creeper.

Gasping for breath, Caleb struggled to his feet, grabbing up the survival kit Danai had left sitting in the middle of the floor. Darkness leaned in at the edge of his vision, narrowing his gaze, but he managed to make it this time all the way to the ruined door before falling against the wall and holding himself up by sheer willpower.

Danai had her knife to the man's throat, but seemed disinclined to use it.

"Well?" Caleb asked. Prompting. Mason could have told her. You did not leave an enemy at your back. Ever.

She looked down. The soldier's face was a bloody mess, nose mashed to one side and upper lip split wide enough to show blood-stained teeth. She shook her head. "He's not going anywhere." Reached down and pried the Intek from his grip. Found the spare battery pack as well. "And now *we* have a rifle."

Now *she* had a rifle. *And* the knife. *And* the only real

idea where they were in relation to the long-abandoned battlefield, Republic patrols, and any sign of civilization. With a plan to escape.

And take Caleb with her? Back to Confederation space? Not likely, Faith defend! She was the enemy. Maybe. Certainly she had her own best interests at heart first. Like the Capellan soldier she was.

"Ready?" she asked. Jumping to her feet. Eyes always on the move as she scanned the still forest, the curtains of black creeper hanging down out of nearby pine and elm, and carefully watched Caleb's face.

He nodded. Took a hesitant step forward and let her catch him by the arm. Dragging it over her shoulders and around the back of her neck to take some of his weight.

Then Caleb's own plan began to take form, as he and Danai set off again, fleeing for their lives.

25

Stranger, perhaps, than the arrival of a Federated Suns command to stand for the freedom of Ronel was the quick and near-painless way in which these First Guards absorbed the Dragon's Fury. It makes no sense, with Davions never having had any real love for House Kurita. Whatever his reason, Sho-sa Katanga remains stoically silent . . .
—Military Correspondent James Collins, RBC News, Ronel, 7 September 3135

Janiper, Ronel
Republic of the Sphere
12 September 3135

Janiper was the last stepping stone for Ronel's capital city. And it looked like a good portion of it was ablaze.

Smoke poured into the overcast sky in a vast, oily-black curtain. The stench carried several kilometers south where Julian fought to gain entrance to the city, tinged with the smell of fuel oil and hot metal. It stung the eyes like fresh-cut onion.

Julian still had no idea what the hell had happened up there, and wasn't likely to for some time as he backpedaled his *Templar* out of missile range. Pulled back the two Condors that had paced alongside him on the probing assault as a line of death walked from the river's edge to the sewage treatment facility spread out over several square kilometers to the east. Dirt geysered up on columns of fire and smoke to come raining back down in a dark shower that pattered across his head and shoulders like an evil hail.

"Jules?"

"We hold," he said, leaving himself dialed for the company-wide frequency. Dropping his crosshairs over a distant Behemoth II, he slashed two ionized streams of energy across its blunt nose. His reactor temperature spiked. His receiver crackled with interference.

The Behemoth rolled back towards the safety of the loyalists' main line.

Julian nodded. "We give her time."

Then a warning flashed on his HUD and Julian sidestepped several paces, bringing up both arms—PPCs ready—as VTOLs belonging to Carter's Corsairs mercenary outfit made another dodge in his direction.

Not after him, but a Po tracked tank that had strayed forward from the wedge formation too far to the northwest. The Yellow Jacket gunboats dipped in, smashing at the Po with Gauss rifles underslung their main carriage. Like Callandre's Destroyer—with altitude, if a touch slower on response times—the Gauss-slinging helicopters were flying death incarnate.

The Po never had a chance. Already weakened from earlier missile strikes and a lucky artillery round that scratched away half of one tread and most of the armor on its right side, the Gauss slugs punched in together to smash deep into the machine's belly.

A gout of flame flashed out from beneath its treads as the fuel tank ruptured in a ground-searing explosion. The tank jumped a good meter into the air before it crashed back down into an ungainly squat, treads blown away and drive wheels bowed out by the force of the blast.

"Jules!"

At least Callandre kept her complaint to their private channel. With Major Dwight Hastings sidelined with a broken foot and dislocated shoulder, Calamity Kell had assumed temporary command over Julian's armor assets.

He still wasn't certain if he should be relieved his Guards took to her as an officer, or concerned.

"We have to give Yori more time," he said, toggling onto their private frequency. "A *Grand Dragon* only moves so fast."

"Way out, Jules. But in the meantime, *my* people are paying the hard price."

Her people. Meaning the armored column, which had less defense in an attack from overhead VTOLs. He nodded. He knew it. "So pay it," he said. "Come back to me when you have good news."

"Luder diensteifer—"

He slapped at his comms panel, cutting off her curse. Just as frustrated and fearful as Callandre that Yori couldn't break through on the enemy's eastern flank.

And even if she did, that his company wouldn't respond to her rally in the same way they might one of their own, or she would pull the plug too early.

Unrequited commitment. It had to work both ways.

Which was one of two reasons Julian led this wedge from the very forward point, letting Callandre and the majority of her armor fan out to the east as he shot the gap between the river's bend and the sewage treatment plant. Pushing Lars Magnusson's *Arcas* out to anchor the west. After the *Grand Dragon*, Lars had one of the best 'Mech weight-to-speed ratios. He wanted the *Arcas* ready to swing around and back any wild play he might need to make.

One reason. The other was the *Rifleman* that held the center of the loyalist line, a linchpin between the regular line troops on the western side and the mercenary groups (Storm Chasers, Carter's Corsairs) holding the east. Always a tempting target, that *Rifleman*, trying to lure Julian forward into the enemy embrace.

Granted, it could be anyone stalking the northern line, baiting this trap, but Julian did not believe so. He watched the *Rifleman* closely. Saw the fluid motion and the near-human mannerisms in the stride and posture of the sixty-ton machine that took a great deal of effort to mimic, or otherwise came only with years of training and experience in a single machine. A true melding of technology and skill.

The kind of faculty one expected in an ex-Knight of The Republic.

Conner Monroe.

"Guard-one, two minute standby."

The transmission came over another of his private command channels, this one linking him back to the Praetorian command crawler that slowed the back of Julian's western line. The channel was usually reserved for his intelligence analyst. But Lieutenant Dawkins did not have such a smooth contralto.

He passed the standby alert along to his senior officers, then cut back to the mobile HQ. "Our appreciation, Lady Zou."

"Todd has a civilian report on the smoke to the north," Ariana said, leaving it up to him whether or not he could afford to take the time to discuss. Meaning it was not necessarily tactical in nature.

He traded long-range PPC fire with a Hasek mechanized combat vehicle. Its particle cannon ripped an unsteady gash along his left leg, chewing apart armor and raining thick, smoking crisps across the ground.

A light flashed for his attention, warning him of a damaged foot actuator. Of all the cursed luck. "G'head," he growled through clenched teeth.

"It's a series of fuel tankers. They went up when some of Monroe's hired guns chanced on our spotter lance sneaking into the local industrial sector. They took cover behind the wrong train."

And overzealous mercenaries had done the rest. Julian was grateful that the heavy pall of oily smoke wasn't an indication of a massive city-wide fire. Still, he could have wished for it not to happen at all.

That was true of so many things this past year.

"Thank you, Lady Zou."

"*Least* I could do," the paladin said. And in a tone suggesting she was not happy about that being the case.

Julian had asked Ariana to hold her *Griffin* in reserve for this battle, so she had opted to ride out the battle in the mobile HQ to contribute however she could at the moment. Her 'Mech waited at a rear staging area along with the First Guards' *Enforcer* and their *Legionnaire*. They were prepped to rotate up in case the battle dragged out too long, letting Julian field a second, fresh line with a commander capable of assuming full command of the battle.

Ready also to hold open a rear line of retreat, should it become necessary. He didn't think that likely. Not now.

Within the next moment, he knew it for certain.

"Contact!" Magnusson said, already throttling his *Arcas* into a run at better than eighty kilometers per hour. Pushing his way up the river's course. "She's broken cover at one eight degrees, range four point five!"

"Bring it," Julian ordered his warriors, and flashed a second signal to the reserve units holding several klicks south. "Forward the Guards!"

Their answering cheers were violent growls, tearing apart the command channels for several long heartbeats while the entire right side of Julian's wedge suddenly swept out in a strong and mighty wing to wrap up towards the loyalist position.

Not that they could do much for it, as they had a dragon in their midst.

Yori!

It had taken her ten minutes longer than scheduled, and in battle ten minutes was an eternity. But she had made it, taking her *Grand Dragon* on a wide, sweeping maneuver under radio silence with nothing much more than a fast-strike lance of Dragon's Fury to accompany her. If spotted early, it would have been a long, desperate run back to safety. But getting slightly north of the loyalist position she had managed to skulk the river and come wading up onto the near bank with weapons blazing, two hover APCs deploying combat engineer squads from the Dragon's Fury while a pair of Maxim heavy hover transports dumped out Hauberk SRM infantry.

A stroke of good fortune, Julian knew, that Yori had turned that first victory on the dry basin into a recruitment push. Trading off her Kurita name for the first time since he'd met her, she'd quickly taken control of the Dragon's Fury, severing their ties to Katana Tormark, who had left them in such straits.

Not that her efforts would amount to much if he didn't back her, and soon! Yori's *Dragon* tangled with a *Shadow Hawk IIC* and a *MadCat III* as well as two Joust tanks. The 'Mechs and machines were painted the blue and silver of Carter's Corsairs. And she did it two kilometers past any effective range of cover from Julian's line.

Julian pushed his warriors forward at the *Templar's* best

speed, ready to add his firepower to the hole Yori had just opened up on the enemy's right flank.

"Guard-one! Gunboats!"

Julian nearly missed them, stumbling through a tortured landscape of exploding warheads and the slashing red and green fire of lasers—the two Yellow Jacket VTOLs winging up from the northwest. He turned onto a sudden oblique line, ducked one Gauss slug but took the second square against his centerline.

The kinetic force smashed armor and cracked internal support struts. His engine temperature jumped several degrees as waste heat bled out through damaged reactor shielding. He staggered forward, splitting off slightly from the eastern line.

"Fill the gap!" Julian ordered. Worried, as his turn opened a slight hole. He didn't want his Guards suddenly pulling back to cover his flank. Abandoning Yori.

They did not. Behind his position, Leftenant Beaufort's *Centurion* crossed quickly at his back from the western flank to the eastern drive. If anything, it added more momentum to the push.

"Got company," Callandre called. Missiles rained down as strategic carriers along the entire loyalist front spread hundreds of warheads into the air as a deterrent against any hard push forward.

Conner Monroe either did not plan for it to work, or did not care if it did. His *Rifleman* led an echelon-right maneuver *away* from the attacking *Dragon* . . .

And into the second fist of Julian's one-two punch.

"Calamity! Now! Right wing, enfold and charge; go go go!"

Within a handful of seconds the full trap had snapped shut. Yori's flanking assault had been a feint *disguised* as a major push. Expecting the Senator and ex-knight to react quickly and efficiently to any threat from the river, Julian had readied his people for a two-prong attack. With her Dragon's Fury in tow, Yori retreated slowly to the south to link up with Lars. As the Guards had waited, trusting her to make the flanking push, now she ran a hard gauntlet back to safety while the *entire* eastern line pivoted around Julian's *Templar* to smash like a hammer into the brittle steel of the gathered loyalists and their mercenary support.

Like quicksilver beneath a mallet, the eastern side of Conner's line crumbled and spattered into tiny, fast-moving clumps. A few retreated back towards the city and the raging fire clouding the horizon. Some of the Storm Chasers' hovercraft took to the river as a natural throughway, skating quickly upriver and out of danger. Most struggled to link back up with the core of the loyalist line, now curling hard away from Janiper.

"Gunboats coming hard around." Callandre's warning came at about the same time a digital clock on Julian's control panel flashed down to 0:00:00.

"Too late for them now," Julian said.

His words seemed prophetic when the first gunboat exploded in midair while still out of range from any large weapons on Julian's line. The fireball roiled out and up, flaming wreckage scattering over several hundred square meters. The burning cloud molted quickly from reddish-orange to a soot-stained bloom that hung heavily against the overcast sky.

Then, like twin bolts of lightning, the two *Sparrowhawk* fightercraft slashed through the cloud. Their jetwash scattered the pall of smoke into a dozen small tornadoes. And then they were gone, winging far, far over the city of Janiper, losing themselves behind the thick curtain of the fuel oil fire before they began to make any turns.

Smart. They could bank east or west, lost behind the smoke, and Conner's warriors would have no idea from which direction they'd next come.

Wave Two slammed down hard and brutal in the next second as artillery fire from distant emplacements walked a hard line of destruction down the backside of the loyalist position.

Like patrons at the back of a crowded restaurant set suddenly ablaze, the units covering Monroe's back pushed forward in a frantic surge to escape the fire and shrapnel and rain of scorched earth.

"That's it," Julian said. "Block up on my position and press forward. Cut them off from the city. We don't want a knock-down brawl, not today. We want Janiper."

He saw the blue-friendly icons on his HUD pulling in around him. Spreading out carefully to the north and west to cordon off access to the city. Yori's *Dragon* now hooked into the line near Magnusson. The Ghost Bear *Arcas* backing up Julian's swinging fist. Dragon's Fury and a few Republic vehicles hanging in there.

All of them.

But one.

"Calamity!"

He didn't need to read the iconic tag SM1-K to know who it was out there, running roughshod over his orders and careful planning. Her Destroyer blasting forward at one hundred thirty kph. Chasing the second gunboat!

The Yellow Jacket, no longer king of the skies with the arrival of Julian's aerospace fighters, had gotten low and fast in a hurry, scraping the earth as it sped through the open ground separating the First Guards from the loyalists. Looking for the treeline on the far side of the treatment plant, was Julian's quick guess, where a VTOL could hover in close, safely, and an aerospace pilot would be suicidal to approach. A single treetop snapped across a dipped wing and the *Sparrowhawk* would be pulled down into the tall timber.

But even shedding altitude for a slight pickup in speed, the nose-heavy gunboat was no match for the raw speed of Callandre's Destroyer. She cut the distance down quickly, before the enemy even knew she was there, slapping onto its tail with her assault-class autocannon, burning a stream of hot metal and white-sparking tracers into the stabilizing rotor.

The Yellow Jacket spun off in a wild arc, clipped the side of the treatment plant's main building and came right back at the Destroyer.

Julian caught his breath, expecting a collision, but the gunboat fell heavily to one side of the hovertank, breaking up over the open graywater pools. While Callandre skated across the shallow ponds, throwing back a tall roostertail, the gunboat splashed down hard and erupted in a dampened explosion that threw tall sheets of water in every direction and spattered the side of Callandre's Destroyer with great, sticking globs of gray muck.

"Crap!" she said. And was a single processing treatment away from the literal truth. But it was only a heavy, sludge-like mud.

She swept around in a wide arc, sliding right back into the western line a moment later as if she'd never left.

Julian was too relieved to have her back whole and alive to worry about a rebuke. Not then. He stomped forward, trading long-range PPC blasts against the *Rifleman's* rotary autocannon. Worried less about the missile range of Monroe's JES carriers (as they crawled back farther and farther to the west) than he was about the ex-knight's targeting ability.

Already Monroe had sliced deeper into the *Templar's* wounded leg and hammered away enough armor from his right side that Julian worried for his engine shielding, his primary weapons systems. It slowed Julian down. Bought Monroe and the bulk of his forces some grace time, letting them organize a well-ordered retreat.

Finally, Julian waved off his forces. Pulled them back into a double-thick line that guarded all approaches to Janiper.

Letting the loyalists go.

"It's just going to get harder," Callandre said, skating her Destroyer up at the side of his *Templar*. "Monroe didn't come to Ronel to get thrown back again. He'll bunker down at Richmond. Gonna be difficult to pry him out of there."

He knew that. He also knew his First Guards were still feeling their way forward, acting under The Republic's visiting foreign powers act. Working so closely with the Dragon's Fury, and Yori Kurita. Accepting Lars Magnusson, and Paladin Ariana Zou with her small Republic support lance. They had responded as well as he could hope. But as a commander he believed in pressing his gains only when the reward far outweighed the risk.

Today, the risk was too great. He'd trade Janiper against a *possible* knock-out blow. Marshal his strength while waiting for just the right time.

The first man to attack blindly is the first man to run out of ideas. Harrison had taught Julian that. Battles were usually won in the planning stage.

Today, they had planned for Janiper. And they had it.

Julian tied in his senior officers, the mobile HQ crawler and Yori and Lars as well. "We've got what we came here for. There's a heavy fire burning down half of Janiper's industrial sector, it sounds like. Haul our reserves forward. I want a double-strength patrol on the city's edge, and everyone else pushing for the city to see what we can do to help contain the damage."

"We do not pursue?" Yori asked.

"Negative. We're into plus-hours now on the mission clock. Freewheeling an assault is too dangerous."

"Tough call." Callandre again, keeping her argument alive but never, never challenging Julian publicly as she might in private.

It was a tough call. And it was his to make. As a leader, there was no other way to approach it. Julian listened to his officers and advisors. His allies. He weighed the risks and considered all sides. But in the end, it was his decision.

Harrison had taught him that as well.

"Not so bad," he said then. "Conner Monroe is our enemy, but he's no Capellan warlord. He'll bunker in around Richmond, likely, but he won't make us tear the city down to get at him. No Republic knight could put people at such risk. Ariana?"

"That would be my read as well, Julian. You can let him retreat. For the same reason, he won't push for a desperate assault against Janiper now. He'll let you come to him."

"*Hai. Wakarimas.*" Yori voiced her quick approval as well. "It would seem, then, that we are of an accord."

"Bargained well and done," Lars agreed.

Callandre was hard pressed to gripe against the consensus. She did, though, in an overly pleasant tone that made a mockery of her agreement. "Well. Since the new Star League has ratified, I see no reason to continue pushing for an amendment. But the member from the Lyran Commonwealth reserves her right to say 'I told you so.'"

Julian couldn't help the thin smile that crept over his mouth. He hadn't heard such a formal bitchiness in Callandre's voice since the week following their one and only attempt at a "date" back in their shared year at the Nagelring. He wondered if she even recalled the awkwardness they had endured. He wasn't about to let it fester now, though. Not again. Never again.

He twisted his *Templar* to one side, leaning it over in an exaggerated bow as if taking a good long look at her muck-splattered Destroyer. "You know, Callandre. I never thought I'd say this about you." He arched back, leaning the *Templar* away again. "But you smell."

26

For the first time, a pro-Kurita rally has dared show itself on Markab. In an impromptu parade, citizens and residents marched on New Bristol's city center. They handed out leaflets and called openly for a return of the Dragon. Officials high in the planetary government are "very concerned."

—Erin DeSalvatore, On the Streets, Markab, 2 September 3135

Richmond, Ronel
Republic of the Sphere
14 September 3135

Storming out of a side entrance to ComStar's local HPG station, pushing ahead of the new security contingent that had quickly learned to give *this* Senator some leeway, Conner Rhys-Monroe shoved into the gusting breeze that pushed the steel door right back into his face.

Needing something to focus his frustrations against, he added the toe of his dress boot to the problem and kicked the heavy door open, far enough so the zephyr caught it and slammed it back against the wall. The gust pinned it against the building's red brick façade.

He exited into a little-used side lot, walled off from Richmond's main avenue of State Street by a tall cinderblock barricade, though it stood open onto a large, private park stretching back several blocks behind the station. Blacktop dove into fields of tall, pale grasses gone to seed and stunted cherry trees in desperate need of water, their leaves curled and browning. A few decorative evergreens, and bark-covered flower beds sprouting with weeds.

Winds barreled in from this open side, spinning dust and trash and the dried husks of cherry tree leaves across the open lot. Dust devils whipped at the edge of his long, black leather duster, pulling it out behind him, and stung his eyes with grit. Limbs shook and treetops tipped over. A can rolled and clattered across the blacktop, was lost beneath one of the dark SUVs waiting for Conner and Melanie and their respective security agents.

Conner squinted as he studied the nearby fields. He could easily imagine it as it must have looked at one time. A well-manicured lawn kept green by hidden sprinklers, drifting deep in pink cherry blossoms in the spring. A refuge. Once. Maybe the ComStar acolytes made half-hearted attempts to keep it under some kind of control, but landscaping had ceased being a priority for several years now by the looks of things.

"No time for the finer points," he said. "Not anymore."

A small group filed out of the door behind him, men and women in dark suits fanning out in a protective circle. One woman wore a stylish, dark blue overcoat, clutching the collar closed tight at her neck with one hand, the other holding a leather handbag against her chest.

"Shouting into the winds, Conner?" Melanie Vladistock moved in behind him, using him for a temporary windbreak. The winds tugged and twirled at her long, reddish-brown curls. "An apt metaphor if ever I saw one."

"Talking. Talking into the winds. To myself." One of the dark suits held open the rear door of the closest black SUV, waiting in frozen pantomime. He'd wait all day if Conner made him. "It seems for all our efforts, that is all I can do at the moment. Talk to myself. No one else is listening."

"Someone is," she said. Watching the tops of nearby buildings. Holding her handbag up to shield her face from the gusting winds and the grit. "I'd feel better inside the car."

"Of course." He swept his hand to indicate both of the waiting SUVs. "Would you prefer your vehicle *with* bullet holes, or without, Senator?"

Irritation flashed in Melanie's dark eyes, but she hardly missed a beat stepping towards the closest of the two vehicles—the one with gray-steel gouges showing in the dark paint and a frosted divot in the rear passenger window. "Oh, with. Naturally."

"You know," she said as he followed her into the spacious interior and the agent slammed the door solidly behind them, "you drive your security agents crazy. I'm not exactly pleased with you at the moment, either." She looked past Conner, through the smoke-tinted glass with its thin spider-strands of cracks. "That could have gone better back there. I didn't appreciate being left behind."

"When you are making a point by storming out of a room, it detracts from the effectiveness when you wait for a woman to gather her handbag."

"Really?" Melanie asked. Dropping several degrees of warmth. "And how long does it take to gather a handbag?"

"A question men have been asking for centuries, is my guess."

She tried to stay mad at him. Gave it a real effort, he saw. Biting down on the inside of her cheeks. Taking a few deep, steadying breaths. But then her demeanor cracked and she smiled. Then laughed.

He liked hearing her laugh. It was the only silver brightening an otherwise tarnished week.

"Conner. You bring a certain something to being a Senator. It may be sophomoric, but it suits."

With a quiet rumble, the vehicle's engine fired to life. With an easy grace the two-SUV caravan wheeled out from the lot and through a guarded gatehouse to merge into light traffic. He noticed Melanie did not sit close to the window, even though the armored ferroglass had proven its worth very recently. She shifted closer to him instead.

"May I ask what threatening the local ComStar officials gained us back there?"

"I did not threaten. I accused them of taking direction

from Terra. To keep us isolated, from what little there is to stay connected *with*."

"You're worried about Lina Derius."

"I'm worried about Liberty. And Ozawa. And what's happening back on Markab. This whole Faith-cursed alliance of Senators that relies on constant and accurate communications. Yes, I'm worried about Lina."

If that was a flash of jealousy darkening Melanie's face, Conner might have told her not to worry. But he didn't. He left her to work out her own feelings and insecurities. He had enough trouble with his own. Wrestled with them constantly. As now.

Meanwhile, Melanie leaned forward and busied herself with the suburban vehicle's small bar. Nothing much more than a cooler for one bottle of wine, and half a dozen plastic flasks with a sample of the usual suspects. Two local bourbons. A tequila. Whiskey (Glengarry Black Label). Northwind vodka. Sake. The plastic bottles tapped together as she dug one of them out and poured heavy splashes of crystal-clear alcohol into two thick-based highball glasses. She left his sitting on the non-skid counter and settled back into the plush, leather wrapped seat with her own, cradling it with both hands.

The elusive scent of the alcohol—spicy?—mixed with the warm scent of leather interior and Melanie's perfume.

"I am, too. Worried. Though more for a lack of reports from our agents on Northwind than anything out of Prefecture X. But, as to that, I see two possibilities. Lina is unable to respond. Or she is unwilling to respond. Do you believe she has hung us out to dry?"

He gave it a moment's thought. Shook his head. "No. She needs us more than we need her at this point, trapped as she is within Prefecture X, too close to Terra and the exarch's reach. And did you see the face of Demi-precentor Burns back there? When I *suggested* he was taking orders from Terra?"

"When you—"

"Something to that effect." Conner waved aside her correction. "He stared off into the corner. Not to avoid me. Worried for his own people and his station. I think Terra may have cut them loose."

Melanie took a sip of her drink and wrinkled her nose at it. "But ComStar's base of all operations resides on Terra."

"Exactly. These people are on their own, for the moment at least."

"And yelling at them?"

He spread his hands in an open shrug. "Gets them thinking about the allies they might need to start making out here. I convinced Subhar Usuha of that."

"You practically held a gun to his head."

"Whatever works. Everyone needs friends."

She stewed on that a moment, and Conner looked out the tinted, cracked ferroglass to watch gray-faced buildings fall by the wayside as the two-car caravan sped through Richmond for the south side military grounds. The one his loyalists had taken away from the Dragon's Fury.

The garrison post that Julian Davion would now try to wrest away from him.

"So," she finally asked, "what if your . . . conversational techniques convince ComStar, and others, that they do need allies. And they decide to lean in favor of Davion and his motley force?"

He shrugged. "I'll learn to duck more often."

"That's not funny, Conner. You were lucky the sniper was likely some yokel with his hunting rifle. Next time, they might have military grade weaponry. One sabot-loaded bullet and it's all over."

He thumped a fist against his thigh. "All right. You and this floating security perimeter surrounding us have to get it into your heads that I'm not going to let that bother me. I get the idea that most Senators are more than a little self-conscious about their security. But that is *not* me. I routinely take the field in a 'Mech where some of the weapons aimed at my head will do worse than spill a little blood. It is a very real possibility I might be brought back in a shoebox. Enough ashes to fill a small jar, or a bloody paste scooped into bucket. You think a single rifle shot is going to scare me?"

"Fired from an apartment building in broad daylight? It should."

"If they're shooting at you, you must be doing something right."

That set her back for a heartbeat or two. Melanie put

the drink into a holder built in the door panel. "Excuse me?"

Now where . . . Conner leaned forward, mouth suddenly dry. He'd spoken out without thinking, dredging the words from deep in his memory. They left an acrid taste behind. Like fresh gunpowder.

"Something my father once told me," he said. "After his first death threat. Got a lot of those, from time to time, you know. I imagine you do as well."

She nodded. "And my staff takes them fairly seriously."

"So did my father. To a point. But he never let it stop him from going where he needed to go and doing what needed to be done. When I asked him about that—I think I was fifteen, sixteen at the time—he said, 'If they're shooting at you, you must be doing something right.' I'd forgotten that." Until now. Missing his father roiled inside Conner like a cold hand tying knots in his guts.

"You must be doing quite a few things right lately."

"That's military. That's different. But the guy with the rifle." He raised a hand to the window, traced one finger along the thin crack that spread through the smoked glass. Tapped the finger against the small, frosted white star of the bullet impact. "That was a personal thing. Political."

"You think military operations aren't political? They don't count?"

He hesitated. Started to speak. Hedged.

Finally, "If Julian Davion were sitting in this car right now, I'd never worry for a second that he might draw a gun and shoot me in the head."

"And Ariana Zou? Yori Kurita?"

Okay. "You get a slight twinge of doubt for Zou. Only because I didn't know her well among the knights and she might be fairly hot for my head on a pike."

"You really believe in that difference. Don't you?"

Didn't he? Wasn't that what he had devoted a large part of his life towards? And Julian Davion led a similar life inside the Federated Suns. Julian had turned out, in fact, to be a more impressive (and dangerous) adversary than Conner had ever thought. For the very same reasons that made him worry, that Julian Davion might have the momentum behind him now to push Conner off Ronel, so did he respect the man and extended the same courtesy he himself would expect.

"Yes," he finally said. The only way to answer such a question.

Melanie flopped back against the seat. "They're going to miss you and hit me," she groused. Paused. Looked sideline at him. "That is not the reason," she explained, getting ahead of herself, "but I *am* leaving."

"Leaving?"

"As you pointed out, we're too isolated from what else is going on. I need to contact our worlds in Prefecture II, those not yet under the Dragon's claw, and it would be good to touch base with Subhar Usuha in person. I will also hand deliver the personal video you have for your mother."

"I don't have a vid for her."

"You will. You'll record it tonight, Conner, and encourage her to vocally support the recent rise of pro-Kurita fervor on Markab. As an exercise in freedom of speech, for now. This way, while you work on the alliance's present, I'll be able to take certain steps to ensure our—yours and mine—future." She reached forward to pluck the second highball from the tray and handed it to him.

He took a small sip. Frowned in disappointment. "Sake?"

She nodded. "Get used to it. Because if we lose Ronel, and Liberty falls, we'll be caught between a rock and a hard place. I, for one, plan to get on the other side of the rock."

The Combine! "You think my mother can make contacts within House Kurita?"

"If she can't, we'll be in very bad shape once the Dragon turns its attention away from Dieron and recalls that Ozawa and even Markab were also once Combine worlds. Let's avoid the rush, and get in line early."

Conner sipped again at the warm rice wine. The bite wasn't so bad on the second taste. He could get used to that, he supposed. "The definition of modern leadership," he said. "Sense which direction the mob is going to push, and jump out in front." He didn't have to like it, but there it was.

If Melanie ever worried about the idea, she had already made her peace with it. She shrugged. Smiled. "As you said," she offered. And toasted him with the warm sake.

"We all need friends."

= 27 =

It's chaos at the leading edge of House Kurita's forward thrust! Warlord Sakamoto is dead following a terrible catastrophe two days ago on the Dovejin Ice Cap. Local forces are reportedly falling under the nominal control of Katana Tormark, though it remains to be seen how smoothly such a transfer of command can and will go. And the fighting continues, as the Dragon digs in tenacious claws.

—Mikhail Suvich, *Second Limited Press*, Saffel,
7 September 3135

Janiper, Ronel
Republic of the Sphere
19 September 3135

The news came like a swift punch in the gut, and Julian sat down hard. *Collapsed* might have been the better description of how he all but fell back into the roll-around executive chair he'd pulled up at the head of their makeshift table. His knees gave out; his strength fled like a puppet with its strings cut. A metallic taste dried his mouth.

The backs of his legs bumped the boardroom-style chair and it nearly got away from him. He caught the edge of the leather seat, slouched back into its comfortable grip, and rocked back and forth a few times as he processed the enormity of what Aaron Sandoval suggested.

Exarch Levin had truly yanked the rug out from beneath them? All of them?

"This doesn't make sense," Ariana Zou said, breaking the awkward silence. Her voice echoed thin and reedy inside the cavernous, glassed-in room. "You are saying that Jonah Levin has sacrificed—or plans to sacrifice—nine-tenths of The Republic? How could he even enforce such an order?"

Callandre Kell gripped the arms of her chair with strong claws. "Well, that tears it!" She shoved away from the table. Left her seat spinning in lazy, slowing circles as she paced one side of the large showroom floor beneath a drop-down red-white-and-blue banner advertising BANNER DAY SALES!

Julian had commandeered Stillson Motors for his command post shortly after taking Janiper. An abandoned automobile dealership on the city outskirts, it had a blacktopped lot large enough to accommodate every armored vehicle under his command as needs be. A separate building with six maintenance bays was quickly converted to servicing the APCs, hovercraft, wheeled assault vehicles and even some of the lighter tanks. And a large showroom hall glassed in on three sides as well as overhead, with offices along the back, now served as a communications room and logistics coordination center.

Moving in, the place had still smelled of car wax and tire rubber. It had not been out of business long.

Now it smelled of spilled coffee, nervous smoking, and recent hot metalwork a pair of his astechs had performed in constructing the large table at which (most) everyone sat. Two girders cut up and rewelded into heavy sawhorses. A large sheet of raw armor stock forklifted in and laid across. Draped with a large flag bearing the crest of the First Davion Guards, their Roman helmet set over the Davion Brigade sunburst, it had comfortably seated twice their number for any of the dozen tactical planning sessions held here in the last five days.

Just eight of them for this. Julian, who had pulled Leftenant Todd Dawkins inside as well, wanting his personal intelligence aide in on the primary meeting. Lars Magnusson beyond him, moving around the table to Julian's left. And Yori Kurita, who sat stiffly but calm as she looked inward to whatever deep pool of reserve she harbored.

Lady Paladin Ariana Zou at the far end, looking nauseated. But also . . . thoughtful? As if remembering something.

Duke Aaron Sandoval's personal aide sat in between Zou and himself, allowing the lord governor to split the difference between Julian and Ariana, claiming the middle of one side. Then the empty space where Callandre had sat at Julian's right hand.

Of all the reactions around the table, hers seemed the most honest to Julian. A gut-check response, throwing *Calamity* Kell into immediate overdrive. She had come in fresh from patrol for this meeting of the core command staff, still wearing the padded vest and heavy fatigues common to most armor crews. Her hazelnut hair, spiked with platinum highlights today, was matted down from sweating inside a helmet. Her fingers dove into the tangle, began combing it into place. Meanwhile she continued to grind her frustrations against the gray-tiled floor, beneath the heels of black, spit-polished cavalry boots.

Always one to wear her emotions openly, Julian knew.

Not that she was the only one. Lars Magnusson had also scraped his chair back, a straight-backed seat he'd dug out of a back office rather than take one of the more comfortable executive-style chairs. Never a follower, he contented himself watching Callandre's pacing. Or perhaps he'd only wanted some space.

But overall it was Ariana Zou's reaction that most interested Julian. The Republic's representative on Ronel, and Julian's *de facto* ally if not exactly his partner. He wrote off pulling any meaningful thoughts from the preset expressions of Aaron Sandoval or his man—Gavin?—who demonstrated a tight poker face. No, it was Ariana first and foremost. A woman Julian had believed he could trust.

Much as he had believed of Jonah Levin?

Ariana Zou, looking around the table, caught on to Julian's interest. Her dark gaze settled on him. She shrugged. "How is it neither of us were informed? Or warned, at the very least."

She had moved past questioning the news to wondering aloud about the specifics fairly quickly.

A shift Callandre did not miss, either. Paused in midturn, she glared down the table's length towards the paladin. "How about because your exarch is a backstabbing duplicitous bastard who could give a Lyran money-changer lessons in perfidy?"

If Callandre's bite struck home, Ariana hid it well. "I wasn't aware you knew so many large words," she said.

Callandre smiled. "Then whose ignorance is showing, yours or mine?"

That registered. Ariana's eyes widened every so slightly. Julian prevented any further sniping by leaning back into the meeting and slapping one hand down on the table's cloth-covered surface, hard enough he felt the solid metal beneath stinging his palm.

"Enough! This isn't helping, Calamity." He knew his friend would escalate any verbal match to critical temperature, partly out of a defensive reflex.

More, he suddenly suspected, to test Ariana Zou.

She glared at him, a look he knew well. One that said *I know what I'm doing*.

Well, so did he. And now was not the time to force a divide in the small group. "Sit down, Callandre."

She did. With obvious reluctance.

"Good. All right. Now . . . fine." Julian reined in his emotions and confined them to a back seat while marshalling his own thoughts. A well-ordered mind and rational debate could overcome any obstacle. Even one dropped on him like a bombshell. First order of business: additional intelligence gathering and confirmation. "Exarch Levin has instituted some kind of Republic-wide shutdown. Duke Sandoval, you are certain. There is no leeway for interpretation?"

Aaron Sandoval had sat calm and careful since delivering the news. Before, he had hardly been able to sit still, storming into the meeting within moments of his private VTOL landing him outside. With the ice broken, however, he sat back and watched, idly stroking the fringe of blond beard highlighting his strong jawline.

"The orders have been coming in for weeks, actually. Nothing too obverse. Pulling troops back from problem areas, consolidating force strength on worlds such as Kawich and Acamar."

And Northwind, Julian realized. Saw the same flare of suspicion mirrored at the far end of the table, on Ariana's face. That explained a great deal as to why Northwind had gradually cut back on support of Julian's drive.

"I can also tell you that nearly one hundred percent of Republic forces brought back to Kawich for 'temporary rebilleting' were recently loaded up and pulled all the way back into Prefecture X. Gavin?"

Julian had thought the lord governor's aide a much older man at first. But the way he pounced at his name, like an eager puppy, had Julian wondering. And where had he seen this man before? Something about his eyes, and the generous mouth, reminded Julian of someone...

Gavin set two data crystals on the table. "One report from a ship's purser, with documentation to prove the troops held at the Kawich staging facility were relocated to Liberty, which is now under martial law and a system-wide blockade." He tapped the second. "Verification that Prefecture IV has been, for all intents and purposes, militarily and politically isolated from Prefecture X, Terra, and the exarch."

Aaron looked around the table. "Exarch Levin also passed several executive orders through confidential channels, expanding further the emergency powers he granted local governors after disbanding the Senate. Including direct oversight of local military forces. I also do not think it a coincidence that some very few military legates were called back to Terra, and replacements appointed for them."

"Ariana?" Julian asked.

She hesitated. The entire table saw it. "It would explain things I have seen—or was *allowed* to see. Some of the doubts and concerns Exarch Levin expressed in my presence." She would say no more about what those concerns might be. "Julian, I knew nothing about this."

"And if you had known?" Lars Magnusson asked, cutting to the quick. "You would have told us, *quineg?*"

As Magnusson expected, Ariana shook her head. But, "I don't know. If I had been under orders, but still placed in the field with you on Ronel, it might have . . . I don't know." She laughed, curt and brittle. "I suspect this is why I was not informed. I could not have offered the First Davion Guards my—what did you call it, Lord Davion?—*unrequited commitment*."

"Few of us could have," Yori Kurita said. Slowly, as if mustering her strength, she stood. Stared down at the table, with its golden sunburst on a red field. "Now I find myself, as well, in the unenviable position of withdrawing. I will remove the local Dragon's Fury from this world at once."

Julian stared down and across the table, stunned by her resolute tone. If Yori removed the Dragon's Fury, who else might be tempted to abandon the fight? Aaron Sandoval's Swordsworn troops might balance out any losses, but they could no longer guarantee a victory.

"We don't know that Exarch Levin is truly pulling up the drawbridges, Yori-*san*. Give us time."

She shook her head. "There are . . . other considerations. The death of the Benjamin Warlord on Saffel. And *Sho-sa* Katanga has received word that his forces were to rotate to Halstead Station. It is best that they—that we all—follow our natural course in this."

Callandre leaned forward. "There is still a battle to be won here."

"This I understand," Yori said. Then she looked up towards the head of the table. "But I can no longer countenance our involvement in this action. I have stretched Lord Toranaga's orders to their limit as is, to appraise the strength of The Republic and its allies. *Sumimassen*, Lord Davion. So sorry. But this is the way it must be."

So much for avoiding a divide within the group. *And* unrequited commitment. Dammit! He half rose from his chair. "For the sake of camaraderie alone—"

There she stopped him with a raised hand. "You think I did not consider this? My honor is lessened no matter what course I choose, so now I look to the Combine's past as well as our future to guide me. And I see that we cannot afford to be friends."

She stepped away from the table.

"No one can say where the Dragon will next turn its

attention. Perhaps towards Vega and Prefecture I. Perhaps towards Markab, and eventually to Ronel. When next we meet in battle, I'm afraid we will not be on the same side."

No one spoke, or moved, as the scion of House Kurita abandoned the table and quietly strode from the room. If she felt the six pairs of eyes burning holes in her back she showed not the least bit of discomfort. Julian noticed that Aaron Sandoval did not turn at all to follow Yori's departure—seemed quite comfortable with it, actually—and wrote that off to the centuries of the Sandoval dynasty's wars with House Kurita.

He also caught Lars Magnusson hovering on the edge of following Yori, obviously caught in the same web. Lars had taken leave from the Dominion to better understand the troubles faced by The Republic, and to get a feel for the true strength of the nation. He had, and not in the terms he'd thought to have proven.

Either the bite of Exarch Levin's decision stung less or he was simply too stubborn to admit defeat. He planted himself back in his chair with a solidity Julian appreciated, voting with his presence.

Aaron Sandoval was first to break the new silence.

"I still have a company and change brought down with me," he promised. "And more on the way, I hope. Regardless, Julian, they are pledged to your service for the campaign on Ronel. If you are still for it."

That was the question. And never was it thrown more into doubt than at any time since he'd accepted the exarch's charge, on behalf of Harrison's final wishes for a strong relationship between House Davion and The Republic of the Sphere. But Harrison lay silent and Caleb had torn the thin fabric of any earlier accord, and now there was the possibility of Levin himself turning his back on all Julian had done in the name of prince and possibility.

And still he nodded. Slow but sure.

"As Callandre said, there is still a battle to be won. We cannot go back without knowing what awaits us. We cannot hold steady. There is only the future, now." He looked down the length of the banner-shrouded table. "Lady Zou?"

She nodded without hesitation. "I am with you."

And Lars. And Aaron. Both men nodded once, firmly.

Callandre leaned back in her chair, arms folded defiantly. "Try to get rid of me again, why don't you?"

He nodded. "Then we wait for more out of Terra, and Exarch Levin. And in the meantime, we finish this."

There had never been another choice for him. He had to trust in what he had started. What he was doing.

Because, otherwise, there was nothing left.

Genève, Terra
Republic of the Sphere

"Two weeks," Jonah told his two closest paladins. "That is all the more we'll need."

Both Gareth Sinclair and Heather GioAvanti sat on the leather divan in the exarch's private office, looking uncomfortable in the Bullet for the first time in so long that Jonah knew a moment's misgiving. He sipped at his golden-spice tea, stared at the two over the rim of the bone china cup, and ruthlessly throttled the inner voice that had first warned him of trusting anyone else with the plans for Fortress Republic, and now had turned treacherously on *him* to argue that perhaps he hadn't taken enough time and enough counsel to make the best decision possible.

The die was cast and they were well past the point of no return.

Gareth nodded. He set his cup down with the beverage cooling and untouched. "But the Isle of Skye?" he asked.

"It's not the most stable region, I know." He swallowed hard. The spiced tea left a bitter aftertaste on the back of his tongue. Or perhaps it was the politics involved in this latest order. "That is why I'll need you there. One of you. With Jasek Kelswa-Steiner gone missing and presumed dead, and the Jade Falcons in a staring match with House Steiner, I'll need a paladin on the ground. To mind our interests."

Heather sipped her own tea, for politeness' sake if nothing else. Then, "I'm sure you appreciate that your paladins—any representative of the military, in fact—will receive a suspicious welcome. At best. Geoffrey Mallowes was a *very* popular duke with wide-spread family ties."

"And Mallowes led the Senate's treachery against The

Republic," he said. "Which is why Skye concerns me so much. I can't have a direct threat rising too soon, and it is the most likely region to mount such a challenge."

The two paladins traded glances.

"Can it be prevented?" he asked as a soft knock fell against the office's outer door.

Héloïse Montgolfier cracked the door open, slipped inside and shut it softly behind her. Her green eyes were heavy with news. She clasped her hands behind her and leaned back against the wall.

"What resources would we have, and to what lengths would you authorize us—the one of us—to go?" Heather asked in return.

"Not much. And you will be acting upon whatever authority you can muster for yourself." He shook his head, the only apology they were likely to receive. "You cannot expect *any* political cover from Terra."

"How far are you *asking* us to pursue this, then?"

A glance traded with Héloïse. "As far as necessary. And maybe a step beyond that."

Gareth slumped down against the divan's stiff backrest. "You are that worried for the Isle?"

Jonah spread his hands. "It is our most uncertain quarter," he said. And caught the warning glance from his chief of staff. "What?" He saw her frown towards Gareth, and Heather, and waved that concern aside. Too late for such worries these days. "What has happened?" he asked. But already a sinking feeling promised that he knew, he knew.

Héloïse nodded. "Harrison Davion has just died."

28

In a move more stunning than the slow build-up of military forces on Acamar, every last soldier was mustered aboard ship this eve and left in a series of DropShip launches that shook the ground and rose dozens of bright, blinding stars into the gathering dusk. The Republic, it would seem, has abandoned us.
 —The Evening Report, Acamar, 15 September 3135

Midlake Transfer Station, New Hessen
Federated Suns
20 September 3135

This woman was insane!

Caleb clambered over the rubble of the fallen wall at Danai's side, choking on a haze of dust and smoke, and half-falling down the far side as the jagged spill of cinderblock and ferrocrete shifted beneath their weight. Dusk was settling into evening, the worst of all possible lighting. There was no way to be certain this side of the overland shipping station was even clear of infantry. A gun nest? Razor wire strung low to the ground or in shallow trenches into which they could fall. Deep pits with bayonet blades sticking up from the bottom. Anything might lie ahead of them.

What he could see: A series of long, low warehouses. A distant switching yard crammed with boxcars standing along on spur rails. A MASH van tucked away behind the nearest building. The tall outline of a Praetorian command crawler.

And there! Distant flashes on the horizon, accompanied by hollow *thumping*. Followed a few seconds later by a series of sharp, insistent whistles. Growing louder. Shrill!

The air was screaming. Warning him!

He threw himself forward, falling into the shallow, smoking crater of a recent artillery strike. Danai landed heavily on top of him. The gravel and scorched clods of earth were still warm to the touch. It smelled of cordite and fire and sweat. His sweat, her sweat; after the last two weeks it was hard to make such a distinction.

Danai crabbed over until she lay half atop Caleb, half beside. Studied the tortured ground ahead, preparing to make a run for it. The incoming artillery fire hammered down in five, six . . . seven sporadic bursts. Bright columns of flame tore into the ground and zipped shrapnel and gravel through the air.

"Now!" Danai said. Her voice sounded husky and strained. "Twenty seconds."

Timing an artillery barrage was playing with fire. And shrapnel, and immense concussive forces. Still they scrambled back to their feet. Danai held the Intek laser rifle across her waist, covering the open ground to one side. She led the sprint.

"Crazy. Faith defend."

Caleb glanced back once, searching . . . then followed. He gripped their one survival knife in his left hand. He thumbed the lower edge of the blade, testing it. Feeling the cold metal slip into his skin again, and again. Had to be sure. If the blade went dull, he had to know at once. Be ready to toss it aside and then *take* the rifle Danai carried.

The one she had taken off the infantry trooper, and had never let him touch.

The only power she had over him now that his body was on the mend. Fewer blackouts. Fewer moments where the darkness rolled in and swept over him in a cold sweat, and all he could think about was Mason Lambert. Who had abandoned Caleb back on that battlefield. He must have! Unclipping his restraint harness (and then fastening them up again?) to climb out of the shattered M1 Marksman.

Going for help. That was the only thing that made sense. Mason had run for help, to Lord Faust or even New Hessen's uncertain field commander. Caleb had to believe that, because he knew (he did!) that his friend would never have left him alone and hurt and dying if he could help it. There was no distance Mason would not go for him. No secrets that could not be shared. No deed so terrible that it would affect the two of them in any way.

But where was he?

"Not here," Caleb whispered. Some middle-of-nowhere transfer yard where rail cars were switched and cargo warehoused and tractor-trailer trucks might be brought up a service road to load up cargo for local towns.

A local command post for Republic troops, by all signs.

One under attack! By Liao or Federated Suns forces, neither he nor Danai knew. And she did not seem to care.

Insane . . .

Into the shadow of the nearby warehouse, pressing themselves up against a wall of heavy metal sheeting, Danai reached back for the front of Caleb's uniform and pulled him along the wall towards one corner and into a narrow alley between two such buildings. Caleb grabbed her wrist but did not wrench her grip free. Hesitated. Glanced back over his shoulder.

"There is no one back there," Danai hissed. Mistaking his search for concern about a Republic patrol following up on their heels. "We're clear."

Or they were. Twenty days of running, of hiding. Bathing in muddy creeks as they cut cross-country. Leaving behind two towns where they picked up some food, and he might have left her then if she hadn't seemed so sure of where they were going. So *determined*.

If she hadn't grabbed his uniform and hauled him along. Him, a prince—the . . . *the* prince—of the Federated Suns. Baggage.

He tested the edge of the knife again, felt it slice a shallow groove into the edge of his thumb.

"There *is* something back there," Caleb insisted. Just not

Mason. "And ahead. And to either side. Danai, what are we doing here?"

They hurried up the midnight alleyway, feet scuffling against asphalt as behind them artillery fire ripped along the walls and this time found one end of the warehousing as well. Metal shrieked as the blast ripped it apart. The ground trembled, and Caleb felt small pinpricks stab up into the soles of his feet.

Tested the blade. Cold. Sharp.

He slowed, tugged her back to him harder than he'd intended, coming body-to-body with her in the darkness. Only a dozen paces or so from the near end now, a spill of red emergency light washed into the narrow causeway and showed two side doors to the warehouse on either side of them. One of the doors hung halfway off its hinges.

Shouts ahead. The grinding of armored tracks against ferrocrete. And an almost-familiar rattling sound that took Caleb a few extra heartbeats to place. Tank treads clawing their way over railroad tracks.

"What are we doing here?" he asked again. "Assaulting a Republic post with a laser rifle and a knife?" Cold. Sharp. "We should be circling *north*. Find a flanking patrol of whomever is attacking—your forces *or mine* (his! he bet on his!)—and seek rescue."

"I haven't been trying to get rescued, Caleb."

A red bolt of pain lanced between his temples. "Are you mad? Not trying—"

But Danai turned away. Turned her back on *him*. Led them carefully down the alley, pressed up against the side of the building as they approached the mouth. Crouched at the corner, she gestured out into the open yard. A wide, flat expanse littered with blocky boxcars and tankers, and a few military vehicles crammed in between the several spur lines.

. . . cold . . .

And no, she hadn't been trying to get rescued. What she had been doing was just what it appeared. Tracking the Republic forces as they moved across country and looking for their staging posts. Correction: one of their staging posts. Not for their main force, but an auxiliary—likely a temporary maintenance facility or salvage center.

The kind of place that might be tucked away on a rural route, at a transfer station like this one.

What Danai had wanted all along rested out in the yard on the back of a J100 salvage-recovery vehicle—a large crane-and-winch system on a heavy tractor cab, capable of hauling even the heaviest 'Mech onto its large, flatbed trailer.

A sixty-ton *Centurion*? Not much of a problem.

Yen-lo-wang.

"Your 'Mech? That's what this has been about?" The reason she had dragged him across a good portion of New Hessen's backwoods?

"It's mine and I'll have it," Danai bit back. Real fervor in her voice now. "You had your chances to bail out. You chose to stick. And I appreciate that." She glanced back. "I do."

More shouting. And men running across the yard close enough so that Caleb heard their boots pounding against the asphalt and kicking through cindercone gravel even over the distant echoes of autocannon fire and pounding missiles. Though the artillery had finally stopped . . .

"The 'Mech," Caleb repeated. Still trying to wrap his mind around the fact. And when she had pulled him out of the ruined *Marksman*, had it truly been for his benefit, or was she seeking a bargaining chip to help ransom herself *and her BattleMech* off of New Hessen if necessary? He felt cold sweat beading on the back of his neck. His grip tightened on the knife. "You were more worried about Yen-lo-wang."

Which should not have been as surprising as it was. A storied 'Mech with a long history associated with the Liao dynasty. Of course she had come for it.

. . . sharp . . .

Danai shrugged. "A girl has to have her priorities," she said. Not exactly unkind. "I'd like to think that—"

Whatever she had been about to say, a storm of fire and brimstone pouring out of the sky and into the northeastern corner of the expansive switching yard interrupted her. Half a hundred missiles ripped through another part of the high, heavy wall that protected the transfer station. A coruscating whip of blue-white energies slashed in through that opening, along with white-hot tracers from heavy autocannon fire.

Then the crimson and bright-blood tint of laser fire,

spearing down from the heavens as a pair of night-cloaked VTOLS thundered overhead. Strafing through the yard. Finding the fuel tank on a VV1 Ranger parked over near the tall command crawler. The vehicle burst into flame, coloring the station in a flickering yellow-orange light.

By the light of that initial fireball, Caleb counted three Warrior H8 attack helicopters come slashing over the yard's main gate. Missiles rained onto the guardhouse. A few warheads hammered down around the MASH truck, the J100 salvage vehicle.

Around Danai's precious *Centurion*.

"No!"

She leaped forward, but Caleb caught her by the back of her tan windbreaker and hauled her back. And a good thing, as secondary volleys of missiles from outside the yard walls suddenly pounded down in overlapping waves. Tossing one boxcar off its wheels. Slamming into the corner of the warehouse and ripping free several long strips of metal that whipped out across the open yard like a storm of mangled blades.

She struggled briefly, but Caleb managed to get an arm around her chest and put her into a lifeguard carry. Hauling her back away from the firestorm, he kicked open the sagging warehouse door they'd crawled past earlier and shoved her inside. There wasn't a great deal of room. Crates and barrels stacked floor to ceiling, draped with tarps and canvas wraps. Just enough of the red emergency lighting from outside eked in through the open door to let him find Danai's shadowy outline.

"That's *my* machine out there!"

"And a major push by someone who doesn't like The Republic very much."

Caleb blocked the door with his body. Held the knife down at his side, thumb pressed hard against its lower edge. He felt the blood well up. It dripped slowly down the length of the blade to spatter against the side of his combat boot. In the warehouse, with the firefight outside muted by thick, steel walls, he could hear the gentle *pat, pat, pat* of the blood drops striking leather.

"Damn you, Caleb Davion. Get out of my way."

She levered the Intek laser rifle forward. Actually pointed it at him. She *dared*!

"I will not. It's death on a platter out there, and you know it."

She scoffed. "Trying to save me, Caleb?"

It seemed so unreasonable? Hadn't he held off his own gunner in the middle of their battle, when the Marksman's Gauss rifle could have punched through her cockpit and killed her? Why did people question his motives at all times—and now above all others? Question his bravery. His commitment. His sanity!

. . . coldandsharp . . . coldandsharp . . .

"If I must," he said. "I'll hold you here for the same reason you pulled me out of the M1. I might need a bargaining chip." That's all she was to him now. An asset. He kept telling himself that.

Never trust a Liao.

Danai stepped at him. Thrust the barrel of the laser rifle towards his gut. "Step aside," she said, voice cold and flat.

He stepped right back at her. No longer caring. Letting the madness of the moment sweep him away with sudden power. A prince of havoc. Cold sweat stained his neck, turning hot very quickly.

The barrel pushed against his lower belly. He stared straight back at her. "Shoot," he taunted.

She didn't. He sensed her hesitation even before the pressure against his gut relaxed marginally. Knew she had surrendered to him.

Finally! From the moment he'd met her aboard the *Stargazer*, that had been what he'd wanted. Her surrender. After learning her true identity, having it thrown in his face at the Exarch's Ball, he'd accepted that it would—could—never happen. The insult and the humiliation were too great. The divide too wide between their heritages.

But she was Liao! And Liao should be used to surrendering to Davion demands after so many centuries!

He knocked the rifle aside, tearing it from Danai's grip in a swift, violent motion. He stepped up against her, pinning her back against a canvas-draped wall of crates with the knife up near her throat and his thumb still riding that magic edge (*was it still sharp? Oh yes, yes it was, cold and sharp!*). His skin flushed and crawling with tension. Every muscle vibrating, the pounding of his own heartbeat overpowering the sounds of nearby battle.

A thunderous ovation.

He crushed his mouth down against hers. Tasting the dirt and sweat of their travels on her lips. And something sweet as well. Overripe, like bruised plums. The taste and the scent of her overpowering him.

"Caleb . . . no . . ."

But she did not mean it. He felt it in the tremble of her body as it responded to him. This was how their game had originally been meant to play out, and they both knew it. With her

(fear)

complete surrender. One hand bunched into the fabric of her tan windbreaker, holding her in place, he tasted her again. Remembered her earlier comments, and took them for his own.

This was his.

And he'd have it.

Midlake Transfer Station, New Hessen
21 September 3135

In the waxing hours of morning, with dawn's arrival pulling back the shroud of night and coloring the sky with bloody reds and deep, burnished gold, Erik Sandoval-Groell walked his *Enforcer III* up to the *Phoenix's* lowered ramp.

An *Excalibur*-class DropShip, the large, egg-shaped vessel towered over the ruined Midlake Transfer Station like God Himself had reached into some city to pluck up a skyscraper, carried it across New Hessen and then planted it again over the wide, expansive yard. Erik knew The Republic force that had held the transfer station until only a few hours ago had likely seen it as much the same thing. God's own fist lowering out of the sky. Blazing with fire. Dropping ramps so Erik could lead out fresh troops in support of the forces he'd deployed earlier with Brevet-Colonel Hedges. Their third in a series of quickly planned operations.

This one netting Erik the true prize to be found on New

Hessen. The man who waited at the foot of the DropShip's ramp, surrounded once again by a full contingent of armed security agents and (now) a second line of battlesuit infantry as well.

Caleb Hasek Sandoval Davion.

The Federated Suns' new prince watched as Erik's armored column limped back aboard. Counting the Swordsworn crests proudly displayed on every vehicle, and catching the three or four left of the troops Erik had *borrowed* from Count Brisham Vicore. Like the DropShip, which did not display a sunburst crest but rather a design that centered the silhouette of a *Phoenix Hawk* against an inferno of flames twisted into the wide outline of a large bird.

Erik throttled down, bringing his *Enforcer* to an easy halt. He set it in a wide-legged stance and deactivated all command functions, which locked out weapons and sensors but left open the maintenance protocol that would allow a technician or junior MechWarrior to walk the *Enforcer* up into the DropShip's massive bay when it was time.

He had better things to do than wait in line.

Shelving his neurohelmet into its overhead cradle and then popping an egress hatch, he thumbed a control stud and spilled the chainlink ladder out of its storage compartment beneath the hatch. He clambered down, and moved (slowly!) to greet the prince.

Rescuer or not, the security team made him wait—one man holding him back with an upraised hand and another walking back to get verbal approval from Caleb. Which he gave, and Erik was allowed forward without the slightest insult taken. Three weeks of rough, cross-country travel and who could say *how* many harrowing moments, the man had earned a little cautious paranoia. And a whole lot of rest, was Erik's guess as well.

Caleb had looked far more . . . polished, last time they'd met. At the viewing before Victor Steiner-Davion's funeral, that had been, with Caleb in dress greens and well groomed. Now the prince wore a soiled and torn tanker's uniform, had several weeks of growth bearding his face, deep scratches on the side of his neck, and a vacant stare that seemed to pass right through Erik as if Caleb looked for someone behind him.

Erik resisted the urge to turn and look.

"Prince Caleb," Erik said by way of greeting. "Never a dull moment."

Caleb also remembered their exchange, apparently. He smiled thinly. "When we are at war," he said, finishing the sentiment they had shared during the viewing.

"We are tying up some loose ends here, Prince Caleb. Then we would be honored to escort you back to Jarman City's DropPort where the *First Sun* awaits."

"Loose ends?"

"A few vehicles left to salvage. And we are investigating a battle-communications report of a large vehicle or tank that broke free during the fighting and pushed off towards the southwest wilderness. We did find some tracks leading away from the station's ruined walls. Fresh. Wide enough and deep enough to be a loaded J100 salvage vehicle. But we can't really say if it had been coming or going."

Caleb's dark eyes flashed out once again over the nearby ruins. Then he nodded. "Let it go, Erik," Caleb said.

Which implied that there *had* been such a vehicle.

This time Erik bristled. Just a bit. Felt the hairs on the back of his neck rise. "This is your world, Prince Caleb, and we are here on questionable terms, I do appreciate that." It had taken some serious browbeating of Brevet-Colonel Hedges to even get permission to land. "I would not be doing my duty to my own people, though, if I did not point out that this mission to help throw Liao *and* rogue Republic units off New Hessen has cost us. That salvage could be useful."

"And if I guaranteed your losses?"

Careful! Erik knew that Caleb would not make such an offer casually. There was more at play here than he knew. "I would hesitate to accept. Sire, I came here to offer you *our* assistance, and serve Tikonov's needs in stopping the Liao advance. Not to take advantage of the situation." Not in *that* way, at least.

"But if you ask it of me, I will leave off our search. As . . . a favor."

That was part of a language every political leader knew. The language of compromise and barter. Caleb's eyes drifted, his gaze searching among the rubble and returning men. Even checking around him from time to time as if someone might simply appear within the tight circle of security. Someone dangerous? No, it didn't seem that way.

Someone missing. That was all.

"Very well," Caleb said then. Nodded to himself. Distracted. "I can appreciate that. If the Swordsworn won't take my bounty, I assume you do have a favor I can offer in return."

It wasn't a question, but Erik nodded nonetheless. "Just a moment of your time, Prince Caleb. To discuss some of the latest happenings within The Republic. And a potential future."

"The Swordsworn are looking for new allies?"

Close. "The Swordsworn are looking for a new home," Erik said, throwing his hat into the ring. A move he had never thought to make on his own, and made possible thanks to Exarch Levin's decision to close the borders of Prefecture X. Isolationism was a knife that cut both ways.

Erik planned to wield it like a scalpel.

Caleb stared down at his own feet. Thinking? Considering? Finally, he nodded. Glanced up. Evaluated Erik with a measuring gaze. Nodded once, decisive. "By all means. Let us sit down and talk." Then he turned to lead the way back into the *Phoenix*.

Erik paused for a few seconds, letting the security team close up around their charge, then followed at a discreet distance. He spared only a brief thought for Aaron, stuck on Ronel and sniffing around the scraps left to Prince Harrison's table. Never appreciating that the feast had been moved.

And now dear uncle, dear cousin—there is no going back.

29

Northwind is under military blockade. Attempt no DropShip landings or you will be fired upon. Do not approach the local recharge stations or you will be fired upon. You are allowed no aerospace patrols, no active sensor emissions. Retreat from this system within six days. (message repeats)
—Automated message received at Nadir Jump Point, Northwind, 16 September 3135, relayed by Captain Jack Trader of the JumpShip *Achilles Best*

Richmond Lowlands, Ronel
Republic of the Sphere
26 September 3135

"**N**ow!" Julian called out, having pushed his flanks as far forward as he dared before Conner's loyalists thought to clip away one of the thinning wings. "Go! Hard and fast. Forward the Guard!"

Almost immediately his *Templar* stumbled, right leg shoved back as a Gauss slug buried itself in his armored thigh.

An M1 Marksman had pushed forward just enough to throw a hitch into Julian's stride, letting Leftenant Andrew Giles take the lead as he pushed his *Legionnaire* forward at its full flank speed of nearly one hundred twenty kilometers per hour.

Julian wrestled with his controls, fighting the forward pitch of his war avatar by arching backward, using his own equilibrium to adjust. Deep within the *Templar's* armored body, the gyroscopic stabilizers screamed in protest, but obeyed.

He dropped crosshairs over the M1's blocky nose, his targeting computer acquiring solid tone almost at once despite the distance. Like coiling serpents, the particle cannon streams twisted outward along a running path, sliding together into one great, sinuous beast before they smashed into the M1's right forward corner and slagged armor into charred, useless crisps. A dream shot. Julian could only thank the weather for holding off long enough to get it.

It would not remain so for long. The rain had fallen all day long in brief, desperate squalls, some of the strangest weather he had ever seen. First pounding down so hard against his armor he could hardly tell when the rain ended and the autocannon fire he took from Conner Monroe's *Rifleman* began. Then, as the black, leathery clouds pushed hard to the west on Ronel's autumn trade winds, a wide sun break baked the sodden ground and stepped up humidity percentage point by percentage point until the air shimmered with collected moisture.

Just now they were between cycles, with a thickening cloud cover the dingy gray-white of overwashed shorts. And growing dingier as missile exhaust trailed across the battlefield and chuffing gouts of oily smoke boiled up from Julian's burning Behemoth.

Callandre still wasn't taking that loss well, he saw, skating her SM1 Tank Destroyer right on the edge of suicide as she edged out again and again to the fore of Julian's advancing line. Already she'd caught a VV1 Ranger and a lone hovercycle where they never should have been, leaving both of them piled up for scrap, but hardly an equitable trade.

She grew bolder by the minute as the loyalist forces all but ignored her; the missile-laden JES carriers having learned not to chase after her with their depleted supply of warheads and most others unable to track her well enough at one hundred thirty kilometers per hour. Waiting for their shot.

Julian would not let her hand it to them so easily. "Back away, Callandre."

His voice-activated mic picked up the command and relayed it over a general officer's channel. Levering his arms forward, he sniped at a *Warhammer IIC* that crossed Conner Monroe's line of fire, and burned away a good amount of armor from its left leg. Gem-colored laser fire and arcing missiles criss-crossed back and forth over the flat lowlands.

"They *want* you in close," he said. "Don't give it to them."

"I'll give them something," she snapped back. But she did pull her Destroyer back into the shadow of the allied forces. "Just let them—right flank!"

She called it first. Saw the defensive hook slip in past a thin stand of ponderosa pine. Two Pegasus scout hovercraft leading in a *MadCat III* and a *Shadow Hawk IIC*. Elements of the Storm Chasers mercenary force under Conner's employ, sliding in from the western approach. Trying to throw off his advance without realizing that this one was different than the ones that had come before.

"On it," Ariana Zou said before he had a chance to pass along any order. Her *Griffin* anchored the right wing, sweeping far out in a possible envelopment or pincer maneuver. Always on the edge, to keep Conner guessing from where the other shoe would drop.

"Guard-West forces, with me."

She led out a brief foray, StarFire missile launcher belching out flight after flight of LRMs while her extended-range laser probed and prodded with a lance of scarlet fire. A pair of Fulcrum heavy hovertanks guarded her flanks, adding their own missiles and lasers to the ceaseless barrage. A Fox armored car brought up the rear, on picket detail, there to make a quick pick-up should a crew (or Ariana herself) end up stranded.

The *MadCat III* had good reach with its long-range missile launchers, but against the kind of firepower and accuracy Ariana Zou could throw at it, the mercenaries quickly retreated.

Ariana anchored herself to the pines, taking temporary refuge within the stand as the rest of Julian's line pushed forward to catch her. Julian raced after the advancing *Legionnaire*. Guided Lars Magnusson up on the eastern flank where he held a mirror position to The Republic paladin.

Lars's *Arcas*. Ariana's *Griffin*. Julian's *Templar*. The three 'Mechs held flanks and center of the allies' bowl-shaped line. Julian had kept Leftenant Giles's *Legionnaire* in close on his position. Split the difference to Lars and Ariana with his *Centurion* and his *Enforcer III*. Half a dozen 'Mechs, backed by armor and infantry, and then a second line of reinforcements under Aaron Sandoval's command pushing up right behind them. The lord governor crawled along the back lines with Julian's command staff in the First Guards' Tribune mobile HQ.

More autocannon fire hammered away at him, cutting deep wounds across his 'Mech's chest and upper arms. Conner Rhys-Monroe, holding the forward edge of his own line, bending his flanks back in a slight wedge. He'd done that in response to Julian's possible envelopment. A game of strategy and tactics at which both men excelled. Guessing *and* second-guessing every order, every maneuver.

Conner had pulled back into a wedge, protecting the lowland access to Richmond and encouraging the attempt to envelop. Giving up ground for time and as a way to stay out from under Julian's artillery, which was now left far in the backfield out of effective range. Waiting for Julian to try for the envelopment, at which time he'd spear forward to either side, rolling up Julian's line.

"Not going to happen." Julian raced after the *Legionnaire*, calling Giles to throttle down, and started counting the seconds until they passed the make-or-break mark.

Thirty-five . . . and Callandre powered into a wide turn to ease out from beneath the guns of a squadron of attacking VTOL gunships. Warrior HW copters and a pair of Peregrines.

Aaron Sandoval moved forward the Swordsworn's Aesir AA vehicles to drive back the VTOLs with their quad-linked twenty-mills.

Twenty . . . The first, fat desultory drops of rain smashed into Julian's cockpit ferroglass, leaving long spatters. "Flanks thin. East and west. Giles, back down."

This time the M1's Gauss rifle took Julian high in the left side of his chest, smashing armor into shards and splinters that rained down over the ground. The shot left them strewn over several dozen square meters.

Conner's rotary autocannon slashed across from shoulder to shoulder. A handful of bullets *spanged* into the side of the *Templar's* head, throwing Julian against his restraint harness and making his ears ring.

Sixteen . . . fifteen . . . fourteen . . .

"Giles?"

Fire intensified against Julian's forward line. A stiffened defense on the part of the loyalists. Ruby lances burned in all around him as the *Warhammer* cut loose with first one pair of lasers, then the other.

Ten . . . nine . . . eight—

Not soon enough.

Tempted by the same disdain the loyalists had shown Callandre earlier, ignoring him for the *Templar* that followed, Andrew Giles had pushed his *Legionnaire* forward too far, too fast. He got caught out as the *Warhammer* pilot hot-cycled his weapons and put three of the 'Mech's four lasers dead center into the chest of the fifty-ton machine, followed by long pulls from the *Rifleman's* RACs and a sudden spread of warheads as the retreating *Mad Cat III* spun about, raced in on an oblique, and piled more misery on the Davion Guards' warrior.

"GILES! Dammit, Giles, no!"

The *Legionnaire* had caught a bad break, with so many of the *Warhammer's* lasers spearing into its centerline. Armor melted and runneled to the ground in a fiery stream, leaving a gaping wound for the rotary autocannons and the infalling missiles to exploit. No telling which of them found the weakness, or if both did, but one moment a fifty-ton machine stood there with its own rotary autocannon blazing, dishing back a measure of the horrific damage being served it, and the next the 'Mech was bleeding golden fire out of every seam, every ruptured joint as its fusion engine let go in catastrophic failure. The air shimmered and pulled to one side as the pressure wave washed out from the explosion, and the 'Mech flew into a thousand fiery pieces.

So close and running up fast, Julian's 'Mech took the brunt of the explosion right against its front. Armor plating turned into 'Mech-sized shrapnel, several large pieces cratering huge webs across his ferroglass shield. At least one fist-sized chunk crashed through to slam into the back of the cockpit, leaving a gaping hole in the shield's lower left-hand corner.

Buffeted, shoved off kilter, he had to throttle back. He barely kept his balance as the *Templar* stumbled forward and into the scattered, burning wreckage that had once been one of Julian's strongest machines.

One of his best warriors.

And then the heavens opened up once again, and down came the rains to drop a heavy gray fortress of solitude around him.

Eject eject eject!

Even as he held into extra-long pulls out of his rotary autocannon, hammering the struggling *Legionnaire* with a razor storm of hot, fifty-mill slugs, Conner Rhys-Monroe had been hoping to see the cockpit split open and the MechWarrior rocket to safety on his ejection thrusters. Knowing the machine was doomed from the moment his *Warhammer* pumped so many megajoules of energy into the *Legionnaire's* chest. Doing his duty by his people and his own honor, dropping crosshairs dead center on the 'Mech and, along with the *Mad Cat III*, hammering in the killing blows.

Watching the great machine come apart like a paper doll soaked in fuel oil and set alight by the strike of a match.

Then Ronel's terrible, autumn showers had hammered down once again, falling by buckets out of a sky of dark, boiled leather. Dropping a curtain across the stage. Putting him back on sensors again.

He made the switch with practiced ease. Checked his own formation first, counting icons by groups as they fanned out across his HUD. Carson's Corsairs in silver-blue, spreading out over the eastern flank, while his left side—*Mad Cat* and *Shadow Hawk IIC*—led forward a spreading envelopment of their own to enfold Julian Davion's line (and pull that paladin's *Griffin* once and for all time).

And the Storm Chasers in dark blue, clumping up in a

tangle to the west, to his right. *Pack Hunters* stalled in their own charge . . . and Captain Kremmen's *Ocelot* actually in retreat! Quick-stepping backward at fifty klicks per.

Half of his loyalists' armor assets had pushed west regardless, though now they, too, stalled.

"Beta-flankers, hold and secure!" He toggled up a tactical screen and drew his targeting reticle over the silhouette of Julian Davion's *Templar*. Outside, through the gray veil of downpour, the eighty-ton machine was a shadow lost against the gray backdrop. "Captain Kremmens, your Storm Chasers should be swinging out west. West!"

He pulled into his triggers, chopping at the distant *Templar* with short, controlled bursts.

His automated warnings beat Kremmens' response by about half a second, filling his cockpit with a wailing siren and the sharp, piercing ring of a proximity alert.

"I'd be swinging west if the Davion Guards weren't punching up our gut!" Kremmens shouted back.

A good thing he did, or Conner might have lost him against the alarms and the sudden, deafening ring of angry hammers beating his armor into fresh scrap.

The *Destroyer*! Racing forward under cover of the early downpour, front edge bursting through the curtains of rain like the prow of some armored cutter, it sped out of the gloom, fishtailed into a side-slipping glide, and barked out with its assault-class autocannon to savage his left side.

Before he could even *think* to drag his crosshairs down, depressing his weapons at the close range, the Destroyer turned tail and powered into a sharp-angled retreat. The damnable crew no doubt cheering their quick taste of blood.

. . . up our gut . . .

Like a message queue, his brain jumped from alerts to communications to alarms to his tactical screens. Tracking down the immediate threats, sorting out and discarding the chaff as quickly as it could.

Not quick enough. What the Storm Chasers' commander had warned him of was true. Julian Davion's line had not thinned out into the envelopment he'd threatened to deploy, or a pincer that was the next most likely maneuver. Conner had planned for either one, stretching his wedge, ready to spread out in a quick push and then collapse over both wings of the Davion Guards. Chewing them apart before the Swordsworn line could push forward and reinforce.

When the *Legionnaire* fell, Conner had pushed forward with his own counter-assault, knowing the kind of weakness he'd just chewed into Julian's center line.

Except that the Guards were collapsing! Flanks not bending out and around, or even swinging forward on an oblique attack, but cutting the corner off and racing inward to rendezvous behind and around Julian's *Templar*! *Arcas* loping in at eighty-plus klicks per from the west, trailed by a *Centurion* and the two safeguarded by a line of armored vehicles ranging from a twenty-ton Fox armored car to fifty-ton Maxims, the heavy hover transports leading in Anat APCs as well.

Worse news on his eastern flank, where the Corsairs had committed the same fatal mistake as Conner had. They'd *assumed* they had covered their bases, and as the storm-squall raged at the wrong moment, they pushed forward on a preset plan without checking instruments, without verifying targets or even sticking their heads out of a turret hatch to *take a look!*

The Corsairs' *Mad Cat* led the charge south and east, followed quickly by the *'Hawk* and a line of armor including both Goblin APCs, Pegasus scout craft and a squad of hoverbikes. But Ariana Zou had ducked beneath that line, curling in as her *Griffin* led an in-sweeping charge of an *Enforcer* and some Kinnol main battle tanks.

The equivalent of putting every last gram of strength into a left hook, only to have your opponent duck inside for a body blow deep into the gut.

And that was about how Conner felt as he backpedaled his *Rifleman,* called quickly for his line to fall back, fall back and *regroup*! Gut-punched. Nauseated; hollow inside. Head swimming as he tensed for the knock-out blow to follow. So many 'Mechs and vehicles swarming in against one spot, the storm about to be unleashed would make a Ronel autumn squall pale to the level of a gentle spring shower.

"Center-down," Conner ordered. "Pull in. Pull in! Grab some terrain and *hold*!"

Then he stumbled back as a particle cannon whipped out from the storm, slashing the rain apart into a sudden mist as the manmade lightning slapped against his right side and burned a wide, red-tinged weal.

Julian's Guards did unleash a storm. Like hell itself had opened up and its fires unleashed, a furious assault of laser fire burned out of the gloom, slashing at three well-chosen targets in different spots along Conner's line. The *Warhammer IIC* that carried his best firepower, the M1 Marksman with its Gauss rifle and missile support, and a Hasek MCV that still had its infantry loaded, burning through the armored sides and rolling it into a fireball that claimed the lives of four battlesuit infantry as well.

And here came Julian Davion's *Templar*, storming the gates like a paladin of old, forging forward at the side of Ariana Zou, a paladin of more recent vintage.

Conner burned his crosshairs over the advancing *Templar*, ignoring the haze of shadows and rain that danced outside his ferroglass shield as he relied entirely on electronics. Chewing though several hundred rounds of ammunition, his rotary cannons lit up the gloom around him with long tongues of flame and a flurry of white-hot tracer fire. One of his rotaries blasted into the side of the *Templar* and missed. He caught a piece of a Fox armored car with the second, but mostly buried too many rounds of razored metal into the rain-softened earth.

It was Julian's second salvo, fast-cycling the *Templar's* particle cannons, that finished off the *Warhammer*. A powerful blast cored through weakened front armor, skewered the machine's heavy gyro, and then sliced all the way through the back of the eighty-ton 'Mech. High velocity metal and spatters of molten composite sprayed out both sides of the stricken machine, which shook with mechanical palsy and then collapsed forward. Hard. Burying one shoulder and the side of its head in the earth.

"Box formation," Conner ordered. "VTOLs swing around their back door and kick them in the ass!"

He throttled down on his initial retreat, was joined by a Schmitt and a pair of *Pack Hunters* as Lieutenant Minor led the Storm Chaser 'Mechs in to tuck them against the side of Conner's loyalists. Strength in numbers. At his back, the crippled M1 rolled in, barely escaping the Guards' fury. Then a pair of JES tactical carries and from far, far afield Conner's remaining Behemoth.

What they had was a wall, now. A solid formation, being joined every moment by more 'Mechs and vehicles. Kremmens' *Ocelot*. A *Spider*. A lance of Jousts paired with Goblin APCs.

The Corsairs were also pulling back, but too slow, too slow.

Conner tightened down on his triggers, firing quickly though he continued to spend his ammunition in short bursts. Conserving ammo as the Guards came together in a solid column three wide and dozens deep, and punched in against the wall.

Punched in, and shattered.

Somehow, from whatever deep reserves his warriors had left, they held up as the Guard speared in to point-blank range, then threw the enemy back. First once. Then again. Lasers slashing back and forth like quick, stinging blades out of the night. White-fire lances of particle cannon streams. Missiles arcing out and down, out and down, hammering armor from both sides into new scrap.

Julian's PPCs slashing at *Rifleman*, Marksman, a line of Hauberk infantry spreading out of a nearby APC. The best target of the moment.

Conner doing the same. Digging into the side of Julian's *Templar* as the tide of battle threw them together, then ripping in half a Condor hovertank the moment the two leaders were swept apart again.

Rising and falling. Slashing. Probing. Hammering. Vehicles rolled over and burning. The fight quickly degraded into a short-range slugging match.

Which would be won by whoever was willing to pay the higher price.

30

> *To all captains in port, to be relayed to all ships at space among the trade routes. Attempt no jump across the borders of Prefecture X, as redefined in the attached cartographic file. A zero tolerance policy will be in effect as of 1 October 3135.*
>
> —Transmitted first from Towne, 22 September 3135

Richmond Lowlands, Ronel
Republic of the Sphere
26 September 3135

Too high a price. Too much blood.

Julian's vision swam as the heat build-up from hot-cycling his weapons turned his cockpit into a sauna. The place stank of scorched metal and fresh mud and gunpowder. The acrid stench clawed at the back of his throat, shortened his breath. Nothing he could do about it, with his ferroglass shield cracked and a fist-sized hole shoved through it. Nothing he could do but wait for the next stream of autocannon fire to walk across the ruined shield and slash through the cockpit like a frag grenade. Wait, continue to maneuver in the close-quarters battle, and lay about on all sides with his particle cannons and lasers.

Turn, throttle forward. One PPC. Two. A blister of four ruby darts and maybe—maybe!—his TharHes SRM four-pack when he thought he could afford it. Which wasn't often.

"Swinging behind," Callandre called out, skating her hovercraft right in at his heels. There was a tremor and a slight swoon as the *Templar* rocked hard to the left.

"Are you crazy?"

"You have to ask that?" He checked his rear monitor, saw the Destroyer fishtailing across a muddy stretch of torn earth, a hulking weight hanging off its left side. "I have a hitchhiker to scrape off. Coming around again!"

Two lasers criss-crossed over his 'Mech's left shoulder, drawing in too close to his cockpit. Julian stepped back, pivoted, and sank to one knee in a quick duck-aside that left the lasers searching through empty air and Callandre's SM1 barreling in at his planted leg. Trusting her to make the course correction, he dropped his crosshairs against the side of her hovertank, and used his left-arm medium laser. He scored a large glowing gash down the side of the Destroyer, cutting off an arm and slicing away a large chunk of helmet.

The Infiltrator trooper peeled off to the side like dropped baggage, bounced hard against the ground, and slid into a muddy pile.

"*Verdammt*, Jules! That cost me . . . armor."

A burst of static interrupted her as he triggered his right-arm PPC into the nose of a charging hovercycle.

"And at no extra charge. Now slide around on my left and prepare to fall back on my order. Cover the crippled vehicles best you can but don't you dare hit the slow side of ninety."

"Retreat?" Aaron Sandoval asked. They had been transmitting on one of the officers' channels. "Julian, you can't hand Conner Monroe this . . . victory and expect a second chance like this one."

More static. His second PPC. Stagger-firing kept his heat levels from building up to dangerous levels. Shaved a few degrees off his reactor temperature every other volley or so.

He knew Sandoval had a point. A good one. Julian's strategy had half-paid, rolling up the loyalists' eastern flank as Carter's Corsairs struggled again and again to break back through the line of death Ariana Zou had set. Her *Griffin* and the Guards' *Enforcer*, and a pair of Swordsworn Fulcrum hovertanks for support, had already dropped the *Mad Cat III* with a busted right femur and some gyroscope damage. The *Shadow Hawk IIC*, as impressive a design as it was, simply couldn't get the job done by itself.

Neither could Julian's First Davion Guards, though. Every push was thrown back with a high cost of armor and blood on both sides.

"It's a butcher's bill out here, Aaron! What do you expect us to do?"

"Pay it!" Callandre jumped back in. "We pay it, Jules. For Giles and for every warrior who has already put up the—*Verflucht*! Hard right!—the down payment."

Unrequited commitment. That was still what it came down to. Julian had never set a goal on the battle for Ronel except that he would see it through to the end. It was the pledge *he* had made to Jonah Levin *and* to Harrison Davion. To his people. And they had pledged it right back to him.

A Pegasus made an end-run-around, strafing a squad of Cavalier infantry troopers. This time Julian damned his heat curve and put both PPCs into the side of the hovercraft, stripping away its lift skirt and spilling the air cushion. Its nose dug into the soft ground, crumpled, and then the back end kicked over as it tumbled end-over-end and right into a loyalist Hauberk squad.

"Ariana?" Julian asked, gasping for air as the *Templar's* reactor spike tortured the atmosphere in his cockpit.

"Pay it."

And Lars echoed her. "Sometimes you do not get to make the choice for yourself," he added.

Julian nodded to the empty cockpit. This was also what Harrison had taught him. "To lead. To win," he said. "But at what cost?" A question he asked of himself more than the others, just as the loyalists' VTOL squadron shot the gap between his front line and the advancing Swordsworn reinforcements, burning down a Fox armored car that had strayed too far from cover.

"I'm not sure how much coin we have left," he said, and made the final call. "But we put it all on the counter. One final push!"

"As to that," Aaron said, voice strong and confident, "perhaps we can offer a bit more. If you are still ready to lead, Julian, my Swordsworn are here to follow."

"And all of us," he said, "are here to win."

Conner Rhys-Monroe struggled his *Rifleman* back to its feet. Blood tasted warm and salty in his mouth. His chest ached where the harness straps had caught him after the rough face-plant.

"Someone . . ." Chips ground between his teeth. He spit dryly, clearing them. Clacked his teeth together twice to check them present and accounted for. "Someone draw a bead on that Destroyer and chase it the hell away! Skyhooks," he ordered up what was left of his VTOL squadron, "handle it."

Twice now, that damned skating assault cannon had slid into his blind spot, using the heavy downpour as cover. Twice it had savaged armor from one side or the other, and escaped back into the sheeting rains.

He checked his weapon systems, his control systems. All good, except for a wrenched lower upper arm actuator. A bad shoulder joint. And there, a flashing telltale light that warned of an ammunition jam in the same-side RAC.

Okay, not so good as he'd first believed.

"On my order, back another two hundred meters. Hook left, left! Thin the distance to Carter's Corsairs." He checked over his HUD, ran mental lists. "Can anyone break that line on the east?"

"We're on it!"

Lieutenant Blake Minor of the Storm Chasers. He'd lost his second *Pack Hunter*, but had snagged a JES tactical carrier to guard his flank and deliver close-in damage to anyone who fixed overmuch on the 'Mech. He backed out of line, running down the backfield.

"Then go!" he ordered the bulk of his forces. "Minus two hundred . . . now."

About two seconds too late.

He had throttled back on his own stick, walking his *Rifleman* at a good clip towards the rear to put a *little* distance between himself and Davion's First Guards. Buy some breathing room. Save lives (if only to hurl them back into the grinder once he could set a better battle plan than "keep slugging at them"). A dozen long strides . . . Two dozen . . .

. . . and straight into a storm of falling missiles and lancing fire.

Warheads erupted in overlapping waves, falling out of the dwindling skies to geyser clods of muck and scorched earth and fire and smoke back into the air. Several score slammed iron fists into his *Rifleman*, cracking armor, crushing it, digging deep for critical systems.

The rains were lessening, so instead of vague shadows on the other side of his ferroglass shield, there were quite a few low-to-the-ground definite shadows that looked like Demon wheeled tanks and Condors, a trio of laser-packing hovercycles and a Fulcrum hovertank. All circling around him in wide, sweeping arcs. Throwing back roostertails of mud, drive fans chopping the rains into a fine mist that swirled up in miniature funnel spouts.

And with weapons slicing as they wheeled by, each turning onto one of three different headings to spear deep behind his main line.

"NO NO NO!"

The Swordsworn! Driving forward on suicidal runs, pushing so deep behind his lines there was no going back. Spearheading the Guards' final and hardest-hitting push. Cracking his line in two . . . three different places as they rolled in, chewed up armor and shoved around his smaller vehicles.

Getting in the way of Blake Minor's charge to the Corsairs' assistance.

Tripping up Kremmens' *Ocelot*, the light 'Mech sent sprawling with an Anat APC dropping Cavalier infantry in a quick swarming attack. Leeching onto the thirty-five ton machine. Working away at it with hand lasers and sharpened steel claws.

And following in right behind, Julian Davion's *Templar*, hurling fistfuls of lightning around the field. Crippling Conner's remaining Schmitt. Dancing electrical discharges up and down the sides of the nearby *Spider*.

Conner dropped crosshairs over a troublesome Demon,

the wheeled tank plowing through one of his infantry lines as if the armored troopers were little more than bowling pins. He reached out with his rotary autocannon and smashed it flat. Then he drifted the targeting reticle over to a fast-moving Maxim heavy hover transport leading forward a second Anat. Saw the crosshairs flash between red and gold—a partial lock—and chanced it.

Missed. The left-side weapon dug into the ground far short, jamming yet again, and his right arm RAC passed high over the turret.

The Maxim never slowed. But it did roll back its main door as it charged up on the backside of Minor's *Pack Hunter*. Without pause the Maxim dove in front of the *Pack Hunter*. A squad of Elemental-style battle armor soldiers jumped free of their carrier, rising on fiery lifters, their arm-mounted lasers already spiking scarlet daggers into the *Hunter's* side.

The *Pack Hunter's* PPC caught one in mid-air, blowing it apart. One tumbled while trying to adjust for his high-speed exit. Two of them leaped over the wide chasm to grapple onto the machine's side.

"Get them off me! Where are they? Get them OFF!"

Minor's JES hover carrier slid in, possibly thinking to use any of its several short-range missile systems to peel the Elementals away from the 'Mech. Like swatting at mosquitoes (deadly ones that they were) with a knife. The battlesuit troops would not survive. But the cost to the *'Hunter* would be terrible as well.

It never got the chance. The Maxim, having disgorged its infantry, ran head to head against the carrier. A combination of machine guns and SRM launchers spread out a few light punches.

Which the JES took, and then spat back a knock-out blow of its own. Eight six-pack launchers, spreading out a curtain of fire and smoke across the front of the Maxim. Shredding armor down to internal supports. Carving into the forward launchers, detonating a new round of warheads. Blossoming fire deep inside the crew compartment.

Throwing the stricken transport out of control as it powered ahead blindly and rammed into the JES's forward corner.

The Maxim had weight and momentum on its side. It

plowed low and left, then grounded out to slide to a graceless stop.

The JES was not so lucky. It jumped up onto the ruined nose of the transport, the impact throwing it up and back as it sailed in an awkward pirouette through the air to land on its roof. It tumbled side-around, crushing launchers and spilling out a trail of unfired warheads like garbage falling out of a rolling dumpster. Several missiles detonated under stress and impact, blossoming what was left of the vehicle into a rolling, roiling ball of fire and metal.

"Get them off!"

Minor had yet to realize how much trouble he was in. And Conner was too far to reach as the Anat APC, which had snuck up in the Maxim's wake, slid to a halt nearby and dropped a combat engineer squad. Lightly armored, and armed with grapple rods for scaling BattleMechs, the engineers quickly swarmed up the back and sides of the *Hunter* with every intention of cracking open the cockpit hatch and taking the machine captive.

And all Conner could do was watch it happen through the drifting, silvered rains. Listen to the mercenary's shouts over the communications band, and then the sudden silence. Hope they tasered Blake and weren't forced to kill him.

Limping forward now as his leg actuator gave out in a burst of sparks, he swatted at a nearby Fulcrum. He took the long trigger pull this time to carve a wide, deadly swath down the side of the tank.

Sent it fleeing, listing to one side.

One weapon torqued out of alignment, the other low on ammo. Leg scraped down to the titanium skeleton. The armor that had once protected the *Rifleman's* chest and arms also more memory than material. It was everything Conner could do just then to hold his part of the battle as his line broke apart into three disparate pieces, each working hard to join back up with the others. He still held the bulk of his forces in the center of the field, but his force was rapidly depleting in numbers.

All slipping away from him. The battle. The alliance. Everything he had worked for since his father's suicide. Two more months. If Jonah Levin had waited two more months before this shutting down of the borders, isolating Terra and Prefecture X from the rest of The Republic, the alliance might have had a chance to get firmly rooted. Link up through Liberty. Force the exarch back to the table, or rally enough of a public outcry to set the entire government on its ear. But that hadn't happened.

And now, Julian had put Conner's back to the wall. Again, dammit! Again.

All Conner's plans. His life as a knight, thrown aside. For nothing?

His father's death. For nothing?

The Republic? Stone's dream?

"No!" Railing against the odds stacked against him, Conner swung the *Rifleman* around in search of his tormentor. Shuffling in an awkward walk, gazing through the light misting rain that fell from a lightened sky. Searching . . .

There! The *Templar*.

Conner cleared his jammed rotary, and from several hundred meters fixed his crosshairs firmly against the side of Julian Davion's BattleMech. He pulled into his double-triggers and kept his finger firmly mashed against them.

His weapons spat several hundred rounds of raging metal across the field, ignoring wounded tanks and a struggling *Arcas*. Tearing long, gaping wounds into the *Templar's* side.

The eighty-ton 'Mech teetered on one leg, but righted itself. Then it twisted at the waist and levered both long-barreled arms forward.

Hellish lightning streamed out in an azure cascade of energies. It snaked quickly across the field, slashed apart Conner's hail of autocannon slugs for just a moment, and then carved deep into his left side and right leg.

"To me," he called. "To me!" Rallying what was left of his armored column, his Senate loyalists, his scattered mercenary forces. Never looking to see who rallied, who didn't.

Shoving his throttle forward, he limped into his best speed of only fifty kilometers per. Again he slashed out with his autocannon. And again. Moving for Julian even as the *Templar* turned into the embrace and came at him with lightning in the grip of each fist.

Another gash carved down his centerline, coring through engine shielding.

And again, chopping through the last of the brittle armor

protecting his hip. Freezing that joint as well as armor composite melted, ran into the coupling, and then refroze into a wax-looking wash that looked softened but was hard as steel and not about to bend again.

He hobbled forward, rotary autocannons blazing.

... Stone's dream ...

Saw on his HUD the Destroyer racing in, putting itself into harm's way one final time to draw fire from the *Templar*. Left it to his remaining M1, which punched a Gauss slug into the skirting and shattered lifting vanes.

The craft grounded, leaped back into the air and nearly overturned. Then it slammed down for one final, long, mud-streaked slide. Bent its steering rudder over and powered into one final turn, pointing its one hundred twenty-mill autocannon right back down the throat of the advancing M1. Let go with all it had left to tear the turret from the Marksman's deck.

... Republic ...

Conner slashed the final spin of fifty-mill rounds out of his left-arm cannon, walking them across the *Templar's* chest. The shots chewed down into the savaged armor. He used his right-arm RAC to saw off the *Templar's* left-side PPC, then spun the last hundred rounds out of that weapon as well.

He throttled forward, pushing for every last meter, every bit of momentum as he charged into point-blank range. Ready to take his enemy with him. One last great act of defiance.

... his father ...

That was what his father had reached for in the end as well, wasn't it? One last great act of defiance?

No!

That hadn't been it at all.

Conner blindly grabbed for the throttle, wrenching it back through a full stop and into a powered reverse. So hard, so fast, momentum alone still carried him forward, overtaxing the gyro.

He stumbled and fell, right into the final discharge from Julian Davion's last PPC.

A blinding flash. The smell of ozone and the sound of shrieking metal. And ...

... for nothing ...

31

Imbros III. Liberty. Denebola. Devil's Rock. Outreach. New Home. Hall. Northwind. (list continues . . .) These worlds are now under the aegis and protection of Terra. Attempt no landings. Anticipate no communication. Expect no exceptions.
—Communiqué delivered simultaneously to all worlds surrounding Prefecture X by transmission from Zenith, 29 September 3135

Richmond, Ronel
Republic of the Sphere
30 September 3135

The Richmond DropPort was a small town in and of itself, located a full twenty kilometers outside of Richmond proper with a large house complex as well as full amenities for restaurants, clubs, shopping, and recreation. On most other planets, the area would be worth its own charter. On Ronel, the capital had no desire to give up such a lucrative venue for collecting city taxes as well as planetary ones.

Just one more thing for Julian to keep in mind when he

arranged for the Senate loyalists to ransom themselves, paying a stiff fee into the planetary coffers as well as giving up a portion of their military equipment—though hardly a major fraction—in salvage rights.

There was nothing to do for the spilled blood, of course, except pray for those who were still alive but fighting for it. And mourn those who would not live to fight another day.

Another thing to keep in mind. Which was what brought Julian out to the DropPort early. To stand silent vigil in the light rain alongside Viscount Markab, Conner Rhys-Monroe, with Ariana Zou on his other side and Callandre watching his back, as always.

The wounded and the dead had been collected. From morgues and hospitals, and from those recovered only recently off one of the forgotten battlefields on Ronel. All of them cleaned and cared for. Loaded into MASH trucks or collected by personnel carriers. Driven out to Richmond's DropPort and right up the ramp into the waiting bay of the *Union*-class vessel.

Conner waited at the foot of the ramp, having already kicked the dirt from Ronel out of his boots. Standing at full attention, frozen in salute as one truck after another passed by in a slow procession, each one bearing the wounded or the dead. Each one afford the same courtesy.

Julian waited with the ex-Senator, blinking rainwater out of his eyes and not caring how slowly-but-certainly the light fall was soaking his uniform through. He waited until the last truck boarded and Conner rendered final honors with his sharp salute.

Then Conner turned and offered him a hand. Julian accepted.

"I appreciate your being here. You are a credit to the Federated Suns, Julian Davion."

Julian nodded. He studied his former adversary. Conner's military bearing—or perhaps he had first learned it as a noble of Markab. The man's direct manner, as if ready to take on the world at any given moment. No wonder men and women had followed him to such extremes. Why the Senators had turned to him as their champion.

Conner Monroe also had a slightly unfocused distance lurking behind his peridot eyes. A way of not quite meeting another's gaze, though Julian knew it was not an intentional snub. It had taken Conner several days in the hospital before his eyesight came back enough to walk unaided, flash-blinded by Julian's final PPC discharge. If the *Rifleman* had fallen any slower, stumbled another half-meter closer, instead of carving through the top of the 'Mech's head the blast would have cremated Conner inside his cockpit.

He still might never pilot a 'Mech again. How much his eyes healed would take weeks and months to determine. Perhaps years.

"This was never personal," Julian said. "Though it was not easy to remember that at times. You fought to keep something from dying. I fought to help it live for so long as it was possible."

"Such a careful distinction." Conner shook his head. He looked to Ariana and Callandre as well. "It would seem we should have been on the same side."

"It would seem," he agreed.

The other man turned to go. Paused. "I nearly made that mistake, you know."

"Which one?"

"Making it personal. There at the end. I saw the prize slipping away, never willing to admit that it was an illusion I had begun to chase." Maybe he saw a look of triumph in the face of Lady Zou, because he looked to her, not Julian as he continued. "Not my stand on Terra, nor our Senate alliance in which I still firmly believe. But here, on Ronel, I let my desire to win a military campaign get in the way of what truly mattered. The need to *defend* our rights. Not enforce them upon others."

Gracious in victory, if not accepting his point, the paladin nodded. "I wish we could convince you otherwise, that your rights did not need defending."

Conner smiled sadly. He looked up into the gray skies and let the light rains wash a fine mist over his face. "We might wish a lot of things, Lady Paladin Zou. It does not change what is. The dream of The Republic has died. For me, it died in a gunshot. For some others, it died in a proclamation." He looked from Julian to Callandre to Ariana. "Perhaps it has not died with all of you yet. But it will. And I do wonder how it will be when that happens."

Julian nodded. "The Republic was never my dream," he said. "But I take your point, and I'm sorry for your loss."

"Thank you. I believe that you are. And thank you for your generosity in letting us ransom our equipment as well as our freedom. Markab and Prefecture III will need our strength in the coming months and years."

Julian was not so sure. "Even with the exarch walled away inside of Prefecture X?" he asked.

"Even so. And as to that, I can only wonder . . ."

"What?"

But Conner was no longer in a talkative mood, having said his piece and treated well with them all. The only hint he dropped, if it were a hint at all, was to ask, "Have you ever heard of an old Scots fable, Julian? Hector's Wall?"

"Can't say that I have. Is it important?"

"You know, I'm still not sure. You should ask Tara Campbell about it, if you ever see her again."

And with that, Conner turned on his heel and strode up the ramp with barely another nod for Julian, Ariana, or Callandre. His boots rang smartly against the ramp as he followed the truck bearing his final cadre of loyalists. Ready to lead those who would still follow, and bury those who were no longer able.

Julian watched the man depart, and wondered just how much he would end up having in common with Conner Rhys-Monroe.

For better or worse.

"Are you certain?" Ariana Zou asked as they stepped away from the ramp and watched it fold up into the DropShip. The trio moved to a nearby armored sedan and stood outside it, for the moment no longer caring about the gray, wet day. "Letting him leave?"

Julian shrugged. The high moral ground was well and good for treating with the enemy, but in the end he was also a practical man. "What else was there to do? Keep him in chains on Ronel? Encourage other Senators—Vladistock? Usuha?—to come here after him?"

He looked askance at Callandre, who shrugged her opinion. "It isn't like we're welcome back on Terra. Any of us, at the moment."

Those orders had come down through the local legate. Those and no others. *Remain on Ronel. Attempt no return to Northwind, or into Prefecture X.*

Julian nodded slowly. "Besides, if Yori was right, and

the Dragon comes knocking on the door to Prefecture III, Aaron believes there may be a chance to quickly move Markab under Tikonov's sphere of influence. And with it comes Ozawa and the resources of half a dozen worlds. Until we know what Exarch Levin has left for us out here, or I hear from Prince Harrison or . . ." he hedged, then, "or Caleb, I have to think about the potential of such an alliance."

"With the Senate loyalists?"

"With anyone I can find to help keep this border secure for the Federated Suns. As I said, Lady Zou, The Republic is not, and has never been, *my* dream."

"But it *is* mine," she said.

"And that," Julian said, opening the car door and holding it for both women, "is why I still believe there may be hope, and help forthcoming, from Exarch Levin and from Terra. Because no man or nation could command such . . . unrequited commitment. Not without a firm foundation to build upon."

That pulled a laugh out of Callandre—a mocking bark he had heard many times before, and likely would again. "Same old Jules," she said. "You still put a great deal of faith in the better nature of men."

"I do," he said. He stepped one leg in through the open door but spared a glance back at the towering DropShip. "I do," he whispered.

"Until and unless they finally let me down."

32

> *Rejoice, citizens of the Federated Suns! Your prince is rescued and well, and soon returns with important tidings from The Republic Territories! Forward the Suns!*
> —Relayed message from JumpShip Dark Chaser, transmitted first to Sonnia, 5 October 3135

Kai Lampur, Tikonov
Federated Suns
7 October 3135

Sweat beaded on the back of Erik Sandoval-Groell's neck. His mouth felt cotton-dry. His skin vibrated with a special intensity as he worked the room, signed a dozen or more noteputer documents thrust into his face by eager aides and advisors, and listened for the call from the door that would be his cue to drop everything and hurry forward for the most important day (so far) of his life.

So much to do, he could almost—almost!—wish his uncle back to Tikonov to take up part of the load.

The exarch's recorded address, delivered to Tikonov by special courier just the day before, was nearly finished playing. After which Prince Caleb Hasek Sandoval Davion would conclude his own statements. And still Erik worked tirelessly behind the scenes, in command of the lobby at the Dao Xi office complex. Security personnel and staff administrators working for Erik and Caleb had commandeered the building's reception hall, turned it into a combination military command post and political action center. Here Erik had brought, bought, or bullied just about every leader Tikonov claimed.

Planetary Governor Vitucci; now about to be retired, comfortably, to new estates.

Legate Maureen Keeting; due for a promotion.

Minor nobility. Religious leaders. Economic moguls. Pop culture icons. None had been fully immune to Erik's reach, thanks to the system of careful influence the Curaitis Organization had helped him build. Not all were on board, but enough to secure Tikonov. And with it, a half dozen worlds (or better!) that recognized Tikonov's leadership and the Swordsworn's strength.

Senator Brisham Vicore was the final cornerstone laid into that foundation, giving Erik the political boost he'd needed. His uncle had overlooked that possibility, too intent on Julian Davion. Too certain of Erik's ultimate trust, even after nearly getting him killed.

Erik slowed his way across the lobby, leaving behind his last impromptu meeting and heading for the intimidating wall of security agents who protected the "green room." He brushed the front of his new uniform flat, then counted the worlds he was certain to secure, ticking them off against raised fingers.

"Vicore delivers Caselton and Schedar." Two. "Between Caselton and Tikonov we apply more than enough pressure to swing Mirach and New Rhodes III." Two more.

On his own he had leveraged Ankaa (even with Aaron's interference) and possibly Hoan and Alrescha as well. Almost certainly Hoan (which put him into counting fingers on his other hand!).

"And the gem in my crown: Tigress."

Once a stronghold for the local military prefect, who had gone over for the Steel Wolves several years back, the Clan-inspired faction had abandoned Tigress. Left it open for the taking. Aaron had always overlooked the world as beneath him. But a vacuum wants to be filled. Erik had filled it. Cemented the Swordsworn position there in his name—*his*, not Aaron's—and with that, he pulled together one neat and tidy package.

Pulled it together, and dropped the entire thing into the lap of Prince Caleb Davion.

The "green room" for today's event wasn't much more than a large corner of the building's vaulted lobby, screened off by tall, cubicle-style dividers with underlays of ballistic cloth. Erik subjected himself to yet another security scan, and tolerated the Syrtis Fusiliers captain who escorted him through security and into Caleb's presence.

"Well?" Caleb snapped. He continued pacing. "All is in place?" he asked back over his shoulder as he turned along a new direction.

Erik smoothed his polished façade, counting to three in his head before answering. Dialing up a calming voice. "My ambassador to Tigress believes there will be no problems. The new legate is trusted, and will be granted extensive estates once he trains and delivers a cadre battalion."

Caleb stopped. Glanced around. Searching. "Perhaps I should speak with him."

In this state? Not a chance. "I've handled it for you, Prince Caleb. This transition will go smoothly. You have my word."

"Yes. Well. It has been good so far."

A new prince. A harrowing ordeal on New Hessen. With who knew what problems waiting for him back on New Avalon. Yes, Erik could forgive Caleb the nervous energy, the paranoia.

Especially once Caleb delivered on his end.

"Time," a nearby officer in the Syrtis Fusiliers called out. "Advance teams, move forward. Flankers are set. My prince?" He gestured forward, and stepped aside to fall in right at Caleb's elbow.

It was a short walk. Along the mirrored glass wall and then out through an entrance way with the regular doors removed for ease of access. Out into the courtyard of the Dao Xi complex, where a large, red-and-gold awning had been erected to shade the building's entire front as well as the ferrocrete steps. And for the added protection it afforded against snipers. On his last day in Kai Lampur, and on Tikonov, Caleb (or his security, at least) was allowing for no mistakes. Not after New Hessen. The crowd gathered within the courtyard had been carefully screened (and well paid), and only two video crews were allowed to record. Their raw feed would be fairly split off to all the major news agencies.

"Coming back live," a nearby production manager said. "In five, four . . ." He counted the last three seconds down silently, showing fingers only.

"What you have watched, and witnessed," Caleb said, "was Exarch Jonah Levin's final words to you, the former citizens and residents of The Republic of the Sphere. I cannot begin to understand how they must have affected you. I will not try to offer any explanations of the minds or machinations of the men and women who chose to abandon their responsibility, and leave rudderless this vital, important region."

Perfectly in character, Erik was relieved to see. He stood off to one side, waiting. Wearing his new uniform. He tugged the hem of his green jacket straight. Shined a few of the gleaming brass buttons with a cuff. Then clasped hands behind his back in the semblance of a military parade-rest posture.

Caleb continued:

"I do know that extraordinary times call for extraordinary measures. Certainly we have seen little more extreme in circumstance than the past few years, as the Inner Sphere entire suffers under the cold and merciless grip of the Blackout. Trade disrupted. Alliances sundered. Violence." He paused. "War."

War. The word hung alone for a long count, letting the listeners think back on the recent events that had all but shattered The Republic. The rise of factional militias. The invasion of the Capellan Confederation, the Jade Falcons, House Kurita's Draconis Combine.

Every disruption and challenge to the status quo, brought about by an unprecedented level of isolation.

Not even Erik was immune. The weight of such solitude had already bent and broken many men. He had certainly felt it as well.

"My father and I visited Terra in the spirit of peace and goodwill and the idea of cooperation between men and nations. It is sorrowful to see such an opportunity wasted, but wasted it has been until these last few weeks when a leader stepped forward to do what was dangerous, what was needed, and what was right. His example has since been multiplied a dozen times over, with offers of aid and pledges of alliance. And it has pressed me to accept his hand of friendship, to consider his counsel, and to raise him up yet again as a leader who deserves your support.

"Which is why, in the absence of any true *lasting* leadership on Terra, I accept the pledge of the Swordsworn, of Tikonov, and of so many other worlds besides, and declare this region a *Davion protectorate*." And here some in the crowd began to clap and cheer. Right on cue.

"A protectorate that I will bring the full power of my realm to safeguard and maintain."

More enthusiasm. The stage was set. Erik came to attention, and tugged into perfect order his uniform of the Armed Forces of the Federated Suns.

"A protectorate I gladly place under the aegis of your own forward-thinking leader. My rescuer. My friend. And here, I declare, my *Prince's Champion*.

"Lord Erik Sandoval-Groell!"

Epilogue

There is nothing more to say, nothing more to endeavor, that we have not said or attempted in the last ten months. And so it is with great sorrow but firm resolve that we put this to you, the people of The Republic of the Sphere, that the time has come for drastic and irrevocable action. To save what we can for the future.
—Opening, Exarch Levin's "Final Address," released among the Territories beginning 1 October 3135

Richmond DropPort, Ronel
Republic of the Sphere
12 October 3135

For Julian Davion, it was a day for good-byes.

Aaron Sandoval was first to gather his people together and bid Julian a curt farewell. He left a short company of Swordsworn armor behind to assist in the garrison of Ronel, though their loyalty would be suspect for some time given the news coming out of Tikonov and the call hitting many worlds for all Swordsworn to "come home to the Federated Suns."

"Too soon!" Aaron had complained, raging at his nephew's treachery. And just a touch of admiration as well? "As usual, Erik has done the wrong thing for the right reasons. And he's accomplished it beautifully this time."

Aaron was going back to Tikonov. He promised "to beat some sense back into that nephew of mine."

Given Aaron's flushed face and the obvious effect to which Erik Sandoval-Groell had stolen a march against him, Julian doubted the trip would produce more than a few new ulcers. Or, worse, a Swordsworn schism he was determined *not* to fall in with.

Lars Magnusson then decided at the last moment to hitch a ride on Ariana Zou's DropShip, lifting off that afternoon, catching up to an outbound cargo vessel bound for Ozawa, then Towne and beyond.

"It's time I returned to the Dominion," he said. "My report will certainly shake things up." Then he frowned, dark and heavy. "When I start using Inner Sphere slang, and contractions, *it is* time to be home."

They had traded grips. Then again, Julian with Ariana. "You will both be missed," he said.

Ariana nodded. But, "I will not be far, Julian. Only on Sheratan. Tara Campbell may still be there, in seclusion. And I do have my orders." She had paused then. "If you have need of me, call. I will come back."

Her *Seeker*-class vessel had rocketed away from Ronel with Julian watching from the main concourse, where he then checked on the two inbound vessels and saw them both still slated for afternoon arrivals on the following day. Sandra Fenlon would be aboard one of those incoming DropShips, having been sent away from Northwind before the final curtain fell across it and another half dozen or so worlds. And Prefecture X.

Sandra, heading back to the Federated Suns; to either Chesterton or New Syrtis. Heading home. Arriving with the last of some troops off Northwind: a few of Julian's First Guard, and some Highlanders who had not taken well to the exarch's final solution. Arriving tomorrow, for a short stay at best. Amanda Hasek would not leave her long in Julian's company. With Julian out of favor—replaced as prince's champion and all but forgotten—it seemed unlikely any more matchmaking would occur. Not until and unless Caleb called him home as well. Which appeared less likely every day.

So, no arrivals to welcome. Just good-byes. Julian had seen off all of his allies and friends now. All but Callandre, who had disappeared this morning and had yet to turn up.

For a moment, on the drive back out to the *Markeson Pride* where he would remain for now, he considered the idea that Callandre would leave without saying good-bye at all. It would be just like her, he knew, to hold a grudge for the seven years they dropped out of contact, and get some payback by walking out on him without a word or a note.

But no, he finally decided, pulling up into the DropShip bay, welcomed by its cool shade and spit-and-polish care. No. She was still around. He felt it.

If for no other reason than to finish fixing up her injured Destroyer, currently in a state of disassembly in the *Pride's* third maintenance bay. And then likely she would try to steal it on her way out the door.

The DropShip had an air of exhaustion about it now that the heavy fighting was over with and repairs and maintenance protocols were once again the order of the day. The injured were being cared for at Richmond's best hospitals. Salvage crews had taken over a large warehouse on the DropPort's tarmac. What was left was a chance to rest and refit, and add a bit more bright polish to their home away from home. Julian passed two painting crews and a trio of mechanics tearing into one of the ship's high pressure air stations as he made his way up to officer's country and his stateroom. He stopped long enough to see how far along the mechanics were, then promised to pull some dungarees and join them.

A task he would never get to. Not today.

The man waited for Julian inside his stateroom, behind a locked door that only three people had a code and the clearance to open. The room itself was nothing special. Four metal bulkheads painted sky blue, decorated with photographs of family and a watercolor painting of an ocean scene off Markeson slid into metal frames permanently welded in place. A desk of dark steel and crushed chrome, with the corners and edges padded by leather wraps. A double-wide rack penned in with safety netting and using a civilian mattress—Julian's one nod to creature comforts while traveling.

"You have good security," the man said as Julian reached for the panel that controlled the room's main light. Giving him a start.

The man sat at Julian's desk, in a chair bolted into the floor to prevent trouble during zero-gravity conditions. The desk lamp was currently the room's only illumination. The light soaked into his dark outfit, tight-fitted shirt worn beneath a leather vest, showed his empty hands splayed against the desk's ferroglass-inset top. No hidden weapons. None within easy reach, anyway. He had square shoulders, a strong chin. The shadows crept in to give him a dark mask from the nose up.

Julian did not step fully into the room. Not then. He let his eyes adjust, checking the room for companions to this man. Breaking and entering was not conducive to trust.

"Not good enough, apparently."

"Could be better."

Something familiar about him. Still, in the low light it took an extra moment. Then he had it. Gavin! Aaron Sandoval's advisor and intelligence aide. "Didn't you miss your flight?"

"I'm not bound back for Tikonov. Everything that could be done there, has been. Now we wait."

"For what?" Julian asked. He tensed, expecting an attack at any moment.

But the other man simply shrugged. He stood up and gestured Julian to his desk. "Maybe to see what you will do, Julian Davion. Riccard Streng believes you to be worth watching."

He knew better (he did!) than to respond so easily to a familiar name. But it was the right name. Streng was—had been—Harrison Davion's spy master and counsel. A man of many secrets, he was one of few people Julian knew who likely knew more about the darker side of the Federated Suns' history than himself. And future plans.

"Riccard sent you?" He moved into the room. Heard the door whisk shut behind him, and paused. "No. You don't work for him." Except for the deepest of cover agents, Julian had a feel for the kind of men Riccard Streng preferred to use as intermediaries and day-to-day operatives. Even then, something about this man said he was . . . other.

Still, Julian accepted the chair to his own desk as Gavin stood nearby. Mainly because, with the door closed, his best access to comms and alarms was there. Should he need them.

"I work for myself, mostly," Gavin said. He had a strong voice and an older man's confidence, but put a uniform on him and he might have passed for a green lieutenant as well. His fresh-faced smile. The chestnut-brown hair clipped into a simple Caesar cut. Only his eyes, a stormy gray-blue, hard as steel, went with the voice. "I work for . . . let's call it a 'local concern.'"

"Local to Ronel, or Tikonov?"

"Yes."

O-kay.

"We did a favor for Erik Sandoval-Groell. And he employed me for a time after that. I left when my work was finished. Aaron Sandoval approached me, but he has proven . . . too *inflexible* in his thinking to appreciate what we could do for him."

We . . . Me . . . Julian did not miss the implications of when this man changed pronouns. He had an idea that very little was left up to interpretation.

"So you hope I'll hire you?" Which worked well no matter if they were talking about the man in front of him, or something larger. "I don't know you."

"True." The man thought for just a moment, then stuck out a hand. "Allow me to introduce myself. I am Gavin Marik."

Again it was the name. The name and the resemblance. It startled Julian enough to begin to reach for the offered hand before he froze, forcing Gavin Marik to reach forward and give Julian's hand a perfunctory shake. "Victor's grandson?" The family traits were there, some so strong that Julian couldn't believe he hadn't recognized them before, from years of looking into a mirror. "Gavin Marik-*Davion*?"

"Gavin. Just keep it to Gavin."

He wasn't certain what else to say. "You weren't at the funeral."

"That's family. This is business." He reached into his

coat pocket and pulled out a pair of thin wafers about the size of a small coin. Data-storage devices. He set them both on the desk in front of Julian. "Caleb is not fit to sit the throne of the Federated Suns," he said. "And this documentation will convince you."

Julian scoffed. "Because he is not a MechWarrior?"

"Because he is insane. By the most clinical definition. Paranoid schizophrenia, Julian. And it has started to get worse. That bottom wafer contains all the evidence Prince Harrison planned to hand you himself, eventually. All of Caleb's records, from the time he was diagnosed."

"In MechWarrior training," Julian said quietly. Nodded. A few odd-shaped pieces in the pattern of his life suddenly fit together. "Testing him for neurological suitability. They would have discovered it." He looked up. "No. Harrison would never have . . ." He stopped.

"You had to wonder, at times." Gavin stepped back from the desk. Leaving Julian to the pool of light, dividing his gaze between the two innocent wafers and the man who had dropped such news on him. "Why you? What was Harrison's interest? Why show such favor to a distant cousin? It's on the wafers as well. Your records. You were being groomed, Julian, as a warrior and—"

"As a leader," he interrupted softly, recalling Harrison's final words to him.

"Yes."

"I don't want this." That was Julian's first reaction. Give it all back. He'd never asked for the responsibility, and he damn sure hadn't asked to be drawn into such trouble after the fact.

"Trust me, Julian, you will want those files. What you do with them is up to you. The second wafer contains a sample of reports we've collected from Terra. From New Hessen and Tikonov. From worlds under attack by House Kurita. You may find the first one of particular and immediate attention."

Then he stepped forward, reached into his vest pocket and plucked from it a black business card. He laid it on the desk in front of Julian. There was nothing on it except an exchange number. Printed in silver, and centered.

It didn't even say what worlds it would work for. Somehow, Julian doubted that mattered.

"The first taste is always free," Gavin promised from the door. He'd moved away stealthy as a cat. "After this, it costs."

The door whisked shut behind him.

Julian sat there for the better part of an hour, staring at the data wafers. At the shut door, after the man who had left him such a terrible gift. He replayed several important moments from his life, reviewing them from the different angles opened up by what he now knew. And once he knew more? Once he had reviewed *all* the information? What then?

What more might he discover about his family, and himself, that he did not want to know?

He pushed the wafers back and forth on the desk, thinking about that. The first taste was free. Always a danger. That was how madness started so very, very often. And yet . . .

He picked up the bottom wafer, thumbed it into a tiny slot on the side of his desk and waited as it fired his computer to life. The inset ferroglass glowed with sudden resolution, projecting a screen filled with data above the desk's steel and glass surface. The first file. That's what Gavin had said. There it was.

SISTERS OF MERCY.

The hospital to which Harrison had been admitted.

Always a danger.

He stared at the blinking file name.

Which was where Callandre Kell eventually found Julian. Sitting at his desk, leaning far back in his chair to stare up into the shadow-cloaked overhead. His holographic screen was still aglow with letters and numbers, all awash in multiple files opened and then tucked away behind different tabs.

"Missed you at the DropPort today," he said after she'd keyed her way into his quarters. He hadn't bothered to lock the door. Wouldn't have mattered if he did. She had the code.

"I was there. Making arrangements for . . . what is it?"

Callandre moved into the darkened room. She came up to the desk. The desk lamp's reflected glow played off the red highlights currently streaked into her hair and spiked a terrible glow into her doe-brown eyes. "Something happened." She looked ready to go jump into . . . well, *someone's* tank and head off.

"What arrangements?" he asked. He leaned back to stare up into the ceiling again.

"Sandra. She's coming in this evening. I got the captain to pour on some extra burn. Thought after this morning, you might need a little pick-me up from your girl."

"She's a friend, Calamity."

"Uh-huh. Anyway, you can meet her DropShip on pad seven and head off to a late meal."

"What about you?"

"Sure, I'm hungry. But three's a crowd."

He kicked at one corner of his desk, turning his swivel chair back and forth, back and forth. "You aren't leaving soon? Back to Lyran space? The Hounds have got to be missing you."

"Let 'em get off their duffs and come looking. I've got better things to do than sit on Arc-Royal and run training exercises the next two years. Besides, someone has to be here to watch your back when you run off to find more trouble."

"I don't have to run anywhere anymore. I can just sit here and wait for trouble to come looking for me, apparently."

"What!" She flapped her arms, hands grasping at the air like she would grab and shake the answers from him. "What happened now? Jules?"

He rocked forward, leaning into his desk with hands splayed across the smooth surface. He pressed himself up into a leaning stand, and looked his best friend straight in the eye. And saw that she knew. It was the news Julian had been dreading for months.

He nodded. "Harrison is dead. Levin wasn't even going to inform me of that, apparently."

"Want to go take Terra? We can do it."

Almost, *almost* the ghost of a smile tugged at the corner of Julian's mouth. "Tomorrow. Maybe tomorrow."

Alive or dead, Harrison had left him a final charge. Levin's offer of alliance firm or broken, Julian had also pledged himself to Ronel, at least for a time, as its defender. Insane or healthy, Caleb Hasek Sandoval Davion was First Prince. So much to weigh. So much to consider. And he would.

Now that the wheels had been set in motion, there was no turning back. He would see it through to the end.

He reached forward and palmed off his computer.

But not today. "We have time," Julian said.

DropShip *First Sun*, *Tikonov Outbound Federated Suns*

"She made it away."

Caleb nodded at the mirror, and his reflection nodded back. Maybe a split second late, but still in agreement.

The lavatory in the prince's stateroom was nearly the size of a regular officer's berth. All steel and chrome and plastic molded to resemble real marble tile. A fully encased shower cubicle large enough for two people to enjoy at once with floor-to-ceiling jets. Multiple sinks of deep red porcelain. A huge mirror of silvered ferroglass. When microgravity returned, all but useless. But while under the one-gravity burn of acceleration thrust, to be enjoyed.

Space. One of the greatest luxuries of space travel. He had plenty.

And didn't want it.

Caleb leaned over one of the sinks. Right hand propped against the cold steel and porcelain. Left hand dipping into a sink of cold water, palming up thin handfuls and scrubbing it over the back of his neck in slow, measured gestures.

"She did. All reports are the same. Three outbound DropShips from New Hessen, all within a forty-eight hour period of Erik's arrival and our . . . my rescue. Liao, every one of them. She

(*Danai*)

must have made rendezvous."

If she hadn't, there was no word from New Hessen of a captured warrior or new guerrilla activity. And Caleb had left *very* strict orders with Lord Faust and Brevet-Colonel Hedges that he should be sent word at once. No word of a discovered 'Mech. Same orders.

"She could have waited. Should have. I'd have let her ransom Yen-lo-wang off New Hessen." His reflection looked at him with dark smudges under both eyes and a shadow of doubt flickering in their depths. "I would have!"

"Caleb?" Sterling McKenna called from within his stateroom. "Did you need something?"

He dropped his gaze to the water. Stirred it with two fingers, and then scrubbed a new handful over his face. Let the water drip back with tiny trickles and splashes.

"No," he said. "No." But he did not raise his gaze.

Softer, he said, "No, I didn't hurt her. I wouldn't. No point to that. I mean, she is Liao, and so not exactly human. By most Davion standards. But there was . . . something. Between us. That she encouraged and I was . . . powerless to help." He leaned down, took up two large handfuls of water and scrubbed them over his face, trying to wash away the dark smudges. "Her fault."

He scooped up more water, sipped it out of cupped palms and swished the cold wetness around in his mouth. The water stung his gums, drilled a deep ache into his teeth. Pushing himself back up, he looked again in the mirror.

A dark-eyed creature looked back at him with hollow, dead eyes and a snarl curling his lip.

Her fault.

Caleb spat his mouthful of water against the silvered glass, erasing that image. Thinking to wash it away and have done with the creature once and for all. Not there! Never again!

And as the water sheeted down, revealing once again his distorted reflection, Caleb saw that he was no longer alone. Finally! After six weeks apart, he breathed a sigh of relief to know that his friend had, in fact, survived New Hessen. One worry, at least, he could set aside. He would not be forced to face the trials ahead by himself.

Mason Lambert stared back out of the mirror, standing just behind him. Mason, who gave his childhood friend an encouraging nod and reached a gentle hand toward his shoulder.

"Everything is going to be fine," Mason promised. "We're just getting started."

MECHWARRIOR: DARK AGE

A BATTLETECH® SERIES

#1: GHOST WAR	0-451-45905-1
#2: A CALL TO ARMS	0-451-45912-1
#3: THE RUINS OF POWER	0-451-45928-8
#4: A SILENCE IN THE HEAVENS	0-451-45932-6
#5: TRUTH AND SHADOWS	0-451-45938-5
#6: SERVICE FOR THE DEAD	0-451-45943-1
#7: BY TEMPTATIONS AND BY WAR	0-451-45947-4
#8: FORTRESS OF LIES	0-451-45963-6
#9: PATRIOT'S STAND	0-451-45970-9
#10: FLIGHT OF THE FALCON	0-451-45983-0
#11: BLOOD OF THE ISLE	0-451-45988-1
#12: HUNTERS OF THE DEEP	0-451-46005-7
#13: THE SCORPION JAR	0-451-46020-0
#14: TARGET OF OPPORTUNITY	0-451-46016-2
#15: SWORD OF SEDITION	0-451-46022-7
#16: DAUGHTER OF THE DRAGON	0-451-46034-0
#17: HERETIC'S FAITH	0-451-46040-5

AVAILABLE WHEREVER BOOKS ARE SOLD OR AT PENGUIN.COM

Roc Science Fiction & Fantasy
COMING IN NOVEMBER 2005

DAYS OF INFAMY by Harry Turtledove
0-451-46056-1

The master of alternate history takes on Pearl Harbor Day. What if the Japanese followed their air attack with an occupation of Hawaii? What if they were prepared to use the island to launch a military attack on America's western coast?

WINDFALL by Rachel Caine
0-451-46057-X

In Book Four of the Weather Warden series, Joanne Baldwin's stormy personal life is taking a toll on her patience—and her powers. Now Joanne is torn between saving her lover, saving her powers—or saving humanity.

SHADOWRUN #1: BORN TO RUN
by Stephen Kenson
0-451-46058-8

This all-new trilogy begins on Earth, 2063. Magical forces have awakened and the world is changed. Kellan Colt has come to Seattle only to learn that in this world, there is only one law: survival.

Available wherever books are sold or at
penguin.com

(0451)

The Bestselling
DEATHSTALKER Saga
by Simon R. Green

Owen Deathstalker, a reluctant hero destined for greatness, guards the secret of his identity from the corrupt powers that run the Empire—an Empire he hopes to protect by leading a rebellion against it!

Praise for the DEATHSTALKER Saga:

"[Simon R.] Green invokes some powerful mythologies." —*Publishers Weekly*

"A huge novel of sweeping scope, told with a strong sense of legend." —*Locus*

DEATHSTALKER	454359
DEATHSTALKER REBELLION	455525
DEATHSTALKER WAR	456084
DEATHSTALKER HONOR	456483
DEATHSTALKER DESTINY	457560
DEATHSTALKER RETURN	459660

Available wherever books are sold or at
penguin.com

R411

Roc

The *Retrieval Artist* series
by
Kristine Kathryn Rusch

In a world where humans and aliens co-exist, where murder is sanctioned, and where no one can find safe haven, one group is willing to help those in danger...

Meet the Retrieval Artists.

The Disappeared
0-451-45888-5

Extremes
0-451-45934-2

Consequences
0-451-45971-7

Buried Deep
0-451-46021-9

Available wherever books are sold or at
www.penguin.com

ROC

The Stardoc Novels
by
S.L. Viehl

STARDOC
0-451-45773-0

BEYOND VARALLAN
0-451-45793-5

SHOCKBALL
0-451-45855-9

ETERNITY ROW
0-451-45891-5

BLADE DANCER
0-451-45946-6

Available wherever books are sold or at
penguin.com